The Pittsley County Chronicles:

Juckets and *Swamp Yankees*

BY

Joyce Keller Walsh

ISBN 0-7414-4671-5

Published by:

INFINITY
PUBLISHING.COM

1094 New DeHaven Street, Suite 100
West Conshohocken, PA 19428-2713
Info@buybooksontheweb.com
www.buybooksontheweb.com
Toll-free (877) BUY BOOK
Local Phone (610) 941-9999
Fax (610) 941-9959

Printed in the United States of America

Printed on Recycled Paper

Published May 2009

For my husband, John,
who gave me inspiration

and

for Kathryn and Robert Keller,
at long last.

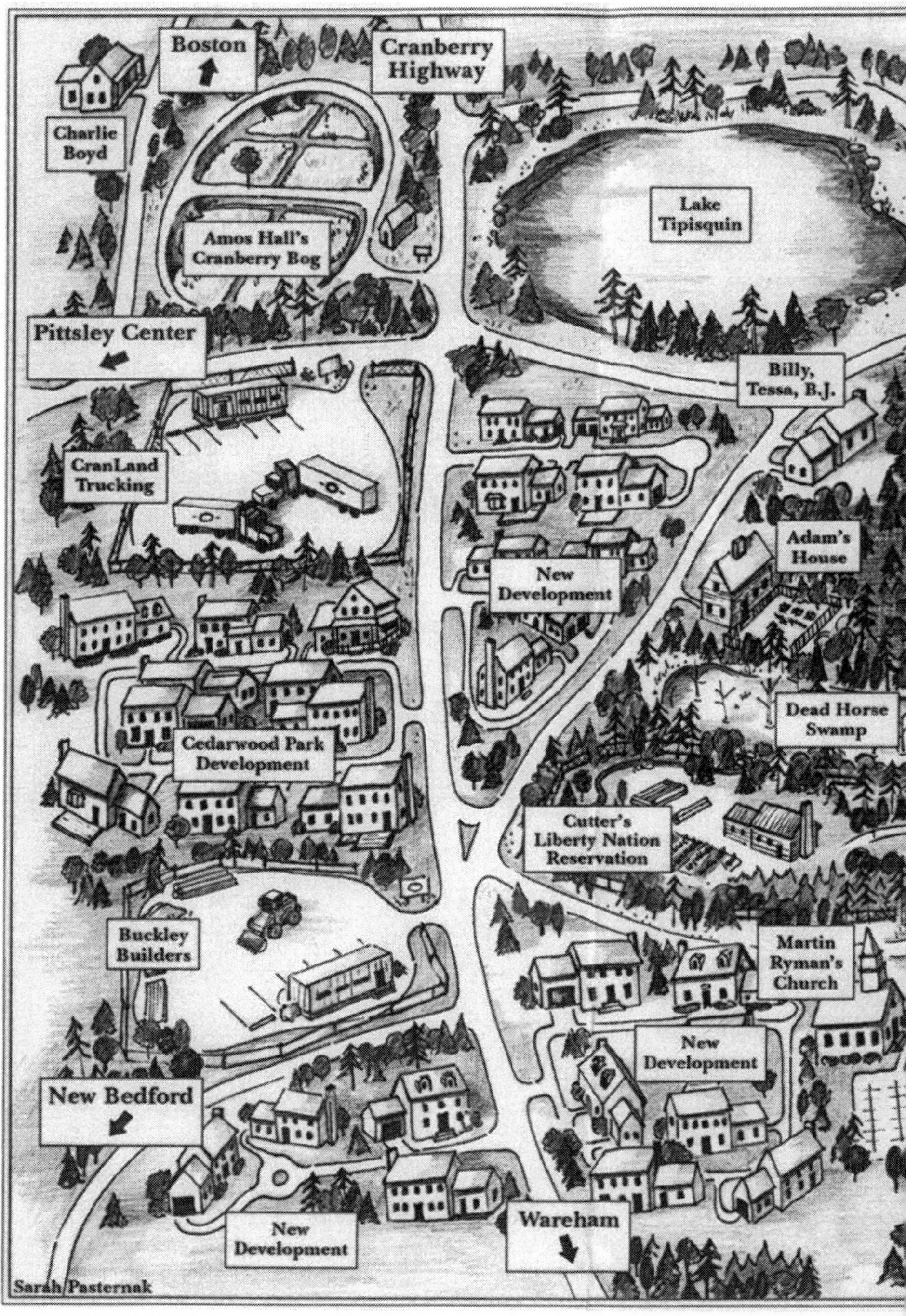
Boston
Cranberry Highway
Charlie Boyd
Lake Tipisquin
Amos Hall's Cranberry Bog
Pittsley Center
Billy, Tessa, B.J.
CranLand Trucking
Adam's House
New Development
Dead Horse Swamp
Cedarwood Park Development
Cutter's Liberty Nation Reservation
Buckley Builders
Martin Ryman's Church
New Development
New Bedford
New Development
Wareham
Sarah Pasternak

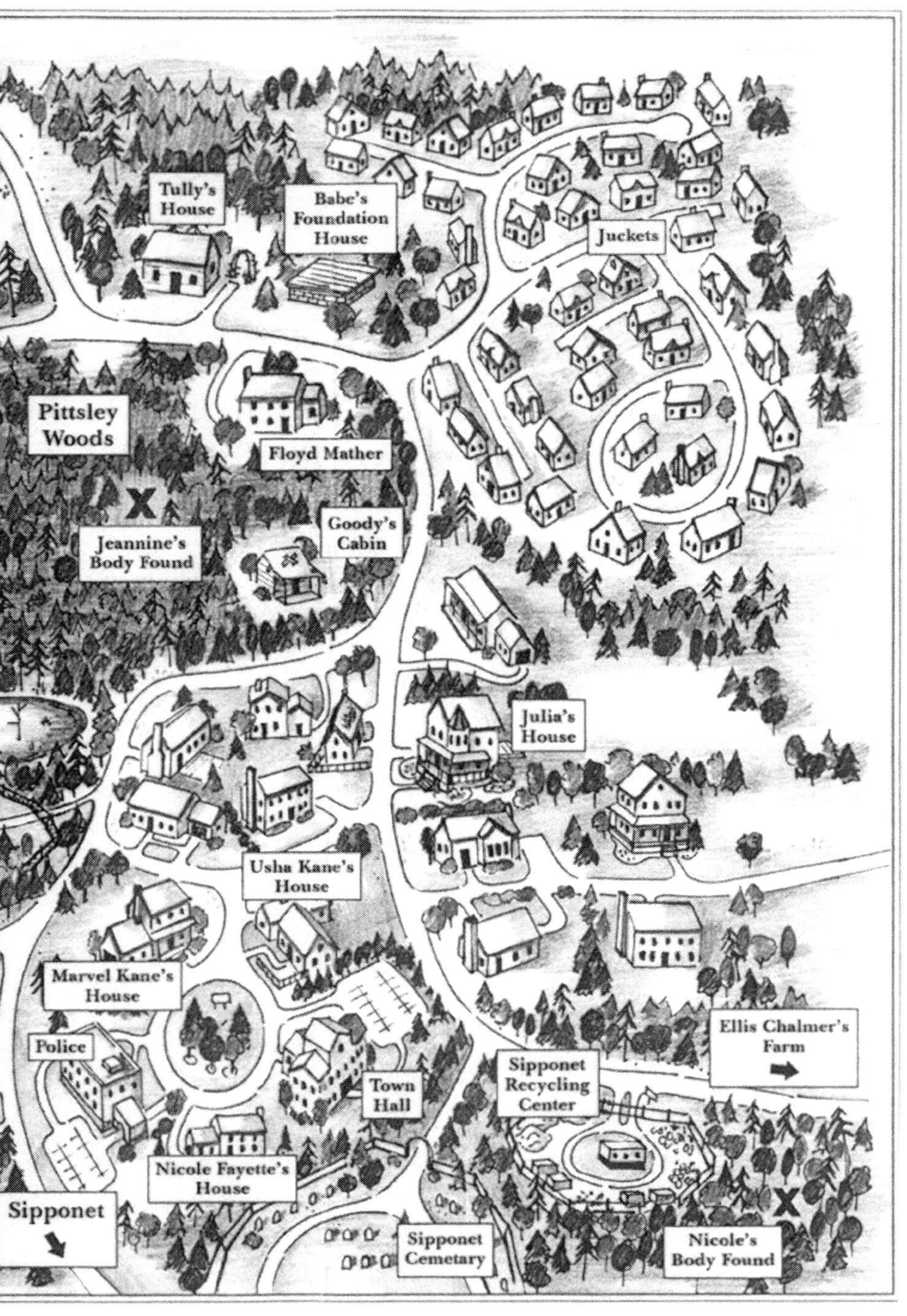
Tully's House
Babe's Foundation House
Juckets
Pittsley Woods
Floyd Mather
X
Jeannine's Body Found
Goody's Cabin
Julia's House
Usha Kane's House
Marvel Kane's House
Police
Town Hall
Ellis Chalmer's Farm
Sipponet Recycling Center
Nicole Fayette's House
Sipponet
Sipponet Cemetery
X
Nicole's Body Found

Juckets

WINTER

SATURDAY, JANUARY 12th

"Heart's no good. Can't use it."

"So what'll we do?"

As he walked a crooked deer-path through Pittsley Woods, his mind replayed the events of the previous day. It had all gone wrong.

"Discard it."

"Alright."

The snow had begun at dawn this morning. All around him, ice crystals coated every dead leaf and pinecone, and the ground swelled up like a pregnant bride.

"We'll have to start over." Then, a blur of crimson on white.

"Yes. But not right away."

"No." The rustle of starched material was the only sound leaving the room.

Now here he was, a lone dark figure with a black ski mask, trudging through the skeletal forest with a bundle on his shoulder. 'If you want something done right,' he thought, 'you best do it yourself.'

SUNDAY, JANUARY 13th

"Click-click. *Bang!*"

Cutter aimed an imaginary rifle at the ceiling, his left arm extended straight to a pointed finger, right fist triggered under his chin.

"So Pa takes his Winchester and starts shootin' up the damn cherry-picker."

Standing with his legs at an "A," he pumped his fist, miming the repeat-lever action of the rifle and sounding out the double-clicking lever noise and shot.

"Click-click. *Bang!*"

Cutter's voice rose as it gained momentum. "And that Electric truck takes off down the road with the guy still up in the bucket. The guy in the cab is strippin' gears to get outa there and the guy in the bucket is duckin' bullets and wettin' his pants. And Pa's shootin' and shoutin,' 'It's gonna piss power-company!'"

Nodding perfunctorily, Adam Sabeski continued ladling steaming hot stew into a white cereal bowl from the cast-iron pot atop his woodstove.

"And," Cutter stroked his black Lincolnesque beard, his aquamarine eyes glittering, "we ain't paid for ee-lectricity since."

Billy Jensen laughed obligingly from the depths of the worn armchair on the opposite side of the wooden-spool table. His eyes crinkled, but his empty gaze remained fixed on the floor.

Adam passed the first bowl through the centrifugal circles of cooler air towards the storyteller, who wore a rusty .38 special on his back hip. The spoon stood mast-upright in the center of the thick stew.

"Try that, Cutter."

Cutter obediently took the bowl and tasted the contents, a few dewy particles clinging to the ends of his moustache. Beard and mustache joined into a ring around his lips.

"Not bad, Ski." Three quick vapors of steam pulsed out of his mouth.

"Not bad, my ass," Adam replied as he filled a second bowl and passed it across the low table.

"Here, Billy." Adam guided the younger man's left hand around the bowl and his right hand to the spoon.

Billy raised the bowl to his nose and inhaled. Then he lightly touched the surface of the stew with his fingertip, and scraped the spoon along the side of the bowl into his mouth.

"Umm, real good, Adam."

"Plenty of barley," Adam explained. "It's not stew without barley."

"Hey, anybody hear anything about that pink-eye kid being missing?" Cutter asked, blowing on his spoon.

"Which kid?" Billy asked.

"Bradburn. Father works at Seaspray. Jeannine, her name is. You know them, don'tcha, Adam?"

"Know the family."

"How old is she?" Billy asked.

"I dunno," Cutter answered. "Twelve or thirteen, I guess."

"Same age as Billy Jr. How long has she been gone?"

"Day before the snowstorm."

"She could even be in his class." Billy's voice became edgy with concern.

"She's probably home by now," Adam said to mollify him, "or maybe they just miscounted noses to begin with. You know the old saying: 'Juckets are perennial and their kids are annual.'"

Billy smiled wanly.

Adam tasted his stew and concluded he'd done a respectable job. He grew his own vegetables during the Summer; in Fall, he canned or froze the ones that didn't go into the root cellar—the potatoes, butternut squash, onions, in particular. There was a competitiveness among the local gardeners. Each noticed, in passing, how far the other had got to plowing, harrowing, and planting. The height of the corn, the yield of the tomatoes, the size of the peppers, were all cause for comment and character judgment. The worst insult one could make about another was that his (women were exempted) garden (never meaning flowers) was feeble—meaning everything from ill-planted to ill-attended—indicating that the gardener was lazy or ignorant. That said it all.

"You putting in a garden this Spring, Cutter?"

"Nah. Can't be bothered." Cutter found his rhythm between eating and speaking. "I got big lumber to cut. No time to waste on weeds."

"That's fine, I guess," Adam drawled without lifting his eyes from his bowl, "if you happen to have a sawmill that happens to be working. Me, I don't mind investing a little bother on weeds, as long as I get something edible for my labors. Can't eat sawdust."

"Don't you worry, the mill will run. Soon as I get that friggin' motor to work." Cutter's voice was strident. "I'll be neck deep in sticks by Spring. Just a little problem with the friggin' motor is all."

Adam simply smiled and Cutter quickly engineered a new topic of discussion.

"What's Tully up to these days, Adam? I ain't seen him in months. Still driving truck for Conny Cranshaw?"

"Far as I know."

Adam crossed the uncarpeted floor to the wood bin at the far side of the livingroom. Like its owner, the room was functional, without excess. Places to sit, a surface to put things on, light and warmth. The ceiling had exposed hand-hewn beams and the walls were tongue-in-groove barnboard. Realtors might deem it New England Primitive or Country Original if they were trying to sell it, but in private would call it ramshackle. What was unexpected, however, was the heavy oak desk with bronze knobs, and a collection of small animal skulls in the bookcase along with books whose titles spoke of veterinary medicine.

"Scumbag," Cutter pronounced.

"Who? Tully?" Billy asked.

"No. Conny."

"Why?"

"Ain't you heard? Conny's bought half of Pittsley Woods. He's puttin' in a concrete plant right behind your house."

"He can't do that!" Billy said, agitated.

"Can, if they let him. This area's still zoned wrong. Shoulda been anything except industrial. But he already submitted the site plan. With an access road down there." Cutter gestured towards the left side of Adam's house, and then reminded himself that Billy couldn't see. "Right down the laneway."

Billy's fingers nervously played his thighs. "I didn't move my family from Revere into the country just to belly up to some damn concrete plant!"

"Don't worry," Adam assured him, "it still has to get past the planning board, and that won't be easy."

In reality, Adam was less certain than he sounded. Even in the few years since Billy had moved to Pittsley, so much had changed. The town had originated as an historical blip in a rural county, bought, like everything else, from the Wampanoags, which then became, through the usual route of conquest, an English stronghold. After King Phillip's War in 1675, only a remnant of Wampanoags remained, although artifacts of their lives—arrowheads and shards—could still be uncovered in marshes and fields and near the hollows of rocks they had used to grind corn. Little trace of the English settlement remained except for descendents who had long since misremembered their lineage.

For three centuries, Pittsley was forgotten territory. At its height, it was a stop along the old coach-road to Cape Cod; but it was bypassed decades ago by the new highway. And so it stayed from that time forward, unaltered. That is, until one Conny Cranshaw recognized that city people would drive an hour-and-a-half to work in Boston if they could come home to live in the country. So, what once was all farms and woodland was being transformed into a bedroom community, or rather a back door, of metropolis. New houses had gone up on practically every street, and not the kind of shacks that Adam and Cutter lived in, but big two- and three-car-garage homes with paved driveways and brass lamplights. As the new people moved in, they began inexorably changing the landscape—as though the things that attracted them in courtship, after wedlock became irritants. The piggery was the first target. Neighbors in the upscale cul-de-sac down the street mounted a protest to the Selectmen. Then on to the Department of Environmental Protection and further to the Environmental Protection Agency. The piggery closed. Then the newcomers voted an override to raise taxes because more children were in school now and they needed more teachers, classrooms, computers.

Cutter said it was rumored that town water and sewerage were going to be discussed at an upcoming planning board.

"Hell, they'll be wanting sidewalks next," Billy murmured.

Had Conny Cranshaw been an outsider, they could have suffered him easier, for then he would have been merely one more exploiter. But he was one of their townsmen. Conny's success in real estate at the expense of his kindred was nothing less than betrayal.

Adam searched for and finally located his pipe. He determined the small amount of tobacco left inside was just enough, and he poked at the bowl with a two-penny nail to loosen the residue. "I'm going ice-fishing next weekend. Anybody want to come?"

"Su-re," Billy drew the word out into two Massachusetts syllables, shoe-wa. "Okay if I bring Billy Jr.?"

"Fine with me," replied Adam. "What about you, Cutter?"

"Can't."

"Why not?"

"Got a little gal comin' by."

"Have her come by some other time."

Cutter stroked his beard. “Her husband ain’t gonna be gone some other time.”

Adam chuckled as he lit his pipe. “If you don’t keep it in your knickers, you’re going to get in a pecker of trouble one day.”

“Why don’t you get a wife of your own?” Billy admonished Cutter.

“I’d rather borrow somebody else’s.”

“You’d change your mind if you had a really good woman.” Billy clearly implied his wife, Tessa.

“That’s okay if you like good women. Me, I like ‘em bad. And then I like ‘em gone.”

Billy shook his head amiably, his curly brown hair brushing his shoulders.

“You want something to wash that stew down, Cutter?” Adam asked.

“I never say never.”

Adam took a green glass bottle from the bookcase. “How ‘bout it, Billy?”

“Well, maybe a short one.”

The routines of their socializing were constant as the seasons, with an order and repetition to them. Food, conversation, drink. Each repetition, both familiar and new. Like prehistoric gatherings in caves, the three men had spent many such Sunday afternoons together, especially in Winter when the weather was harsh and there was little else to do except tell tales and chew hide. They were an unlikely combination, drawn together by Adam who preferred their company to any other. They were perfectly content with the sameness of things. Part of Pittsley was still a time warp and everyone in the room wanted to keep it that way. In fact, they drank to it into the late afternoon—until the sound of tires in the driveway brought them all to attention.

Before the vehicle had come to a halt, Adam was at the front door. Although only four-thirty, it was already dark out. From the reflection onto the snow from the kerosene lanterns inside, he could just make out a small woman struggling to lift a bundle out of her car.

* * *

"Are you the veterinarian?" Julia called breathlessly to the man in the doorway. She had managed to carry her Golden Retriever a few steps forward, but the dog was heavy and the ground was icy.

The man advanced quickly towards her and opened the pink blanket to make an assessment. Then, before Julia could protest, he unceremoniously took the limp dog from her arms.

"Come inside," he instructed.

She followed his quick steps into the house and closed the door behind her.

"Wait here," he said brusquely as he left the room with her dog.

Julia scowled as this tall unkempt man disappeared from sight, dismissing her peremptorily without any discussion.

As she looked around, she decided the house didn't look at all like a veterinary clinic. And he certainly didn't look like any vet she'd ever seen. But according to the phonebook, A. Sabeski, DVM, was the closest veterinarian around. What choice did she have?

She slowly straightened out her arms, her muscles aching, and she gingerly rubbed the back of her neck.

"What's happening?"

"Her dog's been bloodied."

Julia quickly turned to locate the source of the men's voices and discovered there were other occupants in the room. Occupants who had observed her come in and then gone back to their own business. The younger man was saying, "What do you think, is there something we can do about that concrete plant?"

"Town meeting," she heard the bearded man reply. "We just got to get enough opposition is all."

"I don't know, with all these new people moving in…."

The bearded man glanced over towards her and she suddenly felt unwelcome. It took several minutes before she realized that the younger man was blind. As she contemplated the two men, one blind hippie and the other looking like Charles Manson, she wondered what she was getting into. Even the veterinarian seemed as though he belonged more to the southern bayous than southern Massachusetts.

As the two men continued their animated discussion, Julia stood aside quietly listening. Over the course of their conversation, the topics ranged from rising property values, to violations of personal privacy, and what *right* does a government have to tax all the things that it does, even liquor? That's when she realized they were drinking moonshine.

'I've fallen through the rabbit hole,' she thought, trying not to look stunned.

* * *

Downstairs in his operating room, Adam set the injured dog on the stainless steel table. He removed the pink blanket and folded it under her head. She resisted his hand and growled weakly at his touch. He spoke to her calmly, reassuringly.

"All right, girl, we'll take good care of you." He stroked her head and let her sniff his hand. She stared at him but didn't move. "I just want to have a look. It's alright, we're going to make it better."

He washed up to his elbows with antibiotic soap, passed his hands under the blower, and snapped on latex gloves.

Dried blood was caked on the fur around the cut in her abdomen. He cleaned it with sterile water on a gauze pad, his touch firm but careful. Then he applied lidocaine to numb the area and examined the wound. The gash was about four inches long but not deep. His fingers gently explored the cut and he was pleased to find it had not penetrated any organs.

The Golden accepted his ministrations. He talked to her continuously, with compliments on her shiny fur and assurances about her pretty face and soft eyes.

"If I talked like that to a woman," he said ruefully to the dog, "I'd have to marry her."

Next, he set up an I-V for an anesthetic and waited until she was under and breathing regularly. Then he adroitly began the job of cleaning out the wound and stitching it. There was a precision to his needlework that his vet-school classmates had teased him about. He never felt the need to mention to them how he'd spent so many childhood hours watching his mother stitch leather-uppers to lowers in Brockton, the now-defunct shoe capital of America.

When he was finished, he applied antibiotic salve and a bandage, and injected the dog with another antibiotic. Lifting her carefully from the table, he took the patient to an adjacent room and placed her in a large cage to let her sleep. He laid the pink blanket under her head for a familiar smell.

Returning to the livingroom an hour later, Adam found Cutter and Billy gone. The woman was sitting next to the stove, her shoulders hunched and her elbows tight against her sides, hands clasped. He took inventory of the black wool slacks, black leather boots, expensive white parka. Of course, she had to be from one of the new fancy developments.

She looked up at him expectantly. She wasn't exactly young, mid-forties perhaps, but attractive if somewhat pinch-faced. Upswept chestnut hair. Frank eyes.

"Is she all right?" she asked with urgency in her voice.

He nodded, then asked, "How did it happen?" His own voice was calm and practiced.

"I don't know. This is how she came home. Is the wound very bad?"

"Fortunately, whoever cut her wasn't thorough. Or the dog may have been too quick for him." *Or her*, he added mentally.

Her grey eyes registered shock. "Are you saying she was stabbed?"

Adam walked to his desk. "Any idea who might have done it?" He studied her expression.

"No." She shook her head in dismay. "Are you sure that's what it was?"

"Yes."

"But she'll be all right?"

"She should be. I'd like to keep her here for a couple of days."

As she nodded assent and put her hands to her temples, there was no wedding band. Her fingernails were manicured with clear nailpolish, not red or pink. That was in her favor, he thought. And she did seem acutely distressed. But he was not easily swayed. He'd known too many cruelty cases, too many guilty owners.

"I have some questions for my report."

"What report?"

"Incident report." He pulled out a white, printed report-pad and a fountain pen from his desk drawer. He sat down to fill in the questionnaire. "Can I have your full name?"

"Julia Arnault." She pronounced it Ar-know. "A-r-n-a-u-l-t," she spelled. "And you're Dr. A. Sabeski, I presume?"

"A for Adam. Your address?"

"966 Myricks Street."

He nodded. "The old Steeples place. Did you buy it?"

"No, I'm renting."

"How long have you been there?"

"Three months."

"Where did you live before you moved here?"

She took a deep breath before answering. "Boston. Why?"

Without replying, he added that information to the form, then continued. "Golden Retriever. Female. Spayed?"

"Yes."

"Dog's name?"

"Cat."

He arched a skeptical eyebrow.

"As in Catastrophe," she added with a slightly patronizing air.

"About five years old," he continued without inflection.

"Five-and-a-half."

"And you say you *just* found her like this?"

"Yes." She unzipped her parka and reached out to the stove to heat her hands.

"The wound's not fresh."

She stiffened. "Meaning?"

"Meaning it didn't happen today."

"That's entirely possible," she replied, narrowing her eyes. "I let her out yesterday morning, but she didn't come back. I looked for her all afternoon in the snowstorm. I had to quit when it got dark. But I went out again this morning and I still couldn't find her. Then she crawled home this afternoon, and I found her on my doorstep like this. So I brought her here. *Immediately*."

"And you have no idea who did it?"

"Of course not. How could I?"

"Do you live alone?"

She pursed her lips at him. "Yes. Why?"

"Well, sometimes there's a husband or a live-in who doesn't like the dog and—"

"I live alone," she said icily.

"Sorry if I offended you," he responded routinely. "I have to ask. For the report."

"Who gets this report?"

"Me," he admitted somewhat sheepishly. "My records, that is. I investigate and prosecute animal cruelty in the county."

"Oh." Her tone seemed to soften slightly. "Why would anyone want to hurt her?"

Adam shrugged in a way that said he'd seen it too often to even respond.

"Do you ever catch them?"

"Sometimes."

"But not often?"

"Not often enough."

* * *

She was too close to the woodstove. Her face was burning from it. Or perhaps it was from anger at the bastard who'd done this to Cat. Or anger at the bastard who'd just implied she knew more than she was telling. 'Or maybe it's just another damn hot flash,' she thought wearily as she rose to walk over to the window.

It had begun lightly snowing again. From the light of the kerosene lamp on the windowsill, she watched the flickering pattern of herself in a foreshortened shadow on the snow. Her hand went automatically to her hair. It felt dry, lifeless. Had she become suddenly old, falling through the looking glass into this netherworld? Was this perhaps her alter-self?

"Occupation?"

"What?" Julia turned back and saw him still writing in the report. "Oh. I teach psychology. I'm at P.C.C. this term." She deliberately anticipated his next question. "And before that, I taught at B.U. for ten years. And before *that*, I was at Radcliffe." She didn't want even *him* to think that Pittsley Community College was the apex of her academic career.

Adam put down his pen. "So what compelled you to bring psychological enlightenment to the hinterlands?"

"Missionary zeal," she answered without affect.

In truth, she hadn't wanted to leave Boston University. But *he* was still teaching there, so she couldn't stay. Sometimes it felt as if she were in religious exile for her misdeeds. Guilty of Bad Marriage. Sentenced to Divorce. Banished to Coventry. Why did *she* have to leave? And why had she moved here? If she hadn't left Boston, this never would have happened to Cat. It was all her fault.

At the sound of an approaching motor, Julia glanced out the window again to see the outline of two figures in the cab of a pick-up truck.

"You have company. A black truck with a red and white bumpersticker on the front." She squinted but couldn't make out the letters. "I can leave if you're finished with me." She looked at Adam for confirmation.

"Not yet. Besides, you might find this interesting, as a psychologist. Tully's probably your first pure Jucket. The rest of us are assimilated."

"What's a Jucket?"

But 'A-for-Adam' just sucked his empty pipe, so she sat down again. After seeing his other two guests, Julia wondered what more to expect. She had to admit to a perverse curiosity.

Seconds later, there was a loud knock at the door that hardly waited for an invitation.

"Come on in, Tully."

The man who entered wore the typical green chino jacket and pants, green visor cap, and rubber boots of most of the farmers Julia'd seen since she moved here. He was in his late fifties or early sixties, she surmised.

Behind him trailed a teenage boy who was about the same height as Tully, with the same nose and eyes, and similarly dressed except the boy's cap was on backwards. Whereas Tully had entered brash and confident, his son came in like a whipped cur, sullen and uncommunicative.

"Hello Tommy, how are you?" the veterinarian greeted the boy.

Tommy did not respond but instead removed his cap and shook the snow from it onto the back of Julia's neck, startling her.

"Tommy, don't shake your hat at people!" Tully shouted. "You'll get everybody wet, goddamit!"

Despite Tully's warning, Julia again felt the spray, and glanced admonishingly at Tommy's father.

"Tommy, if you don't stop, I'm gonna stuff that cap up your grommet." Then, without missing a beat, Tully turned to Adam. "Thought I'd come by and see what you're doing tomorrow night. What to go to the auction? Who's this pretty little lady?"

Julia looked at him blankly.

"I meant you. Didn't no one ever call you pretty before? Shoot, you got a nice little figger and everything. Don't she, Adam? You ain't so old yet. You got to think positive."

Julia was speechless. Then Tully smiled and his front teeth were like a rabbit's. Adam merely grinned as she threw him a chilly stare.

Tommy meanwhile moved around the room, examining everything, especially the animal skulls.

Had Julia been able to identify them, she would have realized that Tommy passed over the small mouse and rat skulls to finger a squirrel's eyesockets. Then he moved on to an opossum, a raccoon, and stopped at a bobcat, touching the fangs and running his fingers over the sharp points as though testing whether or not it would bite him. On the shelf above were the larger skulls of a dog, pig, cow, and horse. And on the shelf above that were the exotics—a capybara, crocodile, several jars of poisonous snakes' heads, and the prize of the collection, a jaguar skull. All the latter had been given to Adam by friends in various wildlife departments from animals found dead or confiscated in illegal transactions. Adam had studied them assiduously, knowing he would never see them in the wild. Although he'd encountered his share of jungle animals in Vietnam, that hadn't been his priority then.

But all Julia saw was a somewhat odd, somewhat scary young boy who appeared to be fascinated with animal skulls, which, after all, probably wasn't so odd or scary in a boy his age.

"So what do you say about the auction tomorrow night?" Tully asked Adam. Then, in the same breath, he turned to Julia. "You oughta get Adam here to take you. It's a real country auction. They have all kindsa things. Even old muffin tins and cream separators, like your great-grandma used. I bet you ain't seen nothing like that. You don't work for the Welfare, do you?"

Julia looked to Adam, who offered no assistance. "Uh, no," she answered.

"What do you do then?"

"I teach."

"Yeah?" Tully leered with his rabbit smile. "Can you teach an old dog new tricks? Huh?"

Before she could think of a response, Tully laughed at his own joke and moved on.

"You hear about the little Bradburn girl, Adam?"

"Is she still missing?"

"Yup. They still got some kind of search-party out looking everywhere."

Out of the corner of her eye, Julia noticed Tommy's staring at her while the two men talked. The boy had picked up a small rodent skull on the bookshelf and was playing with it as he watched her. 'As if from a lair,' she thought. She tried smiling at him but he was unresponsive. Adam and Tully seemed a million miles away to her, in some other universe. Here, there was only Tommy. Tommy, who might pounce on her with some snarling noise.

"Put it down, Tommy, it'll break." Adam's composed voice brought her back to safety.

"Put it down," Tully echoed, "and get over here! Put it down and come here!"

Tommy glowered at his father and Julia shivered at the look that passed between them.

"Break that and I'll crack *your* head!"

"It's all right. He won't break it, will you Tommy?" Adam said easily.

Slowly, Tommy put down the skull.

"Well, keep your hands off that stuff." Then Tully turned to Adam. "I been getting him on weekends. I'm going to court and see if I can get him back permanent. Boy his age ought to be with his father. I can teach him a trade. They ain't teaching him nothing at that place he's at. I can teach him about motors and welding. Carpentry. Pouring cement.

Things he can earn a living at." He looked at Julia. "It ain't right. The Welfare took my kids. That Mrs. Carlson, she's got it against me. They ain't got no right to do that. Take a man's kids away from him. You married?"

Off-guard, Julia answered, "Not anymore," a little too brittlely.

"Got kids?"

"One."

"Just one? I thought you was Italian."

"Excuse me?"

"You ain't Italian?"

She shook her head.

Tully persisted. "What are you? Portagee? Huh?"

He stared so intently at her for an answer, she finally capitulated. "Irish on my mother's side. French Canadian on my father's."

"Well, they're good breeders, too," Tully said with conviction.

Julia gave a short incredulous laugh.

Then, apparently noticing Tommy staring fixedly at her, Tully announced, "I gotta get going. I got to get Tommy back to the home by six. Come on, Tommy." He pulled Tommy towards him by the sleeve while addressing Adam. "Stop by the house tomorrow night if you're going to the auction."

Tommy yanked his arm free but Tully grabbed it again and propelled him out the door.

"Well, what do you think, shrink?" Adam said, sucking on his empty pipe.

She was tempted to say what she really thought—that Tully was weird and crazy, that his son was frightening, and that she wasn't so sure about *him* either.

Instead, she replied, "The boy's a charmer."

"All his kids are like that. That's why the State took them."

"When?"

"Oh," he looked up as though counting, "about eight, nine years ago. Tommy's the oldest of the four."

"Will he actually get Tommy back?"

"Time will tell," Adam shrugged. "How long have you been divorced?"

"Three months." An unwanted memory flashed into her mind. It was the day of the final decree and across the judge's chambers she saw the look of triumph on her husband's face. She frowned involuntarily.

"Does your ex- live around here?"

"No."

"Where does he live?"

"Boston."

"What does he do?"

"Why?" It wasn't something she wanted to think about, much less discuss.

When Adam didn't reply, she said tartly, "He experiments with graduate students. That's what he does best." At Adam's unswerving gaze, she became embarrassed about having revealed herself.

"Is there any chance he might want to hurt your dog?"

"Oh, no. No. Phillip would never hurt Cat." It was the first time she'd said his name aloud since that day.

"You have a child?"

"Hardly a child. Karen's twenty-one and working in New York." She narrowed her eyes. "And she doesn't stab dogs, either. At least not around here."

Unfazed, Adam said, "I guess that's all I need for the report. You can go home now if you want."

"May I see Cat first?" She didn't give a damn about his report.

"She's in the ward," Adam had said, leading her downstairs, and Julia presumed he was being facetious. But, in sharp contrast to the rest of his home, the clinic was well-equipped and modern. She noted the large and small cages, sink, scale, table, cabinets, the way it would be in a real animal hospital. The orderliness of it was a considerable relief. She had feared it would be as makeshift as his livingroom.

Cat was lying asleep in one of the large cages, the only patient. There was a medical chart in the holder on the door. Julia blinked back tears at seeing the bandage on her dog's stomach with the shaved area around the edges. The pink blanket was under Cat's head.

'I'm sorry, Cat, I'm so sorry,' she thought. But the dog was oblivious to her presence.

As he escorted her to the door, Adam said casually, "I'm going to that auction tomorrow night, do you want to come? You might find it interesting."

There was that phrase again. Why would she find it interesting? And what kind of invitation was that? Oh well, if she went, at least she wouldn't have to stay home alone.

Her house was still referred to as 'the Steeples place,' even though Mark Steeples had long since died and the place had passed through the hands of five subsequent owners and several rentals. Mark had been found dead in the bathroom some twenty years ago and reports of unsettling disturbances plagued the house—doors closing and objects moving when no one was there—nothing too threatening, just enough to make a point. Few occupants had stayed long. But, in recent years, the disturbances had quieted down and the last owners could finally rent it out on a regular basis.

After three months, it still didn't feel comfortable to Julia. There wasn't much to distinguish the house. It was old, but not antique. Neither small nor large, pretty nor ugly. The kitchen was outdated. And although there was a new bathroom, the bedroom was drafty and frost formed on the inside of the windows in eerie Mondrian shapes that dripped water onto the sills and spilled over onto the floor. She put rolled towels along the sills to soak it up. It was the first house the realtor showed her, saying it would "suit" her. She didn't ask why. She took it because she didn't want to have to make any more decisions.

If she hadn't left to spend Christmas with Karen in New York, maybe she would have decorated the house, and then maybe it would have felt more like a home. But she didn't like the way the house creaked at night, and Cat wouldn't be there for company while she lay in bed alone and listened warily to the shifting noises. The truth was, she'd already spent enough lonely nights over the past year, and some even lonelier ones before Phillip actually left her. She'd cried enough, raged enough, and gone to bed by eight o'clock too many nights out of boredom.

The hell with that.

She told herself that she was just looking for something to do. She certainly wasn't looking for another man in her life. Especially not this one. He was unlike any of the men she was accustomed to. He belonged, in fact, to a world completely foreign to hers.

And yet, this world had a distant familiarity. It reminded Julia of her paternal grandparents' farm in northeastern Quebec province, where her parents took her to visit when she was little. But after they died, the property was sold and the proceeds divided among her father and his brothers and sisters. She never went back.

Her grandmother had been a short, stocky woman with fine white curly hair that Julia's father said had once been pure as sunlight, long and silky. When he was a little boy, he used to watch his sisters brush his mother's hair as it gleamed in the firelight. Grandmére was not unkind to Julia, but neither was she warm and loving. The warmth, Julia's father said, had been driven out of her by the cold hard winters. She had been a city girl, from Quebec, and had never loved the farm in the way Grandpére did. He was a short man also, but wiry and strong and full of life. He always whistled a tune when he was in the field. They grew potatoes. Kenebecs, mostly.

Julia hadn't thought about the farm in years but she had a clear memory of the house. Inside, the walls were some sort of beaverboard, papered over in the livingroom where she slept with an incongruous design of Georgia plantations and horses and carriages. Her bed had been a chair that pulled out into a sleeper. There never had been any running water, and she'd had to use a chipped blue-and-white porcelain chamberpot during the night and the outhouse otherwise. (She recalled the 50-pound bag of quicklime that stood next to the stall for ladling copious amounts of the white calcium-oxide powder through the toilet seat and into the hole. The small screened window was always open, even in winter, and there was never any odor to Grandpére's outhouse. She used to play there sometimes, pretending it was a clubhouse.)

Grandmére drew water from the well and cooked on a woodstove. They drove miles to an ice house to get ice for the ice box. She recalled how they wrapped the block of ice in burlap and tied it onto the front bumper of the car. On cold nights, of which there were many even in June, they warmed the house with kerosene heaters. Julia had been only ten when her grandparents died, but she remembered those summers with a mixture of affection and sadness. She had loved the country. 'In fact,' she reminded herself, 'I came here to get away from the city, didn't I?' She had wanted a new life and she wanted it to be far from her old one.

So she said "Yes" to the auction.

Driving home with mixed emotions about leaving Cat, she passed the little white Congregational Church on the corner. A sign still displayed the sermon for that morning: *"A Cold Day in Hell.*"

She involuntarily nodded.

* * *

"Too bad about Chief Kerwin," the old man said, seated on his cot with his knees spread.

Adam sat across from him in the only chair in Goody's one-room cabin set back from the edge of Pittsley Woods.

Elmer Goodson was a small man in his 70s, with gleaming little fox eyes that saw everything. He was a contradiction of a man, both a practical mechanic and naturalist, uniting disparate worlds of matter. Gnarled with arthritis, he wore baggy pants and layers of clothing to keep himself warm.

It had taken about an hour for Goody to get around to this nugget so Adam would not deprive the old man of the pleasure of giving him news. "What about Bill Kerwin?"

"You ain't heard?"

Goody was a purveyor of information, or, as he called it, 'intelligence.' His sources were a mystery.

"Nope."

"You ain't heard about Chief Kerwin?"

"No. I ain't heard and you know it."

Finally assured that it was in fact news, Goody said, "Died this afternoon. Heart attack. He was out searchin' for that girl and he keeled over just like that. That little Jucket girl. You heard?"

"Yeah." After a pause, Adam reflected, "Bill was a decent Chief of Police."

"I figure he wasn't much over fifty-one, fifty-two. Smoked too much." Goody counted it a defect to die so young.

"Who's taking over? Do you know?"

"Nope. But I bet he won't be local. Not with all them city people moving in. It's all going to change around here. You know that, don'tcha?"

Adam surveyed the room, unchanged in all the years he'd known Goody. There was a metal sink, an old refrigerator with worn enamel—patches of black undercoat showing through—some plywood shelves piled with blue-and-white chipped dishes and cast iron pans, a rumpled metal cot with Army blankets, a woodstove sitting on a tin hearth surrounded by short logs ready to throw in, and a stack of paperback books next to the one overstuffed chair with frayed maroon upholstery. In front of the chair, on top of a spool table, sat a Briggs and Stratton engine, *circa* 1925, looking as though it had been dug up from a swamp. The only thing in the room that appeared to be in decent condition was the .12 gauge shotgun with the stock of inlaid mother-of-pearl that stood propped up against the doorjamb.

"You don't happen to know anything about a dog being stabbed around here yesterday, do you?" Adam asked.

"That what you come to find out? Heard it belongs to some city girl just moved here. You fix it up?"

"How'd you know?"

"Intelligence."

"What else?"

"Fact is, that's all. I ain't been out since the storm." He automatically massaged his swollen knees.

Standing up to leave, Adam said, "You need anything, Goody? Provisions?"

"Nah."

"Are you eating regular?"

"Still get my meals delivered."

Those, Adam knew, only came once a day, which is why he had brought—as he usually did—several bags of canned food and fresh fruit.

"I'm putting out the word. In case you hear anything about the dog, you'll let me know, right?"

"Since you asked."

Goody limited his personal contacts to Adam and one or two others, feeling that the human enterprise had long since failed, and very little about very few people was redeemable. Most of his friends were dead, including Adam's father, Harry.

It was common knowledge that Goody had been disappointed in love. The girl he'd wanted to marry was forbidden to him by her parents who, after meeting him, declared, "Jucket is no better than white nigger." And they never allowed their daughter, Lilly, in his company again. Goody began drinking after that. He lost his job and wound up living in an abandoned school bus. Thirty-two years ago, Adam's father found him half-dead of frostbite and malnutrition in the bus and got him to the hospital just in time. Harry paid the hospital bill and Goody remained sober ever after. But some days were harder than others.

Goody and Harry had spent Sundays together, telling stories around the woodstove, much the same as Adam and *his* friends. Goody had taught Adam most of what he knew about the woods. He accepted Adam as a replacement for Harry and, in some filial way, a perpetuation of himself. Adam, in turn, thought of Goody as a cranky Yoda, sprung from legends and myths, who'd lived most of his life in Pittsley Woods.

'What will happen to him,' Adam fretted, 'when Conny Cranshaw builds that concrete plant in here?'

* * *

That night, he dreamed about a Golden Retriever who frolicked in the deepening snow. Overhead, black-capped chickadees played like schoolchildren on vacation. The Golden suddenly caught the scent of something—the only other land creature that hadn't taken cover in the storm. Eagerly, she began tracking the lone human.

The dark figure reached the rim of a hollow deep in the woods and looked down into the center. The voices had told him what to do. With a single motion, he dropped the cigar-shaped bundle down, down into the bottom. Then he climbed down after it.

Slowly and deliberately, he placed rocks on top of the blanket, then made a circle of stones around it. When he was finished, he sucked his lips in and out with perfect satisfaction.

When he rose like an iceberg out of the hollow, he faced a dog wagging her frosty tail. He reached in back of his parka and withdrew a knife from its sheath. Swiftly, he grabbed for the dog and stabbed. She yelped and rolled down into the pit...and suddenly flew back up at him, her shark's teeth closing around his ankle, pulling them both back into the bottomless sea.

He awoke breathing rapidly.

MONDAY, JANUARY 14th

There was no heat in the cab of Adam's pick-up truck and Julia worked at warming her fingers and feet. She made a show of it, but he appeared unmindful. The muffler of the truck was loud and precluded conversation.

When she had greeted him at the door in her rust-colored silk pants' suit and matching suede boots and coat, he seemed to eye her oddly. She thought she looked just right for an auction, casual but smart. But he merely led her to the truck and started the motor before she had time to close the cab door.

'Pretty rude,' she concluded, and was tempted to say so. Most men would try to impress a woman on a first date. Either he was acting deliberately indifferent or he was just obtuse. But after this afternoon, she somehow couldn't believe he was obtuse. Or maybe he didn't consider this a date at all.

Their first stop, by Julia's request, was at his clinic. Cat was still lightly sedated but awake enough to recognize Julia and weakly wag her tail. Julia held her paw and stroked her head.

"Have you learned anything about who stabbed her?"

"Not yet."

But Adam gave her an optimistic report on the dog's progress and they left quietly as Cat returned to sleeping.

There were no streetlights along the back roads they traveled, and all Julia could see beyond the headlights were black trees and starry sky. The cold clear night held hundreds of stars but only a sliver of a moon. They passed a large clearing in the woods where the trees had been logged out for development. Julia wanted to ask Adam about it, but he seemed totally absorbed in private thought.

He actually was rather good-looking, she decided, in a hawklike way. Dark eyebrows and high cheekbones defined his face. His features were sharp, with a thin, long nose and greenish brown eyes that constantly scanned his surroundings. His dark grey-streaked hair was long in back, just meeting the collar of his Army jacket. There was an aroma of Latakia tobacco on him, sweet and musky. She noted that he had shaved for the occasion, and she revised her opinion. Perhaps he really wasn't aloof, but merely shy around women, a country thing.

They turned onto a badly-plowed dirt road. The truck bumped over icy ruts, jostling them. The houses, just small wooden bungalows, lined each side of the street like rotten teeth. Some of the homes were only foundations covered with tarpaper. Most of the yards were littered with junk cars, a boom truck here, a front-end loader there, all rusted and inoperable or broken into parts.

"Where are we?" She had only seen places like this in films of Appalachia.

"Where most of the Juckets live."

"The men I saw in your livingroom yesterday when I came in, are they Juckets?"

"No. Cutter's a Swamp Yankee. Billy's wife is a Jucket, but he's not."

"Swamp Yankee," Julia repeated. "That's like a New England hillbilly, right?"

* * *

'What's the point of correcting her?' Adam thought as he gazed past Julia out the window. Most people never heard of Juckets, and all they knew about Swamp Yankees was pejorative.

While Cutter may have looked and sounded like his origins were in the Ozarks rather than New England, his friend could—if he cared to try—trace his ancestry directly back to the first settlement in Massachusetts Bay Colony, that part of the coastline which later became Maine. Cutter's genealogy would reveal an unbroken line of misbegotten ne'er-do-wells who survived by fleecing the Indians, diddling the Tories, rum-running, and other nefarious, uniquely American pursuits of money. That they were only mediocre at it and never became true robber-barons was touted a virtue. They were people of modest needs whose pleasure lay in meeting those needs creatively. And no Swamp Yankee ever spent his blueberry money frivolously.

Billy, on the other hand was new. But not new like the 'new people,' because his wife was born in Pittsley. He had met Tessa at Boston's Berklee School of Music and they married as soon as they graduated. They settled in a Boston neighborhood—Dorchester—while they kept hoping for that big music break. But after they had Billy Jr., they moved to the country for a vision of their son growing up healthy and safe in a rural environment. Billy played violin, fiddle, and cello. Tessa played guitar, banjo, and mandolin. Billy Jr. was already versatile in several instruments and was becoming very good at oboe. Together, they played weddings, anniversaries, birthdays, and any function that paid or sometimes didn't. What name they used depended on the event. *Foot Stompin' Jug Band* (with Billy Jr. on jug) was one of the most popular, but *Mozart Street* (classical with a party beat) was doing surprisingly well of late. Tessa taught music in the regional high school and earned a little extra by producing the annual musicale. Billy tutored students at home. In the privacy of their boudoir, he played the cello in deep thrumming notes after lovemaking.

* * *

"What exactly are Juckets?" Julia continued.

Adam took a deep breath before answering, "An anachronism. They have their own community, their own ways. Mostly they live hand-to-mouth—junking cars, repairing motors, chopping wood, whatever they have to do to get by. They don't necessarily keep everything legal, and they don't always let the government tell them what to do. They don't fit in this society. And there aren't very many of them left."

"You seem saddened by that."

"Maybe so."

"Why? They sound pretty unsavory."

As soon as she said it, she wished she hadn't. She remembered Adam telling her that Tully was pure Jucket and the rest of *us* are assimilated.

But Adam merely inclined his head towards a particular house, not very different from the others except for the activity inside.

"That's the Bradburn place."

Through the uncurtained window, Julia could see people milling around. She vaguely recalled the conversation between Adam and Tully about something to do with a missing child. But she'd been watching Tommy more than listening. The memory of Tommy came back to her with a shiver.

"Bradburn. Isn't that the little girl who's missing?"

"Yes."

Julia scrutinized the tumbledown house and noticed a police car parked amidst the others on what would have been a lawn, but now was flattened snow. Once, when her own daughter had gone to a girlfriend's house after school without telling her, Julia had spent the most frantic afternoon of her life. She could only begin to imagine the torment in that poor house tonight.

They lapsed into silence again until they pulled into the driveway of another shabby house. Smoke billowed from the chimney. There were no curtains on these windows either, and Julia could see the colored lights still on the dried-out Christmas tree in the livingroom.

Adam parked and motioned Julia out. The driveway was jammed with machinery. There were two rows of old lawn mowers helter-skelter under a shed of corrugated aluminum. Nearby stood a strange-looking tractor with a snowplow on front, and assorted machines with huge rubber tires. There was a bulldozer with equipment parts lying everywhere.

Then she noticed the pick-up with the red and white bumpersticker that she'd seen at Adam's house and she realized that this must be where Tully lived. As she walked past the truck, she made out the lettering on the bumper-sticker—*Smile if you're not wearing undies.*

Julia stopped dead in her tracks as Adam continued ahead. She lifted her chin defiantly and purposely did not smile as she followed him up the decaying wooden steps to the back door.

Three generations of half-wild calico cats huddled on the half-shoveled back stairs like castaway children in the doorways of Bogota. Adam knocked and a sing-song little girl's voice answered.

"Come on in-n-n."

Walking straight into the small kitchen, Julia saw a panorama of the tabletop, stovetop, and sink strewn with piles of dirty dishes, crumbs, and caked-on food. Cat droppings were on the floor close to the bowls of catfood. The floorboards were painted brown and the plasterboard walls were dingy white, streaked with spatter-fat around the stove. Suspended from the string of the one electric lightbulb in the ceiling was a strip of flypaper with Summer flies still affixed like fossils in amber. 'Like a *New Yorker* cartoon,' Julia thought, realizing that probably none of them would know what that was. Stepping into Tully's house was like entering a novel she might have picked up by mistake, where the title page was gone and the author unknown, yet the story drew her on.

It was hot inside. Too hot. The heat from the gas stove combined with the intense heat of the woodstove, making Julia's fingertips tingle in contrast to the cold outside. An odor of sweat and cheap fried hamburger permeated the kitchen.

"Come on in and sit down," Tully greeted Adam from his chair at the table. He was barechested, and instead of trousers, he wore baggy, ribbed, greying long-johns. Though his hairless chest was flabby, his arms were still muscled.

"H'lo, Ad-am," sang a woman with wilted blonde hair in a raggedy Dutchboy cut she had obviously given herself, looking coyly at Julia. Adam introduced her as Tully's wife, Doris.

Doris had no top teeth. She was, Julia judged, no more than thirty. She wore drab brown polyester slacks, ripped sneakers, and a soiled white sweater. Her arms and legs were spidery thin but her stomach protruded in a way that no dieting would ever reduce. 'Tweedledee,' came instantly to Julia's mind.

Sitting at the far end of the table was a man who resembled Doris, although older. His blonde hair was thin at the very top of his head and hung down below his ears in wisps. He had the same pallor as Doris and eyes like oysters. Even the stubble of his beard seemed transparent. His grey flannel shirt was streaked with food stains down the front. His pants were saturated with motor oil and grease. And on closer inspection, Julia noticed a white crust on his eyelids and in the corners of his mouth. Adam introduced him as Babe, but Julia immediately thought, 'Tweedledum.'

"Doris, get something to drink for Adam," Tully bellowed. "What do you want, Adam? I just made some root beer. Have some. You, too." Meaning Julia, who had no time to decline before he said, "Doris, get some glasses, you hear?"

Julia flashed Adam an inquiring look, seeking a cue as to how to behave, but he seemed not to pay any attention. Doris removed two glasses from the cupboard.

"No thanks, don't bother. We're not staying," Adam said, and Julia felt profound relief.

But Tully continued to shout at Doris, "Wash them out! Wash them out!"

Adam leaned against the countertop. "We're just headed for the auction. You going?"

"I was, but I changed my mind. I'm tired and I got to work early tomorrow. This stinking job. And he won't put me on permanent so I can get the union medical. I'm plain disgusted with it."

From the end of the table, Julia heard babbling from Babe. "I'm goin'. I'm goin'. Good stuff. You know I was there. Every time. You know who I seen? That girl there. She's there. I got a egg beater."

Julia listened closely but couldn't follow him. He spoke only in half-formed ideas that trailed off into giggles and spit. It dawned on her that, for Babe, speaking was an act of aphasic self-gratification.

As she looked back at Adam, only a small curve along the corner of his mouth indicated his mirth. She began to think he enjoyed her discomfort. 'Or,' she speculated, 'he's studying me. He's been studying me right from the start. Watching to see how I react, gauging me the same as I've been gauging him.'

She had no time to reflect further because Tully's wife, who had since disappeared, returned holding a spindly little black and white kitten. Childlike, Doris extended the cat to her.

"See my pussy?"

Babe guffawed and Julia felt her cheeks flush.

"Kitties *like* me," Doris cooed as she held the purring kitten under her chin.

"I can see that," Julia replied kindly, while thinking, 'How do I get out of this?' But there was no escape in sight, so she continued to nod politely as Doris patted her…kitty.

After the roasting heat inside the house, the cold air outside was at first bracing, then numbing. As they got into the truck, Julia felt as though she had just climbed back out of the rabbit hole.

Adam turned to her with an appraising gaze.

"Impressions?"

Julia weighed her words. "You have an interesting social circle."

"Don't underestimate Tully. He has a lot of talents."

"Whilst a little short on dress code."

As he started the motor, Adam glanced at her and chuckled in amusement. His eyes had lost their uncompromising look.

"Why does he keep it so hot in there?" she asked. "To breed bottleflies?"

"*Competition* bottleflies. We have the Winter Nationals right here in Pittsley."

"I see. Prizes for quantity?"

"And size. We like 'em really big."

"Umm, well I think your friend has a blue-ribbon crop this year."

Adam smiled, then said earnestly, "Tully hates a cold house. Has to do with when he was a kid. He had a hard growing up." He began backing his truck out of the driveway.

"Neglect?"

Adam nodded.

She nodded in return, more to herself than to him.

Pulling out onto the road in the opposite direction, they passed a concrete-block foundation with a tarpaper roof. Smoke was trickling up out of the stubby brick chimney.

"That's where Babe lives."

"What does he do?"

"He worked in the slaughterhouse for a long time but that's been gone for years. Then he worked in the piggery, but that closed down about and year and a half ago. The town's changing and nobody's raising pigs around here anymore except Floyd Mather, and only on a small scale. Now he works on and off at the landfill and picks the dump for whatever he can sell. Collects cans and bottles. That sort of thing."

"A man for all seasons. Are Babe and Doris related?"

"Cousins. Maybe."

"Strong family resemblance," Julia said dryly and Adam smiled briefly again.

The snow crunched like popcorn under the big tires of the pick-up as they turned into Dawson's Turkey Farm.

Outside the auction barn, the cars and trucks were parked like tombstones in a wintry graveyard. They were, for the most part, old and dented vehicles, rusted, some bumperless where the chrome had been peeled off in accidents, fenders missing here and there. Some of the cars were windowless and patched with what looked like plastic wrap, shrouded in sheet-ice with snowpiles on the roof. Only the fresh tire ruts in the driveway and the cleared windshields proved that the vehicles were actually used, were actually driven to this spot.

Julia followed Adam into the vastness of the noisy crowded barn. Larger than a gymnasium, the barn was lined on both sides with rows of wooden bleachers rising nearly to the high ceiling and filled to capacity with men smoking and talking. Thick layers of smoke hovered over the auction-pit, shape-shifting in mid-air. Most of the men had beards or mustaches, and they wore the green caps and work clothes that seemed to be the local uniform.

There was only a scattering of women, in permutations of Doris with home-cut hair and wearing slightly shabby and mismatched clothes. In her silk pants' suit, Julia felt like Victorian nobility visiting the Marat-Sade asylum.

"Guess I'm a little Lord-and-Taylorish," she acknowledged.

"You mean a little *long* on dress code?"

"Touché."

As Adam made no motion to sit, but stood scanning the crowd, Julia did likewise. In front of the auctioneer's raised podium, goods to be auctioned were stacked and strewn on the ground—a jumble of boxes containing kitchen gadgets and bric-a-brac, old furniture, lamps, mattresses, auto parts, buckets of tar and paint. Amongst the heaps were cages with rabbits and squawking chickens.

Men milled in and out of the piles, examining the items, pointing and talking animatedly among themselves. Most of the women sat in the bleachers, talking or smoking.

Children wriggled in their seats or ran down the bleachers to play underneath. It was noisy as a basketball game, and there was a mix of odors—people, food, and animals.

Julia spotted the bearded man she'd seen yesterday in Adam's livingroom. Was he Billy or Cutter? 'Swamp Yankee,' she guessed. He was standing in line at the concession stand and she watched in fascination while two short women behind the counter scooped what looked like tan-colored lima beans into paper cups. The sign read "Favas." The two women worked faster and faster to keep up with the line.

As she waited for the auction to begin, a thin man in his thirties stood up and nervously cleared his throat for attention. He looked indistinguishable from the other men except for the anxious look on his face.

"I want to make an announcement. You all know that my cousin's little girl, Jeannine, is missing. The police ain't found anything and they been lookin' everywhere for her. We can use some help. All you who can, come to Otis and Cora's house tomorrow morning at daybreak for more searchin'. We can use all the help we can get. Thank you." Amidst nods from the crowd, he sat back down.

Julia turned to Adam. "Could she be lost in the woods?"

"Not likely."

Before she could ask more, Cutter walked over to them with his cup of fava beans. His jeans rode low on his hips, the .38 sagging on his belt.

"Did you hear about Bill Kerwin, Adam?"

"Yeah, too bad."

"We had worse police chiefs," Cutter pronounced. "At least he knew how to handle things. He coulda had my hairy ass on a platter a couple 'a times, but he was okay." It was a eulogy that Chief Kerwin would have found flattering. "I hear they're gonna get a replacement from outside. I don't much like that idea." He proceeded to eat his favas.

Adam continued scanning the crowd. "Conny Cran-shaw's here."

Cutter's gaze swept the bleachers until he found what he was searching for.

"Who's Connie?" Julia inquired as casually as she could, looking for the woman who inspired such attention.

But Adam had already walked away, leaving her with Cutter. He went directly over to the far side of the barn and began climbing the rows of bleachers.

Julia pursed her lips in irritation. First, he treated her as though she weren't there, and now he'd left her for another woman. She turned to Cutter, trying to make it sound as though it didn't matter. "So who's Connie?"

"A scumbag." Cutter spat the last shell of a fava onto the floor and tossed the cup and spoon into a nearby trash barrel.

"Oh."

Julia decided not to pursue it. Instead, she watched Adam finish climbing to the highest row and stop in front of a seated man with a full head of prematurely silver hair and ruddy cheeks, wearing a white cable-knit sweater and jeans.

"Oh," she repeated when she realized her mistake. The more intently she watched, the more she wondered what was going on. There was something in the way he sat back talking to Adam, and the way the men around him leaned forward, deferentially.

"Okay, folks," a voice boomed, "we are commencing to begin." A huge man with a large belly and an ill-fitting red toupee assumed the microphone. He smoked a giant cigar while two young helpers, a slim girl and a slimmer boy, lined up the items. The crowd hushed as though on cue. Julia's attention was drawn back to the spectacle.

"For those of you who don't know me—few though they may be—I am the Marquis de Lard, and it is my pleasure to torture the last penny from your pockets. We got a lot of articles to get through tonight," he continued, "and we're going to get to every one. Buyer's premium, seller's premium, cash or good check only. We reserve the right to pass an item according to our judgment and to refuse a low bid at will. I am your master of merchandise and I am unmerciful. So be it. The first item, please."

The young girl fetched a roasting pan and passed it to the auctioneer, like a handmaiden.

"Item number one. We have here a semi-virgin roasting pan, used only once, on a ceremonial occasion...Thanksgiving." He leered and the men in the bleachers laughed. "No bumps. No bruises. No burns. Almost innocent. What am I bid?"

A male voice rang out, "Fifty cents!"

The bids rose to seventy-five cents, then eighty-five, then a dollar, but Julia turned back to watch Adam. He had placed his foot on the seat of the bleacher between Conny and the man seated next to him, causing that man to shift over. Then Adam put his elbow on his knee and leaned forward just a little. 'Interesting maneuver,' Julia thought. If the seated Conny didn't want to stare at Adam's belt buckle, he had to look up in order to talk.

"Last call. Sold for a dollar-twenty-five."

The young boy, his long brown hair sweeping over his eyes like a pony's forelock, brought over a case of anti-freeze containers.

"Now what have we here? Six gallon jugs of anti-freeze, unopened. Not for drinking, folks, don't confuse it with limeade or Midori. It goes in your vehicle, not your mouth. I know I got to say these things or you'll claim I didn't give you notice. Okay, who'll start?"

"Ten cents," another male voice piped up.

The auctioneer reviewed the crowd. "'Zat you, Babe Hamply?"

Julia looked at the source of the voice and recognized Tweedledum. She hadn't noticed him come in. The invisible man. He giggled at being recognized by the auctioneer and nodded his head vigorously.

"Ten lousy cents," the auctioneer scoffed. "You couldn't get a single rubber for ten cents and that don't go into your mouth either." The audience roared.

Julia's gaze settled on the man sitting next to Babe. Thin as a razorblade, sitting ramrod straight on the bench. He had a receding forehead and short clipped salt-and-pepper hair. Where Babe was slovenly and unkempt, this man was fastidious. He looked as though his clothes were newly cleaned and pressed. Everything about him seemed tidy. She was struck by the contrast between him and the other men in the room.

"Anti-freeze, my friends, think on it. A miracle of the modern age. Without anti-freeze, you know what happens to your water when the temperature drops?"

"Piss icicles!" Babe shouted out his answer like a second-grader.

Amidst laughter, the auctioneer pointed his finger at Babe and poked at the air. "Now there's a man who imbibes the green goddess, folks."

While the crowd cawed approval, the severe man next to Babe said something and Babe stopped laughing.

Julia's attention returned to the bleachers. Conny had raised himself from his unfavorable position on the pretext of searching his pockets for a pack of cigarettes. He found them in his shirt pocket, lit one and offered the pack to Adam, who declined. Casually, Adam straightened up. Being shorter, Conny lost the contest, but never looked directly at his opponent. Instead, he looked around the room and, as he came to Julia, his gaze lingered. She felt a sudden discomfort. Then he moved on to Cutter. Cutter saluted him with his middle finger and Conny saluted back in kind with a half-smile that wasn't friendly.

"I suppose Adam knows what he's doing," she commented, hoping to draw Cutter out.

"Kiddo, I've never known Adam Sabeski to do anything he wasn't meaning to do and I've known him a pretty long time. I suppose you could say I know him better than anybody."

"I guess he's never been married then?"

"I don't answer Adam-questions. You got a question about Adam, you ask him."

Rebuked, Julia squared her shoulders and turned back to the auctioneer, who was holding up a chair.

"Here's a nice little thumbnail chair. Looks like an old piece. Just like my wife. The rushing is gone but the frame is good. Worth a penny or a sou. I don't think it would hold the Marquis de Lard, but if you're some wispy little thing, it'll do fine. Ah, yes, fat, my dears, fat is a sign of high status in some lands, did you know that? And do you know why, laddies? Hmmm? Because *everything* is in proportion, that's why! Start the bidding."

"One dollar."

"Dollar-fifty."

The bidding increased to two, then three. Suddenly, Julia held up her hand. "Four."

"Four. Fourdy-fourdy-four, do I hear five? Five anyone? Five? Four and a half? Do I hear four and a half?" When no one spoke, the auctioneer closed the bidding. "Sold for four dollars. You just got yourself a skinny chair, miss. No ifs, ands, or buts."

"She got the butt for it," a male voice called out.

Julia was suddenly glad that Cutter was standing beside her. Then it occurred to her that that was exactly why Adam had placed her there.

* * *

"What's that?" Adam asked about her purchase. Almost a half-hour had passed between the time he'd left and returned.

"A skinny chair, to fit my derriere."

His eyes dropped automatically towards her backside and Julia quickly added, "Nev-er mind."

He cocked his head as though baffled, then turned his attention to the auction pit as the young helper led in the first goat.

"Here we have a nubile Nubian, folks. Three months of age and—"

Before the offer was completed, Adam stepped forward into the circle. The crowd came to a hush.

"I see it's our veterinary friend again, is it. What's up doc?" the auctioneer bantered.

But Adam did not reply as he strode over to the goat pen. Ignoring the murmurs rising from the bleachers, he entered the pen and began to examine the animals.

"What's happening?" Julia asked Cutter.

"Goats are too thin."

As she looked more carefully, she could see that the goats' ribs were showing. Some of them seemed wobbly, almost too weak to stand.

A voice from the audience shouted, "That there's a little girl goat, doc, be gentle!"

"Woo! Straight in!"

Julia recognized Babe's voice and when she looked, he was giggling. The thin man beside him was staring at Adam like everyone else. Then Julia noticed Cutter fingering the .38 on his hip.

The auctioneer played to the crowd like a Saturday night wrestler. "Dr. Sabeski's looking for a nanny. Can anyone give him a hand?"

The crowd hooted and hollered and began clapping their hands in unison, the rhythm gathering more and more momentum. Finally, Adam straightened up and shook his head 'no' at the auctioneer.

"No goats tonight, my friends," the auctioneer announced. "No kid-ding."

The audience groaned as Adam left the circle.

"What happens now?" Julia asked.

Cutter never took his eyes off the crowd or his hand off his pistol. "He's going to impound them."

Adam waited until the pen of goats was emptied back into the stalls behind the auctioneer.

"Who do they belong to?" Julia asked Cutter.

"That son-of-a-bitch up there."

Julia looked up into the bleachers but couldn't detect any expression on Conny's face.

Adam walked back to Julia and Cutter, saying to her, "Get your chair and let's go."

The auctioneer had meanwhile resumed without missing a beat, "We've got a prize here, folks, three rolls of tarpaper. All new. No nail holes." But the crowd was still making goat and sheep calls as Adam and Julia left.

The auctioneer's voice followed them out of the barn. "Repair to your roofs, gentlemen. Repair to your roofs!"

Carrying her chair like a shield, Julia plunged out into the cold night behind Adam. It was beginning to snow again. In silence, he lifted the little chair into the bed of the truck and covered it with a tarpaulin.

"What will happen to the goats?" she asked.

"I'll come back for them tomorrow. I know a farmer who'll keep them until the hearing."

"Does that mean you're taking Conny Cranshaw to court?"

"Umm hmm."

"Then what? Will he be fined?"

"Depends on whether or not he's convicted."

"Is that likely?"

"Maybe, maybe not."

"I don't understand. If you can't convict him, why go to all this trouble?"

"For the goats."

He didn't speak for the rest of the way to her house, and then it was only a simple "Goodnight."

Back in the safety of her home, Julia wondered how close they had been to real trouble tonight. And what sort of man was this, who both was and was not in harmony with this strange backwoods landscape?

Readying for bed, she missed Cat lying at her feet while she washed and creamed her face. Cat had never been Phillip's dog, even though he had picked her out of the litter and had tried repeatedly to win her to him. She had accepted his affections but her loyalty had always been to Julia. With Phillip gone so often—probably with his girlfriend, Julia realized belatedly—she had spent all her free time with Cat.

But who could have stabbed her? Some young boy? Had to be. Grown men didn't stab dogs for no reason. In fact, if anything, they would beat the dog to death or shoot it for something it did or didn't do. But young boys (and it was gender-specific in most of the research she'd read) generally did a lot more mayhem than one stab wound. Loners like Albert DeSalvo, when he was young, shot arrows into a caged cat. Then there was disemboweling—done mainly by kids in groups. However, the all-time favorite, whether alone or in concert, seemed to be dousing animals with gasoline and setting them on fire. So the more she analyzed it, neither alternative, boy or man, seemed entirely logical. What was the motive? The answer eluded her and that made it all the more distressing. In the end, she was just grateful that Adam was taking good care of her closest companion.

Adam was a puzzle. He obviously had great compassion and caring for animals. But while he appeared to have a number of male friends, there was no evidence of a woman's presence in his life. Adam Sabeski appeared to be a thorough bachelor. And yet, she felt he must have some interest in her. She was not so young and naive, however, to think anything would come it. This wasn't a life she could embrace, should it come to that.

"I'm getting w-aay ahead of myself," she said aloud to the pale face in the mirror. "You know what'll happen if he sees you without makeup? Gonzo."

She ran her fingers over the edges of her mouth, smoothing out the fine lines that started to appear almost mysteriously on her forty-fourth birthday. She was still attractive enough, she concluded, but obviously no ingénue. And the lines would only increase. Somehow she'd have to make her peace with that.

"Nah," she declared aloud, "no truce with traitors," and turned out the light.

In the dark, however, her valor dissolved into the night. Admittedly, she was aging—not old yet, but getting there. No longer was there an infinite future to distinguish herself. 'But there must be something more for me than *this*, mustn't there?' She thought about her father, and how she had vowed to make him proud of her. But that was twenty years ago.

She gradually fell asleep wondering about Tully's father, and what *his* childhood had been like. And about Doris in her childlike simplicity. And about the little girl who had disappeared. Relative to all that, shouldn't she, Julia, just be terribly grateful for what she had?

* * *

He never slept well. Hadn't in years. It was the jungle. Made him alert. Snapping of twigs. No sound of footsteps, just a movement of air and mating frogs. That's when you knew they were there. Maybe just beyond that tree. But how many?

Even worse than the guerillas were the gook women. The one that came into camp crying and bloody, and when the men went to help her, she pulled the grenade pin. He'd seen that. Blew herself to bits and ten men around her. Blew them all to smithereens, but not him. He was taking a shit when it happened.

"Bless my bowels," he laughed.

TUESDAY, JANUARY 15th

After breakfast, Julia drove to the campus of Pittsley Community College. It was the bucolic setting that had attracted her to the school, the acres of fields backing up to Pittsley Woods and a New England look to the somewhat old-fashioned but brand-new buildings. Open for only two years, everything about the college seemed fresh to her when she'd arrived for the interview. A new school, a new start.

'Things are not always what they seem,' she concluded. Because stepping into her new classroom had been disappointing. The students seemed listless. Disinterested. She thought she could energize them, but she hadn't.

As she began walking along the flagstone path to her building, she became aware of a car motor somewhere behind her, idling. Not that a car shouldn't be there, but the slowness of it seemed wrong. She turned around to look, but found nothing. Had there been a car behind her when she was driving in? She tried to recall looking at the rearview mirror. She remembered seeing a truck, a black truck, on the road, but only briefly. Nothing unusual about that. She heard, but did not see, the vehicle accelerate away.

As Julia erased a conjugation of French verbs on the blackboard from the previous class, it evoked sharp memories of her own college French class at Radcliffe. She relived the embarrassment she'd felt when the Parisian instructor had derided her French-Canadian pronunciation—the inflection that Grandpére had taught her. She'd been the only student the instructor had singled out.

"It's *ooooouuuu*, Mademoiselle Arnault, not *e-yu*. *E-yu* is something you say when you step in it."

Each time Julia spoke in class, she was sarcastically corrected. She soon became reluctant to answer, but the instructor pointedly continued to ask her questions. So Julia had transferred to Spanish. She had run away from battle then, just as she did after her divorce. She knew she should have stayed in Boston and confronted Phillip there, but she didn't. She had erased his name like chalk on the blackboard.

Julia turned around to face eight rows of bored young faces. Bodies twisting in impatience. Conversations in undertones. One young man in the back had his eyes closed. She quickly opened the textbook, *Introduction to Psychology*, and turned to the chapter of "Abnormal Personality."

SATURDAY, FEBRUARY 9th

Over the past weeks, Cat had fully recovered and Adam returned her to Julia, but he'd reported that nothing more had been discovered about the dog's attacker. He hadn't asked her out since the auction, so she assumed he'd lost interest. Then he unexpectedly phoned to invite her to dinner and dancing.

"You can wear jeans," he'd advised.

As they entered the dance hall, Julia couldn't conceal her surprise. "I didn't know there were any country-western places in Massachusetts!"

"Civilization's only skin deep," Adam replied non-chalantly.

The Mayfair was one enormous room with a band-stand at one end and a bar at the other, rows of wooden picnic tables and benches on each side of the large center dance floor. Old farm implements hung from the walls and ceiling. There were scythes and hay rakes, cranberry scoops, wooden brass-tipped hames (that fit around the neck of a draft animal to attach the traces) and wagonwheels. In the center of the ceiling, an old horse-drawn sleigh was suspended by chains overhead. As Julia looked around, she realized that the ceilings and walls contained the history of New England agriculture. And yet, here, it didn't seem like history; it seemed as though it were simply everyday life in Pittsley.

The hall was filled to capacity with men and women eating and drinking, dancing a cross between an Irish clog and a Texas two-step to loud country music. Unlike the unidirectional, merry-go-round western dancing, Juckets danced wherever they damn pleased, sliding into pockets of empty space between other couples, monopolizing corners of the dance floor as their own property, sometimes tromping on toes or bumping elbows and hips. Was it a liberty of spirit, a nonconformity from the expected, performance art, or simply bad manners? Julia wasn't sure.

She sat opposite Adam at the end of a long table alongside three other couples eating steamers and drinking beer. They exchanged friendly hellos and some small talk with Adam, but mostly stayed to themselves.

Adam ordered two clamboils and a pitcher of beer as Julia turned her attention to the dance floor. Each couple seemed to have its own motion, inventing steps to the vibrating beat of the band. All the dancers wore jeans and cowboy shirts; the men wore boots and hats, the women wore neck scarves and high heels. Very high heels. One tiny woman with short dark hair and tall red shoes stood out.

"They call her mouse meat," Adam said, observing Julia's stare.

"And what do they call you?" she asked.

"That depends on who you're talking to. Conny Cranshaw calls me a prick. Most everybody else calls me a pain in the ass."

"Are you?"

"I do my best." He smiled ruefully and she smiled back.

They watched the dancers for a few more minutes until Adam held out his hand.

"Want to try?"

Seconds later, they were dancing to "It's a Fine Time to Leave Me, Lucille." Her head reached just up to his chin and she could smell aftershave this time, fresh and salty. No Latakia.

He danced with a kind of abandon that Julia had difficulty matching, but he held her tightly and moved her around the floor as easily as if she were weightless. She gave up any attempt to learn his steps or anticipate his direction, and let herself simply flow with him.

After several more dances, they made their way back to the table just as the clamboil arrived in a galvanized bucket with steamers, corn on the cob, sausages and chorizo, hot dogs, boiled potatoes, and cabbage. Along with that came a pitcher of beer that dripped froth onto the paper tablecloth.

They began with the hot steamers, sliding the dark casings off the long necks and holding the clams like upside-down lollipops to dip first in salty clambroth, then melted butter. She tried to be neat, but the butter ran down her chin and she kept wiping it with her napkin. Adam fared no better as napkins gave way to fingers and the backs of their hands.

"Have you always lived around here?" Julia asked between clams.

"Just about."

"And your family, too?"

He didn't answer immediately, seeming to concentrate on his food until he finally said "Not my father. He was born in Brockton. My mother came from here. She was a Wombart." He looked up at her with those hawk eyes, "And yes, that's a Jucket name."

Julia reacted as though she had been caught rifling through his personal belongings. But, 'in for a penny, in for a pound,' she told herself and probed on. "Do they still live in Pittsley?"

"They died in a car crash ten years ago. The other driver was seventeen and drunk."

"I'm sorry." She did not know how to make that sound sincere. "Do you have any brothers or sisters?" She was inching toward the question she really wanted to ask.

"No."

"Any wives, current or former?" she said casually.

"No."

"Why not?"

He looked at her like someone who'd asked him if he brushed his teeth today.

"Well, it was worth a shot," she shrugged unapologetically. He flashed her a quick smile and she was about to ask more, but the band got into "Orange Blossom Special." The fiddle yowled and the electric guitar reverberated, filling the room so that no other sound could exist there. The music's engine accelerated little by little, faster and faster, the fiddler moving his body in rhythm until the train whistled, took the curves, and accelerated so fast that, at the crescendo, the strings on the fiddle broke apart. At the end, amidst the clapping and shouting, the fiddler laid the broken strings on the microphone.

After finishing their meal, Julia and Adam danced every dance. Finally, the band ended on "When the Saints Go Marching In," and everyone circled the hall in a conga line, ending up at their own tables. As the band members began to put away their instruments, someone called out another song.

"*Kaw-li-ga*!"

To Julia, who had never heard the word, it sounded like Ka-lie-jah and she wondered if they were ordering some unique local dish.

The word echoed around the room.

"*Kaw-li-ga*!"

The demand grew louder. The crowd began stomping feet and clapping hands in unison. Finally, the band acquiesced and took up their instruments again.

The rhythm began slowly, and built. The guitar dominated. The beat was fast and the music was loud, so loud it vibrated through the chairs and tables into their bodies. The clapping began again.

"*Kaw-li-ga*!"

Most everyone stayed seated while the band played, singing out the lyrics of the Hank Williams song in chorus, the tale of the lovestruck wooden Indian and the Indian maiden in the antique store:

"Poor ol' Kaw-li-ga, he never got a kiss..."

Only two young couples ventured out to dance to the undanceable music. The fiddle twanged.

"Poor ol' Kaw-li-ga, he don't know what he missed."

As the sound grew, the crowd stopped clapping and singing, and one by one they turned to one particular table.

Julia recognized one of the men at the table as the man who had made the announcement about his cousin's daughter at the auction. The girl was still missing. She had forgotten all about it.

Then the one particular old man at that table, the one everybody was waiting for, got up on his chair. From there, onto the table. He began dancing by himself, arms and legs jerking and flopping like a marionette's.

Adam sat back in his chair, arms folded, as though waiting for something. Julia, too, became expectant, although she did not know for what.

"*Kaw-li-ga*!"

The old man continued to dance wilder and wilder. The clapping resumed and formed a tornado of noise with the music. The music became impossibly louder and faster, the band sweating and straining to a crescendo.

"*Kaw-li-ga*," and again, "*Kaw-li-ga*"!!!

As the band sounded the last *Kaw-li-ga*, the old man raised up on his toes. Then, on the final note, he dove off the table headfirst onto the floor and knocked himself out.

"Adam!"

"It's okay."

The band held the note, then strummed it to a finish and every clapped. The man lay on the floor as his tablemates tried to pull him to his feet.

"What do you mean, it's okay? Isn't he hurt? Shouldn't we do something?"

"Nope. That's old Elgin Bradburn. Does it every week."

She shook her head. "I feel like I'm in Wonderland and the Mad Hatter just cold-cocked himself."

"Welcome to the real world," Adam toasted with the last of his beer.

"Is it?"

Adam simply inclined his head as if to say, 'You decide.'

Sleep did not come easily to her that night. Her thoughts revolved excitedly around Adam. She was beginning to like him, and the prospect of entering into his kind of life was alluring. She felt as though she were being offered initiation into a closed society.

Then her mood dampened. "But what does he really think of me?" she murmured aloud. This was their second time out together and she still didn't know if he was actually courting her. This evening seemed special, but then when it was over, it was over. She wished she weren't so attracted to him. 'It's only because he's different, and I'm feeling so proletarian,' she told herself. She sighed and felt a soft pulsing between her thighs.

She truly had not wanted a man in a long time. Not after her experience with Phillip. And long before her marriage was over, she had stopped wanting him. As if her body had known what her mind was unwilling to acknowledge, that he really did not want her either. She had begun to think that she did not have any passion left. That she was past it.

So, in a way, it was reassuring to find out that she could still have desire. And yet, she didn't want all the adolescent palpitations and consuming thoughts about whether or not he wanted her too, interpreting every word and gesture, living for their evenings together. The way she'd been with Phillip.

'Oh no,' she thought, shaking her head. 'I'm not going through all that again. There are more important things to think about.' Like work, for instance. It was time for her to recapture her ambition for research and publishing. She should concentrate on that now.

Just then, the telephone rang. Julia raised herself on one elbow and reached over to pick up the receiver wondering if it might be Adam.

"And where have you been all evening?" said the girlish voice on the other end in a mock-scolding tone.

"Is that what happens in my old age, we reverse roles? I suppose you're going to lecture me on safe sex next."

Karen laughed. "Does that mean you were out on a date, Mom?"

"Well, sort of." Julia sat cross-legged on the bed.

"Who with? The vet?"

"Umm hmm."

"You like him?"

"Platonically."

"Yeah, right. Well, anyway, I wanted to thank you for the Valentine's card, Mom. It's very funny."

"Yours, too," Julia replied somewhat glumly, glancing over at the bureau to look again at the front of the card.

"Oops," Karen said quickly. "Sounds like you didn't think so."

"Yes, I did," Julia reassured her, "it just strikes a little close to the bone."

The card depicted a seductive, busty, blue-eyes blonde with the caption 'Happy Valentine's Day to a Special Mom.' On the inside, the blonde vamp was handing a card to a withered old hag, and underneath it read, 'from your sexy daughter.'

She knew it was meant as a joke between them. Karen actually was a blue-eyed blonde like her father, but she wasn't exactly voluptuous. She had, in fact, the same boyishly thin shape as her mother.

"I didn't mean it that way, honest," Karen protested.

"I know. I'm just feeling a little over the hill tonight. Julia pulled her red silk nightgown away from her chest, peered down at her small breasts, and made a face.

"Sounds like you need a good roll in the hay."

"I think my 'hey' days are over."

"Jeez, Mom, you're only forty-seven."

"Forty-five."

"Oh, is that the new math?"

"Brat. Anyway, how are things with you?"

Cat meanwhile had awakened and moved up from the foot of the bed to rest her head on her mistress' lap. Julia patted Cat absently while she listened to Karen. The dog closed her eyes contentedly.

"Great. I love this job. Adele says she's going to train me to take on some of her editing work and she might even let me try writing an article. I thought I'd do it on Grand

Central Station. You know, talk to people waiting for trains, and the vendors and everything. Slice of life. What do you think?"

"Sounds like fun."

"And Paul can take the photos. I'm kind of charged about it."

"How is Paul?" Julia asked with forced enthusiasm.

"Great. He's been getting photography jobs almost every weekend for the past month."

"That's good."

"Yes, it is. I know he's going to be able to make a living at it soon."

When Karen paused, Julia suspected it was significant. 'What's coming now?' she wondered, and was afraid she knew.

"Paul gave me a special Valentine's gift, Mom."

"Already?"

"He's like us, ghastly early with cards and presents. Guess what it is."

"A trip to Jersey."

"An engagement ring."

"Well," Julia expelled it like a held-in breath. "Congratulations, honey, that's wonderful."

She hoped Karen didn't suspect she didn't mean it. When Julia'd met Paul at Christmastime, he had seemed pleasant enough, but she saw something in him that concerned her. Julia's college roommate would have called him, in Yiddish, a *luftmench.* An 'air man' was the closest translation Harriet could give her. A dreamer. A man who spins dreams in the air. (She fleetingly thought she should give Harriet a call in Chicago. Funny, how none of her friends from her married years bothered with her after she and Phillip split up. But Harriet was a pre-Phillip friend.) Anyway, Julia was not happy about having her daughter engaged to a man who took party pictures for a living.

"Have you decided on a wedding date?" Julia prayed not.

"Next year, Valentine's Day."

"Well, good, that gives us time to plan."

'And,' Julia thought hopefully, 'time for plans to change.'

"We're living together now."

"Oh." This was unexpected. "Your place or his?"

"Here."

"Oh." Was she going to have to talk to him? What was she supposed to say, glad to have you boinking my daughter? "Is Paul there now?"

"No, he's working an anniversary party."

Julia could almost see Karen saying this tight-lipped with a wounded look on her pretty face. 'O-migod,' she suddenly though, 'I sound like a crone.' So she hastily amended, "I just wanted to know if I have to memorize a new phone number, that's all. Darling, I want you to be happy and if you and Paul are planning a life together, I'm all for it. I know he loves you. And I know you love him. So, give him a congratulatory kiss from his mother-in-law to be."

"Thanks, Mom," Karen said softly. "I love you."

"Love you too, sweetheart. I'll call you next week."

Julia hung up the phone and leaned against the headboard with a sigh. Then she hugged Cat, who sleepily opened her eyes and gave Julia's nose a warm lick.

* * *

"What, then, is the nature of God that He permits it all?"

"God is weak," he answered, "for He cannot control chaos. Or God is indifferent, for He chooses not to intervene."

"And why does God not exercise His power? Is it that He has none? Or is unaware? Not care? Not there?"

"He is a little girl who tires of her doll and drops it in the mud on the roadside. He is the mother who batters her son."

"What then is the nature of God, that He permits the destruction, disease, and devastation of innocents?"

"Ungodly."

"Amen."

SUNDAY, FEBRUARY 10th

A month after Jeannine Bradburn disappeared, all the intensive searching came to a halt. The effect of Jeannine's disappearance on the town of Pittsley had been immediate and profound, albeit temporary. No children were permitted to play or walk alone. Teachers gave daily reminders about not riding with strangers. Mothers and fathers yelled at their youngsters when they were only five minutes late from school. The town had felt a collective shudder.

In the end, the police concluded, privately and strictly unofficially, that she would not be found. But how and where Jeannine had gone remained a complete mystery. The only lead they had was from a classmate of hers who remembered seeing a black pick-up truck at the stop where Jeannine got off the school bus several blocks from home. But she didn't see Jeannine get into the truck, nor did she see who was driving it because the bus pulled away too quickly. But black pick-ups were a commodity in the area, just about everyone owned one. It wasn't so much a clue as a frustration.

Chief Carson Burke's frustration was intensified even more because he desperately wanted to make good on his first case in Pittsley. Better than good. He wanted this town to think he was as competent as his predecessor, Bill Kerwin. No, he wanted to be better than that hick cop.

Burke's own law enforcement experience was limited to a town in northern Massachusetts where the only real crimes were breaking-and-entering and drug parties. The Pittsley town fathers thought he would be knowledgeable about the growing drug trade spreading throughout the area that stymied the local police. They didn't realize that the only B&Es Burke had handled were more attempted than executed—since the well-to-do estates in Dover Heights had their own security systems and street patrols—and that drug trafficking, if it occurred there at all, was an exclusive and expensive enterprise. Burke, on the other hand, had no idea that his elevation to Chief in a country community would be any more challenging than domestic disputes.

His old nervous habit from childhood of biting his cuticles had returned; they were all but gone now and two of his fingers were slightly infected. Chief Burke was beginning to believe that everyone there thought he was an asshole. Worse, he was beginning to feel like one, despite the fact that he had put all of his effort into this investigation. He spent hours upon hours at his computer. He even hooked up to the national networks of missing children, and tapped the federal files in Quantico on convicted sex offenders and child molesters.

Sergeant Percy Davis conducted the local investigation, talking with Jeannine's classmates, teachers, and family. But he, like Burke, had been thwarted by the lack of clues. And after all that, what did they know for sure? Only (*a*) that she got off the bus, (*b*) a black pick-up was in the vicinity of the bus stop, and (*c*) she never reached home. Did she get into the truck? Or did someone else come along? Did she go with someone she knew, or was she abducted? Where did he take her? Was she still alive? She might be dead, the Sergeant knew, but state law said there was no murder where there was no body. So, the case would remain a missing-child case unless they learned otherwise.

Never did Sgt. Davis consider that Jeannine might have gotten lost. She was too close to home. There were no shortcuts. He briefly entertained the notion that she might be a runaway but in all his interviews nothing suggested any motive or means for it. As much as he hoped for her safety, he knew the odds were against it. And as much as he disdained the new Chief's computer crime-solving, he had to acknowledge grudgingly that, if Jeannine were still alive, it was more likely she'd be long gone from Pittsley. In some ways, she might be better off dead than kidnapped. Being raped wasn't the worst of it. The prospects were all grim.

* * *

Cora Bradburn feared learning what happened to her daughter. She would rather Jeannine remain missing forever than to endure the agony of her death. Or worse, to find her girl drugged and degraded. She knew that whoever took Jeannine had raped her. It's what men did to women.

She, herself, had been raped by a group of older boys when she was Jeannine's age. The unbearable shame of it still haunted her even though the only thing she could remember now was struggling as they held her arms and legs, struggling with all her strength, and struggling until there was no more hope. When she had been tossed out of the car in front of her house and lay crying on the ground, no one had told her it wasn't her fault. No one had said the humiliation wasn't hers. No one had done anything to find the boys. Instead, the family and everyone else had viewed her as sullied. "Cora the whore-a," they'd jeered. So she was grateful to Otis Bradburn for marrying her despite her reputation and she loved him for his love of her. She had been as devoted a wife and mother as she could possibly be. Yet, here this tragedy had come to her. Reminding her of the most terrible time in her life, and tearing up her insides to think about her poor Jeannine.

* * *

Over the course of the month, as with all else, the rest of the Bradburns had accepted the finality of the loss and little by little resumed their daily routines. All except Jeannine's father, who pined in silence for his daughter, and her mother, who remained both tearful and terrified.

Slowly, Pittsley returned to its normal habits, and the air of frightened expectation dissipated. Someone suggested that maybe Jeannine took up with some boy and went off with him.

"After all, she's Cora-the-whore-a's daughter, isn't she?"

"What, at thirteen?"

"You know them Juckets, they ma-ture real early."

Thus, the town relegated the fear into some other compartment that said, 'It wasn't what we thought, it was a Jucket thing. *We're* all safe.'

SUNDAY, MARCH 2nd

Nearly another month passed before Adam called Julia again. This time, it was to ask her over to his house for a stockpot dinner.

Julia presented herself at four o'clock bearing an extra large Black Forest cake she'd labored over that morning. It was covered in whipped cream with ground walnuts sprinkled along the sides and shaved chocolate with cherries on top. Adam showed her in with a skeptical expression as though privately convinced none of *his* friends were likely to eat such fancy cake. He appeared more than a little surprised when they did.

Julia sat on the sidelines as Billy, Cutter, and Adam discussed such weighty matters over stew as the destruction of local trees from gypsy moths, Dutch elm disease, and pine rust. These deliberations occupied at least an hour, with Julia wondering what all the mystique was about and why he'd invited her to this un-birthday party.

Around five o'clock, Tully arrived with a large cardboard carton of cranberries. Each of the plastic bags inside was slit or torn, but most of the cranberries were salvageable.

"I was bringing Tommy back and I stopped at Safeway. Got 'em outa the dumpster. Lookit that. You talk about waste. More food in this country gets wasted than eaten. Nothing wrong with these at all." He held up a bag to Julia. "See that? Couple of squashed berries and they throw the whole thing out. You want one?"

"Thank you, no. I'm not that fond of cranberries." She was, actually, but something told her to demur.

"Don't you make cranberry bread?" Tully insisted. "I make cranberry bread, cranberry relish. Then I'm gonna make wine. I got fourteen more cartons outside. Anybody else want some?"

The others declined except for Billy. "I might take a bag for Tessa," he said, "she bakes cranberry muffins."

"Here, take a couple, I got plenty. Adam, you got a paper bag or something to put them in?"

As Adam went into the kitchen, Tully continued to talk non-stop to Julia. "You don't know what you're missing, but I'll bet you'll be sorry once you taste my cranberry wine."

"You saying she'll be sorry when she tastes your cranberry wine?" Cutter quipped.

But Tully forged on. "I got four five-pound bags of sugar outa the dumpster last week. Canned tuna. Hostess cupcakes. Loaves of bread. Boxes of potatoes. Nothing wrong with any of it."

In the wake of Tully's stampeding conversation, Julia said nothing.

"Lotsa people turn up their noses at dumpster food, but there ain't nothing wrong with any of this. We're a wasteful country, that's what."

What he didn't mention, but all of them knew except Julia, was that Tully also ate road kill. The State police would call him when a deer was hit and Tully would winch up the 200- or 300-pound deer, take it home, dress it off, pop the meat into his freezer and the remains of the carcass into his industrial-size woodstove in his basement. He wasn't averse to picking up a raccoon, either. Nothing about Tully wasn't utilitarian. It was his personal challenge in life to make everything work for him. Food, in particular.

When Adam returned, Tully put three bags of cranberries into the paper sack for Billy. "Here, you take that to Tessa. She make good cranberry bread? I make it with black walnuts. Walnut tree right down there at the intersection. I get a sack of them every year. They're good eating, black walnuts."

"Black walnut trees are the most expensive wood in this country," Cutter commented.

"Why is that?" Billy asked, accepting the paper bag of cranberries that Tully put on his lap.

Before Cutter could reply, Tully answered, “Take the longest to grow, twenty or thirty years for a good size tree.”

“What’s the wood like?” Billy hefted the weight of the cranberries, so much more than he’d expected.

Cutter jumped in. “Hard. Real hard. They use it for spindles, shipping materials, anything that you need hard wood for.” He crossed his arms over his chest.

“Not furniture?”

“Not much,” Cutter replied to Billy, but his eyes were on Tully. “Not much.”

“Veneer,” Tully added.

“Yeah, sometimes,” Cutter conceded.

“There’s a black walnut tree over by the Nemasket Inn,” Tully declared.

“That tree belongs to Mrs. Swanson,” Cutter cautioned.

Tully nodded vigorously. “I give her some of my goose eggs and she lets me pick up all the walnuts I want. She’s too old to bother with them anymore. They’re too hard to crack.”

“How about a piece of cake?” Adam indicated the half-eaten layer cake on the table. “Julia made it.”

“Oh yeah?” Tully glanced at the cake, then at Julia. “I didn’t think you could cook.”

“What made you think that?”

“You don’t make cranberry bread or nothing. I’ll give you some of mine and you see if you don’t like it. It’s the black walnuts, that’s the thing.” He smiled his rabbit-tooth smile.

“Just have some of Julia’s cake, will you?” Adam directed.

Tully patted his abdomen. “Nope. Gotta keep my girlish figger.” Then he turned back to Julia. “You watch your figger, don’tcha? Because if you don’t, no man will.” He immediately returned to Adam, saying, “I want to get these home and wash ‘em off and put ‘em through the grinder so I can get started. Whatd’ya think, twenty pounds of sugar enough?”

"Depends on how many pounds of cranberries," Adam answered practically.

"Well, I got more if I need it," Tully lifted up his carton. "I'll see you later, Adam."

Billy thanked him for the cranberries and Tully left as quickly as he arrived. Julia felt as though a twister had come in, swirled around the room, knocked over a few things, and departed, leaving an impression of rescue from near chaos.

After a minute of silence, Billy commented, "I thought Floyd Mather had the dumpster business for feeding his pigs."

Adam shrugged. "First come, first served."

"Just like the Bradburns used to get all the road kill," Cutter added. "But Tully's been gettin' there with his boom truck before the animals even bleed out. Not that a little sepsis would matter to him." The other two men nodded agreement.

"Speaking of Bradburns," Billy pondered, "they never turned up anything more on the little girl, did they, Adam?"

"Nope. I had a couple of beers with Percy Davis the other night. He said they'd given up looking around here. Whoever snatched her probably took her out of state."

"So the police know she was kidnapped?" Julia asked.

"Not officially."

The three men resumed talking about how the police department was changing with the new Chief. Two of the old-timers had retired and the two new ones were just some smart-ass kids with tight jock straps who gave out speeding tickets. And how the town was changing, too. More big new houses, more new people coming in. Maybe the kidnapper was someone who'd just moved there for all anybody knows. And what's going to happen if Conny Cranshaw paves over Pittsley Woods?

After the others had finally left, and only Adam and Julia sat in front of the woodstove, he asked, not quite ingenuously, "How'd you like my stew?"

"Filling," she replied, being deliberately ambiguous.

"So I'm told," Adam replied with good humor. He slung his feet up onto the spool-table and felt around between the pillows of his chair. "Wish I knew where I put my pipe."

"Do you always do your own cooking?"

He raised an eyebrow. "Gotta eat." Then, laconically, "Or were you trying to find out if I have maid service?"

"Of course not."

"Well, the answer is 'no.' No one's servicing me right now. Was that what you wanted to hear?"

"Don't flatter yourself."

"Oh? Wasn't that *you* asking if I had any wives, current or former, when we were at the Mayfair?"

"Just-making-conversation," she said, clipping her words.

"Umm hmm," he said with exaggeration.

"Anyone ever tell you that you can be pretty irritating?"

"Not in those exact words," Adam said, grinning. "Not exactly."

"Is that funny?" She sounded, she thought, like a schoolmarm with a rowdy pupil.

"Well, yeah. Most women who get riled at me throw lamps, yell and scream, bang doors, or take a roundhouse swing at my head. And you come up with "pretty irritating"? I don't know, shrink, that's some temper you've got."

Julia straightened her back. "You want to know if I have a temper? Is that what you want to find out? Well, I have a temper. I have plenty of temper. Ask my ex-husband." Then she realized how silly she sounded, and that he was laughing at her. "Eat cake."

"With pleasure." Adam smiled and, taking her literally, cut himself a large wedge. "It's actually very good."

"Don't sound so astonished. I'm a very good cook."

"I believe it," Adam said, patently enjoying the cake.

She liked the way he ate. Phillip, she reflected, had a penchant for more exotic food but seemed sometimes indifferent to taste. It reminded her of his lovemaking—setting was everything, execution secondary. But Adam had appetite. As guarded as he was so much of the time, these were occasional glimpses into a different Adam, one who did things with gusto or with compassion. If she had not seen these qualities, she would have found him cold and enigmatic. Or just plain irritating.

"Maybe next time I'll make cranberry bread for your friends. *With* black walnuts."

"Tully's a Christer, isn't he? But I'll tell you, he's always doing something productive. Whether it's working on engines or making wine, he's always got something going. He can build anything with a motor that isn't fuel injected, and he's made more Rube Goldbergs than anybody I know. I admire his ingenuity. If Tully would've had an education, he'd probably solve global warming."

"Except," she countered, "*his* solution would involve wiring junk-refrigerators together with the freezer doors open."

Adam laughed appreciatively, but Julia didn't quite share his admiration for the man whose bumpersticker was intended to make her smile.

"I know I've only met him a couple of times," she said thoughtfully, "and I realize he has lots of merit badges, but I assume the State took his kids away from him for good reason."

"I assume so."

"And Tommy probably didn't get that way all by himself."

"What's your point?"

She wanted to say that Tully was not necessarily the harmless inventor that Adam depicted, but said instead, "It just makes me wonder if Tommy had anything to do with stabbing Cat."

"I've already looked into that."

"And?"

"It wasn't Tommy."

She was tempted to ask if it could have been Tully, but thought better of it.

Observing her silence, he asked, "What?"

"Nothing. Just that you don't seem to have that much in common with your friends."

He got up and crossed the room to get another log for the woodstove. "Birds of a feather don't flock apart."

'I'll try to remember that,' she thought.

"So, what made you go into veterinary medicine?" she asked.

"What made you go into psychology?"

Her gaze drifted to the woodstove. "I guess I've always wanted to know why people do the things they do." She debated saying more but he was waiting quietly as though sensing she wanted to tell him something.

"When I was young," she began slowly, "around eleven, my grandmother and grandfather were murdered in their farmhouse in Quebec by a man who broke in to steal some food. There was no need to kill them. They would have shared whatever little they had with anyone. But he stabbed my grandmother in her kitchen and when my grandfather came home, he stabbed him, too."

She paused for a moment, feeling her throat tighten even after all these years.

"Grandpére didn't die right away. He stayed conscious long enough to write out what happened and then he bled to death with my grandmother in his arms. The neighbors didn't discover them for several days, but the police found the note with a description of the man. They caught him a week later. It was the fourth time he'd murdered. Or perhaps more. And he never took anything except what he could eat. The police told my father that the man—his name was Pierre Sangé—just liked killing. I never got to know anything more about him because the police shot him while he was trying to escape." She shrugged slightly, "Or so they say."

She looked back towards Adam. "I always wanted to know why he did it. Why he had to kill them. So I studied psychology and did my dissertation on serial killers. But I still don't know why." She lapsed into silence.

"I'm sorry about your grandparents," he said, and when she searched his face, she found genuine sympathy in his eyes.

"Your turn," she said somberly.

Such a long time passed, she wasn't sure he was going to answer.

"I don't like to see animals injured or abused," Adam finally said matter-of-factly. "And I wanted to do something about it. Becoming a vet seemed the best way."

"Where did you go to school?"

"Tufts."

"Tufts?" Her voice registered her surprise. This was a first-rate school and big-time expensive.

"G.I. Bill," he said as if knowing what she was thinking.

"Oh. When were you in the military?"

"Early '70s."

"Vietnam?"

"Yes."

She knew she shouldn't ask the next question. "Why did you go?"

"I was drafted."

"Did you believe in it?"

"I didn't believe in dodging."

She didn't think it necessary to mention that when she and Phillip were students, they had protested the war and marched and rallied on the Capitol Mall.

"Were you on the front lines?" she asked tentatively.

"It was a long time ago."

She said nothing more, letting herself become occupied by the thickness of his dark eyebrows, the way they arched near the outer ends.

* * *

He lay in bed thinking about the woods. He called up the memory of his feet crushing the clouds of snow beneath them as he walked. The dampness of his neck where he sweated under his ski-mask. His heart pumping with the extra weight over his shoulder. The length of the bundle fore and aft that made him stride like a high-wire walker. He let himself be carried back to the afternoon it happened. He remembered her bare knees as she sat beside him in the truck.

"But it wasn't a good choice," he muttered. "Not a good choice."

He told himself he mustn't worry because it was all over and done with. Maybe he should have kept her here. But where? No, it was better to have done what he did. The voices told him to. It would be all right. He buried her in the jungle.

The clock struck one. "Go to sleep," he said. "The clock struck one, and down she run. Huckery, duckery, fuck."

SPRING

SUNDAY, APRIL 1st

Julia awoke at six a.m. to the weathered groans of the old house. She lay in bed watching the waves of pelting rain on her bedroom windows. The rain had continued for twelve days and nights, off and on, hard and soft, but always the rain. The house held the dampness like wet clothes. No amount of heat could dry the walls under that constant onslaught. The wind keened through the cracks in the window frame. The two side-by-side windows stretched nearly from ceiling to floor, with nine rectangular panes in each, top and bottom. So much window, Julia almost felt she was outdoors. Shuddering, she gathered the covers up to her neck.

"What a godawful dismal place this is," she said aloud.

Of all the things she had given up in the divorce, the thing she missed most was the comfort of her own home. As part of their settlement, they had sold the Back Bay townhouse and split the proceeds—not very much since the house had been heavily mortgaged. It was the easiest way out, since neither of them was willing or able to buy the other's share. But, with the loss of her home, she had lost her sense of place. That's why she'd kept the furniture and let Phillip take the Mercedes. She thought she had gotten the better deal, but now she almost regretted it. Her modern furniture looked completely wrong here. Too stylish and contemporary. Too Boston. The old flowered wallpaper, the large dark moldings, the pink-glass light fixture suspended from the ceiling were all from a different era. 'A different life zone,' she told herself. Then her eyes fell on the little chair she'd bought at the auction. 'Just four dollars. And it looks better than anything else I own, at least in here,' she thought.

"If I stay, I'll either have to jettison my furnishings or completely re-do the house."

The house groaned and she took it as assent.

She had bought a used car for the same reason she had only rented the Steeple's house. She was not about to make any major investment in this new residence. She had signed the teaching contract for only one term, expecting that she could renew it if she wanted to. Pittsley was just a transition, although she hadn't decided to what yet. There certainly wasn't anything she liked here. Except possibly Adam. And that, she reminded herself, was the last thing she wanted to let influence her.

In fact, the thing with Adam was beginning to puzzle her. So casual. Uncomplicated. No mistakes. At first, she told herself she preferred it that way, too. Then, after a while, she began wondering why he hadn't at least tried to make a move on her. Not that she wanted him to. Then, she started wondering why she didn't appeal to him. Then, she started thinking he wasn't interested in sex. And neither was she, not really. Well, then, of course, he kissed her. And that only made it worse.

It had happened the night before, after their return visit to the Mayfair. The only unusual thing about the evening was that another man came over to their table to ask Julia to dance. She thought he might have been a little drunk. She'd seen him earlier in the evening, a medium-built man in his thirties who sat with a group of people on the other side of the room. He danced every dance with a different partner. She politely declined the invitation and he went off to ask someone else.

Adam never said anything but she had seen him tense when the man approached her and he seemed to glower until the man walked away. Only a few minutes had transpired but somehow Julia realized afterwards, it was a catalyst.

After getting into the truck to go home, Adam did not start the motor right away. She turned to look at him curiously and found him studying her. Silently, he leaned over and kissed her. Gently, at first, waiting to see how she would respond.

Julia kissed him back and felt his arm slide inside her open coat, around her waist as though they were still dancing. His other arm held her around the shoulders drawing her close to him. Almost tenderly, he touched his tongue to her mouth and she opened her lips. His kiss became more insistent and she arched her back, pressing hard against him. When they parted, Adam turned away and started the truck in silence as though nothing had happened. He drove her home and left with merely a "Goodnight."

She understood that he wanted to keep a sea-wall between them. Perhaps that was best. Perhaps it was better to be alone in her own bed. Well, not exactly alone. Cat was curled up at her feet, dug into the covers. Julia turned over to go back to sleep, listening to the insistent rain.

As she slept, on this, the morning of the twelfth day of the downpour, the rain finally and mercifully stopped.

When she awoke again at eight o'clock, the bedroom was bright and cheerful. It was as if the house had been hunched under a huge black umbrella, its back into the storm for days and days, but now had cast it aside to let the sun come streaming in through the windows.

* * *

In Pittsley Woods, the purple crocuses were finally sprouting. The winter snow had shrunk up over the ground like a woolen sweater and fertile trees were in bud with a thousand nipples. In a hollow, a sausage-shaped khaki blanket was exposed through the jumble of rocks.

* * *

By mid-morning, Julia struggled to put her jacket and boots on as her Golden Retriever pawed at her jeans.

"Yes, Cat, I know, I know, the rain stopped. Yes, we're going."

Ten minutes later, they were slogging over a muddy path through the woods. Cat forged ahead as Julia slowed to marvel at the season's transition.

Spring always made her ache for something. There was a wanderlust to it, a feeling that she wanted to go somewhere, anywhere, and discover what it was she ached for. It was in Spring two years ago when she had received a registered letter from Phillip saying he was filing for divorce. As she read the first sentence she'd felt a pressure in her throat as though someone were choking her, or maybe had already choked her and left her for dead. *"Dear Julia, you must know I've been unhappy."* She hadn't known.

After the letter, she had wound up in a short-term private rehabilitation hospital in Vermont. They didn't call it a psychiatric hospital, but that's what Green Willow really was. They only admitted patients with treatable depression. And enough money. "Talk about specialization," she had jibed self-consciously to a somber admitting-nurse. But they were good there. Pumped her with Elevil and fat-free carbs, walked her in the hills, and gave her a therapist—a woman older by ten or more years, who wore black ballet slippers with long, cottony Pakistani skirts—who made Julia believe that her life wasn't destroyed. In the space of three weeks (some others took only two), she was discharged and back to her teaching schedule. But she had glimpsed the abyss and it had frightened her. If pushed from the cliff again, she knew she might not find her wings so readily. She had better be very, very careful not to fall. That's why she'd come to Pittsley. It had seemed a safe choice.

It wasn't until she heard furious barking in the distance that Julia realized for the first time that her dog was out of sight. She walked as fast as she could in the direction of the barking and found Cat standing at the top of a hollow.

Below, Julia saw a khaki blanket under a pile of rocks where the snow had receded.

"What is it, Cat?"

The dog glanced back at her then descended into the hollow. Cat circled the blanket and began tugging at it. A small decomposed leg slipped out. The foot, twisted at an odd angle to the leg, was bare. It took a moment for Julia to accept what she was seeing. In that moment, the stench of decaying human flesh assaulted her. It was an odor she'd never smelled before but it was unmistakable, instinctively repulsive. Julia gagged.

"Cat! Get away from there! Come here!"

Julia ran so fast through the woods, she could barely stay upright. The mud sucked at her boots and she nearly fell, catching herself on a low maple branch and continuing to run. Cat romped alongside as though this were great sport.

An hour later, ignoring the drizzling rain, Julia stood off to the side of the hollow where the police were congregated. Their rain-muffled voices rose and fell as they worked at extracting the blanket and its contents.

The man in charge was the new police chief, Carson Burke. Julia judged him to be about thirty-five. She noticed he wore a newly cleaned topcoat and tie-shoes instead of boots. The mud was over the tops of his shoes and probably inside. He continually got in the way of the other officers as he instructed the men to do things they had already done. One officer in particular, a portly older cop whom she'd talked with at the station, appeared to be directing the others. It seemed to her that Chief Burke never even noticed that Sergeant Percy Davis was in command.

An old man in baggy clothes hobbled over to Sgt. Davis. Julia had never seen him before. Didn't see where he'd come from. He was just suddenly there, talking with the police officer as if he'd casually bumped into him on the street. She thought it was odd but obviously Sgt. Davis didn't, so she dismissed them and concentrated on what was being unearthed in the hollow.

With morbid fascination, she watched as they removed all of the rocks and unwrapped the blanket. When the body was exposed, she could see that much of the tissue was still intact, the decaying process just beginning after the cold winter. What skin was left was the greyish white of a clam shell. Only when they turned the body over did she see that it was a young girl. Burke looked away. She wished she had, too. The limbs were separated from the torso.

The men in the hollow tied handkerchiefs over the lower half of their faces. Julia put her hand over her nose but couldn't filter out the putrid smell. The police wore latex gloves and gingerly picked up the body and its parts and slid it into what looked like a large trash bag. Fleetingly, Julia wondered why they didn't take photographs of the body or perform some sort of forensic work before removing it.

A chill came over her and her face grew numb. She saw the strange old man watching her. Fighting the feeling she was going to pass out, she sat down on the wet ground, cold and queasy. Cat lay down next to her as Julia lowered her head between her knees.

When she was finally able to look back up again, the police had transferred the bag to a stretcher. She looked around to see where the old man was, but he had disappeared.

Sgt. Davis held out his hand and helped her to her feet. "We have all we need from you, Ms. Arnault. I'm sorry you had to be the one to find her."

"So am I."

* * *

Adam and Billy sat on the floor, coaxing an old engine into running. Billy felt his watchface. It was nearly six o'clock and they had been at the task for the past two hours. He listened to Adam describe the reluctant flywheel, the weak compression, the clogged valves. He had felt the metal with his fingertips but could not get a sense of how it operated. He could comprehend the components, he just couldn't integrate them. Times like these, he felt very remote from his friend. It made him feel stupid. He wasn't, but he couldn't help how he felt. It's just the way things were.

"How's Conny doing with the concrete plant, Adam?"

"Planning Board already signed off on the site plan."

"There must be some way to stop him."

"If the Conservation Commission can't find anything, we'll try to stop him at the Board of Appeals."

"Is there a chance of that?"

Billy didn't see the silent shake of Adam's head, but heard a car in the driveway, with one cylinder misfiring.

"That's Julia's car," Billy announced.

* * *

Julia swept into Adam's livingroom, dragging a vortex of moist air behind her.

"Adam," she said breathlessly, "remember the little Bradburn girl? The one who disappeared a few months ago?"

Adam stopped tinkering. Cat shook herself and a spray of rain hit the floor.

"I found her," she continued, "that is, Cat found her. Her body. She was murdered."

"Oh, no!" Billy exclaimed involuntarily.

"Where?" Adam asked.

"Pittsley Woods. I was there most of the day with the police."

Julia gingerly removed her raincoat, trying not to get any wetter, and hung it on a clothestree next to the door.

"This morning, I took Cat out for a walk, and about half-way into the woods she ran off and led me to this hollow. It was as if she knew where she was going. And there was this old blanket at the bottom under some rocks. The way it was rolled, I just knew there was a body in it."

"The little Bradburn girl?" said Billy, caught up in the tale.

"Yes. Cat tugged at the blanket and I saw her little foot. So I ran to my car and drove to the police station." Julia folded her arms, holding onto her elbows to stop from shaking. "Then I had to go back and show them where it was."

In the short silence that followed, Adam tapped the engine with a screwdriver. "Who identified the body?"

"One of the older cops. A Sergeant Davis."

"How was she murdered?" asked Billy, with a tremor in his voice.

As the image of Jeannine flashed through Julia's mind, tears came spontaneously to her eyes and spilled onto her cheeks. She bit her lips and took a deep breath, struggling for control.

"She was cut open." Julia's voice dropped to a whisper and everyone was quiet. She traced the cut from her throat to her navel. "From here to here. And dismembered."

For seconds that seemed like hours, the only sound in the room was the crackling of the fire in the woodstove. Then, Adam broke the silence.

"Do the cops have any leads?"

"I don't know."

"Do you think it's someone from around here?" Billy asked.

"Has to be somebody who knows the woods," Adam speculated. "You don't go burying a body in a place you don't know." He glanced sideways at Julia's dog, lying near the stove. "Well, Catastrophe, looks like you've got a little bloodhound in you."

"I hope they catch the bastard!" Billy said vehemently.

"Might have," Adam replied scornfully, "if Bill Kerwin were still around. Not our new Chief of Police, Carson Jerk."

Moving closer to the stove, Julia warmed her hands. "I'm soaked."

At that moment, Adam got the engine banging and she jumped in fright. "What's that?" Julia asked over the deafening noise.

After Billy left, Julia sat quietly drinking the hot chocolate that Adam had made for her. He continued to work on the engine. She had wrapped a towel around her hair to dry it. She'd been wearing it loose all the time now. It seemed freer and somehow made her feel farther away from her old self.

She drew her knees up and held the cup under her chin. The hot cup warmed her fingers and she inhaled the smell of the chocolate, letting the steam drift over her face. She tried not to visualize Jeannine's naked little body, but she couldn't stop the pictures from flooding her mind.

"She was nude, Adam. And her limbs were—." Her voice cracked. "It was gruesome. I've read about cases like this. I teach them. But I never—I wish I hadn't seen it."

"You can't dwell on it, Julia."

"But you don't know how terrible it was." Her words were muffled as she dropped her forehead on her knees again and closed her eyes.

She was awakened by the sound of a car driving up, followed by a confident knock at the door.

"It's open," Adam called.

Cutter entered in his wet yellow slicker and rain hat, quickly closing the door behind him against the pelting rain. Water puddled onto the floor around him.

"What's up, Cutter?"

"I'm getting pneumonia from this friggin' weather."

Julia sat up straight and unwrapped the towel from her head as Cutter took off his coat and hat and went to the woodstove to warm up. The collar of his red-and-black flannel shirt was drenched, as was the turtleneck of his black sweater underneath.

"Gotta talk to you a minute, Adam."

Adam looked over at Julia. "Could you could make a pot of coffee or something, Julia?" Adam said gently. "Would you mind?"

"I don't mind," she answered as she got up. But of course she did.

* * *

When Julia was out of the room, Cutter said, "I thought you'd want do know, Chief Jerkass just pulled Tully in for murdering the Bradburn kid."

"What?!"

"Cruiser picked him up an hour ago. That's as much as I know about it."

Adam immediately went to the telephone. Cutter listened while spreading his arms to the heat of the stove like a wet cormorant drying in the sun.

"Sergeant Davis, please. Hello, Percy? Adam. Yeah, I heard. What've you got?"

* * *

Julia searched the room at a glance when she returned from the kitchen with a hotpot and a tray of chocolate-chip cookies.

"Where's Adam?" she asked Cutter.

"He said to tell you he had to go out."

"Out where?"

"Guess he'll say when he gets back."

"You mean he didn't tell you where he was going?"

Cutter shrugged.

"Come on, Cutter," she said in a teacherly voice and he relented.

"I don't guess it's no nevermind. Adam went down the police station because they picked Tully up about the Bradburn kid."

"Picked him up for questioning? Or are they charging him with something?"

"Charging him, I expect."

"Why Tully?" In the spool of her memory, she replayed the scenes of Tully and his son, and Tully and Doris. Was he capable of murder?

"Why Tully?" she repeated.

"I guess they got their reasons."

"What reasons?"

"Don't know."

'Of course he knows,' she thought. He knows, and Adam knows, and they probably weren't going to tell her. Damn men and their damn secrets.

"What's that got to do with Adam?" she persisted.

Cutter shrugged again. "'s his friend."

"What about you? Isn't he your friend, too?"

"Not so much."

'Now that was interesting,' she thought. "Did he say anything about wanting me to wait for him?"

"Didn't say."

* * *

"It's going to be a major hernia, Adam." Usually jovial, Sgt. Davis was less than happy right now.

"No, it's not, Percy. You love a challenge."

They'd known each other a very long time. Percy'd helped Adam set up cockfight raids and catch poachers. They had gotten each other out of more than a few tight corners over the years.

"I'll see what I can do," Percy said without enthusiasm, "but it may take a while."

"I've got a while."

Percy walked off towards Chief Burke's office shaking his head.

Adam sat on one of the long pine benches and watched the door.

* * *

As Julia poured hot chocolate into large white mugs, her thoughts were on the news Cutter had just given her. "Do you think Tully did it?"

"He coulda."

"What makes you think so?"

Cutter touched his lips to the rim of the mug but it was too hot to drink. "There's no need of it, Julia."

"No need of what?"

"Prying."

"But I hate not knowing things everybody else knows."

"You best get used to it." He blew at the mug indifferently.

'I have no intention of getting used to it,' Julia thought, but said instead, "I think I can use something stronger than hot chocolate. How about you?"

Cutter brightened. "I never say never."

"Done."

'Moonshine will get him talking,' she thought gleefully.

* * *

Adam waited with the patience of a man used to it. He searched for the pipe inside his jacket and, finding it, saw he was once again out of tobacco. He clamped the empty pipe between his teeth and closed his eyes.

'Why Tully?' he wondered.

It was nearly an hour before Percy finally returned. Adam rose to meet him.

"Sorry, Adam, the Chief says '*Niet*.' Nobody's supposed to see Tully except his lawyer."

"Come on, Percy, you know Tully. He hasn't got a clue how to find a lawyer."

"They'll get him a public defender."

"He's not indigent." Adam stood nose to nose with his friend. "Tell Burke he's going to be in deep shit if he doesn't let me help Tully get counsel. Never mind, I'll tell him myself."

Percy made a gesture of surrender as Adam stalked past him.

"I don't need any help from the State. I'm on top of it."

As Adam entered the office, the new police chief was barking into the telephone. Burke looked up angrily at the interruption and put his hand over the end of the phone.

"Hold on a minute." Then, to Adam, "Get out."

Adam moved to the chair opposite Burke's desk and sat. "I'll wait."

Burke's face reddened. "Who the hell are you?"

"Adam Sabeski."

"I just told Sgt. Davis you can't see the perp, now get out."

Adam sneered. No Pittsley cop ever said 'perp.' In fact, they wouldn't even say 'perpetrator.' Only 'the doer.' As in, 'He did it. He did her. He's the doer.'

"Look," Burke said back into the phone, "I've got a situation here. I'll call back later. I don't need anything, understand? Alright." He hung up the telephone and turned back to Adam. "Now what the hell is all this about?"

Very politely, Adam explained that Tully had diminished capacity in certain areas—such as knowing how to handle himself in this circumstance—and that while he had an income which made him ineligible for a public defender, Tully had no idea of how to engage a lawyer. Surely Burke didn't want to contaminate his case by denying his prisoner representation in the form that he needed. It was a bluff, but Adam guessed correctly that the new Chief didn't really know what he was doing.

* * *

The bottle of moonshine was still on the table. Julia drank from her cup and made a terrible face.

"Awful."

"Supposed to be awful," Cutter assured her.

She took another swallow. Her eyes watered and she grimaced. "Can I ask you a question?"

"Is this an Adam-question?"

"Uh uh." She shook her head emphatically. "I have him all figured out."

"That so?"

"What I want to know is why would Tully kill Jeannine Bradburn?"

* * *

"Are you going to be my lawyer, Adam? I can pay you. I've got enough money."

Tully sat in the corner of the jail cell, looking agitated. Adam succeeded in convincing Burke to let him visit but he was having difficulty calming Tully down.

"I'm not a lawyer," he explained again. "I'm just a special prosecutor."

"But *you* go to court."

"For animals. Not for people. It's different."

"I didn't do it. Honest to God, I didn't." Word by word, Tully's voice became louder.

Adam lowered his voice in contrast. "They have a description of a black pick-up like yours at the school bus stop on the afternoon Jeannine Bradburn disappeared. The man was wearing a green jacket like yours. The police are convinced it was you."

"It wasn't me! I swear!"

"Then how did they find her underpants in your root cellar?" Against regulations, Percy had told Adam what they had for evidence, and it looked pretty solid.

Tully's face went slack. His voice dropped. "I don't know. I don't know nothing about it, Adam, I swear."

"Where were you the day before the blizzard?"

"Driving truck. Pick up and deliver as usual."

"Where? Near the school?"

"Mighta been. I don't know. I drive all over. Why're they picking on me?" Tully's voice turned into a whine.

"Maybe because of what happened before." Adam was just fishing. "They've got a record on you. Right?"

Tully looked distinctly uncomfortable. "That weren't no problem," he finally replied.

'Shit,' thought Adam, but he tried to appear unaccusatory. "Why not?"

"It weren't much of a thing." Tully scraped his foot on the concrete floor. "It was a long time ago."

"What was?"

Tully looked away. “One of the neighbor girls said I put my hands on her but I didn’t.”

“What *did* you do?” He made it sound casual. ‘Take it easy,’ Adam told himself, ‘let him tell you, don’t let him close up.’

“Nothing. I was just teasing her like.”

“And she told her parents?”

Tully squirmed.

“Then what?”

“They told the police and then they dropped it because there weren’t nothing to it.”

“How old was she?”

“I don’t know,” Tully answered with exasperation. “Who can tell when they start developing?”

Adam let out his breath. “What else?”

“Nothing.”

* * *

The bottle of shine on the table in Adam’s livingroom was nearly empty and Julia was quite drunk. Cutter wasn’t even buzzed.

“Well, I gotta be headin’ out now.” He put down his mug.

Julia swallowed the last of the moonshine. Her lips were tingling. “Okay,” she said, more to the cup than to Cutter.

Cutter retrieved his slicker. He headed towards the door, thought about it, and then advised her, “You might want to get some food in you.”

“Yeah,” Julia agreed, slurring the syllable. “I miched lunch.” She corrected herself. “I missed lunns.” She touched her lips gingerly.

Cutter stroked his beard. “Milk helps.”

Julia felt slightly nauseated at the thought. Cutter chuckled, donned his slicker, and left.

* * *

After an hour of pulling out information from his friend, both men were bone-weary but Adam pressed on.

"How did you know the Bradburn girl?"

Tully cast his eyes down at the floor.

"I said, how did you know her?"

"I seen her around."

"'I seen her around,'" Adam repeated sardonically. "What the hell does that mean?"

Tully shuffled his feet. "I seen where her daddy works. I do some hauling from there for Conny."

"And?"

"Nothing. She was in my truck once. I gave her a little ride around the truckyard. That's all."

Adam really wished he had some good tobacco. He badly wanted to smoke because he knew the answer to this next question would not make him happy.

"Anybody see you?"

"Sure," Tully said impatiently. "All them guys on the loading dock. Babe and all them waved to us and stuff."

"Yeah, I'll bet they did. And they'll probably be witnesses at your trial."

"It ain't fair, Adam! Blaming me for what I didn't do."

"You've got a record. You took her in your truck. Her underpants were in *your* root cellar. *You're* the only one who would've put them there."

"I didn't, honest to God. I mighta done some things in my life, but nothing like this. I ain't stupid." Tully held onto his sides with both hands.

"Yes, you are. You're stupid to get caught with your hands up some little girl's dress. And that probably wasn't the first time, was it?"

Tully was silent.

Adam felt his mouth go dry. "Christ, Tully, how many times?"

Tully was reluctant but too tired to protest. "Just one other. A long time ago. Thirty years. Twenty-five, anyway."

"What happened?" Adam's chest tightened but his voice was expressionless.

"I'm tired, Adam, real tired."

Adam waited until Tully finally continued.

"I was married to my first wife then. Sharice." Then he added, meaningfully, "She wasn't much, you know?"

"What do you mean, 'she wasn't much'?" He was afraid he knew exactly what Tully meant.

Tully gave a little jerk of his head. "You know. She wasn't much for it."

"And?" Adam really did not want to hear the details.

"She already had a grown kid by some other guy when we got married. And one day, Sharice saw me kinda touching her. Lottie wasn't no baby and I sure wasn't the first that had a feel of her. Anybody bought her a bag of chips coulda had all the loving they wanted." Tully said this so dispassionately it had to be true.

"What happened then?"

"Nothing. Sharice left and took Lottie with her. But I heard she ran away with some guy after."

"Who knows about this? The cops?"

"No," Tully replied confidently. "Just the Social Service." Tully looked at him expectantly but Adam just gazed past him.

"We'd better get you a damn good lawyer."

"Will you take Doris to her sister's tonight, Adam? You know she can't be on her own."

Driving home from Doris' sister's house, Adam was barely cognizant of the ride. It was still raining as he passed the Bradburn place. One light was on in the back of the house. He came to a full stop at the side of the road and looked over.

He hadn't mentioned it to Julia, but the house behind the Bradburn's had been his grandparents' house. His mother had lived there until she married his father. On Sunday visits to his grandparents, Adam had played with the other boys his age there. When he was twelve, his grandfather died, his grandmother went into a nursing home, and his parents moved back into the house. He sold it through a real estate agent after they died. He was in Vietnam.

He'd known Otis Bradburn back then, although Otis was younger and Adam didn't have much to do with him. Otis' father, Elgin, was always a hard worker and a hard drinker. Both respectable qualities, all agreed.

Adam missed their communality. Driving by, he would see families cooking out on the porch, kids running in and out of the yards, dogs barking. He would wave to them from his car and they would always wave back.

He had been tempted to buy his parents' house from the new owners when he came home from the service. But he realized even then that he could never fit in. It wasn't that he felt superior to them. No. What he felt was alien. And in some ways, envious.

He was surprised to see Julia's car in front of the house when he returned home.

Inside, he discarded his slicker and scanned the empty room, noticing the empty bottle of moonshine and two mugs. He found Julia upstairs, fully clothed, asleep on his bed. She was lying on her side with Cat against her back. His eyes slid longingly over the curve of her hip and the slope of her waist but he did not get aroused. Here it was, the first time she was spending the night, and he was too exhausted. He wished he were feeling more amorous.

Cat's enthusiastic greeting of Adam stirred Julia awake. As she struggled to consciousness, she saw Adam sitting on the bed taking off his shoes and socks.

"Hi," she said groggily, startling him.

"I didn't think you'd still be here." His voice held a mixture of pleasure and weariness.

Julia pushed up on her elbow and held her other hand to her head. "It wasn't exactly optional. I passed out after Cutter drank me under the table."

"That's learning the hard way." At any other time, he might have found this terribly amusing.

"Did you talk to Tully?"

"Yes."

"What's the story?"

"It's complicated."

Julia dropped back onto the pillow. "I can't handle complicated right now. All I want is heroes and villains and happy endings."

"All *I* want is about four hours' sleep," he said apologetically.

"Granted. I'm in no shape for calisthenics."

She turned over and instantly fell back to sleep. He was too tired even to take off his clothes as he lay down next to her. He wondered what it would be like waking up to her in the morning.

* * *

'Maybe it hadn't been a good choice, the woods.'

He was worried now. It he'd put her somewhere else, she might never have been found. He was going to move her but now it's too late. He thought about them digging up his treasure like a pack of dogs digging up buried bones, and he became angry. He never should have listened to The Other. "Put her in the woods. Use again." Whose woods are these? I think I know. You take an arm, I'll take a toe.

He'd messed up. He should have killed the dog. The woman was small and pretty. She looked like a young girl, but she wasn't. He wouldn't tell the Others about her. It was too soon. He was content merely to look at her for now. Just to look. For now.

MONDAY, APRIL 2nd

The morning sun poured through the window of the white-tiled bathroom as Julia poked her head in. Adam stood at the sink shaving. He cocked an eyebrow at her in the mirror.

"So, how do you feel this morning?"

"Shitty. But I earned it." Glancing at herself in the mirror, she concluded she looked as bad as she felt "I know this is a little awkward, but may I use your shower?"

"Sure, I'm finished." He rinsed his face and reached for a towel as Julia entered.

"So what happened last night? Are they going to arraign Tully?"

"Yes."

"I can't believe he did such a monstrous thing. I mean, I guess I *can*, but—," she let it hang.

"How about I make some breakfast?" he offered.

"Oh, no, my stomach couldn't handle it right now. But I could meet you for a late lunch after your clinic hours. I only have one class this morning. I should be ready to face food by this afternoon."

"I'm not having clinic today."

"Oh?"

"I've got to see an old friend. A lawyer. I want him to take Tully's case."

"Why?"

Adam did not respond, seemingly preoccupied. Julia rolled her eyes and retreated into silence. Her head still throbbed from last night. She vowed never to do that again.

"About last night," she began tentatively.

"I never take advantage of a woman's first bout with moonshine."

"Thank you, Sir Knight."

"But I'll take a rain check."

He hung up his towel and, disguising a smile, left the bathroom to her.

Forty minutes later, her car lurched into her reserved parking space on the P.C.C. campus and sputtered to an abrupt stop. Cat, lying on the front seat with her head on Julia's lap, merely blinked.

"The eagle has landed and *it* doesn't want to be here either," Julia said disgustedly to her dog.

* * *

Adam watched Maxwell Kipper sprint down the jail-house steps like a Parson Jack Russell terrier. Approaching Adam, he saluted.

"Major Sabeski. Lieutenant Kipper reporting for duty."

"Good to see you, Kip."

Considerably shorter than Adam's six-two, Kip peered up at his friend out of the corner of his hazel eyes. "How've you been, Ski?"

"As ever—poor but ignoble. And you?"

"A prosperous Jucket," Kip said with a hint of self-mockery. "Now there's an oxymoron for you."

"Some kind of moron, anyway. Did you talk to him?"

"Oh baby, did I. Let's go to Dottie's."

Kipper put his arms around the chunky waist of the no-nonsense sixty-something blonde waitress who came over with a pot of coffee. And when Dottie asked, "So what do you boys want?" the two men answered in unison, "You on a raft with no dressing."

"Yeah, over easy" she replied with a roll of her heavily mascaraed blue eyes. "And what else?"

They both ordered Portuguese sweet-bread French toast with their eggs, and after she left, Adam began by asking, "So you talked to Chief Burke?"

Kip nodded, sipping his four-sugar black coffee.

"So what do you think?"

"I think he's an asshole," Kip replied amiably.

"That goes without saying. I mean, what about the case?"

The lawyer lowered his cup and his voice became formal. "The classmate who saw Jeannine Bradburn get off the bus and saw the pick-up, couldn't identify Tully. Or anyone else, unfortunately. But they've got the underwear. They've got witnesses who saw him give the girl a ride in his truck last summer. And they've got a pretty nefarious personal history. It's enough to indict and probably enough to convict."

"Sound's like you're not anxious to defend him."

"Hell, no. The guy's a walking poster for chemical castration."

"Tully may not be up to your new Brahmin clientele," Adam said evenly, "but somebody's got to defend him or he'll go down the tubes, guilty or not. And what kind of justice is that?"

"All I said was I didn't want the case. I didn't say I wouldn't take it. I still have a conscience, you know."

"Quit masturbating. I want to hear 'Yes' you'll do it, or 'No' you won't. I don't give a flying fuck about your ethics."

"Shit, you never did." Kip sat back in his chair. "Yes, I'm going to do it. You know I'm going to do it. I just need to consider all the ramifications."

Adam leaned back in his chair likewise and assessed his friend. "You know, it's a good thing you're a lawyer, Kip, 'cause if you were a whore, you'd never get laid."

Kip laughed then became serious again. "Look, they're fast-tracking this. The hearing is in four days. There's no chance he won't be bound over for trial."

"Don't be so damned pessimistic."

"Why? You don't think he did it?"

"No."

"Then the question is," Kipper gestured with his mug, "if old Happy Pants didn't do it, who did? The only way to convince a jury that Tully's not guilty is to find someone who looks guiltier. Now there's a challenge and I don't think we can depend on Chief Burke to do our work for us. He's convinced he's got the murderer in his jail." Kipper leaned forward. "And I'm not convinced he doesn't. But if I take this on, I'm going to need your help."

"*My* help?" Adam snorted. "Hell, you're going to need *Divine* help."

* * *

'What do they expect from me, anyway?' Julia thought.

The disinterested class suddenly enraged her. They hadn't read the assignment, weren't paying attention, and made her feel totally incompetent. She wanted to slam the book down on the floor, kick her desk, and walk out. With great effort, she restrained herself. She faced them in infuriated silence.

The clocked ticked loudly on the wall while she deliberated what to say. The seconds eked by at a metronome pace.

Little by little, instead of more talking and twisting, the students began to quiet down. As the minutes ticked on, the room was oddly silent. The longer the silence continued, the more riveted they were.

Slowly, Julia began to regain a sense of control. And then she had an idea. A wonderful idea.

"We're going to do this section differently from the previous ones. We're going to use what's called the case-study method. How many of you have heard of Albert DeSalvo?"

No hands went up. 'Lord, they're young,' she reminded herself, then clarified, "Better known as The Boston Strangler."

All hands now rose.

"How do you know about him?" she asked.

"That barf-y old movie with Tony Curtis," the formerly sleeping young man said, and the others nodded.

"Well," she continued, "we're going to look at that movie and read the book it's based on. We'll talk about F. Lee Bailey's defense, and we're going to recreate some of the courtroom scenes from transcripts of the testimony. We're going to psychoanalyze Albert DeSalvo and profile serial killers. Then we'll take a vote on whether or not DeSalvo was the real Strangler."

Their faces brightened. They were titillated. She had never had to resort to theatrics before but maybe she should have. 'That's entertainment,' Julia intoned to herself.

After class, Julia picked up her mail on the way to her office—a cubicle without a window, large enough only for a small desk, one file cabinet, and two color-coordinated blue and purple chairs. Cat squeezed in under her desk. Papers and books were neatly stacked on two shelves over the desk to conserve space. Julia had made no attempt to personalize the office. No plants, no photos, no artwork. The office was devoid of character, revealing nothing and everything.

She sorted through the mail, mostly school and departmental announcements. Then she spotted the long white stamped envelope typed: *Ms. Julia Arnault Farrell, Associate Professor, Psychology Department, Pittsley Community College, Pittsley, MA.* The return address read: *100 Commonwealth Ave., Boston.*

Julia frowned. It wasn't an address she recognized, but whoever sent it had put both her maiden and married names, as though the sender didn't know which of them she might be using. It could only be from someone who knew of her divorce. As much as she might complain that nobody from her married days bothered with her anymore, she wasn't sure she actually wanted any contact.

She sliced the envelope with the stainless-steel letter opener she'd found in the desk drawer when she moved into the office. It had been the only indication that there had been a previous tenant.

An expression of distaste crossed her face as she read the letter.

"Drop dead," she muttered, and began shredding the paper. She was down to half-inch squares when she was interrupted by the telephone. It was Adam, asking her to meet him.

"I don't really feel much like lunch after all," she said sullenly, anticipating his invitation.

"Lunch? Oh. No, I had something else in mind," he replied. "I want to look at the place where you found Jeannine Bradburn."

"Why?"

"Indulge me."

She did not particularly want to go back there, but neither did she want to be alone right now. So, without enthusiasm, she agreed.

By three p.m., Julia, Adam, and Cat were trudging through Pittsley Woods. As they approached the burial site, Cat ran ahead to the rim of the hollow.

Adam skittered down into the bottom of the hollow and walked around the center, bending to examine the ground. Some of the stones encircling the grave remained but nothing else.

Looking down into the pit, Julia couldn't help visualizing the little decomposed leg. Every time the memories of that day came back to her, she pushed them away. She didn't want to think of the girl's suffering, her terror in being abducted and murdered—the evil that someone did to her, that perhaps Tully did to her.

Julia began reciting "T'was brillig and the slithy toves did gyre and gimble in the wabe…." It was a device she'd used to avoid unpleasantness ever since she'd been a young girl. It had served a useful purpose throughout her break-up. She knew it just delayed the emotion, but if she hadn't blocked out the pain, she couldn't have gotten through the divorce. Sometimes she wondered why she became a psychology teacher when she willfully ignored everything she'd learned when it applied to herself.

As Adam climbed back out of the hollow, Cat began barking fiercely and kept it up until he reached the top.

"Hey, girl," he cajoled, "what's the matter?"

But the agitated dog would not be appeased until Julia commanded her to stop.

"What did you find?" Julia asked with trepidation, peering down into the hollow at the disturbed ring of stones.

"Absolutely nothing."

He took one last look around then began walking back out of the woods, Julia and Cat trailing him.

Julia caught up with him at his truck. "What were you looking for?" she asked as she climbed into the cab with Cat.

"I don't know."

"Now what?" she prodded, as they drove away.

"Now we pay a visit to Elmer Goodson."

"Who's Elmer Goodson?"

"Patience."

Julia gave him an impatient look but did not press it. 'Am I getting used to this?' she asked herself, recalling Cutter's pronouncement.

Driving down a dirt road on the other side of the woods, a one-room shack with a corrugated tin room came into view. An outhouse was in evidence about a hundred yards away, near the riverbank. There was no car in sight and no tire tracks except their own behind them. The temperature was still only about fifty degrees, too cold to go without heat, and the smoke spiraled up from a pipe in the roof.

When they came to a stop, an old man opened the door. Julia immediately recognized him.

"Is he a friend of yours, Adam? I saw him in the woods the afternoon the police took Jeannine's body."

"Goody's ubiquitous."

"Does that mean he's a Jucket?" she asked, smiling.

"He is. And more."

Leaving Cat in the cab of the truck, Adam approached the old man with exaggerated courtesy.

"How do you do, Mr. Goodson?"

"I thought you was my meal," Goody growled, then turned and shuffled inside, leaving the door open.

Julia glanced at Adam, but he was already entering the shack. She followed, grumbling a Cutterism to herself, "I feel like a pimple on somebody's butt."

Adam grinned and introduced her to Goody.

"Seen her," the old man gruffly acknowledged then turned back to Adam. "You come to ask questions about the Bradburn kid?"

"How did you know?"

"I figured it when I heard about Tully."

"What can you tell me?"

"What do you want to know?"

Goody sat on the cot and Adam motioned to Julia to take the chair. Adam stood deliberately silent until the older man decided he was ready to talk.

"Saw her a week or so before they got around to finding her. Guess she'd been there all winter."

Julia didn't even try to conceal her astonishment. "If you knew she was there, why didn't you tell somebody?"

Goody reached inside his shirt pocket for the one cigarette it contained. Before his crippled fingers could find a match, Adam provided him with a light. "Why didn't you tell anybody, Goody?"

"She weren't botherin' nothin'."

Julia checked Adam for a reaction but he gave no sign of one. 'I will never understand these people,' she told herself. 'Never.'

"Do you know who put her there?" Adam asked.

"I didn't go out that week, remember? Storm kicked up my atha-ritis."

"Any ideas?"

"There's lotsa guys goes into the woods for one goddam reason or another."

"Including Tully?"

"He don't never come in here."

This information didn't seem to surprise Adam as it did Julia.

"Make me a list."

Goody regarded Adam as though he had asked him to write *Hamlet*. Meanwhile, Adam took a small red notebook from his pocket.

"I need the names of everybody who comes into the woods on a regular basis."

Goody screwed up his face in disapproval.

* * *

By the time the old man had ticked off everyone he could think of who came into the woods, the list contained forty-two names. As Adam wrote down the names, he crossed off the ones he knew could not be suspects. He crossed his own name and Goody's off the short list and went on to the next, Tully's son, Tommy.

"What about Tommy?"

'Tommy?' Julia wondered. If Adam believed Tully didn't do it—and she wasn't willing to concede that—then Tommy would certainly be a good second choice. Although he didn't drive a truck, of course. But no one saw Jeannine picked up in a truck. That could have been a coincidence. Tommy could have just dragged her into the woods. God knows, he seemed capable of it.

"Tommy has a little hut he built way back in," Goody answered. "He usta spend a lot of time in there."

"Doing what?"

Goody pumped his fist up and down in his lap and Julia averted her eyes.

Adam left Tommy's name on the list. "What about Babe Hamply?"

The name conjured up the Tweedledum that Julia met at Tully's house and saw again at the auction. She could almost guess what kinds of things he did in the woods. She thought back to a time when she and Phillip were walking through the Blue Hills and came upon a cache of slutty magazines in the hollow of a tree. She would expect something like that from Babe. Phillip had taken the magazines, said he was going to dispose of them, but she never thought to ask what he had actually done with them.

"Sometimes he comes with Tommy. But most times by himself. He sets traps. I spring them. Traps is nasty killing."

"Now Floyd here," Goody nodded to the next name on the list, "he's got his own path in from the back of his property. He's a hunter but everything legal. Only takes what he oughta, in the right season." He looked at Adam. "I know that don't make no nevermind to you. Bein' against even the legal hunting that's our God-ever-bearin' right."

Adam didn't bother to reply. They'd argued this subject for as many years as he could remember. So he left Babe's name and Floyd Mather's name on the list and scanned down to the next.

"Judd Vaughan is Jeannine's cousin. What's his business here?"

"He stashes some shine in here once in a while. And once in a while he's short a bottle."

Adam nodded but left the name on the list. "And Cranshaw?"

Goody became animated. "When he first come in, he was making some kind goddam map. Now that he owns nearly the whole damn place, I hear he'd gonna build a concrete plant in here. Goodbye Pittsley Woods." Goody spat onto the wooden boards of his floor and ground it in with the heel of his boot.

He pointed to the next name on the list. "Now this last one, I don't know his name. He's one of the yukkies in those new houses in the development. Got some big silver camper in his yard. He comes in with binoculars and a backpack. Like he was hiking the Himmelays or somethin'."

"Description?"

"About six foot. Blondy hair."

"How old?"

"Younger than me. Younger than you." Good inclined his head toward Julia, "Younger than her."

She grimaced.

"How often does he come in?" Adam continued.

"Oh, 'bout once't a month."

"Anything else I should know?"

"You want me to tell you which actual house he lives in? And when he scratches his croakies?"

"That would be nice," Adam replied dryly, but Julia could see the crinkles of humor around his eyes.

* * *

It had grown nearly dark and Adam and Julia were about to leave when they heard a car drive up.

"My goddam supper's finally here."

Goody got up from the cot by pushing down on his knuckles and lifting himself up by the strength of his arms. He scuffled to the door and looked out. Past him, Julia could see a smiling, dough-faced woman in her late sixties, with curly grey hair and pink cheeks. She wore a cherry-red winter coat and was walking towards the house carrying a covered tray.

"You're late, old lady," Goody grunted.

"Be glad I'm here at all, beagle face," she said affectionately, and nodded in recognition to Adam as she entered.

* * *

As soon as Adam let Cat out of the truck, the dog squatted and pee'd. Julia meanwhile studied the outhouse with distaste. She saw Adam watching her, so she stuck out her chin in determination and tromped towards the half-moon door.

* * *

Adam awoke around two a.m. and lay still, feeling the reassuring weight of Julia's body against his. 'Sober, too,' he thought with a smile. One leg still straddled his and her head rested on his chest. They had made love until they both spasmed with waves of pleasure, and had fallen asleep immediately after.

His mind moved inexorably away from Julia and back to Tully. His friend. He had always known that Tully walked a shaky bridge between normal and not. Maybe he'd fallen off. Worse, maybe he'd always been off and Adam hadn't recognized it.

Further sleep was impossible. He gently extracted himself from Julia's leg without waking her, then quietly put on his jeans and left the room. Cat immediately got up from her spot on the floor and took his warm place on the bed.

Downstairs in his clinic, Adam checked in on a little calico kitten with a broken leg. He softly stroked the cat. She opened her gold-flecked eyes to look at him questioningly, then after a moment contentedly closed them again. Adam imagined they were a child's eyes. He tried to shake it off but couldn't.

Back in the livingroom, Adam studied Goody's list of names with all the concentration he might give to a difficult diagnosis. As though reviewing symptoms, he eliminated suspects, drew a second line through some of the names he had drawn a line through originally, and annotated them.

He again crossed off his own and Goody's names. He added "mushroomer" next to Wheezie Chace and her pal Mattie Hayden. Some of the names were boys and girls Adam knew to be Scouts. He wrote "trapper" next to Babe, "hut" next to Tommy. Two hours passed as he pored over and over the list.

Finally, he came down to four names that kept bothering him. First, was the unknown man Goody had called a yukkie. His name stayed on the list simply because Adam didn't know him. Second, Judd Vaughan. He was Jeannine's cousin and his name remained on the list because things like that could happen in pink-eye village. Then there was Floyd Mather. His name stayed on just because Adam didn't much like him. And finally, there was Conny Cranshaw, because he was Conny Cranshaw.

"All in all,' Adam admitted aloud, "not very scientific."

As he circled the four names, he heard Julia come down the stairs. She was wearing jeans and a blouse but was barefooted like him. Her hair was loose and flowed down her shoulders. She looked cute, he thought, but peevish.

"What are you doing?" She pulled over a chair next to his.

"Grasping at straws."

She scanned the list and pursed her lips. "It doesn't look like much."

"It's all I've got. The police aren't investigating any more. As far as they're concerned, they have their man."

"Perhaps they do."

"And so sayeth the Kipper."

A silence followed until finally Julia broke it with, "I got a letter from Phillip today. Or rather, a notification."

"Of what?"

"Seems he's going to marry his little lab rat. *And* he's been offered a full professorship in the biochemistry department at U.C.L.A." Julia's storm-grey eyes narrowed. "For September."

"So?"

"So?" Julia was beyond pacification. "So, he screwed me again!" The words came out gathering volume. "I left a tenure track at B.U. for a minor league job down here because I didn't want to be anywhere near him. Not even in the same city. So here I am, teaching Freud and Jung to kids who call them 'Siegfried and Freud' or 'The Blues Brothers.' And now that I've given up everything, absolutely everything, now *he's* leaving. In a blaze of glory." Julia waved her arms in the air. "And he has the balls to send me an engraved announcement!"

"I see," Adam said, stifling a laugh.

"It's not funny."

"No, of course not."

"It isn't!"

"I know. So I guess there's only one question to ask in a situation like this."

"Which is?" Julia said acidly.

"What's the appropriate wedding gift?"

She was about to retort rudely when Adam playfully shoved her with his bare foot. She knew he was teasing but she was not in the mood for it.

"It was an announcement," she replied tartly, "not an invitation. I'm not invited. But the putz asked my daughter to be a bridesmaid."

Then, without knowing exactly why, she suddenly found this quite hilarious and began laughing, Adam along with her.

"You're right," Julia conceded. "It's just my vanity that's injured. But he sure knows how to play me."

"Forget it."

"Yeah, I suppose." And somehow she did feel better for having told him.

"You hungry?"

"I'm *always* hungry," she responded.

"Let's cook up a mess of noodles and butter."

"Is that the best you can do in my moment of defeat? Noodles?"

Adam took her hand and pulled her out of the chair into his arms.

"It's not what's cooked, it's how it's served," he whispered suggestively in her ear.

"Ain't that the truth?" Julia agreed, slipping her arms around his neck.

* * *

Only fleetingly did he experience a sense that what he did was wrong. Not wrong in a universe of right and wrong. But only wrong in the way of having an extra piece of cake, or the next cigarette, or the last drink. And besides, His wrong was not as bad as the Others'. It was really the Others who had goaded him into it. The voices that repeated,

"Do it, do it!" until he did. But, in the end, he did it because he wanted to. And he was glad.

He moved his peas around the plate with a three-tined fork. No, he wasn't very hungry. He was sated. Like a lizard that swallowed a mouse. It was a meal that would last him a while.

And he's smarter than any of them. Maybe he has needs that are different. Maybe his needs make him different. But they can't judge him. "I am not to be judged," he mouthed to himself, "because I can to whatever I want." No one could judge him.

"Hickory, dick-ory, dock," he sang, "the mouse ran up the cock."

TUESDAY, APRIL 3rd

Julia was in a buoyant mood. This week, she'd shown her class *The Boston Strangler* movie and they had talked about motivation. She'd posed the question, "Why did he do it?" and challenged each of her students to answer. She charted their responses and obligingly counted each one without comment.

Four students said he was "sick." Four more said "he hated his mother." Five thought "he was impotent" but three others said "he did it for sex" (or, as one put it, "got his rocks off"). Three more thought "he did it just for kicks." Two felt it was "a compulsion," and the sleepy young man in the last row said, "It was the wrong man and the case was never proven."

"In the next session," Julia informed them, "we're going to go through all the evidence and look back at your answers and see where we are." The students had left class still talking about the exercise and Julia was as pleased as she had ever been in her teaching. Maybe things were finally beginning to turn around. After all the misery she'd been through the past year, at last she was beginning to find her own stride. Maybe it wasn't exactly the life she'd imagined for herself, but at least she was doing it on her own. Fuck Philip.

What fascinated her about DeSalvo was the very unlikelihood of his guilt when the police investigation began. DeSalvo had had a conviction and imprisonment for breaking and entering and sexual assault but he had never physically brutalized any of the women. Actually, most of the time he was able to gain their cooperation by telling them he would get them a modeling job. He took their measurements, hence his earlier nickname, The Measuring Man. Sometimes he would even get them into bed. When he confessed to being The Strangler, the police did not believe him. It just wasn't his *modus operandi*. Albert never killed anyone, much less mangle them. Had he not confessed, he probably would never have been suspected.

Julia did not find it illogical, though, that DeSalvo could have progressed from tamer to more and more violent assaults. And then there was the fact that both The Measuring Man and The Strangler were both opportunistic in their methods. In fact, psychological profiling failed because there was no pattern in the killer's victims. The women were young, old, foreign, students, *etc*. As it turned out, the only real pattern was accessibility.

Julia was still thinking about her class as she and Adam drove into Cedarwood Park, the new development of custom-built houses where Goody's yukkie lived. As they passed the sprawling houses, Julia made a lemon face at the street names—Acorn Drive, Bluebell Court, Cowslip Drive, Daisy Court, Elderberry Drive, Forsythia Court, Gentian Drive.

"There it is," she pointed. They turned down Heliotrope Court.

"If this is the right street," Adam said, "the yellow house should be at the end."

They pulled up slowly to the last house, and it was indeed yellow. Creamy yellow with butterscotch shutters and window boxes, and a stained oak door with brass trim. The front yard was landscaped with blue spruce and pink dogwood, and the path to the house was lined with dark yellow bricks. The name on the floral (heliotrope) painted mailbox read 'Wilson.' There was a shiny Airstream camper in back.

"Trust Goody," Julia said, with grudging respect. "Now what?"

"I'm going to investigate a barking-dog complaint."

"What barking dog?"

He looked at her patronizingly.

"Oh," Julia said, feeling a little dense.

"You wait here."

"Why?"

"Because I don't need a deputy for a barking-dog complaint."

Julia pouted as she watched Adam walk to the decorator door of the yellow house. She felt some proprietary rights about this pursuit. After all, *she'd* discovered the body and *she* was the psychologist here. Well, psychology teacher. On the other hand, it was Adam's friend in custody and Adam certainly had more investigative experience than she did. And these were his suspects. Reluctantly, she yielded to the preponderance of arguments.

A young man with 'blondy hair' in his early thirties appeared after Adam rang the doorbell. Wilson wore wire-rimmed glasses and was dressed casually in khaki slacks and a safari shirt. Julia watched Adam talk to this man, hands in pockets, laconic as always. But Julia imagined he was very convincing. Wilson invited Adam in, never noticing her in the truck.

As Julia sat waiting, she reflected on the case as though she were presenting it to her class. This was not just a child molester they were after, it was a child murderer. A mutilator. A sexual sadist.

Julia had not learned, until after her father died, that her Grandmére Arnault had been raped before she was stabbed. Nor had she known that the stabbing was frenzied and brutal. Neither of her parents had talked about it. But Julia had researched it through newspaper articles in the Canadian press. It had been in the province papers.

'What kind of man commits such acts?' she'd asked. There wasn't, she knew, a single profile to fit all of the Dahmers or Henry Lee Lucases. But the literature suggested they most likely came from problem families, especially with alcoholism and physical abuse. The sociopathy sometimes included animal molestation by the young boys. That was true with Jeffrey Dahmer and Lucas. It was also true of DeSalvo. They had all tortured animals. That had been the most notable outcome of her dissertation. She'd tried to find out about Pierre Sangé's background, but there was nothing in the papers and no leads. It probably wasn't even his real name. *Sangé* meant 'blood,' from the Latin *sanguis*. Too coincidental, she concluded.

Engaged in thought, Julia was suddenly startled to see a blonde woman in a white jogging suit appear from the back of the Wilson house. She began jouncing up the walk, her long hair in a French braid swishing under the white headband. About twenty-five or twenty-six, Julia estimated. The L.A. look. 'Like Phillip's fiancée,' she thought bitterly.

Rolling down her window, she called out. "Excuse me, could I talk with you?"

"Not if you're selling anything," the blonde woman replied in a sulky voice.

"No," Julia assured her. "I just wanted to ask where you get your hair done. I just moved into the area."

"Well," the woman responded with flattered interest as she walked over to the truck, "you won't find anyone around here that can do a decent French braid."

* * *

"Danny is beating the pants off me," Wilson explained disarmingly.

Inside the Wilson livingroom, three-year-old Danny was glued to a computer terminal. He and his father had been playing computer games, as they did most days after school.

"Yea!" shouted the towheaded little boy, vaporizing an orange-eyed alien.

As Roger Wilson went to the bookcase and pulled down a thick scrapbook, he said to Adam, "I've had some good findings this year."

Adam focused on the metallic cover of the scrapbook, finally recognizing the design of a space ship.

* * *

When Adam emerged from the Wilson house a half-hour later, he wore an expression of humorous disbelief.

"Well?" prompted Julia.

"Swell guy, Roger Wilson," Adam answered ambiguously and started up the truck.

"For a computer analyst and crackpot, that is," Julia added, trying not to sound too pleased with herself as they began driving away.

"What do you mean?" Adam asked cagily.

"I mean that he's one of those guys who look for archeological markings that prove we're actually Martians or something. Didn't he tell you?"

Adam turned to look at her. "How did you know?"

"Just a guess." Julia gazed smugly out the window as they left the development.

"He showed me his 'sightings' album. It has a picture of the Enterprise on the cover. Apparently, they go all over the country looking for 'traces.' Signs that we've been visited by aliens. He charts everything in detail. He's got the whole thing computerized."

"That's what his wife told me. Holland. That's her name. Holland. She's from Pasadena."

"Uh huh."

"What was he like?"

"Actually," Adam admitted, "he's quite likeable. He's intelligent, loves his kid, real family man. He just really believes this stuff. And he's got his kid believing it, too. But I got a sense there's more to it than that."

"Such as?"

"Well, the way he spoke, I think he's convinced he was abducted."

"Abducted? You mean, by beings from outer space?"

"I know, I feel a little silly just talking about it."

Julia smiled. "It's the new fad phenomenon. Used to be evil possession. Now it's gone sci-fi. I wonder if they took his wife, too. Did you see her when you went in?" Julia asked offhandedly.

"No."

"Good."

Adam glanced at her curiously but she did not elaborate.

"Have you done a lot of investigative work?" she asked.

"On different occasions."

"It doesn't seem to go with being a veterinarian. I mean, it's more like police work," she said tentatively, always tip-toeing around him when she asked personal questions.

"I've had police training. For animal cruelty cases."

He appeared easier with her questions today so she decided to forge ahead. "After you came back from Vietnam?"

"Umm hmm."

She hesitated a moment, then asked, "What was it like? Vietnam."

"Everything they said it was," Adam answered quietly, looking directly into her eyes. Then he cocked his head slightly. "I suppose you were a protester." She nodded gently. "And your husband?" He had never actually asked her about him before.

"He burned his draft card," she answered, a little sardonically.

She had opposed the war and she was not apologetic about that. But she was remembering the big anti-war rally on campus and all the college hippies circling the bonfire in leather vests without shirts, wearing love beads and bell-bottom pants. The real hippies of course had dropped out of school, out of everything, and what was left were the Phillips of their generation.

"2-S?" he asked, giving the code for a student deferment.

"Exactly."

For the first time, she found that ironic. Yes, Phillip burned the draft card that he probably never would have had to use anyway. She began to chuckle and suddenly both of them were laughing. Each felt a release over something so old and still so raw.

Julia settled back in her seat. "Who's next?" She was beginning to enjoy this.

"Judd Vaughan. I think we can eliminate Roger Wilson."

"I'm not so sure. We really don't know enough about him yet. All we really know is whoever killed Jeannine didn't stop at that. The killer could be psychotic, or drugged and hallucinating, or acting out some compulsion. Or he could be mentally deficient and not understand what he's doing. Or he's a sociopath and doesn't care. Anyway, we don't know if any of that fits Wilson. There's no reason to eliminate him just because he loves his kid. Even married men and fathers like Albert DeSalvo can rape and murder."

"Right, teach."

Julia scowled at the implication that she was being pedantic. "So, what do *you* think?"

"I think the man who killed Jeannine Bradburn is evil," Adam replied.

"Of course, it's an evil sadistic act."

"No, I mean *he's* evil."

"You mean 'capital E' evil?"

"Yes."

"Like possessed?"

"No. Just evil."

"Psychology doesn't recognize 'evil' as a diagnostic entity."

"Then psychology is wrong. Once again."

Julia said nothing in response. Apparently Adam didn't hold her profession in very high regard. What, then, did he think of *her*?

She remained silent as they pulled up to the Bradburn house in pink-eye village. Julia had seen it only at night, the night after she met Adam, the night after Jeannine had been declared missing.

In front of the house, in the middle of the bare-ground yard was a leafless maple tree hung with multicolored plastic Easter eggs. Julia had seen other such trees along the road but wondered why the Bradburns had bothered. Or maybe, like Doris' Christmas tree, they never took the decorations down.

As they parked, a thin young girl, about fourteen, with stringy brown hair opened the door.

"Who's that?" Julia asked Adam.

The girl balanced a baby on her hip whom Julia assumed was one of the family.

"Jeannine's sister, Minna." Adam got out of the truck, instructing her to "Stay here."

"What again? Why?"

"Because nobody here is going to talk in front of a woman, especially one who doesn't belong."

Julia was more than a little irritated as she watched Adam walk away again. The worst of it was that he was probably right. The men probably *wouldn't* talk in front of her.

After Minna pointed towards the backyard and Adam headed in that direction, the girl remained in the doorway holding the baby and looking at Julia with expressionless brown eyes. She wore a frilly white blouse and elasticized black pants that ended above the ankle. She had on thin white socks and black low-cut flats. 'Typical teenager,' Julia thought. Then she impulsively decided that if the men won't talk with her, maybe this young girl would. Maybe she could learn something the way she had with Holland Wilson.

Julia walked toward the girl and held out a finger to the baby. "Hello there," she said brightly to the infant. "What's your name?" The baby tugged at her finger.

"His name's Dwayne," Minna responded without inflection.

Playfully, Julia tugged back a little bit on his hand. "Hello, Dwayne. Is Big Sister taking care of you today?"

The baby began to cough and then cry. The girl scolded him, "Quiet, Dwayne. Be quiet." Turning towards the house, she said to Julia, "You can come in." Then Minna opened her blouse and put the baby to her breast.

* * *

Jeannine's grandfather, Elgin Bradburn, stacked the firewood while Judd Vaughan chopped and split it. Both men saw Adam walk towards them, but Judd kept on chopping while Elgin greeted him.

"How'do."

"How're you doing, Elgin? I'm sorry about your granddaughter. I wanted to offer my condolences to your family."

"Appreciate it."

"How's Cora?"

"Not so good. She got a bad heart, you know. Like little Jeannine. Jeannine was gonna have an operation for it. Cora ought to. Right now, it's breakin' inta pieces."

"I have a lady with me who's a psychologist. She knows how to help Cora get through this. Maybe Cora'd like to talk to her."

"Maybe."

Judd Vaughan followed their conversation without looking over at them. His chopping was rhythmic.

"You know they've got Tully in jail."

Elgin nodded.

"What do you think about that?"

Elgin looked over at Judd then back at Adam. "I think if they don't keep him outa my reach, I'm gonna split open his head like a piece of dry oak."

Thwack! went Judd's maul.

* * *

In the impoverished livingroom, Jeannine's mother sat in the corner of a brown and yellow plaid sofa, pressed up against the side. Only thirty-three, Cora was very small and already worn with hard work. She hadn't stopped crying since Jeannine had been found.

Her husband Otis, Elgin's son, sat next to her, a giant of a man with huge hands, fullback shoulders, and a full dark beard. Otis was a gentle man, slow in his movements, not given to great harangues. There had been a playfulness in him that, in past, was not averse to chasing Cora around the kitchen table with a giggle. But none of that showed in him now. Nor, perhaps, ever would again. He held Cora's hand as though she might slip off the sofa and slide down the mountain out of sight.

Both of them looked at Julia as she followed Minna into the room. Minna flopped down into a threadbare armchair across the room, still nursing her baby. She nodded towards Julia.

"She's with the vet-erin-arian," Minna explained, and her parents' glances quickly dropped to the floor, as though they had hoped this city woman might have brought some miracle with her and were once again let down.

No one invited Julia to sit down, so she stood up against the white plasterboard wall and waited. Not only did they not speak to her, neither did they speak to each other. The only sounds were Dwayne's sucking noises at Minna's breast and Jeannine's mother's quiet sobs.

Everything smelled musty and smoky. Julia felt as though she were in a funeral parlor without the coffin and flowers. She wondered where they had buried Jeannine. There were lots of old family cemeteries around. Maybe the funeral had been right here, right in this room.

She was reminded of her mother's funeral two years ago. Her mother had insisted on a closed casket in her instructions, and Julia had complied. She put her parents' wedding picture on the casket cover. Julia's father had died right after she got her doctorate; she was glad he had seen her at the beginning of her career—and not now. They knew, he had whispered to her on his deathbed, that she was going to have a wonderful life ahead of her. But she had not exactly had a wonderful life. Oh, at first, yes. Her mother was thrilled when Julia began teaching, married Phillip, and then had Karen. But as the years went by, her mother began to see through Phillip. 'Before I did.' Julia admitted to herself. Her mother had said pointedly, "The only one he loves, Julia, is himself." Julia denied it because it made her feel unlovable.

After that, Karen became the focus of her mother's attention. Almost as though Julia were all played out, had had her turn and had blown it. At Julia's visits home, her mother's eyes seemed to dwell pityingly on her. Sometimes, after leaving, Julia would pull her car over in a highway rest-stop and cry. Then, hating the thought that Phillip might ask her what was wrong when she got home, she would reapply her makeup and get a chocolate frappe to lift her spirits. When her mother died suddenly of a cerebral hemorrhage, Julia felt as though she had lost all her chances ever to show her parents that she was worth the effort they had put into her. Her mother's dying was almost a recrimination, as if to say "I waited as long as I could."

Julia felt uncomfortable in the Bradburn house. She wanted to back out of the room, out the door, and drive away leaving Adam to his own devices. But seconds later, he entered the livingroom with Elgin Bradburn. The distraught parents' gazes turned hopefully to him.

She recognized Elgin from the Mayfair, the night she had watched him dive headfirst off the table onto the floor.

* * *

"I'm sorry for your troubles, Otis, Cora," Adam addressed the grieving parents in a soft voice.

"Thank you," Otis replied.

"I expect Chief Burke has talked to you already."

"That jerk-off don't know nothin'. We talk to Percy," Elgin snarled, answering for his son.

"Where's Judd at?" Minna interrupted.

"Out back," Grandpa Elgin replied.

Minna got up and walked out of the room, her baby still at her breast.

Adam continued, "What do you think, Otis? You think it was Tully?"

"Coulda been."

"Can you tell me if Jeannine had any boyfriends or boys that she talked about?"

"She wasn't allowed to talk to boys. We already been through that once." He looked towards the chair where Minna had sat.

"Is there anybody else that could have done it, you think?"

"I don't trust nobody but family."

Just then, Judd Vaughan strode into the room with Minna trailing behind him.

"Quit following me, will ya?" Judd griped and crossed the livingroom into the bathroom, closing the door in Minna's face. Unperturbed, she turned around and sat in the armchair again with Dwayne.

"Cora," Adam said, "this is Julia." The woman he addressed seemed to be getting smaller and smaller in front of his eyes. Was it possible to shrink into nothingness from despair? He motioned Julia to come closer. "Julia found Jeannine. She wants to talk to you."

Cora looked up, closed her eyes and began shaking violently.

Julia threw Adam a helpless look, then said softly to Cora, "I'm very sorry about Jeannine." Cora held her head in her hands and began swaying back and forth.

"Is there anything I can do to help you?" Julia offered.

But Cora didn't answer and Otis said, without admonishment, "There ain't nothin' you can do, lady."

* * *

Afterwards, in the truck, it was several long minutes before either of them spoke.

"Will she come out of it?" Adam asked.

"I don't know."

"I thought you might be able to do something for her."

Julia took a deep breath. "I don't work with patients. That's a clinical psychologist. I'm just a teacher." She waited for the look of disappointment she expected to cross his face, but it didn't come.

"Sorry," he said sincerely, "I didn't mean to put you on the spot."

But Julia couldn't help feeling she had failed to pass muster. Maybe not in his eyes, but in her own.

After another silence, she said, "I don't think you ever get over losing a child. And it has to be a million-fold worse to lose her that way. Even for them."

"There's no difference between Juckets and anyone else when it comes to pain and suffering," he said gruffly.

"No, of course not. I didn't mean it that way." But she had, and she admonished herself it. 'This is not the kind of person I want to be, who thinks people who have less *are* less. That's what's wrong with privilege."

"Tell me," she asked in earnest, "where does the word Jucket come from?"

Adam shrugged. "Nobody really knows anymore. Some say it was the family name of some Gypsy settlers. I always figured it was a variation on the Jukes family. Heard of them?"

"Yes. The fictitious family in upstate New York that Dugdale wrote about in the 1800s. I use it in my syllabus. Inheritance determines capability; environment determines criminality."

"Jukes…Juckets. Both inbred, insular communities. My heritage."

"He was wrong, you know. Or at least incomplete."

Adam said nothing and she felt embarrassed to have brought the whole thing up. She went on to ask, "Did you find out anything there?"

"Not really. Otis and Elgin are too broken up. I tried to talk to Judd, but he's a tough case. So we didn't learn very much."

"Except for one thing," Julia corrected.

"Which is?"

"Judd likes his women young."

Adam nodded. "And *vice versa*."

As they drove past the Congregational Church on the way back, she saw the young pastor posting the Lenten sermon, *"Fasting? Prayer is soul food—have another helping."*

Julia wondered if his sermons were as clever as their titles.

* * *

The Others gathered that night, as they had for many years now, their voices increasing.

"It's Spring. In two weeks, it will be Easter. We must prepare.

"The delivery is due this week."

"Excellent."

"It must be healthy."

"Yes."

"No screw-ups, like last time."

"No."

He sat up in bed that night, back against the wall, thinking about Jeannine. How there was nothing she could do to stop him. She got into his truck so shivery and girlish. No idea of how he would hold her thin little wrists and stuff her hair in her mouth. And after he was done, the Others took over. Sharpened the axe and cleaved her in twain.

"I wonder what the woman with the dog would do. Would she scream? Or maybe she would like it."

Maybe it was all right that he hadn't killed the dog, even though because of that they found Jeannine. If he had killed the dog, he might never have known the woman. She was small and thin, too. He'd watched her in her car, watched when she wasn't looking at him. She was a teacher in college.

"Maybe she will be the one. Maybe of all women, she will understand me."

"But she's not a virgin."

SUNDAY, APRIL 8th

As Julia waited in the truck, Adam swung open the long wooden gate across the entrance to Floyd Mather's farm. The ground was still muddy from the recent rains.

"Floyd used to be lazy, kind of no-good when he was younger," Adam explained to Julia as they drove up the graveled driveway. "His parents were old when they had Floyd and he was their only child. His father died when Floyd was in high school. After that, the farm didn't produce. The house was always in disrepair. His mother couldn't manage it alone. She died while Floyd was in 'Nam and the house stood empty a couple of years. But when he got back, he seemed to turn around. Started cleaning up the place. Making the farm work. The war changed him in opposite ways from what you'd expect."

"Is he a Jucket?"

"No."

"Swamp Yankee?"

"No. I guess he'd be an authentic Yankee. Puritan lineage. The family claims relations back to the Reverend Cotton Mather, of Salem witchcraft fame."

"Now there's an interesting psychological study," Julia commented. "He believed in Evil with a capital 'E.' And people died because of it."

"Not just because of him. It was the ethos. They all believed it."

"And they were all misguided. That's the problem."

"I'll give you that. But it doesn't negate the reality. *Any* truth can be misguided."

Julia was ready to argue the point but they were almost at the white farmhouse at the end of the road.

The fields on either side were already half-harrowed and all the preparations for early planting were visible. There was a tidiness about everything, no sags in the barn, even the old equipment was in good shape, freshly painted and lined up methodically, ready to use. The place gave a sense of being well cared for. The Puritan streak, perhaps.

"How would you like to have a piglet?" Adam said impishly.

"*Moi*?"

"They can be housebroken."

"You're not serious."

"It's the only way we're going to get him to talk to us."

"What am I going to do with a piglet?"

Without stipulating, Adam parked in front of the house and Julia and Cat followed him up to the old-fashioned cross door with four panels. Julia noticed that the row of small windows at the top of the door had been replaced with wood.

Minutes passed after Adam knocked, so he knocked again. Finally, Floyd Mather opened the door with a German Shepherd at his side. Immediately, Cat began barking and the Shepherd barked back in kind.

Floyd was as tall as Adam but bone thin. He had an unnaturally broad forehead and pointed chin, accentuated by sideburns. Although she had only seen him once, Julia recognized him instantly from the night at the auction, sitting next to Babe.

"Hello, Floyd," Adam said agreeably. But Floyd remained silent as the German Shepherd bared his teeth.

Cat wouldn't obey Julia's command to stop barking, so she quickly led her by the collar back to the truck, scolding the dog all the way. Mather held the Shepherd's collar as the dog strained forward.

"This lady here," Adam gestured towards Julia, "wants to buy a piglet. I told her you have good stock and maybe you'd sell her one."

"What for?"

"She's starting a 4-H group for the city kids who've moved into Cedarwood Park. They want to raise a pig for competition."

Floyd glanced back and forth from Adam to Julia. Julia tried to look at him levelly. Finally, he said, "They ain't cheap."

"She's looking for quality."

Floyd studied them a moment then reached for a green chino jacket behind the door.

Floyd and his dog led Adam and Julia around the back of the house. There, Floyd opened a wooden storage bin set next to the back door. He removed a pair of shiny clean waders. He wordlessly put on the boots and proceeded to the sty over a muddy path.

Behind his back, Julia looked at Adam and mouthed, "4-H?"

Adam shrugged and they both trudged after Floyd, the mud mounding up dangerously close to the top of Julia's loafers. As she stepped carefully to avoid sinking, she noted that Adam was wearing old leather boots. He might have warned her. The mud was ankle-high in spots between the pens, so Julia stood to the side on dryer ground.

Floyd pointed at a sow with her new suckling piglets in one of the pens. The smell of manure was powerful in the back of Julia's throat. And yet the pen itself was fairly clean. Floyd picked up one of the piglets and brought it over to Adam.

"I can let you have this one when she's bigger. She'll be ready to go in a few weeks. Unless you want a boar."

"No," Adam answered, "a sow."

Floyd passed the piglet to Adam, who looked it over expertly and passed it to Julia. She clutched the warm squirmy little animal and, notwithstanding the odor, held it close to her. She liked this little creature on sight.

"You want her?" Floyd asked impassively.

Julia was surprised to find him talking directly to her. "Yes," she replied.

"We'll take her in early July," Adam said. "It's better for the kids to get her after school's out. We'll give you the right price."

"I'll let you know when to come for her." Floyd took the piglet back from Julia. "Pay me then."

As Floyd returned the piglet to her mother, Julia wondered how he would know which one was hers when the time came. 'Good grief,' she suddenly thought, 'I'm not actually going to own this pig, am I? It's got to be just another ruse. Adam'll get me out of it.'

Adam meanwhile was staring at a dirt path behind the sties that led into Pittsley Woods on the opposite end from the Bradburn place.

"How's the hunting in there?"

Floyd followed Adam's gaze. "I don't hunt anymore."

"I saw the path. Figured you might bag a few raccoons back there."

"No."

Floyd said nothing further as he walked back to the house.

Julia scraped off the mud from the bottom of her shoes on the rim of the truck tire and looked over her shoulder. Floyd was standing in his doorway watching them as though he thought they might steal something on the way out.

She couldn't decide whether she was unfair in disliking this odd man. He seemed sullen and reclusive. 'But,' she reminded herself, 'that describes a lot of people around here.' Just then, she thought she saw the second-floor curtain move.

"Adam, I think someone's upstairs at the window. I bet he has a woman. We probably caught him *in flagrante delicto*. That's why he took so long to answer the door."

"Could be. But Floyd's *always* looked a little *coitus interruptus*."

She laughed as Adam started the truck and headed out the gate.

* * *

"What are we going to do with it, come July?" Julia said on the way home.

"Pay for it and take it."

"Adam, I really can't have a pig. What'll happen if I don't take her?"

"Ham sandwich."

"Oh."

She'd tried being a vegetarian once but she'd gotten anemic and gave it up. Nevertheless, she did not want to be reminded where pork chops came from.

"She's cute and all, but you know I can't take her, Adam."

"I know. Either I'll keep her or maybe I'll give her to somebody. Maybe to Billy's kid."

She inwardly sighed with relief and changed the subject.

"Do you think Floyd's a real suspect?"

"I don't know. All I know is that he lied about not hunting anymore."

"Probably because he knows you're against it, no?"

"Maybe. But now he knows I'm curious. So now we'll see what he does."

"What do you mean, see what he does? What are we going to do now?"

"We're going to take *you* home."

"Then what?"

"Then I'm planning to spend a very uncomfortable night in the woods."

Julia knew there was no dissuading him. She leaned back and tried to imagine what Phillip, or any of her colleagues, would think about all this. They wouldn't understand any of it. Wouldn't understand her fascination with all this; wouldn't understand Adam, either. With some private satisfaction, she realized then how thoroughly she had distanced herself from her former life.

* * *

By sundown, Adam had situated himself in a natural blind at the edge of Pittsley Woods where it met Floyd's property. He carried a pair of small military-issue binoculars in a black gym bag, along with a large thermos of hot coffee, cheese and pickle sandwiches with lettuce and tomato on pumpernickel, and a bag of Julia's chocolate chunk cookies. He looked forward to sitting back later and smoking his pipe, although he would have to be careful to stay undetected. He was dressed in a warm parka. ("Never wore a hat, never will," he told Julia when she suggested it.) He was happy.

Scanning the woods, he observed a squawking cluster of crows settling into the treetops of a nearby fir, squirrels scampering across the ground and up the tree trunks to settle in for the evening, the sounds of Spring peepers, the cacophony of crickets, and then, with particular interest, a salamander. It was an unusual kind of green- and black-spotted salamander, and he watched it crawl into a rockpile not far from a little brook about ten yards away. He spotted a raccoon and shifted to watch it, at the same time knocking his gym bag off a rock, startling the raccoon into disappearing into the underbrush. Adam then settled into a more comfortable position against a tree and waited.

Spring made Adam feel like a horse let out to pasture. There was joy in the smallest signs of life everywhere. Yet here he was, only walking distance from where Jeannine's body had been found. In ways he thought he'd forgotten, it reminded him of how he and his troops and eaten, laughed, slept, and defecated with the bodies of Viet Cong just steps away. Before the war, it had been hard for him to think of killing a human being but after he'd done it, it became hard to remember why it mattered. It was something he'd had to relearn.

The first hour passed quickly. Then at twilight, Adam saw a light go on in Floyd's upstairs window. 'Surly to bed, surly to rise,' he thought.

Another hour passed before his stomach began growling. He hadn't eaten anything since lunch, and that was only a cup of lentil soup and an apple. He reached hungrily for a sandwich in the gym bag but his hand encountered something wet. Everything wet. Sandwiches, cookies, tobacco. Good thing the binoculars were in a waterproof case. But the sandwiches were ruined, the cookies had dissolved into mush, and his tobacco pouch was soggy. Adam cursed under his breath. It was going to be a long night.

* * *

Julia sat at a microfilm reader in the library, scanning through newspaper articles on The Boston Strangler. She finished the last of them, pressed the copy button, and waited for the article to print.

As she assembled her books and papers and began concentrating on the material she'd gathered, she was pleased at a good night's research. Doing what she liked best. She had put together a pretty solid presentation, a model case-study. The more she thought about it, the more anxious she was to present it to her class.

She'd found a useful interview on serial murders with a forensic investigator in the Boston Police Department. He believed the same thing she did—that whenever a particularly grisly murder wasn't committed by a relative or lover, wasn't a revenge death or sudden rage, and wasn't a professional hit, it was likely to be a serial killing (as distinct from spree killing, and the distinction could vacillate). Hate or race crimes sometimes were, and sometimes weren't serial killings. But that was a different sort of genocidal pathology.

"Blood crime is addictive," the investigator concluded. If it happened once, it would happen again. The police had been lucky with DeSalvo, the investigator had said, because the crimes were all local. The biggest problem was when the murderer moved around from state to state. With a few exceptions, serial killers were usually White males past adolescence. The victims varied. Usually female, they frequently used to be hookers or prepubescent girls, but there seemed to be a new trend towards college students, as with Ted Bundy). There were a number of killers like Jeffrey

Dahmer who preferred boys or men but usually there was sexual content in those killings, too. The crimes became more violently sexual with each successive murder. It was a progression, just like any other addiction.

Suddenly, Jeannine Bradburn's name flashed at her as though on a neon sign. "My God, of course," Julia whispered. The shock of recognition pushed her back in her chair. It had never really clicked until that minute.

Julia immediately sought out the librarian and was surprised to find the same woman she'd seen bring Elmer Goodson his meal. Ms. Dudley didn't recognize Julia as she answered her question about the town newspaper.

"Well, you see dear, Pittsley's never had a newspaper of its own. Anything important that happens in Pittsley is reported in the *Tipisquin Gazette*. It covers quite a few of the nearby towns in this county."

Julia watched her search through a huge oak file cabinet filled with rectangular boxes.

"Now these microfilms," the librarian explained nodding in emphasis, "only go back ten years. But the archives go back much further if you want."

"Ten years should be fine," Julia replied, barely containing her curiosity. Were Ms. Dudley and Mr. Goodson lovers? She must remember to ask Adam.

Julia put the first file in the reader. Because the *Gazette* was a weekly, there were five hundred and twenty issues to scan, but only the first few pages were news. The rest was advertising and social notes, editorials, recipes, and high school sports.

It was a typical small town paper, the kind that gave lots of information about the town's history and development. It also contained, Julia was pleased to discover, a police log for each of the four towns the paper covered. She quickly revised her estimate about how long this was going to take, and made herself comfortable.

Julia returned the microfilm to the reference desk at nine o'clock, closing time.

"Did you find what you want?" Ms. Dudley inquired.

"Yes, but I've only gotten part-way through, so I'd like to continue tomorrow. Could you please put these aside for me?"

"Certainly, dear," the librarian said in a grandmotherly voice.

Julia thanked her and left flushed with exhilaration.

* * *

'Time to do it,' Adam decided. It was a little after two a.m. The moon was clouded over and the sky was dark.

Quietly, he straightened up and stretched the kinks out of his muscles. Then very slowly, careful not to make noise, Adam crept down the path towards Floyd's house. It was as though he were approaching the enemy, alert to booby-traps, land mines, cluster bombs. Before his command, he'd been point man on most of the forays, his vision sharper than any others, able to spot anything before anyone else, sensing the unusual, the unexpected. It was a gift he'd had as far back as he could remember. The Army had tried to make him a sniper because of it, just as his father had tried to make him a hunter. But when—on a hunting trip in northern Maine at the age of ten—he saw his father kill a moose, he had cried uncontrollably. His father had slapped him. The young boy stopped crying and stopped talking all the way home. He still recalled his father's fingers tight on the steering wheel, as tight as they'd been on the rifle's trigger. They had never spoken of it again. Nor did he ever go hunting again.

The pigs were sleeping as he passed. For a minute, Adam flashed back to a remote unnamed place in the jungle. The smell of the pigs in the dark reminded him of it. They had secured the village from the V.C., but it had been evacuated. In sweeping the huts, they'd lost three men to booby-traps. There was no one to retaliate against, so one officer shot an M-16 up the ass of a pig. He was about to do it again when Adam forcibly stopped him. The sergeant mentioned something about 'Court Martial,' but somewhere in the conversation with Adam and the other three soldiers, the word 'frag' surfaced. Nothing further transpired.

It was Floyd's barn and garage that Adam particularly wanted to examine although he wasn't sure what he was looking for. Just a chance finding of an article of clothing, Jeannine's books, anything. He decided to start with the garage in case the cows gave alarm when he entered the barn.

Floyd's black winch-truck was in the garage, along with the green and yellow John Deere riding lawnmower, and the tractor parts. Everything was orderly and in place. Scythes hung on the walls with other implements. A long work-bench at the back of the garage held hammers and saws on hooks and screwdrivers in pigeonholes. There were nails and screws in capped bottles, and a drill and buffer neatly arranged on top.

After a futile hour of searching, Adam closed the garage doors and proceeded to the cow barn.

He slid open the door just enough to squeeze by and went in. The barn was dark and warm and smelled sweet. The cows were undisturbed as he made his way around the barn, poking in corners, shifting hay with his foot. After another hour, he had still found nothing.

As he started back for the woods, one of the young pigs awoke, squealing for food. Soon they all took up the call, making a chorus of insistent demands. Adam began running as fast as he could. He just made the cover of woods as the light went on in the upstairs bedroom and Floyd opened the window and stuck out his .30/.30.

Adam crouched, breathing heavily but not moving as Floyd scanned the yard for intruders. After a minute, the pigs settled down and Floyd pulled in his rifle and shut the window.

Adam waited for a few more minutes for the light to go out then went back to his watch. His adrenaline was up and his heart pumped fiercely. He was back in 'Nam and incoming was only a breath away.

MONDAY, APRIL 9th

Patchy sunlight filtered through the trees in Pittsley Woods. It dappled the ground, illuminating the chokeberry bushes at the base of the tree Adam was propped up against in his sleeping bag. He'd been dozing on and off but as he stirred awake, he was instantly galvanized by sounds of activity. Floyd Mather was walking towards the pigpens to slop the hogs. Adam waited, feeling a stiff ache between his shoulders rising up the back of his neck to his head.

He was cold and hungry and sore. It didn't used to hurt so much after a night's surveillance, back when he was doing it pretty regularly. 'Of course, that was a few years ago,' he reminded himself. His knees were sore, too. That was new. He grimaced and imagined himself as the Tin Man with rusty squeaking joints that needed direct squirts of WD-40 just to move again. He quickly bypassed that to focus on Floyd.

Floyd didn't dump the feed in the trough so much as he layered it in. Neat and methodical. Just going about his business. Never even glanced up at the woods. Adam began wondering why he decided to do this anyway. Maybe it was spite. He didn't like Floyd Mather. Nothing to hang it on. Just didn't like him. But no reason to spend a night in the goddam woods playing spy. He didn't much like Judd Vaughan, either. Maybe he should spend a crappy night in the woods out back of *his* house. Actually, not a bad idea.

He shook his head in disgust, thinking, 'I'm being stupid about this. Playing some half-assed game like I'm a genuine cop or something. 'Is it really for Tully's sake or am I just trying to prove something to myself?'

Almost against his wishes, his thoughts drifted to Julia. The softness of the skin on her breasts, stomach, thighs. The smell of perfume in her hair as it brushed his face while they made love. The way they fit together.

Then, forcibly, he stopped himself. Didn't want to be thinking of her when he had work to do. In fact, he'd been thinking of her too much lately. It was something he was unprepared for. And it was unwanted. Maybe she'd turn out to be special to him, maybe not. Too early to tell. And he didn't want to get in over his head. Especially since she hadn't gotten over her divorce yet. And maybe she wouldn't even stay here. Pittsley was a far cry from Boston and she didn't really belong. Maybe she'd move on soon. It seemed like every woman he'd ever been interested in couldn't make the leap. Oh, they all liked it for a while in the beginning, visiting 'the sticks.' But once they took a good look at the underbrush they always bugged out.

Still watching as Floyd finished feeding the animals and began harrowing the field, Adam finally stood up and stretched. All his muscles screamed. He relieved himself against a tree then sat back down and continued to watch.

Another hour passed before he decided there was nothing more to be gained by waiting. 'It was a dumb idea in the first place,' he told himself. When Floyd went back into the house, Adam took note of the spot where he'd spent the night and left.

"You look like hell," Goody said as Adam appeared at his cabin for breakfast.

"Feel like hell."

"That's what you get for sleepin' in the woods."

"How'd you spot me?"

Goody gave him his 'I know everything' look. "So what did you learn?"

"That I'm getting old."

"You want turkey eggs?" Goody shut the door and shuffled over to the woodstove where a cast-iron skillet was already sizzling with pancakes.

"Sounds great." Adam sank into the armchair.

"You find out anything about Floyd?"

"Nope."

"Didn't think so."

"I don't know, I don't seem to be getting anywhere with this. I must be going about it dumb-headed. I can't come up with any suspect that'll hold up in the light of day. Maybe I've overlooked somebody."

"Like who?" Goody lifted out the pancakes onto a plate and put it on top of the woodstove to keep warm.

"Cranshaw, maybe. Tully worked for him. Conny could've framed him. It's logical and it feels right in the gut." Then, shaking his head, "But I just don't have a motive."

As Goody took two turkey eggs from a bowl, he gave Adam a meaningful look. "Since when does crazy have to have a motive?"

"Conny may be mean, but I don't think he's crazy." Adam watched his friend break the eggs in each hand on the sides of the skillet and toss the shells into the sink. "Besides, Conny's married. He's got grown children and about four hundred grandchildren. Why would he want to do that?"

Goody laid two slices of bread on top of the woodstove to toast. "I don't know why anybody does anything. But I know that Conny is a rotten apple in that family barrel. He may be married but that never stopped him from cheatin'. Even when he was married to his first wife."

Adam rubbed the back of his neck. "I know. But that was yesterday and this isn't the same thing." He was starving and longed for breakfast to be ready.

"Bad's bad. Just a matter of direction."

"Yeah, maybe. But why Jeannine Bradburn?"

"Don't you know him and the Bradburns fell out years back?" Goody flipped the eggs and turned the toast.

"Over what?" Adam's stomach rumbled.

"Your married-family-man-grandfather Mr. Conway Victor Cranshaw was one of them that got at Jeannine's mother."

Adam sat up straight, unmindful of any aches or empty stomach. "He was one of the men who raped Cora? Are you sure of that?"

Goody merely lifted the eggs onto the plates, with two pancakes and one piece of toast apiece.

"Yeah, yeah, you're always sure." Adam took the plate of food from Goody's gnarled hand. "So her husband found out?"

Goody shook his head. "Otis never knew any of them that did it. But old Elgin did." He sat down on the bed with his plate of food. "Her own father never did nothin' about it but when she and Otis got hitched, her new father-in-law, Elgin Bradburn, told Conny he'd blow his head clean off if he came near her again. Elgin ain't one to forgive and forget. And Conny ain't one to let anybody tell him what to do. So them two got themselves a feud." Goody dug into his breakfast.

"Who were the others, besides Conny?"

"Conny's cousin, George. He's dead. Cancer. And Bobby Camerona. He's gone. West Virginia. I heard there was another one, but I don't know who."

Between bites, Adam asked, "What makes you think Conny'd take his feud out on Jeannine?"

"He's got a long fuse but when he blows he's got a cruel streak, alright. I seen him take a tire iron to a guy he had a beef with. Banged him unconscious and proceeded to smash just about every bending bone in his body. Toes, knees, fingers, elbows. Went berserk." Goody paused to soak up the yolk with his bread.

"Why didn't I know about that?"

"You was away in the dirty war."

"So what happened?"

"What do you *think* happened?" Goody said contemptuously. "The guy was laid up for six months."

"Did they arrest Conny for it?" Adam cleaned his plate with the toast.

"Nah, guy never pressed charges."

"Why not?"

"'Cause he knew next time Conny'd kill his kids."

"Who was the guy?"

"Ben Bradburn. Elgin's brother."

Goody went back to sopping up his eggs as Adam watched him, still too surprised to say anything.

"Told you. Conny's crazy. Watch yourself around him." Goody screwed up his mouth. "You eat too goddam fast."

"How are you doing, Tully?" In the small visitor area of the jail, Adam sat across from his friend whose pallor was ashen beneath his unshaven face.

"I gotta get outa here. I can't take it." Tully clutched at Adam's sleeve. "Why can't you bail me out? You gotta get me outa here, Adam."

"I can't, Tully. There's no bail."

"I can't stay in here, Adam. I get closed in. I can't take being in a little box." His voice cracked. "I was in jail when I was a kid, Adam, remember I told you? I can't take it."

Adam remembered. Tully had told him the story so many times he could recite it himself. It had happened when Tully was just a young boy, eleven or twelve, on the day his father took him into Boston for the first time. Adam hadn't known Tully's father but he knew the man had worked to organize a trucker's union. He brought his son into the city with him to hand out union leaflets at a trucking company. But when the police came to stop them, Tully's father ran away and they grabbed Tully. Kept him in jail overnight. Tully's father didn't come for him in the morning and the boy had to take the train back to New Bedford and walk the fifteen miles home alone. After that night in jail, which Tully would never talk about, he hated his father with a vengeance for the rest of his life.

"Take it easy, Tully, calm down. You're going to have to do this. There's no choice. It's just a little while longer until the hearing. Just a few more days."

"But what if they say I'm guilty, Adam? I'm not going to stay in here. I'll kill myself first."

"Whoa, one step at a time."

"What's gonna happen next?" Tully whimpered.

"They'll move it along fast now. The hearing on Friday will be for probable cause. And after that, there'll be a trial."

"When?"

"I don't know. You'll have to ask Kipper. Month, probably. Maybe two."

"I can't wait that long." Tully dropped his head in his hands.

"I'm doing my best. But I have to come up with another lead." Adam paused then said, "What about Conny Cranshaw? Did he ever know about the time you gave Jeannine a ride in your truck?"

Tully paused before answering. "Yeah, he was plenty sore about it. Said I was never to take any little girl in one of his trucks ever again or he'd fire me. Hell, he fired me anyway."

"Did he know about the other thing? Your wife's daughter?" Adam watched for Tully's reaction.

"I don't know. He mighta heard a thing or two."

Adam nodded, thinking, 'If Conny did it, and he just may have, he sure knew who to frame.'

"I'm telling you, Adam, I can't stay here. These walls are closing in on me. I can't take it."

* * *

Maxwell Kipper's secretary, Terri, sat on the opposite side of the desk taking notes as he spoke on conference phone. When the second phone rang, Kipper clicked over from conference to receiver, and Terri answered the incoming call.

"Good morning, Kipper and Cummings," she intoned. "Yes, Mr. Sabeski." She looked at her boss with black inquiring eyes and he nodded. She continued, "One minute, he'll be right with you."

Kipper told his party, "I'm going to pass you to my assistant and you can give her the information." He put his line on hold and directed Terri, "Just get this guy's address, will you?" They exchanged telephone receivers. She proceeded to talk to the other party in an undertone as he talked to Adam.

She hung up just as Kipper was finishing his conversation. Terri stared at him under her shiny black bangs. "Any news?"

"Not exactly." Then he grinned. "Only that our client is Mickey Spillane with a pinecone up his bunghole."

The barest smile pulled at his secretary's fuchsia lips.

* * *

The last time Adam had encountered his adversary face-to-face was over two months ago when he charged Conny Cranshaw under the animal cruelty laws for neglecting his goats. In court, Conny had produced a registered bill-of-sale indicating that he had bought the goats that very day, as is, from a goat farm in Tiverton, Rhode Island, and that the goats had been delivered sight unseen to the auction pen. Tiverton might be only a few miles away but it was out of state and out of the court's jurisdiction. Even though all the parties knew it was a fabrication, there were too many convolutions to the case and the judge dismissed it.

Conny was disposed to be tolerant of the incident. Besting Adam had been recompense enough. In Conny's mind, it balanced everything. He had even gotten the go-ahead to put the concrete plant in Pittsley Woods over Adam's objections. Conny was victorious. Incontestably victorious.

Thus, Adam was less than enthusiastic driving through the gates of *CranLand Trucking, Inc.* today. What exactly was he going to say to Conny? "Where were you the day Jeannine Bradburn disappeared?"

What he wound up asking, as he sat across from his nemesis in the well-appointed trailer-office was, "Did you see Tully with Jeannine the time he gave her a ride around the yard in his truck?"

"*My* truck," Conny corrected. "Yes, I saw him"

"And?"

Conny scowled, pushing up the sleeves of the sky-blue hand-knit sweater he was wearing. "I don't allow that. I don't allow any of my drivers to give rides to *any* passengers, and they all know it. Tully's been driving for me for twenty-five years. He knows the rules."

"What was she doing here in the first place?"

Conny regarded him under bushy white eyebrows. "She was here with her kin."

"I thought you didn't do business with Bradburns." Adam crossed his leg, silently thanking Goody for that information.

Conny re-lit his small and obviously expensive cigar. "He's no Bradburn. He's a Vaughan."

Adam took in the distinction. Then he realized *which* Vaughan Conny was talking about.

"You mean she was here with Judd?"

"That's right."

"Her cousin?"

"Whatever. I don't keep track."

"Were they here often?"

"Not often."

"How often?"

Tapping an ash from his cigar into a brass ashtray in the form of a Mack truck, Conny smirked, "Twice as much as half."

Adam was tempted to take a swing at him. But he still needed more information so he tried a different tactic.

"What's your opinion? Do you think Tully could've done what they say?"

"I don't know."

The lush smoke from Conny's cigar wafted across the mahogany desk, making Adam ravenous for tobacco.

"Well, of course nobody knows for sure yet but what to do you think? After all, you fired him, didn't you?"

"I can't afford to have anything like that associated with my business."

"You could've suspended him instead."

"Yes and I could kissed my business goodbye. Because that's what I'd be doing if I didn't fire him. I'm a solid citizen in this county." Conny nodded toward several plaques on the wall honoring him as a member of the Kiwanis and the local development corporation. "I've got a reputation to maintain."

"Your reputation isn't exactly untarnished."

"Meaning?"

"Rumor has it, you had a set-to with Elgin Bradburn over his daughter-in-law."

Conny paused to run his lips up and down the cigar, moistening it. Adam couldn't read him. Had he struck home?

But the man across the desk merely replied in unhurried words, "I explained to Mr. Bradburn that no advantage was taken of anybody that day. Cora was willing."

"The hell she was."

"No complaint was ever made that I know of. Now, unless you were there to see otherwise, you're just going to have to take my word for it. "

Adam clenched his teeth and restrained his impulse to smash the cigar into Conny's mouth. Instead, he got up from his chair.

`"You never answered my question. Do you think Tully did it?"

Conny leaned forward on his elbows. "Whatever the court says is right with me. I put my faith in the American judicial system. Don't you?" He smiled, then guffawed louder and louder.

Julia didn't show up for dinner at Adam's house that evening. Nor had she called. And when Adam phoned, there was no answer. Disquieted, he sat down to read but kept losing interest. Tiredness from the night before finally overcame him and he fell asleep with the latest book on *New England Reptiles* in his lap.

About nine-thirty, a polite knock at the door startled him. The door opened, and before he could get up, Julia was inside saying excitedly, “Adam, I think I’ve found something!”

* * *

Over a bowl of hot chili, Julia showed him the articles she had copied on three other young girls who had disappeared in Pittsley and in neighboring towns over the past ten years.

Adam read the articles and re-read them. Then he laid them down on the table with a sigh. “I don’t see any real link here, Julia. You’ve got a few disappearances—“

“Four, including Jeannine.”

“—over the course of years. Mostly in different towns.”

“But all in Pittsley County.”

“And what about the drowning?” he countered. “One of the girls disappeared while she was swimming. That leaves only three.” Adam regarded her solicitously. “Except for Jeannine, that would be two disappearances in the last five years. That’s probably less than the national average.”

“But there’s a thread here, Adam. If you understood serial killing…,” she trailed off.

“Serial killing? That’s really stretching it, Julia. There’s no reason whatsoever to suspect that this is anything more than a single crime.”

Julia leaned forward. “But what if it’s Tully, Adam? What if he killed Jeannine and he’s killed before? You said yourself he’s got a history with young girls.”

He shook his head slowly. “Not that kind of history.”

“Adam, think about it. Why Jeannine? Why just her?” Anybody who’d do that to Jeannine has a lust for that kind of crime. Doesn’t that make sense to you?”

“Not if it’s Conny Cranshaw.”

“Why Conny Cranshaw?”

Adam explained what Goody had said and told her about his afternoon visit to the trucking company.

Julia got up to rinse her bowl and spoon in the sink. “So you think it’s Conny Cranshaw?”

"He's my best guess right now. I've asked Kipper to check up on him. Conny's got to have a record for *something*."

Julia frowned. But why would he be so brutal? Even if he killed her, why all the rest?"

"Goody says he's got a crazy mean streak in him."

"Is that enough?"

"It's a lead."

"But is it *enough*?"

"Enough," Adam said facetiously, raising and lowering his eyebrows Groucho-style, "to eat you with, Little Red Riding Hood." He slowly got up from the chair, feigning a wolflike approach.

Cupping her hand under the faucet, in one swift motion she laughingly doused him with a handful of cold water.

Adam yelped and jumped towards her as Julia fled shrieking. She was half-way up the stairs when he caught the belt of her jeans.

"I give, I give!" she cried, and within minutes only their clothes remained on the steps.

* * *

Afterwards, they lay sleeping spoon-fashion with Adam's right arm around her waist and his left arm under her pillow. His breaths came softly into her hair and Julia stretched so that all parts of their bodies touched along her back and legs. He stirred, unconsciously holding her closer. She knew he would be ready to make love again if she wanted it, but she didn't. Not right now. She kept thinking about the serial-ness of the murder. Could she be that far off the mark? Maybe. Maybe it *was* Conny Cranshaw. But maybe Adam was too ready to believe it was him, for personal reasons. And those three other little girls nagged at her still.

'What would the murderer be like if he were a serial killer?' she asked herself.

She'd followed Adam's pragmatic lead in investigating his list. But shouldn't she look at it from the other direction? Not with a particular someone in mind, but with a particular personality? The cases she'd studied indicated that most serial killers were seldom prominent or successful men like Conny. They could be drifters like Lucas or marginally functioning like Dahmer. Or living on the fringe. Not well-integrated. Although this killer, she had a hunch, blended in well enough, but not overly well, and had a disturbed interior life that compelled him to violence. He'd probably be schizophrenic and he'd be discriminating in his selection. Only very young girls. Obviously he was sexually aberrant. And what else? What would he look like? How would she know him? How could you tell a smart schizophrenic by looks alone? He might even be attractive. What if he looked like Ted Bundy?

She fell asleep with the image of an evil grinning Jack Nicholson just beyond the window, and he had Tully's rabbit teeth.

* * *

He awoke in a sweat from a nightmare and rolled to the far side of the bed. He was in the woods with a bundle on his shoulder. In the bundle was a woman with chestnut hair trailing on the ground. She was on his shoulder kicking and squirming and when he scrambled down the edge of the hollow to dump her body, her dog was waiting for him with a knife.

He got up from the bed. The Other voice mewled, "Wh-at?" and he answered, "Nothing."

Then he moved to the window and looked up at the sky. The moon was a scythe, a curved blade of a moon. He closed one eye and put his finger up to trace the outer curve of the moon, winding up at the bottom tip.

"I can balance the moon on my finger. I balance life on my finger. I have found my balance. She will balance me and we will become One. I will hold her heart in my hand. And she will hold mine."

THURSDAY, APRIL 12th

Kipper withdrew a manila folder from his black leather attaché case and passed it to Adam. "As far as any documentation goes, Conny Cranshaw is as clean as Mother Theresa."

"I don't believe that," Adam said, flipping the pages.

"Doesn't count."

The afternoon temperature had climbed to a perfect seventy-five degrees; the air was clean and fresh, the sun shining, a rare New England Spring day. A day to go driving in the country or play softball or plant fields of early peas without fear of a late frost. But instead, Adam, Julia, and Kipper were standing in the corridor outside the old courtroom in Fall River waiting for Tully's hearing to begin.

Adam folded his arms across his chest and stared at the ceiling as Kip continued.

"Whatever else he is, Conny Cranshaw hasn't done a thing that would make me or anybody else suspect he was linked to Jeannine's murder. I know he'd double-cross his grandmother for a torn dollar bill, but that's *it*. He's driven by money and not much else. I think it's a dead end, Adam."

"It's him."

Julia and Kipper exchanged glances. Then she asked the lawyer, "Are you putting Tully on the stand?"

Kip shook his head. "They're going to find probable cause whether or not he testifies, so it'll do less harm when he comes to trial if I keep him quiet now."

Adam nodded agreement. Damage control was the only strategy left.

As Julia sat with Adam in the back of the small courtroom, it felt to her like a colonial church. The room was paneled with pine. The windows were tall and flanked both sides of the room, making it bright and airy. But it was stark and unadorned.

Not only was Jeannine's family present but all of the Jucket families as well as curious onlookers. They reminded Julia of the auction crowd and she somehow expected the Marquis de Lard to enter in his toupee. However, the judge walked in looking properly judicial, a plain-faced gray-haired man in a black robe. Julia was absurdly caught between relief and disappointment.

In the succeeding hour, the district attorney presented what seemed to Julia to be a very damning case. He produced the underwear the police had recovered from Tully's root cellar. He brought out a witness, a truck driver who worked with Tully, to say he saw Tully with Jeannine in his cab on at least one occasion at the truck yard. And he called Ms. Carlson, the social worker in charge of Tully's children, to testify that Tully had a file for molesting two other little girls, one of whom was his first wife's daughter.

With each piece of evidence, Tully's head dropped further and further onto his chest. By the end of Ms. Carlson's testimony, he was holding onto the edge of the table with both hands, looking as if he might jump over the table and bolt for the door.

As Kipper spoke to the judge, the district attorney—a man in his forties whose suit was rumpled in contrast to the Kipper's well-tailored one—rolled from side to side in his seat.

Kipper's only tactic was to attack the suppositions made by the district attorney. He called the police officer who found the panties and asked if he saw Tully put them in the root cellar. He recalled the truck driver and asked if he ever saw Tully drive with Jeannine at any other time or place. He even called back Ms. Carlson to specify the nature of the purported molestations and the distant time of occurrence. But the case for the defendant was short and not very sweet.

Tully stared at the judge while Kip was summing up. "It's all circumstantial and the prosecution has failed to forge any direct link between my client and the deceased."

The courtroom audience booed and hissed and the judge called them to order. It made Julia recall how the crowd jeered when Adam walked out of the auction barn. The hefty bailiff made a show of walking around the room and the audience gradually quieted.

Everyone seemed anxious to bring this hearing to a swift conclusion. Chief Burke was seated at the prosecutor's table, feeling pleased with himself, pushing back the cuticles of his thumbs in anticipation. The judge waited for complete silence before speaking.

"It is the judgment of this court that there is probable cause to believe that one Arlo Tulliver may have committed the murder of Jeannine Frances Bradburn. The defendant shall be bound over for trial."

The courtroom erupted with cheers and the judge directed the bailiff to silence them once again. Tully looked over his shoulder at Adam, pleadingly. Julia had never seen such a frightened face. Then slowly, Tully stood up and, little by little, the crowd became silent. He was sweating profusely. Julia could see his shirt was wet in the center of his back and under his arms almost to the waist.

"Don't I get to say nothing, Your Honor?"

The judge turned to the defense. "Counselor?"

Julia watched unblinkingly as Tully and Kipper conferred. Kipper glanced back at Adam somberly then addressed the judge.

"With the court's permission, Mr. Tulliver would like to make a statement."

The judge shifted his gaze to the district attorney. "Any objection?"

"No, your Honor, if it's germane." The prosecutor looked impassive, but behind him Chief Burke leaned forward to whisper something. The D.A. waved him off like a mosquito.

The judged instructed the bailiff to swear in the defendant as he leaned back in his chair and crossed his arms.

Tully took the chair, swiveling around nervously.

"You may proceed Mr. Tulliver," said the judge.

There was an expectant silence in the room, waiting for a confession.

Tully spoke directly to the judge. "It wasn't me, Your Honor. I didn't say nothing before because I didn't think...I didn't think this was going to happen. But it wasn't me. It was Tommy."

The judge seemed to take a minute to comprehend what was being said. "And who is Tommy?"

"My oldest."

Julia watched Kipper to see what the attorney would do, but he was staring down at the table in front of him as though he wanted no part of it. Adam closed his eyes. The courtroom was subdued, with only murmurs here and there.

Julia shook her head and whispered to Adam, "It can't be." He opened his eyes but did not respond. She leaned back, clamping her lips together.

"Are you testifying," the judge's expression briefly lost its neutrality, "that it was your oldest son, Tommy, who killed Jeannine Bradburn?"

"Yessir." Tully's chest heaved in deep breaths.

"On what evidence?"

"He put the underpants in my root cellar."

The judge seemed to mull this over then finally said, "Police Chief Burke, will you please approach the bench?"

The two men conferred at length, with the judge speaking indistinguishably low but clearly irate. Burke appeared to be trying to explain something—most likely, Julia thought, why he hadn't asked the right questions of Tully, why he had not found out about Tommy, and why he had wasted the court's time on the wrong trial.

But Julia knew that Adam *had* asked Tully how Jeannine's underpants got into the root cellar, and Tully hadn't said it was Tommy. Was Tully protecting Tommy then? Or was he lying now?

Tully sat immobile on the witness stand, not looking at anything but the floor in front of him.

Finally, the judge dismissed Tully and called both counsels to the bench. Tully returned to his seat at the table, still looking at the floor in front of his feet.

In short order, the judge directed Tully to be held until his son was brought in for questioning, and Chief Burke was instructed to take one Thomas Tulliver into police custody for questioning. The judge gaveled the end of the hearing.

Julia filed slowly out of the courtroom with the others as Adam talked with Kipper. There was a hush over the room as though they were ashamed of having convicted Tully in their minds. "Still," they said to each other knowingly, "it was *his* son."

Julia spotted the police chief walking down the steps of the courthouse and ran to catch up with him. "Chief Burke," she called out, "wait, please."

He looked at her without recognition and Julia reminded him that she was the one who had found Jeannine's body. She urgently explained that it couldn't have been Tommy. He didn't fit the profile and this was most likely a serial killing. She could document it.

He listened abstractly, engaged in scraping his cuticle. "I understand what you're saying, Ms. Arnault, but even by your own reckoning this 'series' of disappearances goes back at least five years. That would put Tommy at about what age? Ten or eleven? I don't figure him for being that precocious, do you?"

"That's exactly my point."

"But I'm afraid you haven't persuaded me there's anything of a serial nature about this incident. Television has made conspiracy theories and serial killings into a required theme these days. Doesn't happen that way in real life. As far as I'm concerned, this is one murder with one murderer…and that's Tully's mutant son."

"What if you're wrong?"

Burke bit the cuticle of his left thumb. "I don't see that it makes a whole lot of difference. Tommy's a time bomb. He's better off where he is. And if he didn't kill Jeannine, it's just a matter of time until he gets some other little girl."

"Leaving the real killer still loose," Julia protested.

Burke moved to his right thumb. "If it isn't Tommy, it's Tully. And we won't ever stop watching him. Now I've got to go, if you don't mind." Without waiting for an answer, he walked away leaving Julia standing there frustrated.

"What'd Burke have to say?" Adam said as he joined her.

"Nothing of importance. Where's Kipper," she asked, looking around.

"He went back to his office."

As they walked to the truck, she said, "What will happen to Tully?"

"I expect they'll release him once they get Tommy."

"Do you believe he did it?"

"I don't know."

"But you don't believe it was a serial killing, do you?"

"No."

She took a deep breath. There was no point in continuing the discussion. No point whatsoever.

* * *

A mild evening breeze stirred the curtains in Adam's livingroom. No frills, no prints or pastels, just beige and tan stripes. Adam had come to like them. There were other little touches Julia had added, including a bargain sofa she found in a consignment shop. The upholstery was clean, a medium brown Haitian cotton that dated it to the 1970s. Such things were not enough to indicate a woman's full-time presence in the house, but just enough to imply that one had sojourned there.

"I don't understand how Tully could accuse his own son," Billy said. "His own *son*."

Billy and Julia were drinking iced tea. Adam sat at the table, working on a carburetor.

"Is it better for Tommy to be loose on society?" Adam answered. "Maybe do it again?"

The echo of Chief Burke's words made Julia uncomfortable.

"No, I guess not," Billy agreed, shaking his head. "But it just doesn't set right."

They fell quiet. Finally, Billy spoke. "You know, Conny's breaking ground in back of me for the cement plant, Adam. There's no way he should've passed the conservation commission. That land's wet. It had to cost a bundle in bribes."

Adam concentrated on the carburetor. "Probably not. Town wants the business."

"How do you know?" Billy asked.

"If they didn't, it wouldn't get built."

Adam's logic was irrefutable and another silence followed. Then the sound of a car motor driving up broke the quiet.

"That's Tessa," Billy said. "Gotta go. We've got a gig tonight. Tenth anniversary party."

"Whose?" Julia asked.

"New people in Cedarwood Park. Wilson."

"Roger and Holland?"

"Yeah, you know them?"

"Just in passing," she said.

"I think they're a little off. They want us to play every song we know that has *moon*, *stars*, or anything like that in it. But hey, it's their tab."

Julia and Adam exchanged knowing smiles.

The telephone rang as Julia was clearing away the iced tea. "Want me to get it?"

Adam nodded.

Julia heard the urgency in the voice at the other end asking to speak with Adam. She held out the receiver to him, whispering, "Sgt. Davis."

Adam shrugged ignorance and took the phone. The conversation lasted only a few minutes and did not reveal anything to Julia from Adam's side of it. As he hung up, his hand lingered on the phone.

"The cops picked Tommy up," he explained, "but he managed to get out of the cruiser and run off. The whole force is searching for him."

"Why did Sgt. Davis call *you*?"

"He thinks Tommy might be less frightened if he sees me with the police."

"Do they know where he went?"

"No, but Percy wants to meet me at Tully's. I'd better go, maybe it'll help. This whole thing sucks.

Minutes after Adam left, Julia realized she was still standing in the same spot, holding the empty glasses. Still she stood there, believing that she was right about Tommy despite everything. And yet she had nothing else to go on but her own instincts.

"If I were a licensed psychologist, they'd believe me," she voiced into the air. "But I'm just an academic, so nothing I say about it matters."

Julia sat in Adam's armchair with Cat taking up most of her lap. She stroked the dog's ears thinking about her psych class for Monday. The DeSalvo case-study had not gone as well as she had hoped. The class hadn't rallied to the example, after all. She had taken them through the investigation and the victims and tried to get them to think like the police to determine the killer's profile. But of course they already knew it was DeSalvo. Besides, they had said, the Boston Strangler was old news. Before they were born. Boring.

So she had switched to the Bradburn murder as an example of serial killing, and introduced them to other serial killers—Ted Bundy, executed in 1989 as the (then) worst serial killer in American history; and Henry Lee Lucas who, along with a sometime companion, had killed and raped more women than anyone could actually document. Julia talked about parallels with other serial killings and began to guide them, as a class, to try to solve the Bradburn murder. She showed them the articles on the girls in Pittsley County who had disappeared. She demonstrated her theory. They were keen for it.

Even if Adam didn't believe her, thirty-two sophomores did.

She shooed Cat down from her lap and grabbed a pen and pad from her purse. She began making a list of what she knew about the murder that made it unlikely to be Tommy. There was no precedent for instance, for the existence of an eleven-year old serial killer – which is how old Tommy would have had to be at the time of the first girl's disappearance. And what about the black pick-up? Tommy didn't drive one, that's for certain. So how did he lure Jeannine or any others to some place where he could rape and murder them? And what about the weapon? The murderer had opened Jeannine's torso. With what? And where was that weapon?

She made a grid of names of the girls who'd disappeared, dates, places, and method of death, when known. None of it suggested Tommy.

No, the real killer had to be still out there somewhere. And he'd done the most heinous crime. She wondered what he felt while he was doing it. Sexual gratification? Yes, in the rape. But what about the other things? Also sexual? Powerful feelings. Absolute power.

When Adam returned, Julia was sitting in the same chair, writing in a notebook. She watched him go directly to the bookcase and pour himself two fingers of moonshine.

"Tully told the cops where to look. Tommy was hiding in the root cellar, out back of the house."

Julia was surprised by the uncharacteristic bitterness in his voice. "So the police have him now?"

"No. They flushed him out and he ran away before I got there. He ran into the woods. I heard some shots just as I got to Tully's house, but by then it was dark and the cops were leaving. I expect Tommy's holed up in there somewhere for the night. But they'll catch up with him tomorrow."

He drank that shot and poured another. "The thing is, he doesn't even know why he's being hunted. Or what's happening. He's probably going to wind up dead or mangled. And nobody's going to care, not even his father."

Adam went to the bookcase and refilled his glass. He lifted it in a toast, "To fatherhood."

"Tully can't help himself, Adam," Julia heard herself saying. Even if she wasn't sure she completely believed it, she felt she had to soothe him. "You should know that better than anyone. He's like an abused animal. And you're the only friend he has."

"To my good friend, Tully." Adam downed the drink and threw the glass against the wall, but it was too thick to break and it bounced on the floor. He gave a derisive laugh.

For the next half-hour, Adam sat quietly smoking his pipe. Julia didn't know whether he'd found or bought the tobacco. He didn't speak, so she made a pretense of reading until a car drew up outside. Cat growled but soon settled down. A familiar knock at the door followed.

"Come in," Adam said irritably.

Cutter entered, looking chipper. "Good evening, gentlefolks. I saw the light on and figured you was up. Haven't seen you in a dog's age."

"What've you been up to?" Adam asked without inflection. He got up and retrieved the glass on the floor which he took to the bookcase to pour himself and Cutter drinks.

"Business down Maine," Cutter replied as he planted himself in a chair, taking in the glass on the floor and eyeing Adam as if something were amiss. "Me and Driver been lookin' around for woodlots."

"For two weeks?"

Cutter stroked his beard. "Well, there's business and then there's Business." He chuckled.

"Maybe you ought to get yourself a steady woman and concentrate on woodlots," Adam said, handing Cutter his drink.

"Too much like work."

"Who'd have you anyway?" Adam's teasing was half-hearted. "Maybe if you cleaned yourself up and combed the sawdust out of your hair –"

"Ain't no woman worth that. Present company excepted," Cutter gestured with his glass.

Julia made a polite motion of acknowledgement.

"So," he continued, "what's up while I been away?

Adam shrugged a shoulder and shook his head.

"I heard Tully turned Tommy in. What's that all about?"

Adam didn't answer right away and swallowed his drink. Cutter waited in silence. Finally Adam said, "Tully told the court that Tommy killed Jeannine. The cops had Tommy in custody but he escaped into the woods."

"They lookin' for him now?"

"Night tracking?" Adam snorted. "Are you kidding?"

"Yeah," Cutter nodded, holding up his erect index finger on his lap, "Chief Burke couldn't find his hose in the dark except if it stood up in front of him and waves hello." He wiggled his finger.

Julia didn't know whether to laugh or be embarrassed.

"They'll grab him tomorrow," Adam pronounced grimly.

"They're gonna wind up tatooin' buckshot in his back, if I know these boys."

"If the Bradburns don't get him first,"

In the pause that followed that truth, Julia suggested, "Couldn't *you* find him?"

Adam regarded her thoughtfully then looked at Cutter. "What do you think?"

"Not a half-bad idea."

"It's probably the only way he'll get out of there alive. Want to do it?"

Cutter stroked his beard. "What the hell," he said as he got up. "I'll get my hound and meet you at Tully's house."

"Right now?" Julia asked.

"Man," Cutter declared as he reached the door, "we don't want to be out there after sun-up. Not with those Keystone Kops wavin' shotguns."

After he left, Adam began searching the room. "Have you seen my halogen light?"

"No," Julia answered. "Do you really think you can find him?"

"Cutter can. I've done my share of night tracking, but he's the pro. He's jacked more deer than anybody else in the state."

Adam located the flashlight and checked the batteries.

"Cutter's a poacher?" Julia asked, mystified.

"Used to be. You going to wait here or go home?"

"I'll be here."

He looked at her appreciatively, then turned and left.

After a moment of staring at the closed door, Julia went to the kitchen to see what there was to eat, mentally pondering over strange alliances. Adam and Cutter. Adam and Tully. Adam and her.

After Julia and Cat shared a cheese sandwich—the only thing she could find in Adam's refrigerator that didn't need to be cooked—Julia was about to go upstairs to bed when she heard a sound outside near the front window. At the same time, Cat growled a low warning. Julia stood stiffly, waiting.

The next sound came from beyond the front door. Cat's growls turned into full-fledged barking.

Did Adam lock the door when he left? She tried to remember. He usually didn't. Could she get to it in time?

Julia impulsively lunged for the door, but before she reached it, it burst open and she involuntarily shrieked.

Tommy stood in the doorway. His shoulders were taut like a cougar's, ready to spring.

Cat moved between the intruder and her mistress, growling menacingly. Julia's heart was pounding. She waited for Tommy to do something when she spotted the blood on his green shirt.

"Where's doctor?" Tommy said plaintively to Julia, holding his side where it had been bleeding.

"No," she answered raspily, "there's no doctor here."

Tommy pointed to the animal skulls in the bookcase. "Doctor."

It took just a moment to comprehend. "Oh. No, he's not here now."

"Where's doctor?"

"He'll be back later." She didn't know if he understood her and he didn't react, but she could see he was in pain. He made no move to leave, and she wasn't sure what to do next.

"Come in. Come on," she gestured.

He walked slowly into the room. Cat eyed him, then looked at Julia, then apparently decided her services were no longer required. She found a spot to lie down again but kept watch.

Julia closed the door behind him. "What happened to your side?"

"Hurt." He stood unmoving.

"Can I see where it hurts?" Julia reached out a hand but he shied away. "Let me see your sore, Tommy."

She moved cautiously toward him but he backed up. "Let me see," she repeated.

He hesitated a moment then dropped his hand away and lifted his shirt. His ribs stuck out like a thin goat's. The wound was just below the rib cage but didn't seem to be in any vital organ.

She spoke more to herself than Tommy. "It's stopped bleeding. But I don't know anything about bullet wounds." She wondered how much he understood. "Adam's not here, Tommy, I have to call a doctor. A medical doctor."

Tommy vigorously shook his head 'no.'

"Adam's not here and we have to get you to a doctor."

"No!" he answered loudly, and moved towards the door.

"Alright, alright," Julia said to placate him. "Come back. Be calm. I won't call anybody else. I promise. It's all right. I won't tell anyone."

He stopped and turned to her. "Hurt."

"I know. I'll get you some medicine. Aspirin. I don't know what else to give you. Pills. Sit down, Tommy." She pointed to the sofa. "Sit there."

He walked over to the sofa as though each step were an effort.

"It'll be alright," Julia said soothingly. "I'll help the hurt. I'll be right back. Don't leave. Stay there. Stay." She glanced at the telephone but he was watching her closely.

Some few minutes later, Julia returned carrying a glass of chocolate milk and a first-aid kit. She handed the glass to Tommy and he viewed the contents warily.

"Drink it down. It's chocolate milk. You can't taste the aspirin. It's good. Yum." 'Yum?' she thought to herself. 'I haven't used that word since Karen was a baby.'

But he drank the milk hungrily and she was pleased. "Will you let me bandage your sore?"

"Band-Aid?"

"Yes. Band-Aid."

He said neither 'yes' nor 'no,' so Julia gingerly sat down next to him and gently took his hand away from his side. He watched her every move as she lifted the shirt and looked more carefully at the wound. It looked awful close up, with a bloody center and a fleshy crater around the hollow where the bullet entered. She proceeded to wet some cotton with peroxide and clean around the area. Before applying it to the actual wound, she told him, "This will hurt for a minute but then it will be okay. It's going to be okay."

She applied the peroxide and Tommy howled. She automatically flinched and Cat sprang to her feet and began barking. Julia quieted the dog and then the boy.

"It's over now, it's all over," she reassured him. He took deep breaths as she put antiseptic ointment on the gauze and applied it to his side. She managed to do a patchy job on the adhesive over the gauze.

"There. Okay?"

Slowly the tears began to course down Tommy's dirty face, making crooked seams on his cheeks, until at last he began to sob. Julia was at a loss to comfort him.

Slowly, hesitantly, she put her arm around him and began to rock him as she had her own child when Karen was sick.

"There, there," she said, "we'll wait together.

* * *

Adam and Cutter were still exploring Pittsley Woods as the eastern sky began to brighten. They had been to the hollow where Jeannine was buried and they crisscrossed the woods until Cutter's hound brought them to Tommy's makeshift hut. But it was disappointingly empty.

"I hoped we'd find him here," Adam said, standing at the doorway as Cutter looked around inside. The hut was only six feet square and five feet high. Cutter had to stoop to walk around. The walls were constructed of wood pallets. There was no window and the floor was dirt where the grass had died away but tree roots made the ground uneven.

Cutter flashed his light around the bare ceiling, walls, and floor. Something in the corner caught his eye. He bent over to pick it up and looked at it carefully in the flashlight before extending his palm to Adam.

"What do you make of that?"

Adam looked closely at the object, then back at Cutter.

"I guess that lets Conny Cranshaw off the hook."

GOOD FRIDAY, APRIL 13th

Adam stopped short upon entering the living room. Julia was sitting on the sofa with Tommy cradled in her arms, asleep. Cat was lying on the floor with her head on Julia's feet.

"He came looking for you, Adam," Julia whispered. "He's been shot. I don't know how badly but it's stopped bleeding. He wouldn't let me call a doctor."

Adam approached Tommy quietly, trying not to frighten him into any sudden movements. But as he bent over the boy, Tommy woke up and instinctively recoiled until he recognized Adam.

"It's all right. Let me see, Tommy."

Adam knelt down and peeled away the bandage, examining the wound. "It needs medical attention right away," he said, more to Julia than the boy. Then, to Tommy, he said reassuringly, "You're going to come with me, Tommy, it'll be okay."

Adam reached into his pocket and withdrew the object Cutter had found and showed it to Tommy. It was a plastic tortoise-shell barrette with the initial 'J' on it in flaked gold-painted plastic.

Upon seeing the barrette, Tommy reached for it, but Adam held it away from him.

"Where did you get this, Tommy?"

"Girl hair."

"What girl?"

Tommy looked at him blankly.

"What girl?" Adam repeated, but Tommy shook his head. "Do you know who this belongs to, Tommy?"

Tommy shook his head again. Adam sighed and returned the barrette to his pocket.

"Is it Jeannine's?" Julia asked.

"Yes." Adam never took his eyes off Tommy. "I woke up Otis and Cora to ask them."

"Where did you find it?"

"In Tommy's hut. There's no real question about who put it there."

Julia's thoughts whirled around. 'How could it be true?' She'd spent the night holding this child, humming and rocking him to sleep. He let her touch his wound and take care of him. He trusted her. 'How could I be so wrong about him?' She was supposed to understand psychology; how could she have so misjudged everything? She pressed her fingers hard against her lips.

"I'll take Tommy to the hospital," Adam said. "Call Chief Burke and tell him to meet me there."

Julia nodded bleakly as Adam helped Tommy to his feet.

"I never thought it could be him," she said, looking sadly at the boy.

"Maybe you just didn't want it to be."

"But I should be able to judge something like that. I'm a psychologist."

"But you're not. You're a teacher. So don't beat yourself up about it."

His words chilled her. "You're right. I'm no expert."

"I didn't mean it that way, Julia. It's not a matter of belief; it's a matter of evidence. So you were wrong. It doesn't matter now, does it? We'll talk about it when I get back. I've got to get Tommy to the hospital. Call Burke for me, will you?"

She nodded.

"I'll see you later," Adam said as he led Tommy to the door.

She did not respond, knowing that she had no intention of being there when he returned.

* * *

Their ritual began at sunrise, with the white-robed Others filing into the chamber. The last to enter carried a newborn infant in his arms. Gently, he placed it on the altar. He nodded to Another, who left and returned with a young girl with long dark hair. She looked dazed as the assembly parted for her approach. She was led to the altar.

The Elder stepped alongside her, whispering in her ear. The Others chanted softly. He presented a boning knife to the girl then opened the swaddling clothes. The chanting grew louder and louder and, at the pitch, the Elder whispered, "Now," and the girl plunged the knife into the dog's stomach. The baby's scream and her own were one. She collapsed to the ground.

The Elder opened the dog's chest with the knife, and with his fingers withdrew the still-beating heart. He severed it from the body, laid it on the stone altar, and sliced it into pieces. One for each of them, and one for the mother.

"I am the knife and the altar," he dreamed. "Life and death. No resurrection. The end is the end." What color was the baby's hair? Was it golden like the dog's? The resurrected dog? Am I dreaming?

SUMMER

SUNDAY, JUNE 21st

Julia sat at her kitchen table, staring out the open window at the greenness beyond the backyard lawn. At the edge of the property was a tangle of leaves, wild grapevines, and bullbriars. Beyond that the woods were thick with oak, maple, pine, and arborvitae. But she was not seeing any of it. It was only a point to focus on while she was thinking. A goldfinch darted across the window into the woods, and still Julia did not take notice.

A month and a half had passed since Tommy was consigned to the state hospital for permanent incarceration. He never confessed to the murder. Couldn't. Couldn't be expected to. But it was over, everyone agreed.

The school term had ended three weeks ago. In the beginning, she'd had the students excited over the Bradburn case, but then her theory about a serial killer was swept away with the appearance of the barrette. They insinuated that she didn't know squat about psychology. They had mocked her. "It wasn't a serial killing after all," the students said. "Just a retard Jucket kid." She tried to tell them not to stereotype Juckets but they ignored her. They stopped coming to class. The last three weeks were an embarrassment she never wanted to repeat.

'I'm not a good teacher,' she thought despondently. 'Not even for a Sesame Street class in some second-rate backwater community college.'

She'd always believed she would have done much better by now. Accomplished something. Published a couple of landmark books, a few dozen provocative articles instead of only five pedestrian ones—and all of those had come strictly out of her dissertation. She really hadn't done any original research since then. Her teaching load at B.U. took all her time. And then there was marriage with Phillip. His demands. His expectations. And then Karen. She had tried to be a good mother. She couldn't do everything.

Julia shook her head at her own rationalizations. "No. Nobody to blame but me." And here she was, forty-seven and nowhere. And nowhere to go.

She had always wanted to be a teacher. Never a clinical psychologist. The truth was, she was afraid of psychotics. Partly for what they might do, partly because she didn't think she could help them anyway. Might even do harm. Look at Tommy. No, let the biochemists like Phillip deal with it. Actually, he was a neurobiologist and he had scorned psychology.

She never wanted private practice, either. Didn't care a damn about other people's neuroses. 'Not even my own,' she thought, with a grim smile. Otherwise, she might have to start psychoprobing her real motives—why she never did anything with her life, why Phillip left her, why she ran away from Boston.

Why *had* he left her?

'Because there was no promise left in me?' she wondered. 'We had such dreams when we first got married, and such ambitions. But all the possibilities have been exhausted and I have been found wanting.'

Her contract with the college had not been renewed. Her students did poorly on the final exam and their class evaluations of her were dismal. At least she was salaried through August. But come September, she would have no money and no job. The summer stretched out ahead of her like spilled coffee.

She hadn't seen Adam since the night Tommy came to the house. She excused herself by saying she was caught up with final papers and exams, grades and all. She begged off planting a garden with him. Too busy. Too tired. He tried to coax her to grade her papers at his house but she said she needed solitude.

When Adam had called to invite her over last Saturday, she declined again. She could hear the disappointment in his voice but she didn't care. She didn't want to go out with him. He hadn't trusted her enough. Hadn't believed in her. Didn't take her seriously. Like Phillip.

The last time she drove by his house, she saw that he had planted the field without her. The even rows of vegetables were like notches on a sawblade.

Maybe, she considered, she should visit her daughter, after Karen comes back from her father's wedding. June wedding. First day of summer. Today. But just the thought of making the trip to New York overwhelmed her.

She'd been sleeping later and later in the mornings. Cat had become her only reason to get up before Noon. In desperation, as the morning wore on, Cat would sit politely on the pillow next to her and softly lick Julia's hand to waken her so she could go out.

How had she spent her days this past week? She wasn't sure. She did little tasks around the house, sometimes no more than cooking her meals and washing the dishes. Sometimes not. She read from a stack of books next to her bed, but only the first few pages of each before getting bored. She watched television, talked to the dog, and went to bed too early.

When Adam called again on Thursday, she told him she was coming down with something and would call him back in a few days when she felt better. He asked if there was anything he could do, but she said no, it would all be over in a couple of days. The next time the phone rang, she didn't answer it. She did not want to see him anymore. She did not want him to see her.

She had taken to letting Cat out into the backyard instead of walking her. She left the house only once in the past week, to shop for food. The rest of the time she stayed in her bathrobe. She ate irregularly, what she wanted, when she wanted. Chocolate ice cream in the morning. Cereal at night. With lots of milk and sugar. Frozen foods that she didn't have to put on plates. She ignored time and relied on her own body clock, all the while fearing that it, too, had betrayed her.

There was a time when she had believed that if all else failed her, she could still depend on her own intelligence. She might not be successful at marriage, but she was good at her profession. But she had already been proven wrong on that score. Now she had failed at everything.

* * *

He stood just beyond the tree line looking at the house. He could see her through the kitchen window. She hadn't moved from the chair for the past hour.

'She sees me looking at her. She's waiting for me. She's wearing a bathrobe with nothing underneath because she's waiting for me. I will come for you when the time is right. I will cum, cum, cum.'

* * *

When Adam arrived at Julia's door about seven-thirty, he knocked repeatedly but she didn't answer. Her car was in the driveway so he kept calling her name and telling her to "Open up, Julia, open the door." He was considering calling the police until finally she let him in.

"You look awful," he said, scrutinizing her with grave concern. She wore a navy velour bathrobe, no makeup, and her eyes were puffy. "Have you seen a doctor?"

"No. I'm feeling better now. I'm just not ready to go out or anything yet."

"What's wrong?"

"Just a bug," she replied, sitting down in the armchair.

"Do you need anything? Can I do anything for you?"

"No. I just need a little more rest, that's all."

"Why don't you come to my house? I'll take care of you. Bring you breakfast in bed. *Et cetera,*" he added invitingly.

"No. Thank you. I really need to be alone for a while."

He studied her for a clue in her expression and found none. "Has this got anything to do with me? With us?"

"No. I don't know. I haven't worked it out yet."

"Worked what out?"

"I need some more time, Adam, please."

Julia didn't look at him and he frowned. "That's what you said last week."

"Then I still need more time."

"Will you tell me what's going on, dammit?"

Julia stood up and walked to the door. "I'll call you."

He wanted to shake her, or kiss her, or shout at her that she wasn't being fair. But why should he expect her to be fair? Women weren't. Not in his experience. So he followed her to the door and stifled his response. It was his own fault for letting her get close to him. He should have known better.

* * *

Julia closed the door behind him and slumped against it. If he really cared about her, he wouldn't have accepted her lame explanation. He'd have shaken her, or kissed her, or shouted at her. The fact is, she didn't mean all that much to him.

'I don't care,' she told herself, biting her lip. Playing detective with Adam had been exciting but ultimately unrewarding. She didn't want any part of it anymore. Or of Adam, either. She didn't belong with him. She didn't belong in Pittsley.

MONDAY, JUNE 22nd

When the phone rang that evening, Julia debated answering it, expecting it to be Adam. But she was surprised and pleased to hear Karen's voice. She was less certain however about how she felt hearing Karen's news of the wedding.

"How was California?" Julia asked neutrally.

"Big. Expensive. Beautiful."

Her daughter sounded subdued, Julia thought, and wondered why. "Did you have a good time out there?"

"Yes, it was nice."

Julia realized that Karen was trying to be discreet. No need to tell her old mother what a fab-ulous event it had really been. How much she liked her new stepmother, who actually was more like a friend her own age. Julia's envy twisted into a knot but her voice remained even.

"So you liked southern California?"

"Yes, very much."

"And did Paul go?"

"Yes. He took the wedding pictures." Then there was a pause before Karen added, "We may move out there next year."

"Move to California?" Julia couldn't conceal her dismay.

"We're thinking about it," Karen replied then added hastily, "but it wouldn't be until after we get married."

"I see," Julia said, holding the receiver very close. "I'd really like to see you, honey. Do you want to come and visit with me for a while?"

"I'd like to, Mom, but I've used up all my vacation time. I won't be able to get away from the office again for months."

"Even for a weekend?"

"I'd like to. But that's when Paul has most of his work, and we go together."

"Yes, of course." Julia hadn't realized how much she wanted Karen's company, had counted on it.

"I have an idea," Karen said enthusiastically. "Why don't you come here?"

"Oh, I don't know."

"You can stay with us. You can do city things during the day while I'm at work, and we can be together in the evenings. What do you say? Come on, okay?"

"Well, let me think about it."

"Why, do you have other plans for the summer?"

"I may," Julia fibbed. "Anyway, let me see what I can do. I'll try to spend some time there with you, soon."

"Great."

"So," Julia broached it hesitantly, "how was your father?"

Karen paused, then answered, "He seems happy."

"Why shouldn't he be?" An edge crept into her voice. "Sorry, hon," Julia amended, "but I guess you know ours is not one of those oh-so-civil divorces. Your father and I are never going to be on friendly speaking terms."

"He asked how you were."

"And you said?" Julia hated the idea that he'd asked.

"I said you were fine. Loved your job. Had a new guy. Doing swell."

Julia laughed cynically.

"Isn't that true, Mom?"

"Oh, sure."

"Mother?"

"Yes, it's true. It's all true."

"Mom, you don't sound very good now. Is everything okay?"

Karen seemed so anxious that Julia replied convincingly, "Yes, dear, everything's fine."

"So when do you think you can come to visit?"

"Maybe in a few weeks. Let me work it out."

"Okay, as long as you come."

"You take care of yourself, sweetie, and I'll call you next week."

"All right, Mom. Love you a bunch. Bye."

"Love you too, possum." It was an old affectionate nickname that Karen had outgrown, but it brought back warm memories for Julia. Bittersweet, now.

SATURDAY, JULY 4th

The days that followed—or were they weeks?—had become a blur to Julia. She got out of bed only for trips to the bathroom and forays to the refrigerator. She drew the shades and left them closed. The phone rang occasionally, but she didn't answer it. Sometimes she got up just to sit in a chair, wrapped in a blanket despite the warm temperatures.

Ultimately, it wasn't her own condition that alarmed Julia, but Cat's. The dog had begun mimicking Julia's behavior. Sleeping most of the time. Barely eating. And finally, Cat stopped reminding Julia that she had to go out. After the third encounter with Cat's lapse in manners on the carpet, Julia diagnosed the depression in her dog that she hadn't seen in herself.

She decided not to try to psychoanalyze her reaction until later. Right now, she had to concentrate on behavior. Compartments of her life. She knew that only motion could overcome inertia, so she prescribed her own treatment and forced herself to begin to do the physical activities that came first. Straighten the house, get things in order. Resist the impulse to slow down, to rest, to sleep. She made lists and spent the next two days righting things. Changing sheets, scrubbing floors, washing, vacuuming, dusting. With activity, she began to feel better.

SUNDAY, JULY 5th

In the early afternoon, Billy's wife, Tessa, dropped by Julia's house unexpectedly. Tessa, Julia thought sympathetically, was just about as plain as a woman could be without being homely. She had limp mud-colored hair and large Rushmore features. Yet her warmth and humor and good nature made her seem very lovely. In truth, Julia admired her.

"I haven't heard from you in a couple of weeks, so I thought I'd stop by and bore you with Billy Jr. stories," Tessa said as she settled in the kitchen chair while Julia made coffee.

"Adam sent you, I suppose."

"Did I say that?" Tessa feigned innocence.

"Well, did he?"

Tessa inclined her head. "You can't blame the guy for wanting to know how you are. He figured you didn't want to talk to him for some reason."

Julia poured the water into the automatic coffee-maker. "He's right. I don't.

"Why not?"

"It's hard to explain."

But then, over coffee, Julia found herself explaining everything, ending with, "Nothing in my life is working right now and I'm trying to figure out how to get back on track." Julia looked at the empty cup realizing she hadn't even tasted the coffee. "I screwed up my job and I have no prospects. The one thing I thought I was good at, I'm not. And the guy I thought I could count on, I couldn't. He never even believed in my serial-killer theory."

"But Julia, honey, turns out he was right, no?"

"That just makes it worse."

Tessa ran her fingertips over the edge of the coffeecup. "Isn't that sort of, well, damned if he does and damned if he doesn't?"

"It doesn't matter, really." Julia rolled the empty cup between her palms. "My relationship with Adam is pretty much over."

"But why?" Tessa asked, reaching for another chocolate-chip cookie. "He really cares for you, you know."

"It's not him, so much as it is me. This whole experiment has been a big disaster."

"Experiment?"

"Trying to make a new life for myself here. It's just not happening."

Tessa finished her cookie and sipped her coffee. "Hey, nothing comes easy."

As Tessa reached for another cookie, Julia noticed the worn collar on her plaid blouse, and she caught an inadvertent glimpse of Tessa's bra strap. It was white cotton, washed so often that the paint had come off the metal buckle. Julia suddenly felt a little ashamed. Tessa's life wasn't exactly a bed of roses.

"How's it going with your music these days?" Julia asked.

"Well, school's over so we're just doing tutoring and gigs wherever we can get them. And we're working on a score for an operetta a friend of ours has written."

"That's wonderful," Julia responded genuinely, "how exciting for you both."

But Tessa was more measured. "Not so exciting. I mean, we love doing it, and of course we hope it will get produced somewhere, but really the odds are against it. We've gone through all that before."

"You mean you've written other musical scores?"

"Scores of scores," Tessa answered with a self-deprecating smile. "And a few times we almost got there. A producer or director liked it, but there wasn't any money for a production, or something else came along they liked better, or the producer decided to become a monk, or some such thing. We don't even get our hopes up anymore. We just do what we love doing and wish for the best. Mind if I get some more coffee?"

When Tessa brought her cup back to the table and sat down facing Julia, she said, "Okay if I ask you a personal question?"

"Shoot."

"Me, I love making music. I like to teach it okay, it pays the bills, but I really think of myself as a musician." She looked at Julia for confirmation and Julia nodded. "What about you? Do you think of yourself as a psychologist or a teacher?"

Julia signed deeply. "At the moment, neither." Then she added, "I'm not even sure I believe in psychology anymore." Her gaze fixed on the corner of the ceiling. There was a spider's web she hadn't noticed before, although it might have been there for a very long time. So intricate, Julia thought, and delicate. But there was nothing there. No spider, no fly, nothing. Just a web. An empty web.

Psychology wasn't a science. No therapy was actually quantified in long-term follow-up studies. No one could prove that therapy cured mental problems the way penicillin cured infections. So if it wasn't a science, it had to be an art. A healing art. But if that were so, the practice of the art varied with the artist. Was it any more than shaman healing? Was it as much as that? Or was it just a philosophy, a behavioral philosophy. A construct.

"There as to be something more," Julia finally said.

"Like what?"

With all the new psychotropic drugs, and the new brain-mind physiological approach to 'mental illness'—it wasn't even called that anymore, and patients were being called 'consumers'—with all that, she wondered, what place was there for psychology? The fact is, it wouldn't be long before psychology fell into the same category as astrology. At best, it was enhanced conversation.

"I really don't know," Julia said flatly. "I don't know anything anymore."

Tessa leaned back appraisingly. "You *are* in a pickle, aren't you?"

As Julia nodded in agreement, she admonished herself. She didn't have to *stay* in a pickle. She didn't even have to stay in Pittsley anymore. Or condemn herself to Pittsley Community College. She could go back to Boston now. Now that Phillip was in California, she could leave this netherworld and go back to B.U. and teach again. Get her old life back. Isn't that what she wanted?

Or was it? Maybe what she needed was a new life, a new job, and a new home far away from here. It was something she would have to think about. The house was rented through August and she had her salary through August, so she was safe. Through August.

"I *am* going to get it together," Julia claimed with bravado. "It's just going to take a little time to come up with a new profession."

"What'd you have in mind? The world's oldest?" Tessa shimmied her shoulders.

Julia laughed and swung her leg onto the tabletop and pulled up the cuff of her sweatpants to knee high. "Are you kidding? That, my dear, is a forty-five year old leg. Or thereabouts."

Then Tessa did the same. "This is a thirty-five year old leg. Or thereabouts. Can you tell the difference, ladies and gentlemen? Only her electrolygist knows for sure."

They both giggled and agreed they each had rather good legs after all.

"Honestly, Tessa, you should wear Tina Turner skirts when you and Billy go onstage. You'd have a dozen hits in no time. Your own band—"

"Our own bus."

"A gold album."

"Two."

"You'll headline in Vegas."

"Uh uh, Nashville."

"Consider it booked."

At five o'clock, Julia said, "Want to order in pizza?"

"Can't. Gotta go home and feed the boys. And you should have something more nutritious than pizza and cookies." Tessa pointed accusingly at the ring of cookies Julia had laid out around her saucer.

Julia studied the circle of cookies she had unconsciously put there. "That reminds me of something."

"What, to buy more cookies?"

"That, too. No, really. It reminds me of the stones around Jeannine's burial site."

"How grim."

"More than grim. Deliberate."

"What do you make of it?"

"I'm not sure," Julia admitted. "Just that it's ritualistic."

"Is that something Tommy might do?"

"I don't know."

"Have you been to see Tommy?"

"Who, me?"

"I just wondered if you'd gone to see him, the way he took to you and all."

"He's a murderer, Tessa."

"I thought you didn't believe that."

"I was wrong."

"Who says?"

Julia looked intently at her friend and drew a deep breath.

MONDAY, JULY 6th

The first thing she did in the morning was to call the nearest garage to jump-start her car. The repairman told her the starter motor was weak and would quit on her one of these days. Did she want him to replace it? She told him no, when it broke she'd get it fixed. The New England mantra.

Meanwhile, she had a list of other things to do. The first item was written with an exclamation point. *Plant a garden!* Her own flower garden. No vegetables, not even one.

She drove to the Agway store to buy a selection of seed, bulbs, and plants. She was intent on flowers in the front yard. Lots of them. It was a frivolous desire. Diversionary, even. But that was how she was going to think about things while she seeded and weeded and watched the plants grow over the next weeks. Adam could have his vegetables; she wouldn't plant anything that reminded her of him.

Driving home with twenty-five pots of six-inch-high blue delphinium, multicolored hollyhocks, pink lupine, and white foxglove, Julia's mind was not at all on gardening. She was thinking of Tommy.

The faded visitor's lounge of the third ward of the state hospital was alight with the afternoon sun as Julia sat across from Tommy. The ward doors were locked and a large Hawaiian attendant sat in the corner, watching. There was only one other visitor, a distraught-looking mother of a teenage daughter who obviously had tried to commit suicide by slitting her wrists. They were still bandaged. There were recent scratches on her face which, Julia guessed, were self-inflicted. The girl sat with her hands in her lap while her mother stretched her own arms across the Formica table as though reaching through spatial dimensions. The mother tried to talk with her daughter, but the girl would not speak.

Julia had worked in a psychiatric hospital for one summer when she was a grad student, and hated it. She was on a research project that required her to test the inpatient's motor skills on admission and discharge. It was a silly project, she had thought. But it also scared her because she had to take each patient downstairs to a lab for the tests. Walking the long corridor down the isolated stairway into the small labroom, all alone with a severely disturbed patient, always made her shaky. She never came to any harm but one patient did take off on her and she had had to report it. They found him on the grounds within half an hour. No one thought much of it; he was an habitual runaway. But it unnerved her.

And here she was, sitting within inches of a boy who had raped and mutilated a young girl. Of course, the attendant was there, too. It was all reasonably safe. She had been there an hour already and nothing disastrous had happened. In fact, the opposite.

She brought Tommy a game of Chinese checkers, which he easily learned to play. At this moment, he was setting his orange and white marbles carefully into holes in the tin board. Her marbles were grey and white. He called them eyes and pointed to her own grey eyes. He seemed to be happy, and it filled her with...well, gratitude, actually. Gratitude that she'd been able to connect with him.

When she first arrived, she didn't think Tommy remembered her very well. Not that he was hostile. He just didn't respond to her. She wondered what she was even doing here. She was timid with him. After all, he could be dangerous. But she could not convince herself of it and something made her persist. The sadness of the boy. His loneliness. It all made her want to help him.

She had called his doctor first, for permission to visit. Doctor "Sam" was a part-time staff psychiatrist with a caseload far too large for one person. He told her Tommy was on Thorazine. Julia was pretty sure that Tommy didn't need megadoses of meds to calm him down, but said nothing.

As she watched Tommy finger the marbles, he seemed almost like a normal young man, except for a tendency to flinch at sudden moves. He did not resemble Tully very much at all. Nor Doris, for that matter. He had a keen look, a look that quested to understand more than he did. She remembered how he had examined the skulls on Adam's shelves the first time she met him. There was an intelligence there, somewhere buried.

He had gained a little weight since that night he'd come to the house so desperately. And he was probably cleaner than he'd ever been before. All in all, she had to admit he was better off here than anywhere else right now.

"Leave me alone!" The angry words cut through Julia's thoughts, and caused Tommy to cringe in fright.

The girl at the other table jumped up and ran to the locked ward door and began kicking it. The Sumo attendant was on his feet and at the door in a flash. He talked to the patient in a soft voice, but the girl began hitting and kicking him. He finally pinned her arms, unlocked the door, and called another attendant to take her away. He then closed the door, locked it, and went over to the mother. He said something that caused her to nod while she dabbed at her eyes with a lace-bordered handkerchief. Then the plump woman in her faded housedress got up and left. The attendant went back to his corner without a glance at Julia.

Tommy watched all this, trembling. Although he said nothing, Julia could see the panic in his eyes. 'How could he be capable of killing Jeannine when he seemed so fearful? But no,' she old herself, 'that was inconclusive. He could have an equal and opposite reaction.' So, in the end, she wasn't sure.

She doubted that Tully actually ever struck Tommy; the boy seemed more conditioned to yelling. Julia had not seen Tully since the day of the hearing. She recalled her own words to Adam, that Tully couldn't help the way he was. But, watching Tommy's happy absorption in the game, she couldn't help being angry with his father.

* * *

He called up the image of her slender arm reaching out to touch a flower. Delicate fingers caressing the petals. Almost childlike, bending to smell the fragrance. She belonged with flowers. She was a flower. He would unfurl her petals one by one and, like a bee, sink into her very middle.

He followed her to the institution, but she never saw him. He could have waited there for her to come out, but it was enough to know where she was. Perhaps he would go to her house tonight and look in her window.

The Others were stirring. They wanted to meet again, but he did not. It wasn't the right time. "Not now," he argued. "Wrong time." But The Others complained, wheedled, harangued.

He put his hands over his ears. "I don't hear you. Be quiet." The Others were too impatient. Becoming reckless. He began to worry that he might lose control of them. That would be dangerous. The Others were all blood and impulse, not cunning and deliberate like him. He could not let them have control.

WEDNESDAY, JULY 7th

Tully had driven his bulldozer back into the yard from the edge of the woods where he'd been clearing trees. Anyone else would have shut themselves up in an air-conditioned room on this sweltering day, or at least found a shady tree and fallen asleep in the hammock. But Tully paid no attention to heat or cold, except as they interfered with his machinery.

As was his custom, Tully stood up in the dozer as it neared the place he was going to clear the brush. But this time, he suddenly lost his balance. Before he could right himself, he tumbled onto the treads. His shirt caught on the gear shaft, holding him in place while the tractor treads kept crunching forward, scoring his back. He screamed in pain, but Doris was inside with the television on and did not hear.

He groaned as he tried to reach the gears to stop the machine. By the time he managed to stop the dozer, his back had been badly shredded.

With no one around to help, he half walked, half crawled his way back to the house.

"Doris!" he yelled as he shuffled past his wife towards the bedroom, "Bring the bag balm."

He fell onto the bed on his stomach, closed his eyes and took deep breaths, waiting for relief. It did not occur to him or, naturally, to Doris to call a doctor.

* * *

He had never hidden anything from the Others before. They always knew what he wanted. But not this time. She was his secret. If she came to him, he would banish the Others. Could he do it? Yes, yes he could. Couldn't he?

He was torn between his choices. Not that he loved the Others, but that he was so alone without. He needed them so that he was not tyrannized by his own thoughts. He could not hold the knife in his own hands and drive it into the flesh and bone, but he dreamed of holding it, and of driving it into a breast, cleaving it asunder like firewood.

The only time he did not want to kill was when he fucked. And he fucked like he wanted to kill. But she was a woman and she could take him and soothe him afterwards and take him again when the urge was upon him, and he wouldn't have to kill, only fuck. And then he would not need the Others ever again.

SATURDAY, JULY 10th

"You're damn lucky you didn't kill yourself." Adam shook his head as he checked for signs of infection in Tully's badly scraped back.

"I know." As he lay on his side amidst the rumpled bedsheets, Tully's embarrassment at his folly was greater than his pain.

The bedroom was as disheveled as the rest of the house. An old air-conditioner, layered with grime, clattered noisily in the window against the noonday heat. In the corner was a high-back chair, with a half-sewn pinafore on the seat. Dirty laundry was piled on the floor in a pyramid. Clean laundry was folded in four two-foot piles on top of the bureau. Doris sat on the edge of the bed watching the two men.

"What's new with you, Adam?" Tully asked to avoid any more scolding. "You ain't been by in a long while."

"Yeah, well I've been busy."

"I guess Julia keeps you plenty occupied, huh?" Tully snickered.

"She been to see Tommy at the hospital," Doris informed him.

"How do know that?" Adam asked with surprise.

"The Welfare called me," Tully answered, "to find out if she was a relative, 'cause she been seeing him. Doris has another one in the cooker, you know. Due in December."

"What?" Adam did not quite believe what he'd heard.

Doris smiled bashfully.

"Yep, the old boy's still got it." Tully tried to change his position and moaned.

"The old boy ought to keep it in a sling. Don't you know you're going to have those social workers on your neck again if you have another kid?"

"It's *my* kid."

"That's not the point."

"Besides," Tully argued, "I got another job driving truck next week, so we got a regular income again."

"You had a regular income when they took your kids away the first time. What makes you think it's going to be any different now?" Adam looked back and forth between Tully and Doris, both of them appearing quite unaffected.

"'Cause there's only one this time. Last time there were too many for Doris to handle." Tully smiled his rabbit smile and pumped his testicles. "These old bulbs still got spizzerinktum in 'em."

Doris giggled again, her eyes crinkling in premature wrinkles at the corners. Adam just shook his head in disbelief.

He had come to help Tully as soon as he'd heard about the accident. And whereas Tully might not say so outright, Adam knew the visit was appreciated. In fact, Tully would never say anything that indicated indebtedness to anyone. But, one way or another, he would repay the obligation, whether it was tuning up a lawnmower or giving away some of his garden vegetables. There was a code to it. One that Adam had adopted for himself.

As for what Tully had done to Tommy, Adam was resigned to that aspect of the man's character. Nothing would change it. Tully was as crazy as an outhouse rat. And while there were parts of Tully that Adam didn't like, he would ignore them. So their friendship continued, but it was not quite the same.

Beyond Adam's work, the rest of his life had not seemed quite the same either, not since Julia dumped him. There was no reason to call it anything but what it was. He wasn't sure exactly why she had dumped him, but dump him she did. Tessa finally told him it was because he didn't buy into Julia's serial-killer theory. But how could he support a theory that had been proven wrong? It wasn't rational. Hadn't he given up his own theory about Conny Cranshaw in light of the evidence?

No, there had to be more to it. She probably just came to the end with him. It'd happened before. She took a good look and realized she was never going to embrace his lifestyle or live happily ever after with him in Pittsley. That was for Romantics. Reality was different. He would never admit how much he missed her, and chastised himself for his weakness.

He'd taken to walking Pittsley Woods at the end of each day. He wasn't searching for anything, just needed to reconnect with the outdoors again. It restored him, made him feel independent, self-determining. This was what his life was about. Time to think and observe. Time alone.

Sometimes, he meandered up to the perimeter of Roger Wilson's backyard. The Airstream camper had been gone for the past few weeks. Adam supposed they were off on another alien chase and wondered where. He pictured them backpacking into remote areas with a laptop computer and freeze-dried yogurt and tofu. He presumed they saw themselves as cosmic detectives, but he couldn't bring himself to judge them too harshly. After all, hadn't he had his own infatuation with being Sherlock Holmes?

Frequently, he traveled the woods diagonally from one place to another, past Tommy's hut. And just as often, he passed by the hollow where Jeannine's body had lain all those months. These were places he wanted to avoid, yet invariably he would wind up standing at the edge of the hollow staring down. Then he would skirt the edge of Cutter's property along to the Bradburn's, by the back end of Tully's and Babe's land, around Billy's perimeter and to Floyd Mather's—where he reminded himself to search in his new reptile book for the little salamander he'd seen. Mostly, he kept tabs on the progress of the cement plant. Once in a while, he'd see a leg-hold trap sprung with a stick and he'd know that Goody had been there first.

Elmer Goodson was not above playing tricks on people, Adam recalled with a grin, and not just springing Babe's traps or scooping a jug of Judd Vaughan's moonshine. A few years back, the military orienteers—before they got discouraged and moved elsewhere—used the woods to test their skills. The day before the exercise, the officers would come in and set up flags and checkpoints that the enlistees would have to locate by compass. The orienteers would have to punch a design on a special card to prove they had found each flag. The punch-pins all had different patterns, according to the checkpoint. It was a full day's event to get from the first to the last checkpoint. None of them ever made it.

The games started off well enough, but by the third flag, the rookies were cursing the officers when they had to slog their way into the swamp to punch their cards. Then they found flags high up in the trees and out on branches that they couldn't reach, but when they climbed up there, the pins were missing. Cursing turned to rage when they had to walk through poison ivy only to find the punch for the flag had the wrong patterns, out of sequence. Battered, furious, and helpless, the orienteers gave up at sundown and rag-tagged out of the woods in defeat. An amused Goody had watched their labors always within yards of the group.

Sometimes, Adam got the feeling the old man of the woods was watching *him* from some hidden vantagepoint. Sometimes he felt *he* was becoming an old man of the woods. That was all right, too.

The only time it bothered him that he was alone was in considering that he hadn't had any children to bring here. He would like to have taught his own son or daughter the things he knew. But sometimes kids don't take any interest in what a parent wants to teach. Adam and his own father were proof of that. Odds were that he wouldn't have the kind of kid he wanted anyway, so 'no regrets,' he told himself. Nor did he need a wife. The more time he spent alone, the more normal it seemed again. And yet, when he'd been with Julia, it had seemed better. In frustration, he headed towards Cutter's sawmill.

By the time they finished the bottle of Southern Comfort, both Cutter and Adam were having a great time shooting at flies in Cutter's cabin with his .38 special.

"Seen Julia lately?" Cutter asked as he took a bead on the door.

Bang!

He passed the pistol to Adam.

"It's done with."

Bang!

Adam passed it back.

"You know what I think, Ski?"

Bang!

"No, what?"

Cutter passed him the pistol again and Adam took another shot.

Bang!

The cabin door was beginning to splinter. Adam passed the pistol back.

"I think I'm going to abstain from women forevermore." Cutter aimed at the ceiling.

Bang!

Passed the pistol back to Adam.

"Why?"

Bang!

"Could you have this much fun with a woman? Hell, no, she'd be too damn worried about her windows or something."

Then they both laughed because they'd already shot out both of the windows.

* * *

It was just before midnight and he couldn't sleep. He kept thinking of the...Julia. He was beginning to get restless. The stirrings moved in him. He pressed his knees together and the feeling between his legs intensified. The pulsing began. It was in his arms and chest. In his throat and in his eyes. A chill came over him. Oh, God, he needed it. A strong unquenchable need.

It was a long time since he'd been satisfied. Such a long time. And now the need was upon him. He wanted to scream. Dig his fingers into soft small arms and press his mouth on a soft small mouth and bite. Hard, hard, hard. Slam himself against her. Jam himself into her. Again and again and again until it was quelled, this feeling. But it was risky, much too risky.

MONDAY, JULY 11th

Julia awoke at six o'clock with a sense of purpose she hadn't felt in a long time. She knew it was because of Tommy. It had been going so well. His own doctor, Dr. Shing Wu— whom everyone called Dr. Sam—was pleased with her progress. Dr. Sam always surprised people because on first appearance they assumed he was from Beijing on a green card. He had the youthful face of a fifteen-year-old, with slightly rounded cheeks and rimless glasses. But he was born in Boston, graduated Harvard Med, and as soon as his patients heard his flat New England accent they generally relaxed. His primary appointment was at the prestigious McLean Hospital and he was maneuvering to get Julia on staff at the state hospital as an adjunct psychologist in order to take some of his overload. He'd already spoken to her about assisting with the angry young woman Julia had seen in the visitor's area. He even talked her into signing up for the few extra courses she needed to get licensed.

'Can't believe I'm becoming a staff shrink,' Julia thought. But, to her amazement, she was liking it. It had almost made her a believer again, and she had decided to stay in Pittsley for a while longer. She'd continue renting her house until she saw where all of this was leading.

Since she wasn't scheduled to be at the hospital until afternoon, Julia spent mornings gardening. The garden was looking very fine. In fact, there wasn't too much more to be done with it now. She had created something reminiscent of an English Victorian garden, a little tangled but profuse in variety and color.

As she stopped to pull at stalks of grass invading the budding hibiscus bush, she thought of Adam weeding his vegetable garden. She hated admitting that she missed him.

Mostly, when she thought about him, it wasn't the lovemaking she dwelt on, so much as it was his way of teasing, and the way he put her in unfamiliar situations to see how would adapt, how he guided her through *terra incognita*. But she was still angry with him for not believing her, even though she was wrong. She had felt the same when Phillip abandoned her. She tried to tell herself not to confuse them, that what happened with Phillip was totally different. But, in the end, Adam wasn't steadfast either, so it was the same thing after all.

Later that afternoon, Julia sat next to Tommy at the hefty oak chair and table in the visitor's room. She looked around as if she were seeing everything for the first time. The walls of the stark room had chipped pale-green paint and the floor had worn grey linoleum tiles. It was clean but used, just what she had come to expect from a state facility. It was reassuring in a way. No neurotics here. Of course there were plenty of psychotics, but she could get used to it. She had gotten used to Tommy, hadn't she? She looked down at his head bathed in a shaft of light through the barred windows as he pointed to the large letter 'B' on the page of the kindergarten book Julia had given him.

He sounded it out, "B," then "boy." He looked at her, moving his head out of the sunlight to see her better. His pale-eyed gaze held a question, and Julia nodded in response. He turned back to the book, dipping his head back into the bright light, and repeated the lesson.

While Julia knew she had gained his trust, she had no real idea of how much Tommy could learn. The tests she'd administered were confounded by his inability to tolerate even the slightest frustration. If he felt thwarted, he would simply throw down the test materials, or fold his arms and begin rocking. Julia was not even sure what she hoped for. But she found it harder and harder to believe that Tommy had had anything to do with the murder of Jeannine Bradburn, or anyone else.

Her thoughts were interrupted by Tommy saying, "C, cat." He turned to her quizzically. "I *see*?"

Julia shook her head. “This is a different ‘C.’ This is ‘C’ as in…car. It’s a ‘kuh’ sound.”

Tommy said nothing for a moment, then dove back into the sunlight to turn the pages of the book to ‘K.’

“Kuh,” he said and looked at Julia.

‘He’s made that connection already,’ Julia realized with astonishment. How was she going to explain the difference between ‘C’ and ‘K’ to him? She’d better find a grade-school primer to help her, fast.

Driving home, she couldn’t stop thinking about Tommy. How unlikely a killer he was. ‘Why can’t I let this go?’ she asked herself. Because she believed she had a sense of the murderer. In fact, she found herself returning to her idea of a serial killer. If it wasn’t Tommy, it *had* to be someone who killed repetitively. It might not be any of the four men on Adam’s list, either. There had to be other potential suspects. But first, she would have to prove that Tommy didn’t do it.

That night, she went to a box on the shelf where she kept all of her notes on the Bradburn case, and the copies of newspaper articles she’d found. She brought the box over to the coffeetable and spread out the newspaper articles into four piles in order of disappearance:

Judy Eastgate,
Sally Menzes,
Roberta Kingman,
Jeannine Bradburn.

What she needed to do was find out more about the missing girls. She read the dates aloud, then reflected, ‘It’s not consistent with one a year. But it’s possible there could be others no one knows about.’ She suddenly felt lightheaded.

*FRIDAY, JULY 15^h^*

Julia waited unto mid-morning to visit Judy Eastgate's home on the other side of Dighton at the edge of Pittsley County. It was, as far as she could tell, another Jucket village. The Eastgates were a very extended family occupying four different houses (at least) that looked as though they were one-room bungalows with one room added on.

Entering the house through a pantry stacked with old newspapers and magazines, Julia had found a clutter of paper in the livingroom. There was hardly any place to sit down without moving *The Inquirer* or some other pile of tabloids and gossip magazines. The one on top of the stack on the end table next to Julia showed Hillary Clinton with an alien baby. 'I'll bet,' Julia said to herself with amusement, 'our Roger Wilson has the original photo.'

The person Julia had come to see was Judy's grandmother, a portly woman in a sleeveless housedress and a stocking cap over what may have been a bald head. She had blue thyroid eyes and furrows in her forehead and chin.

Grandma told Julia that her daughter, Judy's mother, had not been married when she "caught" Judy, and she wasn't around since Judy was born. No, she didn't know where she was. Judy was thirteen when she disappeared, and the grandmother thought she might have gone looking for her mother. Grandma was obscure about the details, but seemed quite unconcerned about either of them, her daughter or her granddaughter.

"Did Judy take anything with her? Clothes? Any of her things?"

Grandma shook her head. "Just the clothes on her back."

Try as she might, Julia could not get any more information out of the old woman. In desperation, she asked if there were anyone else she could speak with. But the old lady shook her head.

"Only the men are left. They don't know nothing. They never do, do they?"

Julia nodded agreement but thought Grandma was not much help either.

"What about Judy's friends? Did she have a close girlfriend?"

The old woman nodded. "Donna, she's the closest. Two doors down."

Judy thanked her and crossed her fingers that Donna was closer to Judy than just two doors down.

"Damn ducks." Donna's father said as he came tromping through the squalid livingroom where Judy sat talking with Donna. By now, Julia was familiar enough with the Jucket lifestyle not to be disconcerted at what she found inside their homes, but even she was astonished to see five soiled white ducks padding past her into the kitchen.

"Track the damn cattails all over the house," Donna's father complained as he followed their single-file.

Donna, with large unblinking eyes, swore that Judy never ran away. Now almost sixteen, the teen was experimenting with makeup and had put black eyeliner on top and bottom lids, making her look, Julia thought, like a kewpie doll.

Julia tried to remember if she had ever looked like that at Donna's age, but thought not. Her mother would have hit the roof. Sometimes she felt she had missed out on growing up like other teenagers because she had had to work after school and weekends in the family's convenience store. There were times when she had wanted to run away and never go back, so why not Judy?

"Why don't you think Judy ran away?"

"She didn't," Donna replied earnestly. "She was scared of her own shadow. She would never be able to go off on her own."

"Judy's grandmother thinks she may have left to find her mother."

Donna made a face. "Judy's grandma always smacked her, but she still would've been too scared to run away. Besides, she thought what her mother did was wrong. Believe me, I'd know if she ran away, we were blood sisters. And no matter where she was, she'd let me know. No way she ran away."

"Not even with a boyfriend."

"She didn't have a boyfriend."

"Are you sure? Girls keep secrets sometimes, even from their best friends. Could she have been pregnant?"

"Judy was a virgin."

"How do you know?"

"We told each other *everything*."

"You wouldn't happen to have a photo of Judy, would you?" Julia asked hopefully.

"I got one somewhere."

In short order, Donna produced a plastic brown wallet out of her green vinyl purse and presented Julia with Judy's picture. It showed a pretty little girl with straight blonde hair down to her shoulders. It was a class picture and Judy looked slightly past the camera as directed. It was a stock pose, Julia recognized, but somehow it seemed as if the girl were looking towards a future that wasn't there.

"What do *you* think happened to her?" Julia asked.

Donna looked sad. "For a while, I thought her grandma beat her to death. But," she shrugged, "I guess I don't think that now. I was home, sick, the day she disappeared. We were having a math final and I had to make it up. Judy was always good in math. Then I thought maybe she was hit by a car or something, and they took her to the hospital but then she died, or she had amnesia and nobody knew her name. But I don't think so now. I think she's dead. Killed. Because I'd know if she was alive; she'd write me. That was over three years ago, you know."

"Yes," Julia said, "I know."

The young woman tossed her long, straight brown hair. "Nobody talks about her anymore." Then she added, "But I miss her."

Sally Menzes' home was at the end of a dead-end road in Pittsley, next to the town dump. Mr. Menzes had converted his land into a junkyard where he scrapped metal and glass. Julia found him at the end of the driveway burning the rubber sheath off copper wire. There were piles of metal all around, and barrels of broken glass. The smoke from the burning rubber was acrid, and the fire burned blue and green. Hunched alongside the barrel, feeding in the wire, he seemed to Julia like some imp fueling the hell fires. That was probably unfair, she told herself, but the image lingered.

Rather than interview him, Julia asked for Mrs. Menzes. He pointed to the second floor of the two-story house that had add-ons, making it look like a child's first game of blocks.

She found Mrs. Menzes on her knees washing the old brick-pattern linoleum kitchen floor from a bucket of strong-smelling pine liquid. When the woman stood up, she was majestically tall. Taller by far than Mr. Menzes. Both looked in their middle fifties, and her hair was almost completely grey.

"Did you talk to Manny?"

"Mr. Menzes? No, he seemed very busy."

Mrs. Menzes motioned Julia to sit at the kitchen table. It, too, was so old that the white marbleized Formica had rubbed off in spots. But everything in the small kitchen was spotless, even the old gas stove with chipped enamel.

"Night and day he's busy. You know why? They didn't renew our license to operate a junkyard. You know why? They don't want a junkyard in town anymore, not even back here. We've been here for almost thirty-five years, and now nobody wants a junkyard. That's the way it is. You know why? It's that new development. They're the ones. So he's trying to dispose of his inventory before they get the EPA on us."

Julia expressed sympathy but Mrs. Menzes went on to ask, "What is it you want to talk about?"

"I wanted to ask you a few questions about Sally, if you wouldn't mind."

Mrs. Menzes' eyes went immediately moist. "Why?" she asked softly.

Julia drew a breath. There was no point hedging with Mrs. Menzes. She would be insulted if Julia didn't tell her everything.

"In light of what happened to Jeannine Bradburn, I'm just trying to talk with parents of any other little girls that have disappeared through the years."

Mrs. Menzes frowned. "What others?"

Julia flattened her hands on the table top. "Well, over the course of a few years, there've been some others."

"How come we never heard about it?" Mrs. Menzes' voice was accusatory.

"I don't know. Each case was different, and in different towns."

"And you think they're linked?"

"I just don't know."

Mrs. Menzes folded her hands in her lap. "What do you want to know?"

But, in the end, all Julia had learned was that Sally was their only child, a late unexpected gift. They had prized her so much they probably spoiled her with attention, Mrs. Menzes explained without apology. "I'm glad, at least while she was with us, she knew she was loved."

Sally disappeared on her way home from school five years ago February. Mrs. Menzes always believed she was kidnapped. But nothing more was ever found, and thirteen-year old Sally never came home. The Menzes had never stopped grieving.

Julia suddenly had a different image of Mr. Menzes. No imp gleefully stoking the hell fires, but rather a man condemned to trying to keep from thinking about his daughter by working himself to exhaustion.

"Didn't the police investigate?"

"Only a little. Just a little. There wasn't anything to go on. Like she fell into a black hole or something. But don't you think," Mrs. Menzes looked straight at Julia, "someone should have kept on it?"

Julia solemnly nodded her head. "Do you have a picture of her I could borrow?"

"Of course." Mrs. Menzes immediately went to the family album, flipping through several pages of photos before picking one out.

"This is the most recent. The Autumn before she disappeared."

The picture of Sally Menzes showed a thin, dark-eyed brunette with bangs and braids, laughing in mid-swing in a large tire hanging from an oak tree with red-gold leaves over the junkyard driveway. Julia did not remember seeing either the tire or the tree when she came in, and surmised they must have cut it down.

"Someone took her," Mrs. Menzes said convincingly. "Just snatched her out of our lives. For what? For what?"

Roberta Kingman's mother had since gone back to being Ms. Paula Marchuk, after her husband left her and their son. Roberta, she told Julia, had been swimming in Cedar Pond while her fifteen-year-old brother, Kevin, was supposed to be watching her. But he went off with his friends and when he got back, Roberta had drowned. Mr. Kingman, "that useless bastard," had blamed her for putting Kevin in charge.

"Why are you asking me about that now? That was two years ago. You from some insurance company?" Paula Marchuk was only about thirty-five but there were hard lines around her heavily lipsticked mouth, and her short curly blonde hair had been overbleached to nothing but split ends.

Julia told her the same thing she had told Mrs. Menzes, but Ms. Marchuk's reaction was entirely different.

"No, Roberta didn't disappear. We know what happened to her. She drowned."

"Did you ever find her, Ms. Marchuk?"

"Call me Paula. Nope. Never did." She lit a thin cigarette and took a long drag, leaving the imprint of rose red lipstick on the filter.

"Was your daughter a good swimmer?"

"Like a fish. But she wasn't much of a diver. They think she hit her head on something." Paula tugged at her tight white shorts. "Him, he couldn't handle anything. Left me to handle it all. Everything, you know? No body to bury. Hardly any kind of funeral."

She took another drag and exhaled slowly through her nose. She tapped the ash into the ashtray three times, took another drag and tapped it again, long red nails on the white wrapper.

"I hate the son of a bitch."

Fleetingly, Julia thought of Phillip. Then realized she hardly ever thought of him anymore, and when she did, she didn't care what he was doing or who he was doing it with. She almost smiled in relief before she realized that Paula would not have the slightest idea why and might be offended. So Julia nodded her head knowingly.

"Roberta was how old?"

"Twelve. But people took her for older. She was an early bloomer. Like me." Paula pulled at her pink tank top. "I was pushing out at her age, too," she said matter-of-factly, "and I just kept on growing."

Julia glanced at Paula's ample breasts and avoided looking down at her own. "Just one last question. How long was it between the time your son went off with his friends and came back to look for Roberta?"

Paula Marchuk bit the inside of her lip while she thought, then took another drag on the cigarette.

"At first, Kevin told me five minutes. But then he said it was fifteen minutes and he made Robbie promise to stay out of the water and he'd bring her back an ice cream. That's where they went, him and his friends, to get ice cream from the truck they heard. You know, the bells? So I guess he was gone for a while."

"Would Roberta go into the water after Kevin told her not to?"

"That's an extra question," Paula said as though catching Julia in a mistake. Julia nodded, still hoping for a reply.

Paula ground out her cigarette in the aquamarine plastic ashtray. "I guess she did, didn't she?"

The sharpness left her then, and the façade crumbled and she began to sob uncontrollably.

"I'm so sorry," Julia said with sincerity. She got up to put her arms around the younger woman's shoulders. Paula buried her blonde head in her chest and leaned against Julia.

Julia remained silent until Paula stopped crying and then asked her for a picture of her daughter, promising to return it. It was the only one the mother had.

Roberta Kingman was another brunette, but with glasses framing her blue eyes and long hair that curled waywardly like her mother's. What was even sadder in the picture was that standing next to her was her big brother, Kevin, playfully making devil's horns with his fingers over her head.

"How has your son dealt with all of this, Paula?"

"I worry for him. He's withdrawn from all his friends. He just graduated high school and he's not working yet. He's gone all day and I don't know where he goes or what he does. He won't say."

"Has he seen anybody about it? A psychologist?"

"No. What for?"

"I'm going to give you the name of someone to call. He might be able to help." Julia wrote Dr. Sam's name and phone number on her notepad and tore out the page for Paula.

"We can't pay."

"I think he can work it out with state services. I'll talk with him. Call tomorrow, okay?"

Paula nodded ambivalently.

'Who is he, this killer of little girls?' Julia asked herself on the drive home from Paula Marchuk's. She was convinced that Roberta didn't just drown. They had dragged the pond for her body and never found it. They should have, if it was there.

The three girls, and Jeannine as well, had all been between twelve and fourteen. Not fully women, and relatively or completely inexperienced sexually. That made psychological consistency, as perverted as it was.

While she didn't know how the others were killed, or whether they were mutilated, she knew that Jeannine was. Why? Rage? The raping and the mutilating were on two different levels of gratification. More and more, he was sounding like a schizophrenic. The one thing she knew for fact was that he kept trophies—at least in Jeannine's case, with the barrette and underpants. And if Tully didn't do it, how did Jeannine's panties get into his root cellar?

When she got to the Bradburn house, she didn't have the heart to interview them. Fortunately, only Minna was at home, and she was able to give Julia a photograph. For a reason Julia couldn't yet fathom, she could not look at the picture. She put it into her purse and left it there.

Ruminating about the results of her interviews on the way home, Julia had to acknowledge that except for one link, the girls' ages, she'd found no other similarities. The girls were all Caucasian, but otherwise they differed in appearance. Blonde, brown-haired, brunette—no pattern there. Brown eyes, blue eyes, glasses, no glasses, heavier, thinner, taller, shorter. Age and geography seemed the only things they had in common.

'Well,' Julia thought dismally, 'that got me nowhere.'

* * *

"My son's calf has been killed, Adam." Billy said over the phone.

It was only two o'clock when Adam saw the last of his patients, a Spaniel with a nose full of porcupine quills. When the phone rang, he assumed it was for an appointment.

"How?" Adam thought Billy must mean in an accident.

"Somebody killed her and hacked her up."

Adam quickly closed up the clinic, forgetting to turn off the air-conditioner, and headed over to Billy's.

It was a humid ninety-four degrees Fahrenheit as Adam and Billy walked up behind the house, with Billy hanging onto Adam's arm. Both men were sweating.

"Tessa found the calf right before I called." Billy's tight grip on Adam's forearm indicated his distress. "She was all right at the morning feeding, so it had to happen after that. It's Billy Jr.'s calf. He doesn't know about it yet."

The back of Billy's property abutted the land being cleared for the cement plant. The land looked scarred where they'd been doing site prep. As the two men walked up the trail, Adam could smell blood. It was a rusty, sweet, sickly smell he knew well.

The dead calf had been left in the corral but the gate was open. The underbelly had been carved open, the entrails spilling on the ground. The snout was tied with a rope. Her eyes were covered with blowflies. The limbs had been separated from the body. Bees circled, landed and circled, landed and circled. Fly larvae wriggled in the open wounds.

"Judging by the larvae, this must have happened in the early morning. This heat accelerates everything," Adam said, disengaging his arm from Billy.

As he walked into the corral, he noted that there were so many dry ridges in the ground; there was no hope of getting a footprint. He hunkered down next to the carcass.

"Did Tessa go near the calf?"

"No. She came back to the house as soon as she discovered it. Has she been dressed off, Adam?"

"No." Adam carefully reviewed the remains. "She wasn't killed for meat."

"What, then?"

"Pleasure."

Adam got up and walked around the carcass. There was an uneven circle of stones around the calf. Blood was splashed on a few of the rocks, and others looked as they had been kicked or trampled out of the way. He had seen this before.

Billy scowled and took a deep breath. "What'll I tell Billy Jr.?"

"Tell him the truth."

"He doesn't know about things like this," Billy shook his head. "I know he's got to learn that things aren't always the way we'd have them be, but I don't know if it's time yet. How do you tell an Innocent that there's a craziness in people that makes them do this sort of thing?"

"I guess you tell him it's wrong, but it happens. It happens too often. And somehow we cope with it."

After a brief silence, Billy said, "You know, most people think that losing your innocence just means losing your virginity. Not in my book. To me," Billy tapped his chest, "it's when you take that first step into the void—where there's no ground underneath and there's no one to catch you. That's the moment. And I don't want to do that to my son."

"You and Tessa will be there to catch him, Billy. He's got two parents who love him and a lot of years to grow up safe."

Billy placed his hand lightly on Adam's arm as they walked back. "I guess it's could've been anybody," he speculated. "They're using my laneway up back, too. The kids all go through here now. Sometimes they go parking up there. Anybody can cut through these woods. What about Tully? Could it have been him?"

"No. Tully got chopped up on tractor tread two days ago and he hasn't been out of bed. Besides, he wouldn't kill any animal he didn't eat."

They walked on in silence until they reached Billy's house. Then Adam said, "I'm driving back in with the truck to take her out. I want to do a necropsy."

"Why?"

"Let me check it out first."

"What is it, Adam?"

"Doesn't matter unless I can prove it."

"Prove what?"

But Adam was thinking about the circle of stones where Jeannine Bradburn's body had been buried.

Before removing the calf, Adam took photos. It was an old habit from prosecuting animal cruelty cases. Then he unrolled the blue plastic tarpaulin he had in the bed of his truck. Out of the metal case he kept behind the driver's seat, he took a body sling that he used to move injured animals. He went about preparing to lift the torso into the pick-up. It wasn't much more difficult than moving a large dog.

By the time he got the carcass back to his clinic, he was glad he'd left the air-conditioner on.

He spent the following hours examining the remains of the calf, documenting his findings. The rope around the muzzle was standard. The dismembering was clean, at the joints. As he suspected, the calf had been penetrated, but there were no traces of semen. The most remarkable finding, however, was that the heart was missing.

After he'd finished, he sat at his desk, quiet and unmoving. He hadn't eaten all day but he wasn't hungry. He was thinking the impossible.

* * *

When Julia returned to her house, she was dismayed to see Adam's truck parked in front. As she pulled into the gravel driveway, he got out and walked over to her. She felt an involuntary flutter in her stomach.

Adam greeted her without a trace of the awkwardness she was feeling, and added, "Can I talk to you professionally for a minute?"

She watched his gaze take in the foxglove, holly-hocks, and lupine that flowered along the walk.

"Professionally?" Julia asked, with a squint of skepticism, wondering 'What did he mean, professionally?'

"About the Bradburn case."

"What about it?" Since when, she thought bitterly, did he put any stock in what <u>she</u> thought about the Bradburn case? Was this a way for him to start seeing her again? If it was, she wasn't having any.

"Can we talk inside?"

She took a deep breath, letting him see she wasn't pleased about any of this and then said impatiently, "I suppose so." As she opened the door, Cat scampered out to him, wagging her tail.

Inside, she did not sit down nor did she invite him to sit.

"Yes?" she asked.

He hesitated at first, then said, "Remember when you were preparing the case study on the Boston Strangler for your class?"

Julia practically cringed at the memory, but she nodded.

"We talked about how he began his career with torturing animals. And we talked about progression. And I told you some of the things I'd seen done to animals by guys that later did some pretty psycho things to people." He looked at her for confirmation, but Julia remained impassive. "What I need to know is, could it go back and forth? Animals to people, people to animals?"

"You mean start with harming people and then turn to animals? I don't think so."

"No, I mean interchangeably."

Julia considered it for a moment. "I don't know. I've never read of anything like that. Maybe. But somehow I don't think so. It's an addiction. It usually takes more and more to satisfy the urge, not less."

Adam looked distinctly disappointed.

"Why? Have you found something?"

"I'm not certain."

"I suppose," Julia mused, "if the urge to kill or torture couldn't be executed for some reason, the killer might possibly substitute an animal. Not so much back and forth, but as a displacement.

"Billy Jr.'s calf was killed today," he began slowly. "Sliced open and dismembered like Jeannine. I did a *post mortem*. It had been used sexually, as well."

"Maybe it's a copycat. Somebody who knew how Jeannine—"

"Those details were never reported."

"But her family knew. The police knew. The district attorney's office knew. The judge knew. You and Kip knew. I knew. Others could have known." Julia took some satisfaction in pointing out the holes in *his* theory.

He shook his head. "Nobody outside the case knew that Jeannine's heart had been cut out."

"You didn't tell me that!"

"I didn't know. Not even her family knew. Only the police chief, the medical examiner, and Percy."

"When did *you* find out?"

"This afternoon. I called Percy about Billy's calf and told him there was a ring of stones around the carcass, and that the calf had been dismembered. He didn't say anything until I told him the calf's heart was missing. Then he said Jeannine's heart had been cut out, but put back in. And I remembered Elgin telling me that Jeannine had had a bad heart, like her mother, and needed an operation. It looked as though whoever cut it out somehow could tell it was defective and didn't want it. I know that sounds completely off the wall."

Julia sat down on the sofa and tried to clear her mind.

"Are you saying you think there *is* a serial murderer? A ritualistic murderer? And that it's not Tommy?"

"All I'm thinking is that there may be more here than what first appeared." He began pacing. "But I can't figure it out."

"So you think I was right after all?"

Adam stopped pacing opposite her. "Maybe."

She shook her head. 'It's irrational,' Julia thought, 'for me to be so happy over something so grotesque.' But the feeling of vindication could not be denied.

"Then why didn't you believe me before?"

"I couldn't find the connection."

"And now you can?"

"I'm willing to consider the possibility. But that means we're back to square one."

"*We*?"

Adam hesitated again, then confessed, "I could use your help."

"Oh? How?" she asked coolly.

"I'd like to see those newspaper articles again, about the other girls who disappeared."

As Adam looked through the photos she'd collected, Julia related her day's activities to him, concluding, "That's all I could get."

"We're missing something," he said, shaking his head, "but I don't know what."

After a short silence, she finally said, "What we may be missing are more victims."

She then saw the same expression of dismay on his fact that must have been on her own when she first thought it. There was a logic to it. A terrible logic that there could be someone sick and destructive among them and that no one else knew it except the two of them...and the killer. Inadvertently, Julia's hand rose to her throat.

"Should we go back to our original suspects," she inquired tentatively.

Adam paused before replying. "Just to start."

"What about Tully?"

"Tully didn't kill the calf."

"How do you know?"

"He's bedridden. A dozer accident."

Julia looked down. "I guess I'm glad it's not him."

"Me, too."

"It has to be a ritual killing," Julia said. "The heart. The stone circle."

"Yes. That's the conclusion I came to."

"And we know that Tommy didn't kill the calf, either."

"Right."

"So where do we go from here?"

"We need to follow the evidence. We can start back on track tomorrow."

Julia nodded.

Adam paused, then said, "Given the hour, can I interest you in dinner?"

She wanted to say yes, but there was still a reluctance in her. "I can't tonight. Why don't we get together here tomorrow morning at ten, and go over what we've got."

"Fine." Adam lingered in the doorway on the way out. "Well, thanks for your help."

"You're welcome."

He didn't move.

"See you tomorrow then," she said with perfect composure.

"Right. Well, goodnight," he replied, subdued.

"Goodnight." She felt the question in his eyes but she kept her own expressionless. After he left, she wondered if she'd done the right thing. It didn't feel right. But letting him stay would not have been any better.

* * *

Conny Cranshaw's house was exactly the kind of house Conny Cranshaw would have, Adam thought. Large with Grecian columns, overlooking a lake, it reeked of money.

The house was dark as he drove past. He slowed down and turned off the motor. When he rolled the window, the only sound outside were crickets.

"It *was* you, you son of a bitch," he said softly.

He sat staring at the house until his thoughts wandered and he found himself thinking of Julia. He frowned, then started the truck and drove away, putting her out of his mind.

* * *

The night was so still he could hear his own breathing. Unhappy that he had listened to the Others' demand. The animal had not been satisfying. It was the Other who wanted the animal. He wanted the woman. He had had animals when he was younger. When he was a boy, he had pleasured himself with boyish things. But he was a man now, and returning to boyish things was not satisfying. He had grown beyond animals. Perhaps he has evolved beyond young girls. They were too much like animals. Like the wide-eyed calf. They were too easy. Perhaps it was time to change. He would have to think about that.

Why had he succumbed to the Other's need? Reckless, mindless need. He knew better, but he had bent. But he would not bend again. He was in control of the Others, not the reverse. If you don't take control of things, things take control of you. Things are going to change.

SATURDAY, JULY 16th

Adam looked thoughtfully at the photographs on the table. “But is that enough?”

“Is what enough?”

“The fact that they all were roughly the same age.”

“It’s just a beginning.” Julia said. “But there should be something else that links the victims. Something we haven’t seen yet.”

“Right,” Adam nodded. “Why *this* little girl instead of *that* little girl? Multiple opportunities, one selection. So there’s something we haven’t noticed. But what?”

“I don’t know. But let’s try to figure out what we’re missing. Go through the process. Let’s say I’m Jeannine Bradburn.”

Adam felt decidedly skeptical.

“Come on,” Julia coaxed. “I’m Jeannine, and I’m thirteen years old. I live with my mother and father, grandfather, sister Minna, and cousin Judd. On the morning of January 11th, I get up around 6:30 am. I get dressed, have breakfast—write that down…clothes.”

“Why?”

“We don’t know what she was wearing.”

“Is that important?” Then he answered his own question. “Anything could be important, I suppose.”

“Exactly. A red sweater, a white blouse. We just don’t know why he selected her.”

He wrote it down.

“So,” Julia continued, “I had breakfast and now I’m leaving my house. Then what? I walk to school? Or take the school bus?”

“The school bus stops at every other corner along the road. But she would have to walk a ways to get there.”

“Past houses?”

“Woods.”

"Alone?"

"We'll have to ask her mother," Adam said and wrote it down. "Let's say you meet up with friends at the bus stop."

"Okay, then I go to school. Attend classes. Recess. Classes. Lunch. Classes. Then school's over and I leave. Wait a minute," she interrupted herself. "Recess and lunch where? In the schoolyard?"

"Not likely, too cold."

"Right, cafeteria." Julia stretched, wearying of this exercise even though she had proposed it. "We need to check the cafeteria staff."

"I think they're all women. But go back, she didn't leave school right away, either."

"She didn't?"

Adam watched the slight curve of Julia's breast rise as she stretched, and restrained himself from reaching out a hand to touch her.

"No, Percy said Jeannine left later than her friends because she went to the drama club after school. So she left on the late bus about an hour after everybody else except the kids in the club."

"And when she got to her stop, her classmate saw the black pick-up truck. Maybe we've got something there," Julia said eagerly, "opportunity of time and place,"

"There's something else, too. Something obvious," Adam added.

"What?"

"We'll have to check, but all these girls probably went to the same school. It's a regional school," he explained. It's the only public school they can go to. So it's another common thread. They all went to school and didn't come home."

"Except for Roberta Kingman. She wasn't missing after school. She supposedly drowned in Cedar Pond."

"Which is directly across from the school."

"I didn't know that." Julia pondered a minute before speaking again. "Excepting Roberta Kingman, how likely is it that any one of them would have taken a ride home from a stranger."

"Not likely at all."

"So can we assume either they were forced into a vehicle by some unknown man or they knew the driver?"

"Assuming they were all abducted by the same person, yes, I guess so."

"Maybe that's the link, Adam. Maybe he knew all of them, and they knew him. He watched them. Maybe for a long time before approaching them. It could be an older boy in the school, or one who dropped out or graduated. Or it might be a teacher."

He watched a shiver pass over her as she said it and he felt the same.

Adam leaned back in his chair. "I suppose we could see if they had any teachers in common, but there's not much we can do about all the male students past and present."

In the silence that followed, Julia finally said, "What are you thinking?"

"I'm trying to figure how Conny Cranshaw fits into all of this."

"Maybe he doesn't."

"There has to be a connection." Or maybe he just wanted there to be one.

"I don't think we should focus on Conny Cranshaw to the exclusion of other suspects."

"We don't have any other suspects."

"Well, that's our job now, isn't it?"

He took a deep breath. "Yeah, you're right."

"Why don't I go to the school on Monday and talk with the principal? I'm sure the administration offices stay open all summer."

"Okay." He flexed his neck, leaning forward and back. "We've been at this a long time, it's almost five o'clock. How about we take a break and go out tonight? Forget about it for a few hours."

"Oh, yes. I could use an interlude."

He smiled invitingly, but she didn't smile back.

"That's not what I meant," she said hastily.

The smile left his face as he contemplated her.

"I'm sorry," Julia added quickly. "I didn't mean that to sound so...," she trailed off. "I'm just not, I don't know, I'm not ready for anything like that right now."

He said nothing.

"I just want to keep it uncomplicated. Okay?"

"Fine, that suits me. There's a Portuguese fiesta tonight. I can come back and pick you up in about two hours."

"Yes, that'd be good," she said awkwardly.

* * *

After Adam left, Julia began to put the photos back together in a folder. She reluctantly made herself look at Jeannine's picture. Barely able to keep her eyes on it, yet she couldn't bring herself to look away. It was a picture of the three Bradburn women—Cora, Jeannine, Minna—with baby Dwayne on Jeannine's lap. They were all looking at the baby and smiling. It wasn't that Jeannine was so pretty, for she was quite plain looking although she had large brown eyes and long brown hair that shined in the camera's flash. It wasn't that she was so young or so innocent that touched Julia. It was the way she held her baby nephew, loving and tender, that made Julia want to hug and protect her. But of course it was too late for that.

Seeing Jeannine's face made everything more ominous. The full terror of it overwhelmed her. It was as though evil really did exist. Not a psychological aberration or pathology or sociopathy. 'How evil does evil have to be before we call it what it is?' she asked herself.

* * *

When Adam and Julia went to the Holy Ghost Festa that night, it was with the express intention of forgetting about the investigation. The Fair was always held on church grounds, thronged with young and old people, mostly Portuguese. Two bands played alternately: one the traditional rhythmic Portuguese songs; the other heavy-metal rock music. Both bands had their constituents.

The church was decorated with candlelights and flowers, silver balloons and gold ribbons, and the streets were strung with multicolored Christmas lights and paper saints. Stalls encircled the grounds, selling fava beans, chorizo, linguica, homemade wine, as well as hot dogs, hamburgers, New England clam chowder, stuffed quahogs, and french fries. Lines of people queued up to eat, talking and laughing and not minding the wait not even one little bit.

Behind the church, a permanent barbecue pit was constructed of concrete blocks in the shape of a trough. Adam brought a three-foot skewer of marinated fish kebabs and joined the men at the barbecue. The smoke from the searing juices and the smell of pungent spices wafted over the grounds, up over the church, seeping into the nearby houses and calling everyone out to the festa.

Julia sat at a picnic table with Billy, Tessa, and their son. Billy Jr. seemed to be an average young boy, Julia thought, not particularly spoiled or coddled. Yet, there was a far-away expression on his soft face every now and then. And although he would go off periodically to be with his friends, he would return to his parents, looking anxious.

"All he talks about is his calf," Tessa confided to Julia while Billy Jr. was away from the table.

"It's okay that he does," Julia reassured her, "that's normal. Does he ever mention Jeannine?" Julia knew they'd been classmates.

As Tessa shook her head, Billy said, "No. Should we bring it up?"

Julia nodded, then realized only Tessa saw her. "I think it would be a good idea," she said to Billy. "Talk it out."

Billy nodded as Adam brought the blackened kabobs back to the table and slid them off the skewer onto paper plates.

As they ate and drank homemade Dao—Portuguese red wine—they watched couples dancing. Julia noticed

Cutter joined to a bosomy candy-blonde who was looking up at him moon-faced. Her curiosity was aroused.

"Who's that with Cutter?"

"The 'widder' Kerwin," Adam answered with exaggerated formality.

"Who?" Billy asked.

"Angel Kerwin. Bill's wife." Adam added, "Our last Chief of Police" for Julia's benefit.

"Angel?" Tessa commented facetiously.

Adam shrugged and smiled. But as he spotted someone in the crowd, his smile faded.

Julia followed his gaze. The man seemed familiar. She tried to recall where she had seen him before. Then she remembered the silver hair and it came to her.

"That's Conny Cranshaw, isn't it?"

"Is it?" Billy asked, not hearing any answer.

"Yes," Adam confirmed.

"He's broken ground for that damn plant already," Billy complained. "They're going to let him put his access road in."

As Conny passed by, neither man acknowledged the other.

"You don't like him very much, do you, Adam?" Tessa observed. "Because of the plant?"

"Among other things."

"What other things?" she prodded, but Adam didn't reply.

"He's a sleezebag," Billy volunteered. "His trucking company used to run toxic waste to the landfills. The only thing he cares about is making a buck."

As Billy was speaking, the Bradburn clan arrived. Elgin, along with Judd Vaughan, Minna and the baby, and a handful of others (minus Otis and Cora) settled into a nearby picnic table. They brought their own meat and skewers and busied themselves assembling them for the barbecue. Judd poured his homemade shine into styrofoam cups. A shock of black hair kept falling over his eyes, which he repeatedly tried to push out of the way with the back of his wrist. But since he wouldn't put down the bottle, every time he got ready to pour, his hair slid down again. He finally gave up and just tilted his head so the hair moved a little bit out of his eyes. He was already quite drunk and poured almost as much onto the table as into the cup, until Minna held the cup to the lip of the bottle. Rather than mollifying him, it enraged Judd. He grabbed the cup away from her and threw Minna's hand down, striking the table. She stifled a yelp, and quickly put her hand in her lap. Judd went on pouring and spilling.

"He's hammered," Tessa said.

"Who?" asked Billy.

"Judd Vaughan," his wife answered. "The Bradburns are here with Judd and Minna, and the little one, and Judd is pissed as a newt. You'd think old Elgin would do something about it."

"Give him half an hour," Adam predicted, "and Elgin will be in the same condition."

"Is Tully coming tonight?" Billy asked.

"Said he was," Adam replied.

"This really is delicious," Tessa said as she wiped her lips. "I'd love to get some of these spices."

Having handily finished off that batch of kebobs, Adam went back to the pit with more skewers. As he was cooking the food over the coals, Tully and Doris appeared at the edge of the crowd. They looked out of place, Julia thought, uncomfortable at not knowing where to go. What should she do? Pretend she didn't see them? Invite them over? She would like to have simply ignored them, but Doris recognized Julia and immediately walked over to her.

"H'lo-o, Jul-ya," Doris said rhythmically.

"How are you, Doris? I haven't seen you in a while."

"I'm going to have a baby. Are you going to have a baby, Jul-ya?"

"No, Doris" Julia answered.

"Are you?" Doris asked Tessa.

"Uh, no, I'm not. Not right now," Tessa answered, looking sidelong at Julia.

"You stay here," Tully instructed his wife. "I'm going to talk to Adam."

"Sit down here, Doris." Julia patted the space next to her on the bench. Doris sat down and stroked Julia's arm.

"Thank you, Jul-ya, you're just like my mother."

Julia wanted to say she was definitely *not* her mother, but restrained herself.

"When are you due, Doris?" Tessa asked.

"I dunno."

"Have you been to the doctor?"

"Noo-oo. Not yet. I got time yet."

Julia and Tessa exchanged glances.

"Maybe it would be a good idea to see the doctor a little early this time, what do you think?" Julia prompted.

"I dunno." Then, Doris added, "Will you go with me, Jul-ya?"

"Yes, I'll take you. We'll go together, how's that?"

"All-right. There's my cousin."

Doris waved and Julia watched apprehensively as Babe walked over to them. She hoped he wouldn't sit with them.

As Babe reached the table, Tully and Adam returned, brandishing the skewers aloft. Adam slid the kebobs off onto plates and offered one to Doris, who shook her head 'no.'

"Just try a little piece," he coaxed.

"No-o, I don't want any."

Adam then offered the plate to Tully. "Have some, it's nice and spicy."

"I can't eat that spicy stuff no more. We already et. We just come to do a look-around and now we're going."

"Babe, how about you?"

Babe nodded vigorously. He grabbed the kebob off the plate with his open hand and walked away, putting the food in his mouth as he walked.

"You shouldn't give him nothing," Tully scolded. "He don't appreciate it. He's a half-wit, just like her." Then, without interruption, he continued, "You gonna be home tomorrow, Adam? I got a bushel of beans come in, I wanna give you some. I'm going to have a good crop this year."

Meanwhile, Doris' face had swollen and reddened as though she'd eaten a poison mushroom. Her eyes became teary and her mouth quivered.

"He didn't mean it like that," Julia whispered to her. "You're not a half-wit. And if he calls you that, you just tell yourself that he's a *nit*-wit and that's even worse, right?"

Doris looked trustingly at Julia. Like a passing rain cloud, her mood changed. Her face smoothed out and little wrinkles fanned the corner of her eyes as she smiled.

"That's right," Doris whispered back. "He has nits." She giggled and Julia smiled at her and looked at Tessa, who shook her head.

"I got some for you, too, Billy," Tully was saying. "You like beans, don'tcha?"

"Thanks, but we have our own beans this year," Billy replied.

Julia knew that was only partly true. Tessa had told her their garden was a little sparse. Julia presumed Billy couldn't bring himself to accept anything from Tully anymore.

"Well, I'll drop some off for you, Adam. Just came down here to see the crowd. Don't want to keep Doris out too late. Come on, Doris."

As Doris got up from the bench, she put her arm through Tully's and the two of them ambled off.

"How could he say that in front of her?" Julia said to Adam. "Did you see how it affected her?"

"That's Tully," Billy said sourly.

"The way he said it," Adam explained, "was the way you'd say someone is tall or short or even blind. It's just the way he says things."

"But it hurts her," Julia protested.

"Funny, though," Tessa said, looking off where Tully and Doris were walking into the crowd, "if you saw them and didn't know them, you'd think he was very solicitous of her. The way she takes his arm and the way he guides her to wherever they're going."

"Fact is," Adam added, "in his own way, he cares for her."

"Emphasis on *in his own way*," Julia retorted.

"So be it," Adam said nonchalantly. "Eat your food everybody before it gets cold."

Adam excused himself after they'd finished eating and left. Noticing Julia's silence, Tessa suggested they walk around, leaving Billy to mind their son. Julia readily agreed.

There were booths of spinning wheels to win cartons of healthily-incorrect cigarettes and boxes of chocolate candy bars. There were games like pitching the ball at metal milk-bottles to win pink-and-blue stuffed bunnies or plastic dolls; and games to race toy cars by picking the highest number cards where you could win a transistor radio or a strobe flashlight. Mobs of people were playing all the games and there was a winner nearly every time. It would be a great night for the concessions, and a good one for the players.

"You seem distracted," Tessa observed. "Everything okay between you and Adam?"

"I'm not sure really."

Tessa cocked her head inquiringly, but Julia shrugged her shoulders. "Just something I have to work out for myself."

* * *

Adam walked conspicuously over to the Cranshaw table and stood within view of his target. The only way to get anything out of Conny was to rattle him, Adam decided. So, every time Conny looked up, he found Adam Sabeski watching him. Amidst the din and activity of his sons and daughters and grandchildren, Conny could not hear or see anything except this troublesome man glaring at him. Finally, it became too much. Conny got up from the table and bore down on Adam like a tractor.

"What are you staring at, Sabeski?" he growled menacingly.

"Was I staring?"

"Don't play games with me. What do you want?"

"I want to nail you." Adam smiled as though it were a compliment.

"Nail me for what? A few thin goats?"

"For killing Jeannine Bradburn."

"What are you, crazy? Get your Jucket ass out of my sight or you won't have one. Understand?" Conny turned back to his family.

"Just wanted you to know I'm your biggest fan." Adam said pleasantly.

"Go fuck yourself."

Conny walked away and Adam continued to stand his ground just long enough to make the point.

* * *

When Adam caught up with Julia and Tessa, they were leaning on the fence outside the Skydiver, a Ferris wheel with enclosed cars that twisted and rotated as the Ferris wheel spun. Billy Jr. was on the ride with his father. They all watched as the cars rose up high into the air, twirling like automated ballerinas as they gained height. Julia wondered if it was harder or easier to ride such a thing if you were blind. She thought she would probably get sick to her stomach.

After the ride ended, Billy Jr. persuaded his dad to go again. In the line for tickets, Julia saw the Wilsons and their son. Couldn't miss them. Roger was wearing Banana Republic khaki slacks and a pale yellow turtleneck. His Pasadena wife was dressed in white linen slacks with navy-and-white spectators, a navy silk blouse and, over her shoulders, a white cardigan with navy trim. And of course, white pearls. Amidst the jumble of jeans, green chinos, and black and violet spandex, the Wilsons looked like they belonged in a different movie. Julia snickered along with

Tessa, but inwardly envied what's-her-name for looking so damn gorgeous.

Roger Wilson climbed onto the ride with his son while his wife stood watching. They sat in the car behind Billy and, when the ride was over, Roger was still holding onto the bar for dear life, looking yellow as his turtleneck.

"Albert DeSalvo was a family man," Julia murmured.

"But Wilson wasn't around here five years ago," Adam responded.

"Right, I forgot. He was on Mars."

They had played every game by the end of the evening, ridden every ride, and eaten everything there was to sample. They had danced to the music until they were exhausted. Billy, Tessa, and Billy Jr. joined the band onstage and gave a final rendition of "When the Saints Go Marching In" on clarinet, bugle, and drums.

Leaving, they passed by Babe again, standing next to Floyd Mather. Julia recalled seeing them together once before, at the auction. Babe was talking non-stop in his stunted way, babbling and giggling as he had when Julia'd first seen him in Tully's kitchen. Floyd appeared not to be paying any attention. She nodded to Floyd in recognition but he did not return the acknowledgement. 'Just as well,' she decided. She didn't want to remind him about the piglet.

"They're strange friends," she commented, then remembered saying something similar about Adam and *his* friends.

Adam glanced over his shoulder to see who Julia meant. "Floyd and Babe? They're related somehow. Third cousins or something."

"Everybody's related around here," Billy interjected. "You have to watch what you say to whom about whom because they might be kin."

"And if it isn't blood kin," Tessa chortled, "we're related by marriage, adultery, or common law—infusion, injection, or osmosis."

* * *

Adam shut off the engine as he pulled up to Julia's house. There was an uncomfortable silence until he said, "Did you enjoy the festa?"

"Yes, very much, thank you."

He slid his thumbs along the steering wheel, looking straight ahead. "Should I come in?"

"No, I don't think that's such a good idea."

He felt the heat rising to his ears. "Right," he replied not looking at her.

She opened the door and stepped down, saying breezily, "Well, thanks again for the evening. Goodnight."

She didn't wait for his reply, but walked briskly into the house without a backward glance.

Adam lingered until she was inside and he saw the lights go on. He could, he thought, get out of the truck and go to the door. Ask her to invite him in. But he wouldn't. So he pressed his lips together and drove away.

* * *

She was light on her feet and she smiled when she danced. He wanted her. Oh, yes. But who was he kidding? She didn't want him. Clearly not. These women who think they're better than him. What gives them the right to judge? Take his measure and find him wanting. What does he have to do to prove himself?

What is he, just some courting bird, fanning his feathers and bobbing his dance? Why should he bother? She's not worth the effort, no more than any of them.

"I do not love you, Miss Arnault, I do not love you, this I know. I do not love you, Miss Arnault, I do not love your little toe."

TUESDAY, JULY 19th

Over the past two days, Julia had returned to the girls' families to ask more questions. Maybe there was something else—dress, transportation to school, friends, habits—that linked them. She asked about everything, but to no avail. Maybe there wasn't any link.

As a last resort, she had tried to find a connection with the victims' teachers. According to the school records over the last five years, there had been only two male teachers whom the missing girls had in common. One had left the school a few weeks before Jeannine was murdered, severely disabled in a skiing accident. The other was, by Julia's own observation, not a suspect. Diminutive Mr. Claremont was ready to retire and quite incapable of any act more physical than lifting the window shades. So that, too, was a dead end. And yet, the school was their common ground. It had to have something to do with school.

She wondered what Adam was doing. He hadn't called her since the festa. And she hadn't called him. She wanted to talk with him, but she refrained.

* * *

Percy had pulled eight files for all missing girls in Pittsley and the neighboring towns over the past ten years and given them to Adam. Percy well knew that Adam's powers of investigation and arrest were solely for animal cruelty cases. But because Adam was authorized through the state police, technically he could be considered a law enforcement official. Although that was stretching the point.

Percy and Adam had worked on too many raids together to quibble over the fine distinctions now. Adam had demonstrated the connection, however loosely, of the calf to Jeannine's murder, and that was almost, if not quite, reason enough for Adam to ask Percy to go through the files. Percy hemmed and hawed, but, in the end, complied.

"Don't you tell anybody about this," Percy'd said, and Adam assured him he wouldn't.

Returning home with the files, Adam drove past CranLand Trucking, then impulsively swung around and pulled in.

Conny was on the telephone when Adam walked into the office. He was talking with a very expensive cigar in his mouth, facing away from the door. It smelled enticing to Adam as he waited for Conny to finish. But he had quit tobacco, this time for good.

When Conny hung up and turned around, he was startled into a tirade.

"What do you want? Get out of here!"

"Don't want a thing today," Adam replied casually. "Just thought I'd tell you how nice it was to see you at the festa. We have to get together like that more often."

Conny stood up and leaned forward, hands on desk. "You get out of here or I'll throw you out myself."

"I just came to visit, Conny. I don't see a 'no visitors' sign. But if I'm interrupting you, I can come back another time."

"If you ever come back here again, I'll shoot your goddam kneecaps off."

"You mean you don't have the balls to take a tire iron to me the way you did to Ben Bradburn? You're getting soft, Conny."

With that, Adam turned and left, waving a polite goodbye to the man who looked as though he wanted to vault the desk and charge at him.

That afternoon, Adam worked silently, reading and making notes on the police files. He was looking for something, anything, to connect Conny Cranshaw to the missing girls.

'Okay,' he thought, 'maybe there wasn't much of an investigation into Roberta Kingman's drowning because it seemed so plausible.' Although, he reminded himself, they never did find her body. As for Judy Eastgate, well, the police thought she ran away to find her mother. Should they have looked for her? Yes, but they assumed she went out of state. Someone had written, under "Finding": "Status unknown." It was initialed "W.K."

"Bill Kerwin. William," Adam said aloud.

Then what about Sally Menzes? Sally just disappeared and there was nothing in the file that showed the police did anything beyond the necessary. There were two pages of interviews with mother and father; interviews with teachers and friends. They had put out an A.P.B., set up neighborhood watches. Her parents put up posters and Percy Davis went to the school to talk with her classmates. "Finding: Status unknown. W.K."

As he sorted through the files, he couldn't help coming back to the conclusion that it just wasn't very good police work.

He shook his head. There were four more files of girls he had never heard of. Even though there were different towns and years, they were still in Bill's jurisdiction because the other towns were still too small to have full-time police departments.

Adam reached for the phone.

WEDNESDAY, JULY 20th

Adam and Percy met in a booth at Dud's Suds at noontime. There were only two other customers, both sitting at the bar, half in the tank. Dud's was just a hole-in-the-wall barroom where the locals went, usually no women tolerated. The vintage sports photos on the walls were layered with years of grime. Fortunately, as the lighting was so dim, no one paid attention to the dirty floor or the splits in the red plastic-covered bar seats.

Both men were sweating in the steamy air that even the darkness of the bar couldn't dispel.

"I know it's all hypothetical, but that's all we've got," Adam said. "Just heat lightning." It was an expression they always used with each other to indicate a strong hunch with no evidence. Percy nodded acknowledgement.

"And the police investigations weren't very helpful," Adam concluded.

Percy chewed his ham and cheese sandwich with his mouth open. "So you want to know who Bill was protecting."

"Yes," Adam hadn't spelled it out, but that was exactly what he wanted.

Percy took a swig of tonic. "Nobody."

"Percy—," Adam began, but the sergeant interrupted him.

"No, Adam, nobody." Percy sighed. "I know you want to hear he was protecting his cousin, Conny, but it ain't the case. Truth is, Bill was a piss-poor detective.

"What do you mean?"

Percy lowered his voice. "Chief was good with the usual kind of stuff we deal with every day. Everybody liked him. He could talk to people, figure out who oughta be doing what. Knew when to go hard on somebody or when to back off. That kind of stuff. Got a call on a domestic dispute, he was right there. Drunken brawls. Motor vehicle stuff. The petty-ass things we do all the time, he was real good at. But he never knew squat about investigations or forensics or any of that. He wasn't protecting anybody, Adam. He just didn't know how to do it, wouldn't admit, and wouldn't let anybody else know." Percy took another slug of his soda and wiped his mouth with his hand.

Adam sat back and regarded his friend of twenty years. "You never told me Bill couldn't handle his job."

Percy shook his head. "Just parts of it. And besides, that's something no cop in this town would say about his brother. And don't forget, Bill and me started out together."

"Then you should have done the investigation yourself."

"I did as much as I could. But you know I'm not trained for it, either."

"You could have called in the State."

"You read the files." Percy chewed his sandwich between sentences, but without paying any attention to his food. "Not one of those cases was officially listed as a wrongful death."

"Why the hell not!"

Percy glanced at the men on the barstools, but neither of them gave any indication of interest.

"Chief didn't want the State crawling all over his files."

"Shit, Percy, why did you let this happen?"

"Nothin' I could do."

"That's a load of crap. I expected better from you, Perce."

Percy threw down the remainder of his sandwich onto the plate. "How was I supposed to know all those girls were murdered? Shit, I *still* don't know that for sure. And neither do you. You ain't a cop. And all you're doing is blowin' smoke. So don't make something my fault that probably never happened."

Adam got up and flipped some change on the table.

"See you around, Perce."

He didn't wait for a response, and figured he wasn't going to get one.

Opposite Adam, Chief Burke sat with his feet up on his computer table, his navy blue and red-striped tie loosened and one top shirt-button opened. It was his one concession to the heat.

"Air conditioner broke down," he explained with exasperation. "I've got to get another one in here today or I'm going to have problems with my hard drive."

Declining an offer of ice water, Adam placed the eight files on top of the desk. Burke recognized the folders.

"These are PPD case files."

Adam nodded.

"What are you doing with them?"

"I'd like you to take a look through them."

"Why?"

"Just read."

Burke picked up the file on top, Alice Peters. "This case is nine years old."

"I know, but I think there's some important information in there."

Burke glanced quickly at the cover sheet in each file and grimaced. "Three of these aren't even in Pittsley."

"Same jurisdiction back then."

"What are you doing with these files?"

Adam was prepared for the question. "I have authorization." He flashed his wallet card with his State Police gun permit and appointment.

Burke scanned it in a glance and smirked. "You might be able to bulldoze some rookie with that. But you and I both know that you're not even authorized to use the can in the police station unless there's a cat being flushed down the hopper."

Adam conceded that with a half-smile. Then he patiently explained, as he had with Percy, the similarities between the mutilation of the calf with the mutilation of

Jeannine Bradburn, and the connection between the missing girls.

Burke listened silently until Adam was finished. He pondered for a few minutes, scowling. "Leave these here and come back in an hour."

Adam nodded and got up, giving credit to the asshole for at least listening.

As Adam left, Police Chief Burke began looking through the Judy Eastgate file. And began chewing his cuticle.

He sat on the front steps of the police station smoking his pipe. The tobacco burned his tongue and he resolved once again to quit. It irritated him that he couldn't master this habit. Just as, from time to time, it irked him that he had let himself come so close to Julia, a nagging reminder that he was not as self-sufficient as he imagined. But that was all done now. That's the way she wanted it. That's the way he wanted it.

He watched as Percy drove around back with his cruiser. Despite Adam's disappointment with his old colleague, he hoped Percy wouldn't get in trouble over the files. Perce was only a few years away from early retirement.

When Adam returned to Burke's office, he saw an expression of disbelief on the Chief's face.

"No coordination at all!" he barked. "We never knew what we were up against with Jeannine. Seven other kidnappings and no-fucking-body knew it. How did this happen?" He shook his head in despair. "I never pulled up any of these on the computer because they weren't coded as abductions."

"Now what?"

"I've already put in a call to the State Police. Got someone coming over this afternoon."

Adam's estimation of Burke went up a notch when the man didn't deride his predecessor. He just took action.

"You'll talk with the agent when he gets here?"

Adam agreed, studying the man who replaced Bill Kerwin a little more closely. He was younger, college educated, trimmer, better dressed that's for sure, and better equipped to handle the technology that Bill had laughed at. Maybe Carson Burke was the right Chief for the job, after all. Pittsley was changing. Adam saw the metamorphosis in just a couple of years. He realized that, in the next few years, the balance of the town would shift. Fewer and fewer Juckets. More and more yuppies. Just a fact of life. The old Pittsley that had been essentially the same for a hundred…no…*two* hundred years…was being transformed before his eyes like a computer model. There was no room here in the future for backwoodsmen. Maybe not even himself. Oh sure, maybe they could create their own little pocket of the past, but it wasn't likely to last very long and it wouldn't be the same anyway.

Wasn't Buzzard Bartoncourt already complaining that the FAA was closing in on all the barnstorming pilots? Can't do this, can't do that. And guys with old junkheap cars were being forced off the road and hounded on their own property. Event the dump permit cost fifty dollars now, where a year ago it was still five. And everything had to be separated like tupperware cartons in a refrigerator. It was the population spread, Adam told himself. Maybe it's time they were all moving on. 'I wouldn't hesitate to leave if I were younger,' he admonished himself. 'Go someplace more isolated.' If there were any such places left.

Then he looked again at the future of Pittsley across the desk. '*Neanderthal* meets *Homo sapiens*,' Adam thought wryly.

"I appreciate your bringing all of these data to me," *Homo sapiens* was saying. "I hope we can continue to work together. I guess I can always learn a few things from the locals." There was no derision in his voice, only deference. "More than a few, I expect."

Neanderthal eyed him appraisingly, then said with a crooked grin. "Two-way street, Chief."

* * *

Ever since the festa, he couldn't get her out of his mind. Julia. Julia. She was just what he wanted. Small and womanly. But this time it would be different. He wouldn't let the Others at her. No, he'd keep this one. He'd put her where he could have her whenever he wanted her. And she would love him and love what he did to her. She would spread her legs and ask him, beg him, to sting her while she wiggled and giggled with the spider inside her. And then she would bend over and he'd do it again right in her bottom round, so smooth and tight, and she'd wiggle and giggle with the rider inside her, and they would go wee, wee, wee, all the way home.

THURSDAY, JULY 21st

Julia pointed to a picture of a large St. Bernard in the picturebook. “What is this, Tommy?”

“Dog.”

“Right. Do you like dogs?”

He nodded.

“Good. How do we spell ‘dog’? D-o-g. Now you say it.

When he repeated it, she gave him a thumbs-up sign and he looked pleased with his accomplishment. He went back at the book and began forming the word with his mouth. She glanced out the window. It was hot out, but cool as tile in the hospital visitor area.

“You have dog,” Tommy said, and Julia was astonished that he remembered, or even had noticed, considering his condition the night he came to Adam’s house.

“Yes. I have *a* dog. One dog.”

“*A* dog,” he echoed.

“Yes,” she said with approval. She would not tell him her dog’s name was Cat. Fortunately, he didn’t ask.

Then she turned the page to a picture of a young girl in a pink dress. “What’s this, Tommy?” She tapped the picture.

“Girl.”

“That’s right.” Julia hesitated a moment. Then she decided to do what she had resolved. She reached into her pocket and removed a photograph, the one of Jeannine Bradburn and her family.

“Who’s this, Tommy?” She pointed to Jeannine.

“Girl?” he said without any trace of familiarity.

“Yes. But what girl?”

Tommy shrugged. “Girl.”

“Do you know this girl?”

Tommy shook his head. Julia studied him intently, then put the photo on the table and pointed to the barrette in Jeannine's hair.

"What is this?"

"Hair."

"Yes, but what is in her hair?"

Tommy shrugged.

"It's a barrette, Tommy. Do you know what that is?"

Tommy shook his head.

"A barrette to hold her long hair."

"Long hair," he repeated mechanically.

"Yes, she has—"

Suddenly Julia felt cold. Her heart began pounding her fingers tingled with pins-and-needles.

'Is that it?' she asked herself.

She tried to recall the other photos. Didn't all the girls have long hair? Could that be the connection? So obvious. So simple. But it had to mean something important. Julia shivered as she remembered Jeannine's hair had been short, very short when Julia saw her. That's why she hadn't realized it was a young girl until they turned the body over. Maybe the killer had cut it. Another trophy.

As soon as she collected herself, she ended her visit with Tommy and found the public telephone in the corridor. 'Good, the Bradburns are listed,' she thought.

She dialed and waited for what seemed like a very long time for someone to answer. She hoped it wouldn't be Cora.

Minna answered, "'Lo, who is it?"

Julia identified herself and got right to the point. "Minna, did Jeannine have long hair?"

"'Course."

"I mean, did your sister have long hair when she went to school that day?"

"Yes-s-s, of course," Minna replied impatiently.

"Did you see her that morning?"

"Yes-s-s, I was up with Dwayne."

"And Jeannine hadn't cut her hair short?"

"'Course not. I gotta go. Baby's cryin'."

Julia was still holding the phone to her ear after Minna hung up.

She then dialed Adam's number, but there was no answer. She slammed the phone down in frustration.

Julia pushed through the heat outside to her car. It started with a lurch and bucked before settling into gear. She turned on the air conditioner but turned it off again when only hot gusts of air blew out.

When she reached Adam's house, she saw his truck was gone. Not knowing what to do next, she headed for home.

She couldn't stop thinking about her discovery. Was it really a discovery? So all the young girls had long hair, so what? Lots of young girls had long hair. But the killer cut Jeannine's hair off. Why? Probably to keep looking at it. The fact that they had long hair told her, perhaps, how he chose his victims but it didn't really tell her about him. So the murderer liked long hair. So what? Plenty of men like women with long air. Even Adam liked—

She stepped on the brake and the car stalled to a stop.

Adam had a black pick-up.

'No, that's crazy,' she told herself.

But he was a veterinarian. He'd know how to cut open a body. And he was so secretive. Had such black moods.

"No," she said aloud. "It can't be Adam."

She sat in her car on the empty road, her hands tight on the steering wheel as if she might fall out.

"I can't think that" she said aloud. "I can't let myself think that. No, he wants to find the killer as much as I do."

Her mind raced. 'But what if the killer he's trying to find is himself? What if he wants to stop himself? There've been cases like that. What if he's schizophrenic? What if he's a multiple?'

He could have this other side to him. He had so many sides. How well did she know him, after all? Look at his friends. His life. His profession. He could have multiple personality disorder. Have alters.

"No."

'But what if?'

Shaking now, she started the car. It hesitated, then caught. She swung the wheel around and headed back to the hospital.

"Sam, do you have a few minutes?" Julia entered Dr. Sam's office tentatively.

"Sure. Come on in, Julia. How's everything going?" He motioned her to sit down across the desk from him.

"I need to talk with you about something."

"A patient?"

"No."

He scrutinized her. "What's the problem?"

He removed his glasses and wiped the lenses with the edge of his lab jacket as she began telling him about Adam.

After ten minutes of non-stop talking, she concluded with, "I think it's possible he might be a multiple, Sam. Everything about him is splintered. The way he lives. How he works. Even the approach-avoidance way he is with me."

"All right," Sam replied, fitting his glasses back on, "let's be specific."

Julia tried to describe as much as she could about Adam and it all came out conflicted. Then she told Sam about the serial killer.

"Adam has a black pick-up. He's a veterinarian and could easily have…oh, God, I don't know what I'm saying."

"What you're saying is that he's so completely fragmented that he's investigating his own crime without consciously know it." Sam rested his elbows on the dark wooden arms of this black and gold Harvard chair, and interlaced his fingers.

"That's possible, isn't it? It if was one of his alternate personalities?" Julia asked, hoping for reassurance that it wasn't. "He seems convinced that there's something evil going on, and I don't mean just bad or horrible. Actual evil.

And I'm only this far," she measured a short distance between thumb and forefinger, "from believing it myself."

"Tell me, Julia, are you in love with this man?"

She took a deep breath and let it out slowly. "I don't know. Right this minute, all I am is afraid of him."

Dr. Sam nodded. "Do you think it's possible that you're projecting your own ambiguity about your relationship onto him?"

She rubbed her forehead. "I don't know."

"Maybe you should explore that first. It's a little more plausible than what you're proposing. What do you think?"

She nodded dubiously. "I suppose so." She paused, then asked again, "But it's not impossible that Adam could be the one, is it?" She waited anxiously for the answer that was slow in coming.

"From what you've told me—no it's not impossible. That's the short answer. But we both know there's a lot more to it than what is simply possible. Let me ask you—is it *probable*?"

"I don't know. I honestly don't. I wish you knew him."

"So do I. But in the absence of that, what do you intend to do?"

"What do you think I should do?"

"I think you have to resolve this conflict."

"Should I talk it over with Adam?"

"Under no circumstances. If you're wrong about him, you will only sabotage your relationship. And if you're right, the risk is too great. I suggest that you tell the police your suspicions and let them handle it."

"The police chief is completely out of the question."

"There must be someone there you can talk to."

'Maybe I could take to Sgt. Percy,' Julia thought as she drove home. 'Tell him my discovery about the girls and tell him my concerns about Adam. But will he believe me?' She wasn't sure she even believed herself. And if Sgt. Percy talked to Adam, then Adam would know what she suspected. And if it wasn't true, he'd hate her forever. But what if it *were* true?

As she passed the Congregational Church, she saw the pastor at the display board, putting up Sunday's sermon. *"If God Exists, Why Not the Devil?"*

Julia squealed her car into a sharp turn up the driveway, startling the pastor.

His study was quite modest, plain but tasteful in mahogany and Wedgewood blue. Pastor Ryman listened without interruption to Julia's story. "I suppose," she ended without mentioning Adam by name or profession, "I should have gone to a Catholic priest; they seem to know about these things, but I saw your sermon."

Ryman chuckled. "We Congregationalists get short shrift in the Good *versus* Evil department." Then he grew somber. "But I actually co-teach a course with Rabbi Edelstein on cults at the State Police Academy. Most so-called cults are more like gangs of kids that tip over gravestones and kill animals as initiation sacrifices. Our local veterinarian took the course because of his experiences in that arena."

"Adam Sabeski?"

"Dr. Sabeski, yes. And then there are religious cults that absorb the minds of their communicants. I make a distinction between legitimate religions and religious cults that I won't go into now. Then there are the true Satanic cults. These, too, are divided into types. Black witches and warlocks who are mostly attention-seekers. Groups of men and women who practice aberrant sexual behavior under the guise of devil worship. And lastly, the unexplained ones. What drives them…who drives them is another matter."

"Satan? Is that what you're saying?"

"Satan manifest. Demonized humans. Dybbuks. So corrupted in their souls, they're unredeemable. Are they devils, or The Devil? Who can say? All we know is that their actions are unholy."

Julia remained silent.

"Does that blow you away?"

She smiled briefly. Ryman was about her age, unassuming looking, but she could sense the strength in him. "I have a hard time with the concept."

"Most people do. We're all so secular in our rationales for behavior these days. But if you believe in God—do you believe in God, Ms. Arnault?"

"I…just don't always know. Yes, I guess so, down deep."

"Then why not Satan? Is it any harder to believe one that the other? However, if it's more comfortable for you to think it's just a multiple personality, or even a quasi-cult, you're still dealing with some pretty heinous crimes."

"Yes."

"In either case, you might want to be careful for yourself."

"For myself?"

"To reveal either one puts you in jeopardy."

For the first time, she felt a chilly fear.

"If you need my help at any time, Ms. Arnault, please call on me."

"Julia."

"Martin." He held out his hand.

In shaking his hand, she felt somehow comforted. "Thank you."

His blue eyes held hers. "I'm serious, Julia, be careful."

The phone was ringing as Julia entered her house. She thought it might be Adam and she wasn't ready to confront him yet. She debated for another ring, then finally picked up the receiver.

"Hello?" she said tentatively.

On the other end of the line a deep voice said, "It's time. Come get your pig."

"My what?" Then she identified the voice as Floyd Mather's. "Oh, the pig." She had forgotten about it. "Thank you but I'm not going to need it now."

"It's your pig. And I'll take my money." And with that, he hung up.

Julia frowned as she put down the receiver. Then she rummaged through her purse for her wallet. Counting her money, she scowled.

She quickly changed into jeans, then took her purse and called Cat to go with her. She'd get the pig, and then she'd go to the State Police about Adam.

The two dogs, Cat and Floyd's German Shepherd, began barking at each other as soon as Julia drove up to the house. The German Shepherd was chained to a tree out front, so Julia left Cat in the car as she followed Floyd out to the pigpen.

Before he handed her the pig on a rope, Julia gave Floyd the sum total of the money in her wallet. It was just enough.

By this time, the Shepherd had quieted down and only Cat was barking. Julia hoped she wouldn't give the little pig any trouble. It was an awfully cute little animal.

"Is she housebroken?" Julia asked facetiously, but Floyd did not react. "Just kidding," she added unnecessarily. She fleetingly wondered whether she actually wanted to see him smile, and how would his teeth look? If he had any. She'd seen a lot of Halloween-pumpkin mouths around Pittsley.

"What should I feed her?"

"Dog noses," he replied in a monotone.

"Excuse me?" Her face betrayed her.

"Just kidding," he said unsmiling.

"Good one." She did not even try to sound sincere.

As she lifted the piglet into the front seat of her car, Cat investigated the new arrival. Both animals seemed a little hesitant with each other.

Julia got in and turned the ignition key, but nothing happened. She pumped the gas and tried again. Again, nothing happened.. After the fourth try, Julia hit the steering wheel with her fists.

"Damn this car!"

Beads of perspiration formed along her hairline. She thought about B-movie heroines whose cars suddenly flooded when they were in danger, and whose engines wouldn't start until the last minute when they peeled away in safety. But she wasn't in danger and there was nothing sudden about her car trouble. How stupid could she be? She should have had it fixed weeks ago. Months.

"That's what I get for procrastinating," she muttered. But it hadn't been procrastination so much as defiance. Defying a car? She angrily tucked the wayward ends of her hair at the nape of her neck into her haircomb. "How stupid can you be?"

As she glanced in the rearview mirror, she saw Floyd Mather standing in the doorway of his barn, watching her with an unreadable expression.

Julia took a deep resigned breath and turned off the ignition. Under the circumstances, it was foolish she knew, but turning off the key was too strong a habit to break. She left Cat and the piglet in the car and started walking back towards Floyd.

"May I use your telephone?"

"What for?"

Was he being deliberately obtuse? Julia wondered. "To call a mechanic to fix my car." 'And get scolded for not listening to him about the starter motor,' she thought.

"Don't have a phone."

"But you called me earlier."

"I was at the store."

She looked overhead. Weren't those telephone lines leading into the house? Or were they for electricity? She didn't know.

"Do you think you could give a look at the motor? Maybe we can figure out what's wrong with it so I can be on my way."

Julia walked around the front of the car to open the hood. Not that she knew anything about engines, but maybe, just maybe, this very unpleasant man did.

The hood was unlatched and she wondered how long she'd been driving around like that. Probably since her last oil fill. When was that?

She lifted the hood and stared uncomprehendingly at the engine as Floyd came up behind her. Julia turned to look at him and his expression was completely blank. 'Bland affect,' she thought and became suddenly wary. Something felt wrong. Or was she just overreacting? He didn't really seem as though he would make a move on her. Maybe she was getting paranoid. Too much the urban guerilla. 'But this is how women get raped,' she thought. She had better get out of there.

"I can leave my car here if you could drive me to the nearest phone."

"Who are you going to call?"

"A mechanic."

"Doesn't anyone know you're here?"

It was a question that should not have been asked and she began to realize how vulnerable she was here. She would never have put herself at risk this way in the city.

"Yes, my friend Tessa does," she lied. "She wanted to come with me to see the pigs but her baby was sick. She lives down the road. Maybe you could drive me to her house. Her husband's a mechanic."

As she started to close the hood, she noticed one of the wires was in two pieces. Two clean pieces. Cut, not frayed. But Floyd couldn't have done that, he was with her the whole time. She slammed down the hood, pretending she hadn't seen the wire. As she looked down the long driveway away from the house, she couldn't even see the road.

She was in trouble.

Floyd turned his head to look towards the barn.

'He's not going to get me in there,' Julia thought as she began walking away from the car.

"Actually," she said, "I could walk to Tessa's house. It's not that far. I'll just leave the car and come back for it later."

"Nobody knows she's here," Floyd shouted towards the dark interior of the barn.

'Who's he talking to?' Julia looked towards the barn, hypnotically fascinated.

A man's figure appeared out of the shadow of the doorway. Julia squinted against the sun for a second before she realized he was swinging an axe at his side.

* * *

So, how's the new job going, Tully?"

Tully didn't answer Adam right away so Doris piped up. "He's not workin' there no mo-wa, Adam." Tully shot her a forbidding look and she clamped her mouth closed and looked down.

Tully was sitting on the ground repairing a lawn mower while Doris stood under the grape arbor, plucking and eating the pea-sized unripened Concords.

"What happened?" Adam asked.

"They found out about Tommy. Said they didn't want no killer family working for 'em."

Adam was tempted to tell him that Tommy didn't do it, but he had yet to prove that. He couldn't let anyone else know he had his sights on Conny. "Tell me something, Tully, what made you think Tommy killed Jeannine Bradburn in the first place?"

"'Cause he had the underpants hid in my root cellar."

"Is that the only reason?"

"Ain't that enough?"

"How do you know it was Tommy who hid them?"

"Nobody else goes down my root cellar."

'But,' Adam reasoned, 'they could have. Anyone could have. Even Conny came around to talk to Tully now and again. Conny could have put the underpants there to frame Tully.' He looked around the yard, at the root cellar, at Tully's house, and then at the foundation-house next door beyond the root cellar.

The juxtaposition started him thinking.

"Is Babe home?" Adam asked Doris.

"Na-ow," she answered.

"He's over to Floyd's," Tully added.

"Floyd Mather?"

"Ye-ah," Doris said as though he should know that.

"What for?"

"I dunno."

"He's always over there," Tully explained. "Floyd has him do some work around. Paint, slop hogs, whatever. I don't reckon he does very much. But Floyd hires him during the summer when Babe ain't got any work for Conny."

Adam was instantly on alert. "Babe works for Conny?"

"Conny has the trash contract for the school and Floyd picks up the dumpsters every day and Babe works with him. There's no school in the summer, so there's no work. So Babe works the farm for Floyd. Been doin' it for years."

'That's the connection to Conny,' Adam thought, elated. He had to get to Babe to ask him some questions.

* * *

Julia gasped at seeing Babe with the axe. She lunged into the driver's side of the car, locking the door behind her. Cat started to growl. The little pig huddled on the floor.

She tried frantically to start the engine as she watched Babe's approach in her rear view mirror. Her hand shook. 'Of course it won't start,' she reminded herself. It must have been Babe who cut the wire. 'Oh, God, what do I do now?'

She yelped when Babe suddenly struck at her trunk with the axe, denting it.

As Floyd walked around the car, Cat began snarling. Floyd was now on her side, with Babe on the other, shaking the axe menacingly at her, drool dripping down his chin.

Cat continued to bark and growl fiercely at Floyd, but he just laughed and smacked the palm of his hand against the window.

"Hello again, dog."

Cat tried to bite him through the glass.

Julia hit the horn but there was no sound. And no one to hear it even if it could work. No one knew she was there, no one. Sweat dripped from her neck.

Floyd gestured to Babe, commandingly. "Come here."

Babe immediately went to him and Floyd whispered something in his ear.

"No, I don't wanna," Babe whined in response.

"You do what I tell you. This isn't the place. You wait here until I tell you it's time." Then Floyd walked purposefully toward the back of the house.

Julia shuddered as Babe returned, his face contorted into a temper tantrum. He tried opening each of the doors and grew even more exasperated. He whacked the axe against the car door. Julia jumped in fright and Cat stopped barking for a split second.

Thwarted in his urge to kill Julia right there, right then, Babe circled the car with the axe, swinging it at the hood, the doors, the fenders.

'I've got to stay in control,' Julia told herself, 'no matter what happens.' She took deep breaths and rubbed her eyes. The salty sweat burned. 'I've got to get away.'

But even as she was telling herself that, Floyd was driving his black pick-up truck up the driveway to Julia's car. There was a winch on the front bumper and a rifle in the rear window.

* * *

It was even better than he dreamed, Floyd thought. He had her here and they would have a time with her. Now that he had her, he didn't want the Others to find out. Only Babe knew. He had to move the car out of sight. And then they would party.

He'd have to control Babe. All *he* wanted to do was to chop and quarter. Could only come in her carcass. But Floyd didn't want her dead.

Floyd backed the truck up to the rear of her car. He got out of the cab and saw what Babe had done with his axe.

"You stupid-ass Jucket, not here in the front yard! Can't you wait for a minute? Why do I always have to go through this with you. We've got her. You don't need to smash the car."

"But I want to."

"For Chrissakes, aren't you ever going to learn?" Floyd shouted. Then his voice turned more soothing. "Look, we've got something good here. Real, real good. This one's a full-gown woman. And she's got long hair, all wrapped up, nice long Rapunzel hair. We're going to go nice and slow. We're going to have a good, good time."

He looked in at Julia. "Rapunzel, Rapunzel, let down your magic hair."

Then, calmly, Floyd went about hooking Julia's car onto the tow cable.

* * *

Although terrified, Julia couldn't help thinking that Floyd had the words wrong. It was "let down your *golden* hair." And was long hair his obsession, or Babe's?

As Babe pressed his face full against the window with his mouth open and his tongue out, she shrank back in the opposite direction. She looked around wildly. If she jumped out of the car, how far could she get? Nowhere. Not with Babe there, waiting for her. But if they took her behind the house, out of sight, she was doomed. Terror washed over her as she realized there was no escape.

She heard the clang of the heavy hook locking on her rear bumper. Cat was barking so close to the rear window, she left saliva on it. As the winch tightened the cable, the back of her car slowly rose up from the ground. Higher and higher. Julia slid forward on the seat up against the steering wheel.

Babe climbed onto the back of Floyd's truck and sat in the bed with the axe at his side.

* * *

It all began to make sense to Adam as he drove to Floyd's house. Babe and Conny were linked. That's how Babe got hold of Jeannine's underpants and put them in Tully's root cellar, and how her barrette got into Tommy's hut. Babe must have taken the items from Conny's place.

Without realizing it, he had jammed his foot down on the pedal and was doing sixty-five on a road posted for thirty. As he screeched into a turn, he told himself to slow down.

"There's no rush. Conny doesn't know I've found him out, and Babe will still be at Floyd's when I get there."

* * *

Julia's car rolled inexorably backwards as Floyd began towing it. Her heart pounding, Julia calculated her chances of getting out of the car and running. She put a hand on the door handle but saw Babe reflected in the sideview mirror, palming his axe, and realized she couldn't make it. But she knew Babe couldn't see into the car now that the back end was hoisted up. So she quickly opened the glove compartment and did an inventory. There was the car handbook she never opened. A red scarf. Extra lipstick. A roll of mints. And a screwdriver and pliers. She took out the screwdriver and slid it beneath her thigh. It wasn't much, but it was all she had.

When they circled around to the rear of the house, Floyd stopped the truck. He lowered the car abruptly, letting it bounce. Then he got out and unhooked the tow chain.

Babe jumped down from the truck and walked around the front of Julia's car. He climbed on the hood and sat with his axe, peering in at her.

The most frightening thing to Julia was that she couldn't find any normalcy in that face looking at her.

Nothing to appeal to. No force of reason or compassion. His watery eyes were alight with pleasure.

Julia sensed they were not going to kill her quickly. That they would do everything to her they did to Jeannine Bradburn. And more.

Her breaths came in quick short bursts.

Floyd returned to the cab with a sledgehammer. Coolly, he tapped it against the trunk of Julia's car. Cat renewed her barking, frantically trying to push her way through the window.

With at sudden *Wham!* Floyd struck the windshield. Julia flinched, covering her face with her arm. The force of the hammer broke through the safety glass and made a circle of cracks around the center like a rock thrown on pond ice.

"You see?" Floyd said to Babe. Babe laughed and drooled.

Floyd walked slowly around to the passenger side of the car and leered in at Julia. His face frightened her even more than Babe's mindless glee—the purposefulness of his look, the expectation, his thin lips turned up. He was the dominant one, Babe the submissive. Like body to brain.

Floyd then tapped the passenger-side window lightly with the sledgehammer, teasing in a threatening way. Cat pawed at the window, growling frantically. The two men laughed.

"What'll we do first? What'll we do first?" Babe demanded.

"We're in no hurry," Floyd answered. "Everything counts."

"What's first, though? What's first?"

"First," Floyd said patiently, "we get her out."

While they were temporarily distracted in conversation, Julia swiftly lifted the lock-button on her door. She was going to make a run for it and hoped she could get a few seconds' head start.

'They're going to kill me anyway,' she thought, 'I have nothing to lose.'

She grabbed the handle of the six-inch screwdriver and tried to think where she could stab Floyd badly enough to buy her some time.

Methodically, Floyd moved to the rear window and lifted the sledgehammer over his head. Babe moved out of the way to stand at the driver's side. Julia waited to time her escape with the oncoming blow. Standing alongside her door, Babe was busy watching Floyd.

'Now or never,' she decided.

As the sledgehammer came down onto the rear window, Julia thrust open the door with all her might against Babe.

He stumbled back, lowering his axe. Julia jumped out and plunged the screwdriver into Babe's throat. It went in easily and she left it there. Then she began running without looking behind her to see how seriously she had wounded him.

As soon as Julia was out of the car, Cat leaped out and immediately attacked Floyd as Julia hoped she would. Julia headed towards the woods.

* * *

Floyd kicked at the dog with his foot. But Cat had grabbed onto his leg and would not release it.

"Get her!" Floyd shouted to Babe. But Babe had fallen to his knees, bleeding from the throat.

Floyd swiped at Cat with the sledgehammer and it glanced off her shoulder. She yowled in pain, letting go of his leg and running from him, limping.

Floyd went directly to Babe. He swiftly pulled out the screwdriver and at the same time, pressed a neatly washed and ironed handkerchief against Babe's wound.

"Hold that there. Press hard. I'm going after her."

He pushed Babe's hand hard against the handkerchief at his throat, then went back to the tow truck. Cat growled at him from a safe distance, but did not approach him again.

Floyd grabbed the rifle from the back window and ran towards the woods. He would have shot the dog but didn't want to lose even those few more seconds. His leg was bleeding from where she had bitten him, but he did not feel it.

* * *

Adam heard a dog's distressed barking as he drove into Floyd's driveway. At first, he thought it was the German Shepherd chained to the tree, but it came from behind the house.

Pulling around back he immediately recognized Julia's car, but became instantly alarmed at the smashed windows. Then he saw Babe sitting on the ground, holding a handkerchief to his bleeding throat. Cat was standing on three legs, barking at the woods.

Adam vaulted out of his truck and yelled at Babe.

"Where's Julia?!"

Babe made a gulping motion with his mouth like a fish, but couldn't speak.

"Where's Floyd?"

Involuntarily, Babe's eyes darted towards the woods. Adam quickly began running up the path. Cat limped behind him.

"No, Cat, stay!" Adam commanded and the Golden Retriever reluctantly obeyed.

* * *

Floyd listened carefully to the sound of footsteps moving through the brush. He knew these woods, knew the path she was likely to take, knew where she would leave the path, and where she was likely to hide. He smiled confidently.

He would do this one alone. He let Babe have his way too often. He didn't need to carve her up and eat her heart like the Others. All he wanted was to hold them by the hair and have them scream and struggle. He'd enjoy this one the most.

* * *

Julia ran until she could no longer lift her feet. Her calf muscles spasmed in pain and she seemed to run as slowly as though she were in a dream. She stopped, out of breath. She was making too much noise. She felt like a hunted deer. The sound of her feet crushing the underbrush and leaves was deafening. She had to stop making noise.

She leaned up against a tree and tried to control her breathing. Her tee-shirt was wet with sweat and the pine bark scratched her skin. If she breathed too hard, she was certain he would hear her. If only she could make herself small, disappear under a leaf, crawl into a hole. She couldn't outrun him, he knew these woods too well. She had to find a place to hide. She slipped down to the base of the tree to make herself invisible, trying to decide what to do next, trying to be quiet. There was no point in running. Her legs wouldn't hold.

'Think! Think!' she urged herself, looking around.

Nowhere to hide. Could she climb a tree? Or would he find her? He was a hunter, of course he'd find her. She'd be better off trying to ambush him somehow. He'd have his rifle. What could she do against that? She could wait for him to go by her and jump him. That was her only alternative.

'I've got to find a better place,' she concluded and forced herself up onto her feet. Trying to be silent, she crouched as she moved, looking for a place to catch her pursuer unaware.

* * *

Adam could hear movement in the woods but he couldn't tell if it was Julia or Floyd. He headed in the direction of the sounds, tracking very fast. He didn't worry about Floyd hearing him. He only worried what he would do when he caught up to him if Floyd were armed.

* * *

Julia found an outcropping of boulders and took stock. If she left a trail to the right, he would follow it and pass by underneath. Then she could jump him.

'Jump on him?' she questioned. 'What kind of plan is that?'

But realizing it was her only option, she circled in the direction she wanted him to follow and climbed onto the boulder. She squatted down where she could see a wide angle in front of her and looked around for a rock to hit him with. She found a tree limb the size of a club that would do better. She couldn't escape him, but she could surprise him the way she did Babe. She might catch him from behind.

She waited without moving until she heard him. He made no effort to conceal himself. He was singing.

"I'm gonna git cha, you're gonna love me. I'm gonna get cha, gonna get you...."

She trembled. 'He's spooking me,' she told herself and tried to breathe deeply.

She watched Floyd come into view. He was reading the trail, looking at her tracks, at the leaves brushed aside, the branches turned where she walked through. He observed the boulders, the footprints around to the right. He looked up and beyond.

"Come out. Come out. Come out my pretty kitten, and we'll serenade the moon."

He raised his rifle to his hip.

"You want me to go this way? Alright. I'll do something nice for you and you can do something nice for me."

As he rounded the boulder with his rifle ready, Julia shouted "Now!" and sprang over the top of the rocks, wielding her club.

Just as Floyd looked up to point his rifle, she creased his head with the club and he fell to the ground with a startled groan.

She attempted to hit him again but he turned to his side and put his foot in her stomach and sent her sprawling. He was bleeding from the gash on top of his head and he wiped the blood from his eye with his sleeve. Julia grabbed the club again and immediately hit him with it, this time on his ear.

She raised the club for a final blow but before she could strike again, he had his rifle trained on her heart.

"Don't," he warned.

She wanted to run but she was paralyzed. He looked directly into her eyes and she saw something even more frightening than the madness she's seen earlier. What she saw was comprehension, and something more.

"Stop me, God," he shouted in a controlled voice. "I defy you."

He slowly ran the sight down her torso to her knees.

'Oh, God, he's not going to kill me,' she thought. 'He's going to disable me, then he can do what he wants.' She closed her eyes.

* * *

From a short distance away, Adam heard a shot ring out. A pressure tightened in his chest as he ran towards the sound.

* * *

The rifle fired.

She expected to feel pain. Something. Or nothing, oblivion. But nothing happened. She opened her eyes.

Floyd's body was on the ground. Most of his head was missing. She looked around wildly.

Then Elmer Goodson emerged from behind the trees with his rifle.

* * *

Adam saw Julia standing shock still and Goody toeing Floyd's body with his right foot. He grabbed Julia in his arms.

"Are you all right? Are you okay? Julia?!"

Pressed against him, she murmured "Yes," and held on as though he was the only thing keeping her from hysteria.

"Is he dead?" Adam asked Goody throatily.

"A'course he's dead. I wasn't aimin' to wing him."

"How did you know what was happening?"

"Sounded like a goddam locomotive in here. Couldn't miss it."

Julia, though still shaking, managed to look over at Goody and whisper, "Thank you."

But Goody ignored that and simply turned around and began walking away. "Gotta go get my meal now."

Adam held on to Julia and kissed her forehead and her eyes and her mouth. She leaned her head against his chest, feeling the beating of his heart, its rhythm soothing her.

They stood for a long while holding each other. Then Adam took her hand and they began walking back.

By the time Adam and Julia reached his truck, Carson Burke was in Floyd's yard and the paramedics had arrived. They performed an emergency tracheotomy on Babe to keep him breathing. But as they were putting him into the ambulance, he died.

Julia ran to Cat, who was holding up one leg. Adam gently felt the dog's shoulder. Cat winced.

"It's not broken. Just bruised."

Julia's little piglet had found its way out of the car and nuzzled her ankles.

Adam spoke to Chief Burke. "You'll find Floyd Mather in the woods. No hurry, he's dead."

Burke looked baffled. "You want to tell me what this is all about?"

"Floyd and Babe killed Jeannine Bradburn, and they tried to kill Julia. I came to talk to Babe. What brought you here?"

"Conny Cranshaw came in to find out about taking out a restraining order against you. I talked him out of it, then went to your house to talk to you. When you weren't there, I drove over to Tully's and he said you'd left in a hurry to come here. So I decided to follow you. When I got here I found Babe, and radioed for the ambulance. Then I heard the shot. Who stabbed Babe?"

"I did," Julia replied, "when I escaped."

"Self-defense," Adam said.

Burke nodded. "And who killed Floyd?"

"Fell on his gun," Adam replied.

"Fell on his gun?"

"Happens all the time."

"How about that?" Burke said knowingly. He glanced over at Floyd's house. "Guess I don't need a warrant to go look inside now."

Adam accompanied Burke into Floyd's house. For once, Julia didn't object to being left behind.

Inside, behind a heavy wooden door in the basement, they found a chamber and a stone altar. The altar appeared to be bloodstained.

Along the wall was a series of pegs on which thirteen white robes were hung.

"What the hell's been going on here?" Burke said, incredulously.

* * *

As Julia and Adam sat together in a large armchair in his livingroom that evening, her eyes welled up with tears. She tried to dry them with the back of her hand.

"I guess I'm still a little shaky."

He touched her face and wiped away the tears. "I know." Then he simply held her and she rested against him.

"I think I owe Mr. Goodson a few hot meals." Julia tried to smile.

"Me, too. I came very close to losing you. What were you doing at Floyd's, anyway?"

"He called me to come and get the pig. Oh, Adam, they almost…." She shuddered.

"You're safe now. It's all over."

She blew her nose. "How did you know where I was?"

"I didn't. I was looking for Babe. I thought he might be the one who left Jeannine's underpants in Tully's root cellar. But I had no idea Floyd was involved."

"I think I know what all the girls had in common,' Julia said. "Long hair. Floyd called me Rapunzel. And all the photos of the missing girls showed they had long hair. But I don't think they targeted their victims in advance, so much as looking for girls who were alone."

"And around school. Because Floyd and Babe were there every day, collecting the dumpsters. I thought it was Conny. Conny had the dumpster contract, but Floyd and Babe did the work."

"I didn't know Babe worked there."

"Neither did I."

"I guess we didn't make very good detectives. We missed all the obvious clues," Julia said.

"But you got the most important one. That they were serial murders. And if you hadn't been so adamant about Tommy not being the killer, they'd have kept on doing it."

"So Conny isn't involved. It was just Floyd and Babe then."

"I don't know. I don't know if we'll ever know. There was an altar and what may have been a ritual sacrifice. And thirteen robes."

"Then there are others," she whispered.

"Maybe," he replied softly. "Or maybe it's over now."

"But what happened to the other girls?"

"We found bones in a room behind the altar. In boxes. They're being tested."

"And if they hadn't buried Jeannine in the woods, we may never have known."

Adam nodded. "Because of her bad heart."

Julia's thoughts swirled with unwanted images of the mutilated girls. She buried her head in Adam's chest. They held each other in silence while, in the corner, Cat and the little piglet slept together contentedly.

AUTUMN

SATURDAY, OCTOBER 24th

From an aerial view, Buzzard Bartoncourt thought Pittsley Woods were most beautiful at this time of year. The Fall foliage was at its peak. From this height, the treetops reminded him of a paint-by-numbers landscape, all gold and orange with red daubs of color. The day was bright and crisp, and curls of smoke billowed from the chimneys of the houses in pink-eye village.

Construction on the new concrete plant had been halted. The yellow front-end loaders stood like dinosaurs on exhibit, poised in mid-bite. The dozers were parked end-to-end in a stegosaurus conga line. Buzzard laughed to himself at the mechanical Jurassic Park.

At the edge of the woods, there was a large new sign in orange and black, which read:

Posted—No Trespassing

By order of the E.P.A.

Under that was another sign, with the caption:

Endangered Habitat

Severe penalty if disturbed.

On it was a picture of the red-spotted salamander Adam had discovered.

* * *

A short distance away, the parking lot of the Mayfair was filled with cars. Near the front door, a white Cadillac was decorated with white streamers and bows. A *Just Married* sign was taped to the rear window.

Inside the hall was a crowd of two hundred people in their best party attire, drinking and talking. A hush settled over everyone as the wedding couple stood at the dessert table.

The veiled bride lifted the knife and placed it on the three-tiered wedding cake. The white-tuxedoed groom placed his hand over hers, and together they cut the cake.

As everyone clapped, Cutter Briggs and Angel Kerwin Briggs sweetly turned around and, by custom, mashed a piece of cake in each other's face.

Julia and Adam, Kipper and his secretary, Terri, and Tully and the very pregnant Doris, sat together at one of the tables.

"Cutter looks so dashing," Julia said approvingly. "And Angel looks so…." She couldn't quite think of a word.

"Triumphant?" Terri jibed with a throaty laugh.

"Right."

As Julia smiled at the idea of Cutter married to this formidable wife, she ran her fingers through her new chin-length haircut. She was pleased that Adam liked it, too.

"I hear she comes with a hundred acres," Tully said enviously. "Mostly hardwood."

"She also comes with five kids," remarked Adam.

"That averages about twenty acres per kid," Kipper said facetiously.

Tully lifted his eyes to the ceiling and calculated. "He mighta done better to get a gal with fewer kids and a higher yield."

At that moment, a cheer rose up from the audience as Cutter removed the white lace garter from Angel's fulsome thigh. She coyly protested as though he'd never ventured to that latitude before.

Cutter tossed the garter to his brother, Driver, who tried not to catch it. But the other men of the family wrestled him to the floor and slipped it up his pant leg.

With that, the band—Billy, Tessa, and Billy Jr.—began to play, and Adam invited Julia to dance. On the dance floor, he held her closely, and Kipper and Terri looked almost parentally pleased.

"Quite a turnout of Juckets for a Swamp Yankee wedding," Adam commented.

"You know," Julia eased closer to his chest, "I think I've discovered what that word really means."

"Oh?"

"Want me to tell you?"

"Suit yourself."

"You just can't stand it, can you? All right, never mind."

He swung her around the dance floor until she was dizzy and laughing. "Okay, okay, I'll tell you. I should have thought of it long before. Me, with my French Canadian grandparents."

"French?"

"Yes, I'm pretty sure the word is 'jacquet.' With all the French Canadians around here, it just has to be. They would have called them 'jacquets.' Squirrels."

Adam considered it. "Because we live like squirrels. And we eat squirrels. And maybe we're a little squirrelly, at that. Makes sense. Whether it's right or not." Then he added, "I wouldn't tell anybody else though."

"No, that's just for us. Besides," she smiled as she ran her hand around the back of his neck, "I like Juckets."

"Even Tully?"

"Well, 'like' might be a bit strong," she said as they did a loop around the dance floor. "But I think I understand him better now." Then, she added, "Speaking of Tully, Dr. Sam told me Tommy's going to be transferred soon. To a rehab facility."

"That's good," Adam said. "But where does that leave you?"

"I'm going to continue at the hospital—at least while there's still room for therapy as an adjunct to drug treatment. I should have my license by the end of December."

"Does that mean you're staying in Pittsley?"

She flashed another smile at him. "If you're lucky."

Then one of the crowd called out "*Kaw-li-ga!*" and Billy struck up the first notes on his fiddle. Tessa joined in on banjo, and Billy Jr. on base guitar.

The Juckets began to clog and Adam and Julia moved to the side to watch and clap time with everyone else.

As the rhythm mounted, old Elgin Bradburn got up on the table and began to dance. Faster and faster went his hands and feet. Louder and louder the audience clapped. Then, at the crest of the music, on the final crescendo of "*KAW-LI-GA!*," old Elgin soared headfirst off the table.

-The End-

Swamp Yankees

SPRING

MONDAY, MAY 31st (Memorial Day)

"I hate you," she whispered hoarsely over the bronze gravemarker that lay like a fallen soldier amidst the taller granite headstones.

The sun gradually illuminated the forgotten corner of the cemetery where the young woman knelt in front of the solitary plaque. She brushed away the twigs and wet leaves, revealing the inscription—"*Nicole M. Fayette, 1956-1980.*" It didn't say "cherished wife" or "loving mother" or "dear daughter." There were no cherubs, no weeping roses, no scrollwork, not even a flourish on the initials. The tendrils of Spring grass that framed it, in the coming months would thicken and all but obscure the name again.

She barely remembered her mother now, after so many years. She had been, after all, only a child of five at the time.

"Eeee-a, Eee-a, Eeee-a." The piercing call of the Red Shouldered hawk sounded like a banshee. She looked up to watch it circling overhead. Some small rabbit or field mouse would soon be snatched out of the grass by sharp talons and borne to a treetop. Would the predator make a swift kill? A momentary shock followed by oblivion for the prey? Was that how it happened?

She sat back on her heels and pulled her straight blonde hair behind her ears. The dampness soaked through her jeans onto her shins as she tugged at the new growth to make a moat around the edges of the plaque.

Her grandparents were buried here as well, but she did not visit their graves. They had lied to her for years. "Your mother was in a car accident," Grandma told her.

"Your father died in Vietnam." She was fifteen before she found out the truth. How could so many people keep such a secret for so long?

She had had no reason to doubt them, not until her first date with skinny Mark Robison. After the basketball game, he walked her home and awkwardly tried to kiss her goodnight. "I don't care what they say about your mother," he confided. "I really like you, Sherry."

"What do you mean?" she asked. "What about my mother?"

He looked startled, as though he had stepped on a garter snake, and did not answer.

"What do you mean about my mother?"

"Nothing," he said, and pulled back from her. "I'm sorry. I have to go." He turned and left abruptly without another word.

The following day, she went to see her Aunt Doreen, her mother's closest friend.

A light breeze stirred through the leaves of the trees and lifted strands of hair off her face. She thought about that September Sunday when they buried the small metal box of her mother's ashes. She never thought it strange that so few mourners were there. Only Grandma and Grandpa Fayette and Aunt Doreen. She'd worn the same yellow dress she wore to kindergarten the previous week. The same dress she'd worn two-and-a-half months before that, on her fifth birthday. The dress her mother called her sunshine dress but never saw her wear, for a birthday party she never had.

"Happy birthday to me, happy birthday to me—" she began. But her eyes filled with tears and her voice choked. She heaved a sigh, then slowly and deliberately put both hands up to her face. She sunk her nails into her skin and pulled downward until four parallel tracks of blood trickled over her cheeks. She meant to go deeper, but it was so painful. Then she took out a serrated knife from her pocket and cut quickly across each of her wrists.

"Eeee-a, Eeee-a."

As she looked up, she saw the hawk gliding on the thermals like a big beautiful kite. In the air, on the breezes, with her astride.

SUNDAY, JUNE 6th

Cutter Briggs was in high octaves.

"The building inspector said I needed a permit. I told him I don't need permission from anydamnbody to do whatever I want in my own home on my own land. And if anybody thinks otherwise, I'll show them what No Damn Trespassing means!"

As Cutter leaned forward across the wooden-spool table in Adam Sabeski's livingroom, Billy Jensen nodded vigorously. Although unable to see Cutter's blazing aquamarine eyes, Billy nodded corroboration. In the ten or so years since he'd moved to Pittsley, the changes, Billy said, were "visible even to a blind man like me." He'd recently had his own problems in getting a permit to remodel his garage into a music studio (for himself and his wife, Tessa, and son Billy Jr. to rehearse and record). Billy's sympathies clearly lay with Cutter.

But for Adam it had been a morning of emergencies in his veterinary clinic downstairs and he was tired. He'd made several house calls even before opening his office, to treat a goat with an ulcerated udder and a horse with a fistula. When he got back to his clinic, there was a dog hit by a car, another with a lacerated footpad, and a cat with a torn ear from an altercation with another tom. That was for starters and it continued that way throughout the morning. All he wanted now was to sit back in his threadbare overstuffed armchair with a tumbler of Portuguese red wine and some superficial Sunday-afternoon conversation about motors, gardens, or the weather. As usual, however, Cutter wasn't about to comply.

"No town asswipe is going to tell me what to do with what's legally mine." He pulled on his black beard so hard his bottom lip drooped, revealing alpine sharp teeth.

Cutter's sawmill in the raw end of Pittsley Woods

was the hub of his extended family—five brothers and two sisters and their families, all of whom lived contiguous to each other. Most of them had worked for the lumber mill for over twenty years, before and after Cutter took it over from his father. In all that time, the only thing that ever changed was the saw blade. Then, a year ago, Cutter married the widow Angel Kerwin and acquired five stepchildren with his bride. Plus another hundred acres adjoining his own. But he refused to live in her split-level house (where people could actually watch you come and go or take a piss in the front yard), so they sold off the house lot and kept the rest of the land. The only practical housing solution, then, was to expand his two-room log cabin to accommodate his new family. It seemed like he hardly got it started when somebody official noticed.

"How in bloody hell did they even find out what I was doing? I'm in the middle of a couple a hundred acres of woods and swamp. Is this goddam America, or isn't it? It's a sad day for democracy when these local gumballs know all your business."

"Not only that," Billy vigorously concurred, "but our taxes went up again. I'm paying almost double what I paid when I first moved here."

'Here," was the small rural town of Pittsley. A place with roots back to Massasoit and John Alden that had managed to cleave to its country ways almost into the twenty-first century. A place in southeastern Massachusetts where the names of the town fathers and mothers still harked back to The Mayflower and The Fortune, the first two ships of English settlers in the Bay Colony. But the past two decades had brought rapid expansion and change in exponential numbers. Pittsley had become a desirable community for commuters to Boston, for the Mayflower Bank and the Mayflower Mall, and for contractors to make their own Fortunes.

"They're driving us out, is what they're doing. Half the guys I know have left for Maine or West Virginia. They don't want to live in Taxachusetts anymore. But hell, you have to go practically up to the Canadian border to find any kind of peace. And it's not just happening here. It's everydamnwhere. We're losing all our freedom, our privacy, our independence. Losing it to greedy-eyed bureaucrats."

Adam nodded perfunctorily, knowing that Cutter prided himself on being the town boil. But in theory, he agreed. There were too many restrictions on everything these days. He could put up with some of them if he had to, and skirt the others when necessary. But Cutter was a different breed.

"They aren't getting a penny more out of me. They can send all the demands they want."

"But if you don't pay your real estate tax," Billy said with alarm, "they'll take your land."

"The hell they will. I'm not paying their taxes, I'm not paying their fines, and I'm not going down on my knees in front of any town board." Cutter slapped his rough hands on the table. "I'm seceding."

* * *

It was nearly six o'clock when the last patient of the day appeared at the door. This was Julia's rotation weekend at Bridgewater State Psychiatric Hospital where she'd been working for the past year.

The year had gone by quickly but she was still the newest member of staff with the most weekend rotations and the least desirable office. The psychiatrists got the larger offices; the psychologists, like her, got smaller ones. She suspected it had actually been a file room. But she was allowed, at her own expense, to repaint and refurnish. From institutional green, she changed the walls to the color of tea, and covered the black woodwork with cream-colored paint. She replaced the old green window-shade with venetian blinds and she'd searched the hospital basement for matching almond-colored files and swapped them for the broken grey ones that were leftover in the corner of the room. Then she added a tan Berber carpet and polished the old oak desk and chairs until they were clean of grime the consistency of glue. With the final touches—a mix plants on the file cabinets, a small clock, an old-fashioned blotter on the desk, and pastoral landscapes on the wall—she felt she'd staged the office to be more welcoming.

At home, she preferred bright breezy colors. Primary reds and deep purples. Royal blue and gold. Yellow and tangerine. But in her office, she wanted to reduce the contrasts, mute the extremes. She told herself it was for her patients, but she knew it was equally for herself. To quiet her own extremes, reduce her own contrasts. Julia Arnault was still putting her life together after a contentious marriage, a career change from professor of psychology to practitioner, and the upheaval of her post-divorce move from Boston to Pittsley two years ago.

"Come in, Cheryl. I'm Dr. Arnault."

"I prefer Sherry."

Julia glanced up briefly and motioned the young woman to a chair.

"Sit down, Sherry."

Julia noted the time, marked it on the interview form, then put down the chart and removed her reading glasses. She began wearing them two months ago and was still self-conscious about it.

As Julia shifted her feet, the Golden Retriever under the desk rolled onto her side and yawned. Cat, short for Catastrophe, was disinterested in the office visitors unless she sensed tension in her mistress. There was none as the young woman took a seat on the other side of the desk.

"How are you feeling today?"

Cheryl Fayette had been admitted directly from the hospital after a graveworker discovered her on the grounds of the cemetery, unconscious and bleeding.

"How do I look?" Sherry said tauntingly, "Pretty in pink?"

The chart stated that Cheryl had cut her wrists and mutilated her face with her fingernails. 'Mutilated was perhaps an overstatement,' Julia thought. Yes, there had been deep scratches on Sherry's pretty face, but they were beginning to scab over and fade.

"If you don't pick at the scabs, you probably won't have any permanent scars," Julia replied.

But as she widened her field of vision, Julia observed fresh fingernail gouges bleeding down the young woman's arms below the green cotton hospital gown to the top of her bandaged wrists.

"What happened to your arms?"

"The attendant did it," Sherry said flatly.

Julia was instantly on alert, but she kept her voice neutral. "Which attendant?"

"The big Hawaiian guy."

"When did this happen?"

"Just now. On the way up from the ward."

Julia reached for the phone. "Let's take care of your wounds first."

She dialed the in-house number and instructed the administrator to send up a nurse with a first-aid kit. Then she sat back and regarded her patient.

"Why would the attendant scratch your arms, Sherry?"

"He tried to rape me."

Julia studied the pretty twenty-nine year-old. Sherry was tall with shoulder-length blonde hair and bangs. This was her fourth admission in ten years, but the first time as Julia's patient. Each time, she'd had a different therapist. The first therapist was male and she'd accused him of trying to rape her. When they switched to female therapists, she'd accused the ward attendants of trying to rape her. With each admission, she stayed only until they transferred her out of a locked ward. Then she simply walked away.

"Keoki tried to rape you between the ward and my office?"

"Yes."

It didn't take much insight for Julia to recognize that Sherry had been assigned to her as a challenge for the new psychologist on the block. Julia's transition from assistant professor at Pittsley Community College to clinical psychologist at the state hospital was recent, but she'd been given a thorough immersion in psychopathology. At forty-seven, she was a lot older than most of Dr. Sam's trainees and had a lot of catching-up to do. On the other hand, her age worked for her with certain patients.

Julia picked up the phone again and dialed the ward, disguising the urgency she felt.

"This is Dr. Arnault. Could you please tell me what time was Ms. Fayette signed out to me?"

After the response, she hung up the telephone and feigned reading the chart without her glasses.

"Well, I guess I'll have to change your diagnosis from manic-depression to paranoid schizophrenia, won't I?" She took her pen and pretended to cross out something on the page.

As Sherry caught her meaning, she sputtered, "You don't believe me?"

"And that will be a very different course of treatment." Julia continued without inflection. "As well as a different prognosis. I think we'll start with ECTs. That's electro-convulsive therapy."

"I know what it is," Sherry snapped.

Julia looked up at her expectantly. "Then do you want to tell me why you just scratched your own arms, Sherry?"

The young woman stared without responding, her brown eyes large and penetrating.

"Did you think," Julia continued calmly, "I wouldn't take you seriously because your other cuts are healing?"

The patient flinched.

After treating and bandaging Sherry's arms, the ward nurse straightened up and Julia saw the weary look in Harriet Kern's eyes. Nurse Kern had been at the hospital long enough to recognize a bad situation, Julia thought. Obviously, Keoki had nothing to do with Sherry's cut arms. But somebody was going to have a lot of explaining to do. It was going to generate a lot of paperwork and hopefully the hospital's liability insurance would cover any lawsuit. Clearly, Cheryl Fayette should have been on restraint, even while being transferred to her psychologist's office. That would have been a ward responsibility. There would be an investigation and it would likely be the next subject of Grand Rounds.

"Do you want to go back to the ward with Nurse Kern and see me later?" Julia asked Sherry. "Or do you want to stay and talk?"

"Let's get it over with," Sherry replied, pursing her lips.

After Harriet left, Julia settled back in her chair.

"This is your fourth admission, Sherry. What's going on?"

"Life."

'Okay,' Julia thought, 'the standard bullshit answer.'

"What about life?" she asked.

"Everything."

'Is it bigger than a breadbox?' Julia wanted to ask, but restrained herself. She needed to know the game before playing along.

"Such as?"

"Did you ever plant a garden, Dr. Arnault?" Sherry said in a voice that sounded, to Julia, rather patronizing.

"Flowers or vegetables?" Julia replied in a like tone.

"It doesn't matter."

That, at least, sounded sincere. And Julia had, in fact, spent yesterday planting cartons of multicolored pansies around the borders of her perennial garden. She tried to make the garden bloom from May through September. A week earlier, she had divided and replanted yellow and white tulip and daffodil bulbs in one section, and put in some more tubers of pale pink dahlias and deep pink peonies in another. The back section was all purple iris, foxglove, and deep blue clematis. In the front, by her porch, she had filled the beds with climbing red roses. She thought of the cold moist soil and the feel of her stretched back as she pressed the pansies into the earth. She didn't wear gloves, and dirt caked under her fingernails and roughed up the skin of her forefingers. She involuntarily rubbed her thumb across the first knuckle of her left forefinger where the skin had broken and was painful to the touch.

She'd been instructed never to give any personal information to patients. But this time, she felt there was something to be gained.

"Yes," she answered truthfully, "I have a flower garden."

"Wow," Sherry said facetiously. "My last shrink said something like 'I ask the questions.' I figured you're not allowed to let the patients think that you exist outside this building."

"I *have* a flower garden," Julia repeated.

Sherry nodded. "Then you know how some plants thrive, and some don't. Even in the same garden. Maybe even under the same conditions. Some just don't."

"I have found," Julia responded deliberately, "that there is generally a reason. Whether it's the way the bulb is conditioned, or how the water runs off, or if some insect or cutworm finds its way to one rather than another. There are reasons. Even if it's by chance."

"Sometimes…by chance?" Sherry repeated. "Is it really chance? Or is it a confluence of events?"

"Yes," Julia agreed without showing her surprise, "a confluence of events. Causes unknown or so complex, that we can't comprehend all of them. So we might say chance."

'Whoa,' Julia thought. 'I've got to be careful here. She is smart and she's testing me. But I can't let this waft into some philosophical discussion. I've got to put legs on it.'

"The point is," she continued, "there are reasons for things that happen, whether we understand them or not. Perhaps I phrased the question incorrectly. Rather than ask you what is happening, let me restate it. What is the reason for your four admissions to this facility, Sherry?"

"Each and every one?"

"All right, let's talk about what brought you here this time. What were you doing in the cemetery?"

"I thought it would be easier on everybody if I died where I could be buried," Sherry said flippantly.

"Easier on whom?"

"You shrinks are so humorless."

"Why *that* cemetery?"

Julia tried not to sound irritated, although she was. Her patient made her feel like she had to prove that she wasn't humorless. But she couldn't. Score another point for Sherry.

"Why not?" Sherry said.

"You live in Brockton, not Sipponet." Julia knew Sipponet Village. It was the next town over from where she lived in Pittsley. It was about a forty-minute drive from Brockton.

"I like the neighborhood and decided to move in. It's quiet and it's pretty and I know people there."

"Who?"

"Dead people."

"What dead people, in particular?"

"Just people I knew."

"And you wanted to join them?"

"Something like that."

"And yet," Julia said, "you didn't cut yourself quite hard enough to make it happen."

Sherry opened and closed her mouth and then stared at her. "Are you allowed to say things like that? Aren't you supposed to be nicer?"

"Yes, and we've all seen how well that's worked."

Sherry tilted her head and looked at Julia with renewed interest. Julia decided to take advantage of it.

"Aren't you tired of being hospitalized?" Wrong question, Julia immediately told herself. "Or do you like it here?" Julia amended, looking for a reaction. "Because it's easier than being out there?"

Julia inclined her head towards the window and when she looked back at her patient, the young woman was chewing on her lips.

"Why don't you tell me what you're thinking, Sherry?"

As Julia sat silently and waited, Sherry fidgeted.

"I've been through all of this before. It's all in my chart."

"All right, then, tell me something new. We'll only deal with things you haven't said before. How about that?"

"There's nothing new to say."

"You haven't said why you scratched your face. That's new. Did it give you pleasure?"

"No."

"Then why?"

"I don't like my face."

"You're very attractive. I'm sure you know that. Why don't you like your face?"

"It belongs to my mother."

"You mean you look like her?"

"*Looked*. She's dead."

"So I see by your chart."

"And does it say in the chart how she died?" Sherry asked with an edge to her voice.

"It says she died in a car accident."

"And just because it's in there, you think it's true?"

Suddenly, it was Julia's turn to flinch.

"Isn't it?" she asked after taking a breath.

"Where do you think that information came from?" Sherry said disdainfully.

"Are you saying you lied?"

Sherry got up from the chair. "I think I'll go back to the ward after all. My arms hurt and I don't feel like talking any more. Call me a cab, will you?"

She couldn't make Sherry stay. And she *had* given her a sort of permission to leave. That was stupid. But now Julia had no alternative.

"All right," she replied. "But this time you'll wear your seat belt."

Sherry arched her eyebrows as Julia phoned for another attendant and instructed him to bring restraints for the transfer.

After her patient left, Julia felt a little lightheaded. She had completely lost control of the interview. Her patient had outflanked her several times. And yet, she felt she had made a tenuous connection with Sherry. Plus, she may have learned something useful—Sherry had lied about her mother's death. Julia didn't know whether to be angry with herself for being incompetent or grateful for dumb luck.

* * *

"I can live off my own land without sucking from the State tit."

"If anyone can, Cutter, *you* can," Billy said thickly.

By now, all three men had had several tumblers of moonshine. Meeting at Adam's house was a Sunday afternoon ritual. Frequently, others might stop in and the group would swell to four, five, or six. But the three friends, dissimilar in many ways, were at the core. Adam would make a pot of chowder or vegetable stew; Billy would bring Tessa's homemade desserts; Cutter would bring his home brew. Usually, they got a little drunk.

"Damn right I can. I got everything I need. Good water. Endless wood for cooking and heating. We've already got beans coming and we planted a whole bunch of seedlings that Angel started in the house two months ago. We'll have plenty of vegetables for eating and canning. There's always game in the woods, fish in the brook, and I've got a generator to run the sawmill. I'll just trade off some logs for fuel. That's the way they used to do it. Live by barter. I don't need nothing from no politicians and they ain't getting nothing from me."

"But it's not just you anymore, Cutter. You've got five kids to think about now," Adam cautioned.

"Angel's going to home-school them. She wants to. She's behind me one hundred and ten percent."

"I hear the government takes a pretty dim view of secession," Adam commented wryly. "Something to do with the Civil War, I think."

"The Briggs were here long before any Civil War. My mother's family were renegades for over three hundred years from Maine to Massachusetts, with some Wampanoags along the way. My father's family were all Swamp Yankees, with a couple a Wampanoags thrown in there too, probably. My grandfather-times-seven," Cutter counted seven greats on his fingers, "was Malbone Briggs. And he was the most famous highwayman and horse thief in all New England. Him and his seven sons were all in Charlestown jail at one time or another in the 1800s. Malbone and one of his sons was hung together. Their graves are no more than a hundred feet from my house. Our family ain't never been on good relations with authority."

"That's an understatement," Adam said.

"Things are more complicated now," Billy said, becoming expansive from the red wine. "There has to be regulation of some things to protect the citizenry. Somebody's got to watch out they don't fill in wetlands, or let a septic system overflow into the aquifer. Doctors need to be licensed to perform heart surgery, and meat that's sold in supermarkets can't be putrid. But that's the big stuff. It's all the little stuff that government does, that's like sand in our mouth. Did you know," he said rhetorically, with the hellfire conviction of a Bible-thumping minister, "that the town now requires all cars to face the same direction at the gas pumps? It's a law. You can't face the opposite direction even if your gas tank is on the opposite side. Who in the name of sanity thought that one up? I mean, is there *anything* that we do anymore that isn't subject to some kind of restrictions? We've just become so used to it, we don't even notice half the time. Death by a thousand cuts."

It was a mild source of amusement for Adam that Billy could get so riled up about which way the cars faced at the pump when, because of his blindness, Tessa did all the driving.

"That's what I'm saying," Cutter said emphatically. "What it *is*, is that government is so busy trying to regulate the bad people, it doesn't let the good ones alone."

This time, Adam nodded in agreement.

* * *

"Got a minute, Sam?"

Julia poked her head in the open door to Dr. Shing Wu's office. He nodded and motioned her inside. It may have been her rotation weekend, but Sam seemed to be here all the time.

"What's up, Julia?"

Sam had the habit, when speaking with colleagues, of taking off his wire-rimmed glasses and cleaning the lenses with his pocket-handkerchief. Julia didn't think he did it with patients.

"Cheryl Fayette," Julia said as she sat down across from him.

Sam nodded. "Recidivist."

His lenses cleaned, he delicately placed them back on his nose and eased the arms over his ears. He had manicured nails. In fact, Julia concluded, he was impeccable. His hair was always perfectly cut, his shoes were never scuffed, and his suits were crisply pressed beneath the open starched white lab-coat. She, on the other hand, was usually disheveled. Long work days, too much reading, not enough sleep, and little enough time to think about looking chic. Today she wore a white blouse that she just had cleaned but hung into an overcrowded packed closet. The wrinkles didn't show under her lab coat. She'd caught the hem of her cotton skirt on her heel walking down the front stairs and she'd had to scotch-tape it up when she got to the office. The best thing she'd done was to keep her hair short so it didn't require maintenance. But her pearl nailpolish was wearing off at the tips. She hid her hands below the desktop as she talked.

"I just had a session with her. She gouged both her arms on the way up to my office and claimed Keoki tried to rape her. I had Mrs. Kern treat her, but I expect there will be repercussions. I'm not sure how Keoki didn't see it, but Sherry's very good at hiding things."

"Yes, I've already had Harriet's report. I spoke with Keoki. He thinks she probably did it on the ward just before he went to get her, and concealed it. He noticed that she was holding her arms crossed, but he didn't think anything more about it. Not his fault. She'd been taken off restraint. That's the problem we have to look into."

"There's something else," Julia said. "I went back over her hospital records. When I looked at the dates, I realized that the four times Sherry was admitted were all right around this time of year."

"Really? Hmmm. I don't know why we didn't make that connection. Good work."

"I think it might have something to do with her mother."

"Why do you think that?"

At Sam's expectant look, she continued hesitantly, "We actually don't know what happened to Sherry's mother and father, do we? I mean, independent of her own explanation?"

"No. Although when I reviewed the chart on her admission, I noticed her mother was unmarried. The daughter was raised by her grandparents. No information on the father. Why do you ask?"

"She implied that what she's told us wasn't entirely true."

"She admitted she lied?"

"Not outright. But she's giving me clues."

Sam looked at her with a reserved expression. "She seems to be relating to you."

"I hate to acknowledge it, but—age and vanity aside—she might be associating me with her mother."

Sam removed his glasses again and massaged the bridge of his nose while he was thinking.

"That could be helpful," Julia offered.

"It also could be a double-edged sword."

"I know. And I wouldn't ordinarily do this, but I think I should find out more about her mother. We don't even know if she's actually dead. I think I need some independent verification, if I can get it."

"You want to do some research."

"Yes."

"And you're asking me if I think it's a good idea?" Sam put his glasses back on and his boyish eyes disappeared behind the thick lenses.

"Yes."

"Well I don't."

Julia pursed her lips. Sam was younger than her by several years, and *looked* even younger. She resisted the impulse to contradict him. Instead, she said, "I know it's the patient's perceptions that are important. But there's something going on here that I feel she wants me to find out."

"Then you're playing her game."

"I suppose," Julia sighed.

"You suppose but you're not convinced. Why do I get the feeling you're not listening to me?"

"No, I am. I'm listening."

Sam leaned forward towards her. "Then I'm advising—no, I'm *directing* you not to get involved in any outside research. Just treat the patient. We all—and you, in particular, Julia—need to maintain objectivity. You're still in training. And you can't relate to patients the way you would to your college students."

She nodded in reluctant acquiescence.

* * *

Adam had been waiting in Dottie's Restaurant since 7:30 pm, but it was it was nearly 8:30 by the time Julia got there. He watched her scan the red vinyl booths and spot him sitting in a corner with a partially eaten pizza on the marbled-grey Formica tabletop.

"You look frazzled," he greeted her as she reached the booth. "Tough day?"

"I'm sorry I'm so late," she said, sliding onto the bench across from him and removing her navy blazer. Her white cotton blouse was damp with perspiration and she pulled at it to cool herself, then brushed her hand up over her forehead, fingering her short chestnut hair. As she lifted her arm, her blouse stretched taut over her breast and he felt a familiar desire to caress it.

"I got caught up in work this afternoon. And then I took Cat home, and it's so weirdly hot today that I tried to put on the a.c. in the car, but it needs Freon, so I made an appointment for next week and, I don't know, yes, it's been a tough day."

"I figured as much. Do you want something besides pizza?"

"I wish Dottie would get a liquor license, but no, I'll have iced tea and the pizza will be fine. What's that, linguica?" She fingered a slice with the spicy ground sausage.

"That was my half. Yours is anchovy. Never thought I'd go steady with a girl who likes anchovies," he grinned.

"Is that what we're doing, going steady? And are you going to take me to the hop after we have milkshakes?"

Adam reached for her hand across the table. "No, let's run away to some remote island instead. And go bollocky-bare-ass in the ocean."

As Julia smiled indulgently at him, Dottie magically appeared in all her agile bulk.

"Okay, you two, quit holding hands or you'll give this place a bad reputation. What do you want to drink, hon?"

Julia ordered iced tea and a side salad and leaned back while he told her all about Cutter's plans to secede from Pittsley.

"Isn't that a little drastic? Couldn't he just work on reforming the by-laws or something?"

Adam shook his head. "He's been trying that for the past twenty years. Besides, it isn't just the town. It's what's happening at the state and national level of government, too. It's good old civil disobedience," he concluded.

"In Cutter's case," she retorted, "it's more like civil defiance."

"Whatever it is, he's just wound up enough to try it."

"It's just talk, though, isn't it? He wouldn't actually go through with it."

But hearing her say that aloud made him realize how possible it was. Cutter was a man whose societal veneer ran very thin.

"In a way, I hope he does."

"Why?" Julia asked and he could see she was surprised.

"Because not everyone can do that. And maybe it needs to be done."

"What needs to be done? Breaking laws?"

"Don't you sometimes feel that we're regimented to death these days?"

"I haven't really thought about it. Is that what *you* think?" she asked clinically.

"At times," he answered seriously. "Maybe that's why we need to climb mountains, take to the sea, go into the desert. We can only stomach so much."

He didn't tell her, but once, years ago, he'd had his own ideas about living alone in the woods, like his old friend Elmer Goodson. Except, of course, that Goody wasn't above receiving occasional handouts and meals-on-wheels. But the first summer Adam was back from Vietnam, he'd gone into Pittsley Woods without a rifle, vowing never to shoot anything ever again. He built a lean-to and ate roots and berries, Indian nuts, wild potatoes, and spent his days walking through the bush. He reveled in the variety of the sounds and smells, the infinite colors of green, the scurrying animals. He was never lonely. Solitude was exactly what he wanted.

But as the Summer went on, he lost weight and began to find himself hungry all the time. As the days went on, he began to dream about food and have nightmares about starving. Finally, one desperate Autumn night, he tracked an opossum. He was obsessed with the need to eat something hot and solid and bloody, he didn't care what. It was only after he'd killed the animal with a rock that he realized she had babies. From the dead mother, he gathered up the tiny pink-skinned bodies in his hands and held them warm to his chest as they stopped breathing, and he wept.

That was the Summer Adam realized that while he couldn't live completely within society, he couldn't live completely outside it. And that was the Summer he decided to become a veterinarian.

"This isn't a prelude to seceding with Cutter, is it?" she said interrupting his thoughts.

"Not me," he answered facetiously. "But Billy might."

"Not if Tessa has anything to say about it," Julia added knowingly.

She reached over and held his hand this time, just as Dottie returned.

"Will you guys take it to a motel?" said the waitress amiably. Dottie was past middle-age and her hair had been dyed from white to the color of lemon Jell-o.

"Jealous?" Adam bantered. "I know you want me."

"Honey, I'm way too much woman for the likes of you." As she set down the salad and iced tea, she said to Julia in a mock whisper, "Don't ever let him think he's the one and only, sweetie. You got to keep a man like that on his toes." She nodded for emphasis and swiveled her fulsome backside as she walked away.

Julia laughed and Adam sensed that it was for the first time that day.

* * *

Later that night, she couldn't sleep. Julia lay naked and quiet in Adam's arms until finally he gently disentangled her and rolled over onto his side. They had made love with a passion she hadn't experienced in a long time. Usually, she waited for Adam to initiate sex, but this time she was the aggressor. She had pressed up against him as soon as they entered the house, thrusting her hips at him and kissing him hard and long. Wordlessly he carried her to bed and they coupled like strangers. There were no sounds beyond pleasured moans, no thoughts beyond urgency. Only afterwards did they become themselves again, with tender touches and murmurs. She loved the smell of him and the comfort of his long, lean body next to her. But when he turned away and his breathing became regular and deep, she felt isolated again. If only she had fallen asleep first, she wouldn't have to feel so alone.

MONDAY, JUNE 7th

Julia knew she should take Sam's advice. But she just couldn't.

Since she wasn't scheduled to see any more patients this afternoon, she'd made up her mind to drive into Boston to the Massachusetts Registry of Vital Records and Statistics. Sam couldn't order her what to do on her own time. Could he?

It was warm again, warm enough to put on the air conditioner in her car if it had been working. But, it wasn't. It was going to be a long, hot ride. She turned her radio to Classical 99.5. Ah, Vivaldi. Cool.

The Registry was located on the site of the Bayside Expo in Dorchester. Driving up Route 24 to I-93, she realized that she hadn't been on the Southeast Expressway since the Big Dig was completed and the X-way was rebuilt. She had lived in Boston for over twenty years and it felt strange to be driving a road she'd once known so well and that now seemed unfamiliar. She was alert for the new exits, the new signs in new places, uncertain she was taking the right lane for her destination. It seemed to characterize her life.

When she turned off at Exit 15 onto Columbia Road, she was struck with the difference between Boston's inner-city and New York City, where she had often visited when her daughter, Karen, was living there. Yes, in both places the names of the stores advertised a diversity of ethnicities, and yes there was the urban trash on the sidewalks waiting to be picked up, and indiscriminate trash in front of some houses that would never be picked up—but here there were little patches of grass in front of the rows of triple-deckers, and the street was wide with a centerstrip. It seemed to her more livable than New York, with more horizon and less concrete.

But despite that, Boston was as unlike where she lived now as it was from New York.

In a way, when Julia first moved to Pittsley, she felt like *she* had seceded. From Boston and city life, anyway. Not to mention her ex-husband. It was a little foreign at first, and it definitely felt like she had dropped out. But now, finally, she felt she belonged. But just because she had transformed, had she failed to see what was transforming around her?

The population of Pittsley had doubled in a decade. Sons and daughters of long-time farmers were splitting up their parents' land into smaller, lucrative building lots. Developers were sending form letters to all the homeowners in town asking if they wanted to sell or if they knew of anyone who did. Newbies (the new residents) were clamoring for a town center, replete with park benches, strolling sidewalks, and streetlights. New schools, new library, new police station, new senior center. Progress. Nothing different from a million other rural towns being suburbanized across America.

But the more suburban it became, the more intolerant of deviation it became, too. There were 'eyesore by-laws' voted in at the town meeting. Well, of course, if you build a look-at-me house, you don't want your neighbor's slovenly yard running down the value of your re-sale. It all made sense, and yet there was something perverse about it. In a way, she understood what Cutter was protesting. It was sad that there were fewer and fewer places to live without restrictions. But what was important, Julia decided, was to hold onto what they had.

Pittsley, however, was not the hub of the universe. It wasn't even the hub of southeastern Massachusetts. There was no diverse racial palette, as when she lived on Beacon Street. Nor was there any great cultural or economic diversity. She had twinges of guilt about that. But Pittsley had trees, forests, ponds, bogs, starry skies. Of course it had all the vanities, frailties, honor, and altruism as any other human community. Just not quite as ubiquitous. 'Density exaggerates everything,' she concluded as she turned onto

William Day Boulevard and headed towards the Bayside Expo complex, North Entrance.

Inside the Registry, she signed the visitor's book before entering the public research room. It was smaller than she'd expected, no larger than a small classroom. It was filled with several long tables and stacks of books.

A pleasant clerk with long dreadlocks explained that records since 1980 were computerized; preceding years had to be looked up manually. Julia sat at the only available computer and clicked on "Deaths."

It came up within seconds: Nicole Marie Fayette. Date of death: 1980. Record number: 054287. Age: 24. Cause of death code: 9689. Never Married. No occupation. Parents: Walter and Winifred Fayette. Cremated 10/25/80.

Julia submitted the record number and name to the clerk with long dreadlocks in order to call up the death certificate. She waited her turn, eyeing the other men and women in the room. All six computers were in use by people focused solely and possessively on their screens. More than a dozen others walked hurriedly back and forth between the tables and the stacks of books, looking up record codes. She would like to have asked each of them their business there today. They all seemed so purposeful. Some were probably medical researchers—Boston was rife with epidemiological studies. Some might have been from insurance agencies. Some perhaps were tracing family genealogies. She felt sure that she was the only one there on research that her supervisor told her *not* to do.

The clerk wheeled in a cart of books with the request slips stuck in each volume. He nodded helpfully at Julia and pointed to a particular book. She carried it to a table and turned to record #054287.

The death certificate indicated that Nicole Fayette was found off Pondview Avenue in Sipponet Village and pronounced dead September 17th, 1980 at 6:55am. Massive skull fracture. Interval between onset and death, unknown. Blunt skull trauma. Homicide.

Julia stared at the page. She had seen death certificates before, even her parents', but looking at one that read "Homicide" felt inexplicably eerie.

Questions flooded her mind. "Interval between onset and death, unknown." What does that mean? That she was killed at some earlier time and only found on September 17th? Found off Pondview Avenue, what does that mean? Not in a house, but on the ground, in the woods?

Julia took a deep breath and sat back in her chair. 'If she was murdered,' she thought, 'there should be newspaper accounts of it.' But first, she wanted to see Sherry's birth certificate.

Leaving the Registry, she was not surprised to find it was raining and chilly. 'Such is June in New England,' she thought. Traffic was slow on the highway, but still she made it to the offices of the *Sipponet Village Gazette* by four o'clock. The receptionist showed her to the rear of large room filled with four desks, of which only two were occupied. Every issue had been transferred to microfilm. Julia settled in with her notebook and glasses, and rolled the wheel of microfilm to September, 1980.

Behind her, phones rang and the news staff were putting together copy for the Thursday weekly paper. She concentrated on the microfilm; the office activity receded into the background like waves on a beach.

The first article on September 17th described the discovery of an unidentified and extensively decomposed body of an unclad female lying face down in a gully in the woods off Pondview Avenue. The Sipponet Police Chief characterized the site as a "lovers' parking area."

Two raccoon hunters and their dogs had come upon the body. The woman was estimated to be about 4'10" with brown hair. 'So tiny,' Julia thought, 'just a wisp of a thing.' Police were reviewing reports of missing women in the area. There were at least seventeen. The jaw of the skull was intact and they intended to investigate dental records for a match.

The next day's article declared that the dental records matched those of Nicole Fayette, a twenty-four-year-old woman who'd been missing since the beginning of the previous June. There was a small picture of a pretty young woman smiling. But it wasn't Nicole. It was a photo of another woman attached to an adjacent story about a winning basketball team.

Julia flipped through the microfilm to the next article a week later. Still no picture of Nicole. The story re-capped the prior articles, mentioning that the investigating State Police officer was Lieutenant John McDermott.

* * *

"What's the matter? Are you sick, you old bastard?" Adam asked as he entered the one-room that made up Goody's cabin in Pittsley Woods. He hefted two large grocery bags onto the sideboard. "What's up?"

Adam always closed his clinic on Monday afternoons to make up for being open Sunday morning. He routinely spent this time with Goody, bringing him food supplies. Adam had known Goody almost all his life as his father's friend. After his father died, Adam just slid into that void. Generally, he found the old gnome puttering around on some repair project or another when he arrived. But today, Goody was still in bed with several layers of tattered covers pulled up to his chin.

"It's the atha-ritis," Goody growled. "My joints seized up. Damn rain always does it. Anyways I knew you was coming."

"Let's take the dampness out. I'll light a fire."

Adam went back outside and brought in several arm-loads of wood from the bin. He started up the woodstove, piling small sticks on the bottom and the larger logs on top. Within fifteen minutes the fire was crackling and warming the entire room with a deep penetrating heat.

"Have you eaten anything today?" Adam asked as he emptied the grocery bags.

"Where's your logic, boy? If I ain't got out of bed, I ain't et."

"Where's your spider?"

"In the cupboard, where the hell do you think, up my ass?"

"With you, Goody, I never know."

Spider was an old Yankee name for a cast-iron frying pan, a term that few people besides Goody used anymore. Adam pulled it out and set it on the woodstove. He put a chipped enamel pot of water on for instant coffee. He added lard to the frying pan and beat five eggs in a bowl. As the pan sizzled, he began making scrambled eggs. He placed slices of bread flat on the stovetop for toasting.

"What would you have done if I didn't come by?"

"Hell, I got my meal coming tonight, and tomorrow it'll be warm again. Don't worry about me none."

The old man was as ornery as ever. Adam smiled with relief.

Sitting across from Goody in the only chair in the room, Adam watched his friend eat heartily. Goody had moved to a sitting position on the bed after discarding his worn woolen blankets. Underneath, he was fully dressed in overalls and a brown flannel shirt with white muslin showing through the frayed collar. Adam suspected that Goody didn't remove his outer clothes at night until mid-summer.

"Did you hear about your buddy Cutter's brother?" Goody asked, finished with his food and ready to dispense his 'intelligence.' How he knew what he knew without leaving his corner of the woods was a mystery to Adam.

"Which brother? He's got five of them."

"The one who drives the boom truck."

"Driver."

"That's the one."

"What about him?"

"You ain't heard?"

"No, I ain't heard," Adam said.

Goody nodded with satisfaction.

"Seems there was three city punks came into Dud's Suds last week when Driver was there. He wasn't in no forgiving mood because his truck had broke down and he lost out on a load of wood. There were only one other guy there, Windy, and he's drunk as usual. So Driver is sitting alone, minding himself, when these three guys come in with spiky, colored hair. They're quiet at first, but they're shooting down rounds of ginger brandy and vodka."

"Poppers," Adam added, but Goody shrugged him off.

"So one of the fellas with white hair, who seems like he was the leader says, 'So what do you all do for fun here in hayseed country? You all got a pretty little piggy waiting for you at home?' He directs his remarks to Driver. 'Is that what you do, Farmer Brown? Play leap-frog with piggy?' You know, like Driver's out of that *Deliverance* movie or something."

Before Adam even had a chance to wonder how Goody would know anything about any movie, the old man continued.

"Driver, he takes a drag on his cigarette and says, 'If you want to see what we do here in hayseed country, bend over, I'll show you.'

"Then the orange hair guy says, 'You couldn't show us shit, asshole.'

"And Driver says, 'Why not? I'm looking at it.'"

Adam nodded. "Yep, that sounds like Driver in a bad mood."

Goody pressed on, undaunted. "Then the white-hair guy says to his companions, 'Big mouth here, he wants to dance with us. Is that what you want to do, big mouth?'

"And Driver puts his elbow on the bar and holds up his middle finger and says, 'Dance on this.'

"Well, that's that. The white hair says to his boys, 'It looks like I'm going to have to give Big Mouth here some boogie lessons.' And he reaches inside his jacket and pulls out one very large Bowie knife with a serrated edge. 'See this?' he says. 'This here's a pigsticker. Souwee-ee-ee.'

"Then Driver tells them to hold that thought, he has to go take a piss. And out the back door he goes. Those punks think they scared him off and they're laughing like hell. But Driver comes back. And when he comes in, he's got his twenty-seven-inch chainsaw with him. He lifts it up and pulls the cord. It starts on the first pull. So the chainsaw's blowing out gassy blue smoke throughout the bar and Driver says, 'This here's what we use to dress off billy goats. And it's going to split you right up the middle—balls first.'

"He lunges for the guy's personals, and the city fella and his boys bolt for the door, yelling 'Let's get out of here. This guy's crazy!'

"'You have a nice day now, fellas,' Driver says as they disappear. And as far as anybody knows, they ain't been back."

Adam laughed appreciatively, then shook his head. "I hope that doesn't start some kind of feud with these guys. There's no telling what they might do."

"They shouldn't be messing around here anyways. They ought to stay where they belong."

With that, Goody went off on a tear about the faults in modern society emanating from urbanization. Adam had heard it all before, but waited until the old man eventually sputtered out to change the topic.

"Let me ask you, Goody, how much do you depend on the government?"

"What?"

"How much do you depend on the government?"

"I heard you. But it's a damn fool question. I don't. Government's got no business in my business."

Goody pulled a crushed pack of cigarettes from his pocket and offered it to Adam.

"No thanks, I quit. And so should you, old man."

"Not until I have to," Goody announced, holding the unfiltered cigarette between his gnarled tobacco-stained fingers. "And don't tell me you don't sneak a pipe smoke now and again."

"You own this land, don't you?" Adam asked, going back to the subject.

"Of course I own it. It was my great-grandfather's."

"Do you pay real estate taxes on it?"

"Some. They don't tax me like a house. Just land and building."

"But still, how can you afford that?"

"I get my Social Security. It ain't much, but I don't need much. There's no electricity, no town water or sewer. Low on maintenance. I get by. Why?"

"What about your arthritis? Don't you go to a doctor?"

"Once in a while. To get my prescriptions. Why? You doing a survey?"

"How do you get to the doctor's office? You don't drive."

"COA sends a van, a course," Goody said, referring to the Council on Aging.

"And Medicare helps pay for your doctor visits?"

"What's your point?"

"My point is, you *do* use government services."

"So what? That don't change the way I feel about the institution. You think I shouldn't take what's offered?"

"No. I wasn't thinking that. I was thinking that even a recluse needs *some* government aid, so how is Cutter going to survive without *any*?"

"What's it got to do with Cutter?"

"You ain't heard?" Adam said, mimicking the old man.

Goody just eyed him balefully until Adam proceeded to tell him that Cutter intended to secede.

"Hmmph," Goody commented.

* * *

After dinner, Julia lay on the sofa with her stockinged feet in Adam's lap. She had felt like cooking when she got home from work, not a usual occurrence these days. So she made a vegetable lasagna and chocolate mousse pie and invited Adam over. He brought Sally, his pig, as company for Catastrophe. The two animals lay side by side across the room.

"I never thought you'd actually keep her, Adam."

"Who, Sally?"

Julia nodded. She liked the intimate way he absently massaged her feet in a slow rhythmic motion.

"I can't find anybody else who'll take her. Except for ham."

Julia crinkled up her nose. Buying the little piglet was just supposed to have been a ruse to get Adam and her onto Floyd Mather's farm last year, when they were trying to figure out who killed the little Bradburn girl. Adam thought he would find the little piglet a home. Well, obviously he did—his own.

"They do like each other," Julia inclined her head towards Cat and Sally. "Did, right from the start." But now Sally was at least twice the size of the Golden Retriever. "How much larger will she get?"

"She's a growing girl. She'll go a hundred, hundred and fifty more."

"Good grief, what are you going to do with her then?"

"I was hoping to give her to Billy Jr., but Tessa said 'no thanks.' So I guess she's mine."

Julia raised her eyebrows in amusement. "Does she get along with Horace?"

"Tolerably well. Now that she's bigger than him."

Adam had also wound up with Floyd's German Shepherd because the dog was too mean for anyone else. Adam named him Horace, since no one knew if he actually had a name. Horace, Adam said, was a mortifying name for a German Shepherd and maybe it would take the meanness out of him. It did seem to have an effect. In a year, the dog had gone from vicious to merely cranky. But he still wasn't fit for company.

Thinking about Sally and Horace brought the whole episode of Jeannine Bradburn back to Julia with a shiver.

She had found the little girl's body in Pittsley Woods, the Spring before this one. And from that, she and Adam had discovered the cult killings of so many other little girls. But while Jeannine's killers—Floyd Mather and Babe Hamply—were both dead, the other members of the cult were still at large.

"You look pensive," he said.

"I was just thinking about Jeannine Bradburn. And the thirteen white robes you and Chief Burke found in Floyd's basement, with the altar. Besides Floyd and Babe, there are still eleven men out there who killed all those girls as some sort of sacrifice. And we don't know if they're continuing to kill. We don't know who they are."

"We may never know," Adam said grimly.

There wasn't anything to suggest Nicole Fayette was connected to those other murders. It happened years before the serial killings and it didn't fit the pattern. Nicole was ten years older than Jeannine or the other girls. And she hadn't been dismembered. The only similarity was that her body was left in the woods. But that wasn't uncommon.

"Do you recall the murder of a young woman by the name of Nicole Fayette about twenty years ago in Sipponet?" Julia asked.

"Vaguely."

"Her body was found in a culvert on the edge of the woods, not far from the road. She'd been there all summer."

"That's about as much as I heard."

"That's all?" Julia prodded. "It must have been big news back then. Sipponet Village is so small, and it's just one town over."

"But it's a different county. Our local newspaper doesn't pay much attention to what happens outside the county. Why are you interested?"

Now that she'd brought it up, she wasn't sure how to get out of it without breaking confidentiality.

"Apparently they never found who did it," she said casually.

Adam looked at her dubiously. "Yes, and…?"

"Nothing. Someone just happened to mention it to me."

"Oh?" He stopped massaging her feet. "Why do I get the feeling you're thinking of doing some amateur sleuthing?"

"Not really," she said nonchalantly.

"Good. Resist the impulse."

"Why?"

"In the first place, you're not a detective. In the second place, if it happened twenty years ago there's no way of your investigating a crime that old. And in the third place, it could be dangerous. You kick things over and you don't know what's going to rear up and bite you."

He was probably right on all counts, she thought. And then there was Sam. True, she had all the information she needed in order to talk with Sherry. No need to look further. But she really *would* like to know what happened.

But before she had a chance to go further with that notion, Adam pulled her by her ankles onto his lap.

"I warned you, you tasty young morsel," he said in his best Bella Lugosi voice. "Now I'm going to bite you." He put his mouth to her neck and began playfully nibbling. She dropped her head back and let him kiss her throat and then her mouth, then she thought about nothing else.

* * *

"We're gathered tonight to determine when to resume our rituals. We've lost two members of our circle, Floyd Mather and Babe Hamply, but there are still eleven of us. We need to decide what we want to do and when to do it. The summer solstice is approaching. Shall we have a ceremony? I leave the decision in your hands."

"I think we should continue with our worship, but not a ceremony," said one. "Not yet. It's too soon. Too great a risk."

"He's right," said another. "There's not enough time. We should aim for the autumnal solstice."

"Do the congregates agree? Say 'aye.'"

There were ayes all around.
"Dissension?"
No one spoke.
"Let us bow our heads."

TUESDAY, JUNE 8th

"Be it Known to All Citizens and Governments:
"I, Malbone Briggs, also known as Cutter Briggs, being of sound mind and body, do hereby declare that I and my property (Lots 47-193 in Pittsley, Pittsley County) do hereby secede from the Commonwealth of Massachusetts, as of the date of my signature below:
Signed by my hand ______________________________
Malbone ("Cutter") Briggs
Date: ________________

Witnessed by ______________________________
Adam Sabeski
Date: ________________

"I drew it up myself. Will you come down to the drugstore with me to sign the witnessing, Adam? There's a notary public there. Then I can make copies and send them out."

Adam ran his fingers through his collar-length hair that was beginning to streak more grey than black.

"I don't think it's that simple, Cutter. You're effectively declaring that you're withdrawing from the United States just because you don't want to pay property taxes."

Cutter shook his head vigorously. "It's not just the property taxes. Which is bad enough, plus they even want to charge for what you have inside your house. And it isn't just the federal income tax, the state income tax, the excise tax, sales tax, gas tax, meal tax, and everything else. It's not just *that*."

Cutter spread his hands out on the table, fingers wide apart, as though holding himself down from rising up in a tornado of anger. "I just don't believe that the government is serving my best interests. It's the fact that a body can't move anymore without bumping up against the wall of government. I'm not talking about corrupt government. I'm talking about *this* government. We got people who get elected or appointed to political office who suddenly forget they're supposed to be there for us. They start thinking they're there because they know better than us. And then they figure they know what we want better than we do. They're killing us with good intentions."

"'That government is best which governs least,'" Adam quoted.

"That's it. Exactly," Cutter said. "And I don't believe that anybody can tell me I have to belong to any government when I don't want to. It ain't what this country was started for."

"I can't argue that."

"Why shouldn't I have the right to be left alone?" Cutter said. "I'm no anarchist. I'm not trying to overthrow the government, I'm just taking myself out of it."

"Cutter, they'll nail your skenky hide to the door of the town offices, not to mention the capitol, if you go through with this."

"Let 'em try." Cutter smiled like a fox spitting out chicken bones. "I never signed no paper saying they own me."

If Cutter had had a little more education, Adam thought wryly, he just might be a dangerous man.

* * *

Lieutenant John McDermott, according to the original newspaper accounts, was in his forties when he was worked the Fayette case. Julia had made the appointment to speak with him before her conversation with Adam, so she felt perfectly justified in keeping it. Luckily, the lieutenant was a seasoned veteran at the time he headed up the investigation. It wouldn't be like the Bradburn case, where the police had never dealt with a murder before. And lucky, too, that McDermott was still around.

The desk officer buzzed Julia through the bulletproof glass of the outer office of the regional State Police Headquarters. As she entered his office, Lt. McDermott was on the telephone. She gestured to ask him if she should leave, but he shook his head.

His desk faced the wall with u-shaped arms on either side. The right arm, with a computer on it, faced the window. The left arm was clear except for a triple-stacked in-box. She sat down in the wooden chair perpendicular to him and tried not to look interested in his conversation, which consisted mostly of "yes," "no," "alright," and "we'll see." McDermott was obviously a man of brevity, and he looked it—with a spare frame, buzz-cut grey hair, and a long thin face with a square jaw. She couldn't help thinking of an aged Dudley Do-Right.

When he hung up the telephone, he turned a quarter circle towards Julia.

"What is it you want to know about the Fayette case, Dr. Arnault?"

Right to the point, Julia thought. She would have not expected otherwise.

"I'd like to know what happened to her."

"Why?"

Julia anticipated he would ask that. She would have to be forthright about it.

"Her daughter is my patient."

"Cheryl?"

Julia nodded. She had already decided that telling him this much would not be a breach of confidentiality. It was a state institution and admission records would be accessible to the police.

"But that's as much as I can tell you," she added.

He accepted that and reflected on it. "What happened to Nicole Fayette?" he repeated. "I wish I knew."

Julia's heart sank.

"You mean you have no suspect at all?"

"I have my suspicions. But no evidence."

"Could you tell me what you know about her death?"

"You've probably know most of it. The last anybody saw her was the night she went partying at the dump."

"The dump? The newspaper account didn't say that."

"There was a group of townies, ten or twelve of them in their twenties and early thirties, that would congregate at the dump on a Saturday night. Or a holiday. They could drink and pump up the volume there with nobody around to see or hear them."

"Do you know who they were?"

"Some of them. Not all. They're very tight."

"What did they tell you?"

"That they saw her that night, and didn't see her ever again."

"Did she leave the party with someone?"

"Nobody seems to have paid attention."

How could that be? Julia wondered. Unless they were all drunk. Which was likely.

"Did she have a boyfriend?"

A hint of a smile tugged at the corner of his mouth. "Good question. Nobody will say, and her parents didn't see anybody with her that night. She lived with her parents in the house next to that little church where the road turns. Her mother never knew what Nicole was up to. Sometimes she'd disappear for a couple or three days without notice and then she'd show up again and wouldn't say where she'd been. Basically, the grandparents raised Cheryl even before Nicole died."

"What about Sherry's father?"

"According to the grandparents, he was gone in a flash as soon as Nicole got pregnant."

"Not a suspect?"

McDermott shook his head.

"And nobody would say who the boyfriend *du jour* was?"

"Nope."

"Must be a reason for that." Julia found herself speaking as clipped as the Lieutenant.

"I'm thinking he was probably a townie. Maybe married," he replied.

"Because," Julia said thoughtfully, "if he were an outsider, nobody would care about protecting him?"

"Exactly."

"And if he were married, he would most likely try to be discreet. And maybe only the party group would know about their relationship."

"That's possible." He leaned back in his swivel chair and put his hands behind his head.

And that, Julia estimated, was all he was going to say about *that*. She put her elbow on his desk and cupped her chin in her hand.

"So, after the party, she disappears and her parents don't think much about it when she doesn't show up for Cheerios the next morning."

McDermott nodded.

"But after a few more days, they must have called the police, right?"

"Two weeks," he corrected. "They called the Sipponet police, who searched for a while. But they didn't find her and didn't have any leads."

Julia wondered how hard they looked. And would they have looked harder if they liked her better?

"Then what happened?" she asked.

"Then three months later, the hunters stumbled across her in a ditch. She wasn't so much buried as just placed there. We identified her by her dental records."

"What did the autopsy show?"

"Blunt trauma to the head."

Julia looked at him intently. "Could it have been an accident? Like a fall against something?"

"No."

"Because?" She felt like she was trying to pry up a countersunk nail.

"The force was too great."

"The newspaper said the body was unclad. Was there any evidence of rape?"

McDermott shook his head. "With that much decomposition, there wasn't evidence of anything. But the fact that she was 'unclad' doesn't mean she died nude. We found some clothing at a distance from the body, but animals could have dragged it there."

Julia sat back and rested her arms on the arms of the office chair. "Anything else?"

"It's not being actively investigated anymore."

Julia said nothing for a moment.

"Do you have any problem," she finally asked, "with me poking around?"

"Nope. I'm due to retire next year, and this is my only open case. Wouldn't mind closing it. So keep me informed if you learn anything."

After she said she would, McDermott swung his arms down and turned back to his desk. His attention had already shifted to something else.

She got up to leave. "Thank you for your time."

He nodded absently as he dialed the phone.

"Oh, just one more question," she added.

He paused. "Yes?"

"Where is she buried?"

"Sipponet Village Cemetery."

Julia nodded. As she guessed.

"She was cremated," he added. "Cost, I suppose."

He continued dialing. Interview over.

'Now what?' she asked herself as she left McDermott's office. He obviously didn't think much of the likelihood of her finding out anything. Why did she say she would do some poking around? That was exactly what she agreed not to do. Why was she being so obstinate? What was it in her nature that compelled her along this path? She already knew as much as she needed to for her patient: Sherry's mother was murdered; the killer had never been caught. The end.

WEDNESDAY, JUNE 9th

Sherry wasn't paying any attention to her. The anti-depressant took the edge off, Julia thought, but it made her patient too sluggish. She would talk with Sam immediately about reducing the dose.

"I'm correcting your chart," Julia explained as she was writing.

Sherry did not respond.

"I'm crossing out the information you provided about your mother dying in a car accident."

Sherry looked at her under half-lid eyes. Julia could not determine whether or not what she said had registered. She scanned her for a spark of interest. Or even anticipation.

"Did you hear me, Sherry?"

Sherry shrugged one shoulder.

"I know how your mother died. I know she was murdered, Sherry."

"By who?" the young woman said, unexpectedly reviving.

"Well, I don't know that. They never found out, did they?"

"Right," Sherry said, and Julia thought she saw a sneer on the young woman's face before lapsing back into torpor.

"And you actually signed Cutter's declaration?" Julia asked Adam as they sat together on the swing on her back deck drinking mugs of Irish coffee. The weather was balmy that evening; but it wouldn't be steadily hot until July, when the mosquitoes and flies would challenge them for dominion and would inevitably win. The grass was lush and the trees and bushes had all leafed out, creating an impenetrable privacy wall between her large yard and that of her neighbors'. The sun was florescent orange as it sank towards the horizon and the sky had turned into luminous pink with blue waves. As she concentrated, the moon became solid white and the stars were slowly coming into focus in the darkening sky. She loved looking up with no perceptible city lights to dim the heavens. It was one of the things that she relished about living in the country.

Last year, when she first rented 'the old Steeples place,' she really hadn't intended to stay in this house. She really hadn't intended to stay in Pittsley at all. But when that changed, she decided to buy the house she had originally disliked. Now, it seemed to fit her. She'd spent the entire year renovating it. Replacing carpets, stripping old wallpaper and repainting everything, re-facing cabinets, installing new countertops, adding new appliances, little by little changing the décor—just as she'd done with her office. In retrospect, she realized, she had completely renovated her entire environment…well, actually her entire life. The only vestige of her former self (in Boston with Phillip, fuck him) was her dog, Cat, whom she adored, and her rickety old car, which she did not. It was time, she acknowledged, to get rid of that rattletrap old car.

"I only witnessed that it was his true signature," Adam replied, interrupting her thoughts. "And so did the notary. That's all."

Julia shook her head. "It's one thing to challenge the tax code, but quite another to oppose the government altogether. It seems, well, provocative at best, if they take him seriously."

"I'm afraid they'll have to take him seriously. He's setting up his land as a compound outside government authority."

"How can he do that?"

"I don't think he can."

"So what will happen?"

"I don't know. I guess it depends on how far he's going to go with it."

Adam put his arm around her shoulders and they sat quietly for a while listening to the sounds of the birds settling into the trees for the night. Quick small bats zipped by overhead chasing insects. An owl hooted but Cat did not lift her head from where she lay under the swing.

"Do you think the town will settle with some sort of tax abatement to avoid a confrontation?" Julia asked.

"I'm not sure Cutter would even agree to that. He's got a fixed idea about this."

"Did you try to talk him out of it?"

"All the way to the notary."

"You have to keep trying, Adam. This can turn into something very bad for Cutter."

"I know." Adam sipped his coffee. "I'm worried about it."

Julia was, too. But that wasn't the only thing on her mind this evening. She knew she would have to tell Adam what she was doing because she didn't like keeping it secret from him.

"I talked to the State Police Inspector about the Fayette murder yesterday."

Adam removed his arm from her shoulders and took another drink of his coffee. "Why?"

"I need some information."

"No, I mean why are you getting into this, Julia?"

She closed her eyes. It was the same question she had asked herself.

Opening her eyes, she answered, "At first, I just needed to find out whether my patient had lied about her mother. But I think it's more important than that."

She couldn't tell him anything else about Sherry. She couldn't tell him that she'd discovered that Sherry's birthday was only a few days after her mother's death. Or that her attempts at suicide were, Julia was certain, Sherry's way of trying to get someone to pay attention to her—meaning, pay attention to her mother. It was almost as if a whole town had decided Nicole Fayette's death was insignificant.

"What makes you think you're going to solve this when the state police couldn't? They had trained investigators working this case."

"I thought you didn't know anything about it?" Julia eyed him intently.

"Percy and I had a beer together today, so I asked him about it. "

Sergeant Percy Davis had just retired from the Pittsley Police Department. He and Adam had been close until they had a falling-out over the Bradburn case. Percy had been less than candid about the former (deceased) chief of police. Chief Kerwin had bungled the disappearances of little girls in the area, and Percy knew about it. Adam was irate when he found out.

"Are you and Percy friends again?"

"Not a hundred percent."

"But you met with him?"

Adam shrugged. "I wanted to ask him about Cutter. Percy's known him for as long as I have."

"What did he say?"

"Pretty much the same thing I did. That Cutter is likely to go through with it. And he hoped the police wouldn't be called in."

"What did he say about the Fayette case?"

"He knew about it, even though it was in Sipponet. He was on the force back then and the Pittsley P.D. assisted in the original search when she went missing."

"What else did he say?"

"Same thing I told you. Don't stir up a hornet's nest."

"That's an interesting response from a police officer."

"I thought so, too."

"It sounds like he knows something, doesn't it?"

"Maybe. Or maybe it's just instinct."

"But he didn't tell you anything else?"

"When I pressed him, he said, 'Those young hell-raisers are now grown-up men and women with families and jobs, and they buried whatever they knew about Nicole Fayette's death a long time ago.' Adam put down his mug. "You know, Julia," he said earnestly, "this is out of your league."

She took a deep drink of her coffee and stared at the now black sky. She couldn't identify any constellations except the Big Dipper, and wished she knew more. The idea crossed her mind that she would like to get a telescope and learn some rudimentary astronomy. That appealed to her in a way she had never thought of before. Could that be Orion?

THURDSAY, JUNE 10th

The cattle gate to Cutter's property was chained closed and there was a sign on the post that read, "Liberty Nation—No Trespassing."

Adam sat in his pick-up truck, waiting. It was noontime and a mild day again. Cutter had already disconnected his telephone, so Adam had had to call Driver to say he was coming by this afternoon.

Another black pick-up, an older model but similar to his own, barreled down the driveway towards the gate. It came to a screeching, swerving halt inches away. Five children in the bed of the truck screamed with delight. Cutter got out of the cab, cackling.

"They love it," he explained to Adam as he unlocked the chain to the gate. "Like bumper car."

"What happens if you hit the gate?"

"Even better."

To Adam's disbelieving look, he added, "They all got harnesses, see? I made them. They're strapped up tighter than grandma's girdle."

After maneuvering the gate so that Adam could drive in, then locking up again after, Cutter took off up the driveway as fast as he'd come down. Adam kept pace but stopped as he reached the yard. Cutter kept on going, but slowed down as he aimed for a mattress hanging against the barn. He hit it with a controlled thump. The children squealed happily, then finally unbuckled themselves and jumped out of the truck. One by one, they ran over to the five-seat swing set Cutter had built next to the barn and began swinging as fast and as high as they could. The older ones swung faster and higher, but all of them whizzed up and back in sequence like pistons on a motor.

"They got a lot of energy," Cutter said admiringly as he and Adam walked up to the cabin.

Inside was one small central room with a modest bathroom and bedroom off the far end. The addition, on the opposite side, doubled the size of the original house. It was a partitioned room that served both as the children's bedroom—one side for the three boys, the other for the two girls—and playroom in the middle.

In the kitchen, one-half had a refrigerator, gas stove, sink, counter, and cabinets. The other half contained a table and seven chairs and a well-used woodstove. Adam and Cutter sat at the pine board table across from each other. The tabletop was covered with several layers of polyurethane, giving it the childproof finish of Plexiglas.

"Angel's out in back tending the seedlings. We started them in a cold frame and transplanted them into the garden last week. At least we'll have a good crop of vegetables."

"Did you deliver your proclamation to the town offices?"

"Yep. At the Selectmen's meeting."

"What did they say?"

"They thought I was joking. But I told them," Cutter's voice spiraled up as he pointed with both hands in the air and shook his forefingers at the imaginary Board, "that no one has to belong to a government against their will. And no one should be coerced into paying tribute to a government it doesn't belong to. And that no government—no matter what laws it has created for itself—has the right to impose them on me if I don't belong to it."

"The problem is," Adam said, rubbing his forehead, "I don't think it's true."

"Why not?"

"I'm no constitutional lawyer, but I think," Adam kept rubbing, as though the act of putting his thoughts into words required a physical effort, "that if you're an American citizen, you're in a social contract that is binding with the government."

"But that's the thing, Ski." Cutter's eyes gleamed. "I'm not an American citizen anymore. I'm a citizen of

Liberty Nation. I sent a copy of my declaration to the Governor, then I put a stop-mail order in at the Post Office and took down my mailbox. I called the electric company and the phone company and quit my service. Then I made my last call to the telephone company and took the phone out of the jack and tossed it on our junk pile."

"So I discovered." Adam glanced over at the stove. "No electricity, either? What are you cooking with, propane?"

"We're cooking on the grill. With wood."

"What about refrigeration?"

"We stocked in a bunch of canned foods. Chicken eggs stay fresh for a couple of weeks. We've got the cow for milk. We just do day-to-day."

"For two days so far."

"Nope. We actually started a few weeks ago. I wanted to make sure we could do it before I made it official."

"I know it's possible to live independently in a lot of ways." Adam was thinking about Goody. "But what about medical problems. What happens if one of the kids gets hurt, or sick?"

"I don't have that one solved yet, I admit. But I know I'll figure it out."

Adam dug a pipe out of his jacket, tamped down the bowl with his thumb, and lit it.

"What concerns me," he said between starter puffs, "is what the government will do once they really take notice. Like when they want you to pay income tax. The IRS plays hardball, you know."

Cutter grinned. "Ain't paid income tax in years, state or federal. I do a cash business. I'm not even on their radar screen."

"But you're on the town's radar screen, and they're still going to want their real estate tax."

"They can want what they want. But I'll have it fixed so nobody can get in here without a tank."

"If you don't pay, Cutter, they'll take your land."

Cutter closed his eyes, took a deep breath, and when he opened them again, there was a look that Adam had never seen before.

"The state does not own my land and cannot tax me on it. It was Briggs' land before there even was a town of Pittsley. Before there was a Commonwealth of Massachusetts. My eighth great-grandfather bought it from the Wampanoags, and he did it fair and square. They worked in his mill; he paid them the same as any other labor, invited them into his house, and during King Phillip's War, his land and his mill were spared. The government has pushed me and pushed me to where I don't feel like I own my own life anymore. And now I'm saying, 'Leave me alone.'"

* * *

Where to begin? Julia was at a loss as she drove home from work. She didn't know anyone in Sipponet who she could talk to. But as she pulled into her driveway, she suddenly remembered Martin Ryman, the pastor of the little Congregational Church that was on the corner not far from Adam's house. And wasn't the church just over the town line?

Cat was standing up in the front seat next to her, wagging her tail and eagerly waiting to go into the house. But when Julia backed out of the driveway, the dog resigned herself to disappointment.

"Sorry, girl, we have an errand to do. I don't know if this will be helpful, but we have to start somewhere, don't we?"

Adam teased her about always talking to the dog. But of course she caught him talking to his patients all the time. "I'm just explaining their diagnosis and treatment to them," he told her, as if that were fundamentally different.

She and Phillip had bought the Golden Retriever as a puppy right around the time her marriage began its meltdown. How many nights when he was supposedly working, did she cradle the plump little dog in her arms and run her face along the soft fur on Cat's back to soothe herself? Confiding her fears, her worries, her suspicions. Knowing that the little dog would look up at her with loving brown eyes and lick her nose with a small rough tongue. Karen was away at college then, and more often than not, Cat was the only reason she had to take a walk around Boston Common, and the only excuse she had to drive into the country to let the dog have a run. There wasn't anything in her life that she hadn't shared with Cat over the past seven years. Her best companion.

"I don't know how long Martin's been at the church," Julia said to Cat, "or if he even knows about Nicole Fayette. But he just might have some information that will help. Anyway he was very nice to me when I talked to him last year about the Bradburn case. And I never really thanked him."

Cat merely curled up on the seat, lay down with her head between her paws, and sighed.

Martin Ryman sat at his desk across from Julia. He wore a lightweight navy suit with a white shirt, open at the collar. In his late forties, Ryman looked unassuming with sandy brown hair cut short. His features were even and proportional, but more conventional than handsome. In a crowd of forty-year old, brown-haired male Caucasians, he would not stand out. Yet, Julia found a keenness in his expression and an intelligence in his eyes that suggested he might be an interesting man disguised in cleric's camouflage.

His study was unchanged from her last visit, with heavy mahogany furniture and woodwork. High ceilings, white walls with Wedgewood-blue drapes and carpet. A wooden Protestant cross hung behind him and a *bas-relief* of the Last Supper hung on the opposite wall. There was picture on his desk, in a silver filigree frame, of Martin with a beautiful blonde smiling woman and three teenagers, an older girl and two younger boys. Preacher's kids.

"Your family?" she asked studying the photo. It wasn't a very recent picture. He looked much younger.

He stared at the photo. "Yes. My wife Elaine, and our children, Ruth, John, and Mark."

"I don't think I saw this the last time I was here."

"No. It took me a long while before I could display it. I knew people would ask about them and I wasn't ready to discuss it."

He paused before continuing, then looked away from the picture. "They were in a private plane with a friend of the family. Larry was flying them from Baltimore, where we lived at the time, to meet me in western Pennsylvania after a pastoral retreat. It was going to be our family vacation. Larry was to fly back alone and we'd drive home the following week. But on the way, the plane flew into a freak lightening storm over the Alleghenies and went down. They all perished."

"How terrible. I'm so sorry," Julia said sincerely. "When did it happen?"

"Five years ago. Shortly before I was transferred here."

"I can't begin to imagine how painful it is to lose your whole family."

"Do you have children?"

"A daughter. Karen. She and her husband live in California."

She hadn't seen Karen since she and Paul moved from New York to Los Angeles last year. They didn't live very far from Julia's ex-husband, Phillip, and his new Lolita wife.

"This sort of tragedy can test one's faith," Martin said, putting his elbows on his desk and quite unconsciously clasping his hands together.

"And did it?"

Julia remembered when her mother and father stopped going to Mass after her grandmother and grandfather died so brutally. They hadn't made her go anymore, either.

"Yes," he answered, unclasping his hands and making a wide gesture. "But here I am." He then focused on her. "And what can I do for you, Julia?"

"First of all, I need to apologize for not thanking you for your help the last time we spoke."

"As I recall, all we did was talk about Good and Evil."

"Yes, but it made me think."

"Well, that's sometimes worth doing," he said smiling.

She smiled back. "Second of all," she continued, "I neglected to tell you that you were right. In some measure, anyway. We—that is, the police and Adam and I—found that there was a Satanic cult involved with Jeannine's murder and probably the others."

"I didn't know that."

"It wasn't reported."

"What kind of Satanic cult?"

"Is there more than one?" Julia asked, surprised.

"Oh, yes. Many."

"Well, they discovered white robes and an altar and evidence of some kind of blood ritual in Floyd Mather's basement. Thirteen robes. Of which they could account for only two—Floyd and his accomplice, Babe Hamply."

"And the others?"

"No clue. Does this sound familiar?"

"It sounds pretty generic. Except for the murders. Although it isn't unique. Is that what you came to ask me?"

"Not entirely."

Julia got up from her chair and walked over to the sideboard. A set of Wedgewood plates was displayed, each plate with a different church, obviously privately commissioned.

"I'm trying to find out about what happened to a young woman who was killed here in Sipponet twenty years ago. Her name was Nicole Fayette. I know it was before your time but I thought you might know who I can ask about it."

"Is this related to the cult murders?"

"No."

"But I assume you need to know for a particular reason?"

"Yes. But I can't divulge why."

Given her profession, she presumed he would understand. And, in fact, he nodded knowingly.

"Did you ever hear about the incident?" she asked.

"No. Fill me in."

She told him as much as she knew without revealing anything about Sherry.

"Why don't you just talk to the Sipponet police?" he asked.

"For now, I don't want any town officials to know that I'm looking into it."

"Because—?"

"Because the killer may still live here."

"I see." He thought about it for a moment. "A lot of my parishioners are long-time residents of the Village, but I wouldn't know who to send you to under the circumstances. The only thing I can suggest is to talk with the previous pastor, Benjamin Chauncy. He was here during that time. He's in Groton now. I can give you his phone number. At least it's a place to start." He flipped through an old-fashioned rolodex to look for the number.

"Thank you, I knew you'd help. I didn't know who else to ask."

"Can't Adam help you?"

He didn't look at her and she had a sense that his question was more personal than he'd like her to think.

"Adam doesn't really know that many people in the Village."

"Oh?" He stopped at an entry and began copying down the number on a post-it.

"And it's such an old case."

"I see." He handed her the note paper.

"And Pittsley's in a different county from Sipponet." Why was she sounding so defensive? "But, thank you. I'll call Reverend Chauncy tonight."

"Give him my regards. And please let me know if I can be of any further help." Martin stood up to say goodbye and offered his hand.

"Yes, I will."

When she took his hand, it was warm and inviting, and when he looked into her eyes, she felt a little breathless. She shook his hand brusquely and left quickly.

Back in her car, she turned to the sleepy dog.

"I think, Cat, the good reverend is out of mourning."

* * *

On the way home from Cutter's, Adam stopped off to see Tully. As with Goody, Adam thought of Tully as immutable, never changing with age or circumstance. And after his visit with Cutter, he craved that constancy. He was very worried about where his recalcitrant friend was going to wind up.

He found Tully sitting on the ground in his overalls, taking apart an old lawnmower, one of eight he had lined up in a row behind him in various degrees of repair. They looked like the starting line of a race none of them could win.

"Just picked this up this morning," Tully announced. "I got parts from other ones that'll fit it. People just throw these away when they don't work and there's nothing wrong with them, just a part or two. I'll get it running. People just want to go out and buy a new one when all they have to do is fix the old one. Nobody knows how to fix anything anymore. They just want to throw it away and spend their money on something new. I don't know where they're getting all this money from to throw away. They buy new cars, new houses, new lawnmowers. Do you know how much these things cost now?"

"Hi, Tully," Adam said pointedly, "How're you doing?"

While Tully was as independent-minded as Cutter, he didn't participate in politics, pro or con. He did whatever he had to do to escape notice ever since the State removed his children for neglect. He never understood the Social Service's actions. He provided his children with food, clothing, shelter, and sent them to school. He never beat them. Where was the neglect? And what's 'verbally abusive'? Didn't his own father yell at him? And beat him? And didn't he have to sleep in the drafty cold attic without heat in winter? He had had it worse than any of his kids. Didn't hurt him any.

The one thing he knew was that the State could swoop down and pluck your kids right out of your nest without cause. And after himself having been erroneously charged with the little Bradburn girl's murder, he knew that the State could also pluck *you.*

For those reasons, Tully kept his head down and his taxes paid. He was a vulnerable child in the hands of an irrationally angry parent.

"Doris don't want sex with me anymore," Tully said without preamble. "Ever since the baby was born dead, she won't love me or even hug me. No mouth to mouth. She's not acting like a wife no more."

'That's my Tully,' Adam thought. Tully and Doris already had five children that were wards of the state except one, Tommy, who was now in a halfway house. Doris had had several miscarriages and several stillbirths. With her diminished mental capacity, Adam was surprised that Doris was able to make a decision not to have sex. He was surprised she even made the connection between sex and childbirth.

"It's been four months." Tully continued to work on the lawnmower. "She don't even take off her clothes when she comes to bed. She don't say she loves me no more. I don't even touch her hmm-hmm and she won't touch mine. I need it every day or I can't sleep at night. That's not normal for a woman of her age to not want sex. She used to do it even when she was pregnant. But no more. If she don't love me in a wifely way, I'll get someone who will."

"Maybe she just needs some fixing," Adam said, trying to get Tully to see the analogy with his lawnmowers. But Tully didn't get it.

"All she does is mope around. She doesn't make a meal, not that she was ever much good at cooking. But she don't clean the house or be my helpmate. I do all the cooking. I have to make all my meals, do all my laundry. She won't even do my laundry. All she does is sit and watch t.v. I swear I'm going to throw the thing out the window. I don't need it."

"Maybe you should take her to the doctor," Adam suggested, trying a more direct route.

Tully threw down a wrench. "All they want to do is take your money and pretend they're helping you. They're all cheaters. They charge you just for going there whether they do anything or not. Frauds is what they are. Got no use for doctors. Maybe what she needs is a good cleaning out. Get rid of the body poisons. I give myself an enema every Spring. Flushes out the system. Maybe she just needs a good tonic."

Adam nodded. 'What the hell," he thought, 'maybe that's what we all need.'

* * *

Finally home, Julia put on a C.D. of Respighi's orchestral music beginning with *The Pines of Rome*. Then, she microwaved last night's clam chowder. All true New Englanders, and Massachusetts' connoisseurs in particular, were highly discerning about their chowdah. (Excluding those who prefer fish chowder, specifically cod chowder, or even seafood chowder, whatever that was.) Many still preferred to call it quahog chowder, for the larger size of the clams (compared with little necks or cherrystones). Now there were as many ways of preparing chowder as there were cooks. And although seldom were any ingredients measured, fierce arguments to outright hostilities could erupt over recipes. Purists, however, held to the old ways—salt pork, butter, flour, milk, clams. In the early days, the chowder was often thickened with sea biscuits rather than flour. And in parts of Rhode Island, there was no thickening agent whatsoever. But clam chowder always began by sizzling small chunks of salt pork (or bacon, in desperation, but it was frowned upon) to a firm but not overcrispy texture.

Radical though it was, Julia always added a small amount of minced onions and sautéed these down to transparency. She even tossed in a tablespoon of minced celery, strike her with lightening. Back on the straight and narrow, she melted butter into the mix then whisked in enough flour to make a *roux*. To that, she gradually stirred in milk until it seized up thickly like molasses. Then she added her secret ingredient, a bottle of clam juice, until the soup was the consistency of pancake batter. She added diced boiled 'new' potatoes, a pinch of salt, pepper, and Old Bay Seasoning, and simmered until the ingredients melded. At the very end, she added a goodly amount of fresh chopped clams, and cooked the soup for only several minutes more. Then she let it rest for a while, ideally overnight in the refrigerator. Chowder was always better the following day, like now. She ate it without the topping of oyster crackers that came in little cellophane packets in restaurants and preferred instead a piece of French bread on the side. Other than chocolate, this was, she thought, the ultimate comfort food.

Afterwards, she showered and threw on a pair of comfortable black shorts, cut-off from old sweatpants, and a red tee-shirt that had a Larson cartoon of a wild-eyed dog on it. By the time she made herself a cup of tea and sat down to drink it, it was nearly nine o'clock. Just time enough to make the call to Benjamin Chauncy.

The voice answering the phone sounded sleepy. Perhaps she'd called too late.

"Pastor Chauncy?"

"Yes."

Somehow, she hadn't expected him to answer personally. Didn't they have assistants or something? Julia introduced herself and explained that Martin Ryman had given her his number.

"How is Martin?"

"Very well. He sends his regards."

"Please give him my regards as well, when you talk to him again. What is it that I can help you with, Dr. Arnault?"

"Actually, I was wondering if I could make an appointment to speak with you."

Julia preferred to see him in person and Groton was less than two hours' drive. She apologized for interrupting him and they set a time to meet late the following afternoon.

After she hung up, she stretched out on the sofa. Looking down at her legs, she decided they were still in decent shape for an old broad. She grinned, thinking about the last time she and Tessa, Billy's wife, had sat with their legs up on the kitchen table to make an assessment. Tessa's were damn good. Of course, she was younger. Julia made a mental note to call her. They usually had dinner and a movie once a month, and she always looked forward to it. Tessa made Julia forget that she was ten years older.

During this past year, however, menopause had kicked in, reminding Julia with night sweats and unpredictable hot flashes that she was aging. She was beginning to see more grey hairs in the mirror now. Is that what was driving her? She had squandered so many years of her life in a bad marriage, maybe she had to make up for that. Make up for putting herself on hold for so long. And now she had to admit that there was only a limited amount of time left to remedy that.

She fell asleep dreaming of Adam, but they were in a different place and he did not know her. At one a.m., she woke up sweating again. She took another shower and settled in to bed, alternately covers off, covers on. It was a restless night.

FRIDAY, JUNE 11th

"How are you feeling today?" Julia asked Sherry. The young woman looked better around the eyes, more alert than last time, but she said nothing.

Sherry gazed past her out the window as the seconds clocked by. But Julia didn't get a sense that Sherry was hostile. It was as though she were gathering herself up to talk.

Julia didn't hurry her. She decided to wait it out.

It reminded Julia of when, as a child, she used to go crabbing in the bay with her father. They would bait a thick circle of wire, made from a coat hanger, baited with little silver fish called killies. They would tie a good ten feet of cord on the wire and lower it down into the water. She'd hold onto the end of the cord which was wrapped around a stick or piece of wood the right size to grip in the palm of her left hand. With her right hand, she lightly held the cord through her fingers. Then they would wait without talking. Her father never wore a hat. She did, but the sun glanced off the water into her face anyway, making her squint. She could feel the slight rocking of the rowboat, the hard plank seat, the sound of the swells lapping gently gently gently at the side of the boat, the salt smell of the water, the fishy smell of the wooden boat. There was a metal tub half-filled with seawater at the bottom of the boat between the seats where they would put the crabs. She would wait to feel a little tug at the bait. Not a pull exactly, just a tug as the crab grabbed it with his large claw. Only her fingers could tell her when the bait was taken. Then she would pull it up slowly, very slowly so the crab would not become suspicious and dislodge. It would take several minutes before the hoop, bait, and crab came close enough to the surface of the water to be seen. Just then, freeing her right hand, she'd grab the net to scoop it up. Usually, as the net broke the water, the crab let go of the bait. Then she either caught it or didn't—depending on how quick she was—as it began to sink backwards, stalky eyes upon hers, back down into the murky water. In a whole day, they might only catch a dozen blue-claws. It taught her patience.

Finally, Sherry looked at her again. "I spent that Saturday and Sunday before Memorial Day in a motel with four guys."

Julia waited to see if Sherry were going to say anything more. When more seconds passed and she didn't, Julia asked, "For pay?"

"No."

Julia had a hundred questions but she knew she had to go slowly.

"Have you done that before?"

Sherry looked out the window. "Not with four. Not that it matters."

"Do you mean the number of men doesn't matter, or the fact that you did it at all doesn't matter?"

"Both."

Julia let the silence become palpable before asking, "And what happened?"

Sherry took a deep breath. "Everything."

"Meaning?"

"Meaning they did everything. Everything they could think of. And I let them."

Julia let a little more time go by. "Because you liked it?"

Sherry clenched her jaw, then said, "Because I didn't care."

"Were you drunk?"

"Off and on."

"High?"

"No. No drugs."

"Did they use condoms?"

Sherry shook her head.

"I think we should have you tested for HIV."

Sherry's expression did not change.

Julia had a quick rush of adrenaline. “Are you already positive?” Her mind leaped to the cemetery worker who found Sherry, the EMTs who brought her to the hospital, the four men in the motel, and Nurse Kern.

“No.”

Julia kept silent in relief as Sherry seemed to struggle with herself.

“They used me like a toilet.”

Julia watched Sherry unconsciously dug her fingernails into the arms of the chair.

“Do you understand what I’m telling you?” Sherry said angrily.

“I think so.”

“I let them—every one of them—do whatever they wanted with me for forty-eight hours, and when they were finished, they all took showers and left. They left me naked on the dirty bed.”

Julia stared at her unblinking. “Because you let them.”

“Yes-s-s,” Sherry hissed.

“Why? And don’t bullshit me that it didn’t matter, because it mattered enough for you to try to commit suicide the next day.”

Sherry, suddenly aware of her nails digging in the wooden arms of the chair, clenched her fists.

“Because that’s what I do. It’s what I do when I start feeling like I want to hurt somebody or maim somebody or stab somebody or hit somebody in the head until their brains spill out.”

Julia could have said ‘the way your mother was,’ but she didn’t think Sherry was ready for that yet.

“I hate them,” Sherry said.

“The men in the room?”

“All of them. I hate all of them.”

Julia said nothing.

Sherry shook her head. “I’m not a lesbian.”

“I didn’t say you were.”

Sherry breathed deeply again. "They hate us, too. Men hate us first."

"What makes you think that?"

Sherry glared at her. "Isn't it enough that my so-called-father left us? Or that some sniveling coward of a man murdered my mother? Or that four pigs just treated me like I was the family sheep?"

"Is that all?"

"Is that all?" Sherry repeated, raising her voice. "No, that's not all. You want more? You want to know what my grandfather—"

She stopped short and looked helplessly at Julia.

Julia nodded and Sherry put her head in her hands and began sobbing.

After their session, Sherry was escorted back to the ward and Julia went directly to Sam's office. He had two piles of patients' charts at either elbow and he was making notes. He didn't notice her standing in the doorway until she knocked softly at the doorjamb.

Startled, Sam looked up, pen poised in his hand. "Sorry," he said perfunctorily, "I was engrossed."

"I'm just on my way out," she said. "But I think you should put Sherry Fayette on watch this weekend."

"What happened?"

"She made a breakthrough. Now I expect a reaction."

"Does she need meds?"

"I don't think so."

"Okay, I'll alert the ward. Anything you want to tell me about it?

"Not right now."

"Okay." He dropped his gaze onto his pile of papers. "Go home. Have a good weekend, Julia. I'll see you Monday."

"Thanks, Sam, you too."

But she was not exactly on her way home. She was on her way to Groton.

* * *

The Reverend Chauncy smelled like alcohol.

A corpulent man with sparse white hair, he reminded her of Friar Tuck. His face was flushed and his eyes were slightly glassy. Perhaps he'd had a little more wine with dinner than he should have. And maybe a little more afterwards. As he escorted her into his study, she noticed his gait was unsteady. He stared up at the ceiling while she apologized for seeing him so late. It had taken her a full two hours to drive to Groton in the Friday traffic and she'd arrived at the rectory shortly after seven p.m. After she explained the reason for her visit, she waited for his response. Several minutes passed.

"Pastor Chauncy?"

"Yes?"

She didn't want to suggest that he wasn't listening to her, so she merely said, "Can you tell me anything about Nicole Fayette?"

"I knew her mother and father. They lived next door to the church."

"Did they attend your church?"

"She did. He was sick. He died in 1982. She died a few years after."

"Mrs. Fayette must have turned to you when Nicole was missing."

"Yes."

"It must have been very difficult for them."

"Yes."

"Do you think they knew who killed their daughter?"

He looked at her then, and his eyes were empty.

"Nicole's dead and her parents are dead. Dead things are best left alone."

There it was again, the admonition to back off. "Well, Nicole's daughter's not dead, at least not yet."

"Oh, yes, the granddaughter," he said absently. "I lost track of her when Winifred died."

"When was that?"

"Right before I left the parish."

"Did you preside at Nicole's funeral, Reverend?"

"It was a graveside service. Yes."

"Do you remember who attended?"

"It was a private service." He looked up at the ceiling again. "Just Walter and Winifred and the granddaughter."

"Sherry."

"Yes, little Cheryl."

"That's all?"

"Yes," he said reflectively. "Oh, and Doreen Crawford. Friend of Nicole's."

"Not Sherry's father?"

"No."

"Who was her father? Sherry's birth certificate says 'unknown'."

"'Unknown' would be correct. Winifred never said. Other than that he left town. Some young boy, I expect, not ready for a wife and child."

"There was no other family present at the funeral? No friends?"

"No." He looked up at the ceiling. "They didn't want anyone else."

"Why do you suppose that was?"

He lowered his head and looked at the Wedgewood blue carpet. Julia noticed for the first time that Pastor Chauncy's office was a replica of Pastor Ryman's. Rather, Chauncy had simply duplicated the décor from his previous office. Did he, she wondered, do that wherever he went?

"I suppose," he said slowly, "she'd shamed them in death as she had in life."

'Not very charitable,' Julia thought, but perhaps he was just telling her how Nicole's parents must have felt back then. After all, Sipponet Village was a very small town and Julia supposed everyone would have known about Nicole's out-of-wedlock child. And her party-going. The townspeople probably all had opinions about what Nicole was doing when she was murdered.

"Do you know who killed her, Reverend?"

"Me? No. I wouldn't have any idea."

"No one ever said anything to you?"

"No, nothing like that."

"There must be someone who knows what went on that night at the party. Who do you think I could talk to?"

"I can't think of anyone," he answered too quickly.

"What about her friend, Doreen?"

He didn't think she still lived in Sipponet, but her family did. They had been parishioners. She might find Doreen through them. That was as much as he could tell her.

'Why was he so reluctant?' Julia puzzled on the drive home. He appeared, she thought, to be a man whose conscience was troubling him. Or was she reading too much into their brief meeting?

Julia looked up the Crawford family in the telephone directory as soon as she returned home and called them. After explaining that Reverend Chauncy had referred her, Mrs. Crawford was quite willing to tell Julia that their daughter was currently living in New Bedford. Her name was Doreen Estes now and her husband owned a trawler out of New Bedford Harbor called the Azorean Queen. She had talked with Doreen last night. Their boat was in dock over the weekend but they'd be going out scalloping again the first of the week.

Julia resolved to pay a visit to New Bedford the following day. In anticipation, she rooted through her books for her copy of *Moby-Dick; or, The Whale* and settled down to read.

* * *

Two men sat in a corner booth at Dottie's. Their voices were low and insistent.

"You know what's going on?'

"I know."

"She's asking question."

"I said I know."

"What am I going to do about it?"

"Nothing."

"But she's nosing around, stirring it all up again."

"Calm down. She's nobody, and nothing's going to happen. It'll pass. It's all a dead end."

"But—"

"I said, nothing's going to happen. Now shut up and let me eat my supper in peace."

* * *

The Pittsley Selectmen were meeting in executive session. Albert Carriou, Todd Kingman, and Madison Wentworth sat in Albert's livingroom to discuss freely what they could not discuss in public: the situation with Cutter Briggs.

"You've all read this?" Albert waved *The Pittsley Chronicle* in front of them. The *Chronicle* was a new weekly newspaper, the first that focused exclusively on the town.

Both men nodded.

"How in God's green earth did they find this out so fast?"

Both men shook their heads.

"They're calling him a throwback to Thoreau. *Thoreau*, no less." He read from the first page of the paper, *'Cutter Briggs, in true Massachusetts tradition, has established his own utopian community.'*"

"Bollocks." Albert lowered the paper in disgust. "Briggs doesn't know the meaning of utopian. And this reporter compares it with Fruitlands and Brook Farm as if he were some damn transcendentalist. I will guarantee you he never heard of any one of them. He's no Thoreau, he's a renegade and there is no damn precedent for this kind of thing in Massachusetts. The last thing we need is this newspaper guy making him out to be a hero. So boys, what do we do? We can't reach the bastard by telephone. We can't reach him by mail. And we can't go to his door."

He lit a cigar, forbidden in the town offices, and took a long puff as he looked at the other two men. As president of the Board this term, Albert felt it was only necessary for him to pose the question. It was for the others to come up with solutions.

Madison Wentworth, being the oldest member of the Board and the only lawyer, answered first. "We have to document our procedures, step by step. First, we should get a letter from the telephone company confirming that his phone is shut off. And one from the Post Office saying his mail is undeliverable. Since Briggs hasn't paid the real estate taxes on his land this year, Barstow sent a demand from the Collector's Office but we don't know if it's been delivered. We know it hasn't been returned. If Briggs doesn't respond to the demand, we have to go to the next step; Barstow will have to issue a warrant."

"How's he going to do that if we can't get onto his land?" Albert asked. "The place is sealed up like a national park."

"Maybe we should ask town counsel what to do," Todd Kingman suggested. Todd was the newest member to the Board. He was elected by only 30 votes on a re-count, but he took it as a personal mandate.

"We don't have to spend money on town counsel for every damn problem that comes across our desk," Madison snapped. "I was a practicing lawyer for over thirty years in this town."

"Insurance," Albert reminded him.

"Makes no difference. The law is all about procedures, gentlemen. We follow the procedures, then we dump this puppy in the lap of the State."

That, at least, was an idea they could all agree on.

SATURDAY, JUNE 12th

New Bedford was, in the 18th and 19th centuries, the most ethnically diverse city in America. Of the 10,000 or so men who came to crew on whalers, many originated in the Azores and the Islands. Whalemen were a curious lot. "But think not," Melville wrote, "that this famous town has only harpooneers, cannibals, and bumpkins to show her visitors." For in his day, New Bedford was also the most affluent city in the country. Melville's Ishmael remarked that "nowhere in all America will you find more patrician-like houses; parks and gardens more opulent, than in New Bedford....In summer time, the town is sweet to see; full of fine maples—long avenues of green and gold. And in August, high in air, the beautiful and bountiful horse-chestnuts, candelabra-wise, proffer the passer-by their tapering upright cones of congregated blossoms." Albeit that Ishmael (like Melville himself) arrived in New Bedford in Winter—late December to early January.

There were no avenues of green and gold that Julia could see as she drove on Route 18 into downtown New Bedford that morning with Cat sleeping in the back seat. Instead, she found herself tracing the commercial history of the city in its architecture. The old maritime buildings had become just modest tourist attractions in the form of museums and art galleries. But there were still pockets of extravagant sea captain's homes in a city now riddled with low-income housing.

After the disastrous whaling industry declined, then came textiles. But by the mid-20th century, the textile industry succumbed to cheaper labor down South, foreign imports, and synthetics. The manufacture of electrical devices came and went from the 1940s to the 1970s, leaving another sort of disastrous legacy in the form of pollutants. The once-active three- and four-story brick factories were either boarded up or were used to house social service agencies. Fishing, by default, became the next dominant industry, but it wasn't enough for this city of about 100,000 people. New Bedford reminded Julia of a wealthy old woman fallen on hard times.

New Bedford Harbor lay at the mile-wide mouth of the Acushnet River, gateway to Buzzards Bay and the Atlantic Ocean. Although Ishmael was determined to join a whaler out of Nantucket, where he began his voyage on the Pequod, the twenty-two year old Melville actually embarked from New Bedford in 1841 on the Acushnet, a three-master registered in Fairhaven, the city across the water. Melville writes scantily about New Bedford Harbor as Ishmael leaves the port, other than to extol the soul-lifting smell of the sea.

In more recent years, the smell of the coastal waters was less uplifting. The Harbor went through a catastrophic illness during the last several decades of the 20th century, as a result of contamination and over-fishing. Ultimately, in the 1980s, it became the site of a massive clean-up of PCBs and heavy metals from the electrical manufacturers who had discharged waste into the water both directly and through the sewerage system, polluting the Harbor for at least six miles around. It took more than ten years and a federal 'superfund' program to remedy the problem in the upper harbor.

The fishing industry suffered not only from the effects of the contamination, but then from government quotas imposed on their catch because of low fish stocks up and down the East Coast. Fishing boats had lain dormant, tied up three deep along the docks while the fisherman sat smoking unfiltered cigarettes in local bars or sitting on green-and-white woven-strap lawn chairs in their driveways looking longingly to the east. Fisherman in New Bedford were still mainly Portuguese, with a long tradition of taking to the sea. If they couldn't fish, there was nothing better they wanted to do.

By the beginning of the new century, with the Harbor cleaned and the quotas increased, the boats were back in business and the fish storage and processing plants were thriving. Trucks carrying iced fish destined for national and international markets crowded the roads, passing Julia on the way to Boston and Logan Airport. New Bedford was again the premier East Coast fishing port.

The dock that Julia drove onto was a cement pier about four car-lengths wide and several hundred feet long. The first thing that struck her was the number of masts against the skyline—masts, struts, and cable strung like cobwebs between the masts. They looked like open fans with only the 'bones' showing. There were a hundred boats or more docked along the pier. There was activity everywhere. Hammering against steel. Welding. Burnishing the rust off metal. Scraping barnacles and painting hulls. There were men on every boat and walking along the dock in jeans and sweatshirts, in red or yellow waders, and speaking in Portuguese. Seagulls circling overhead sounded out, and several walked goofy-footed on the concrete pecking away at a discarded donut. The sounds were the sounds of an active and thriving industry.

Julia parked her car at the near end of the dock. The smell of diesel fuel, seaweed, fish, and paint mixed together on the cool breeze off the water. The sky was filled with wispy clouds. The harbor was calm, with small ripples of murky water that shimmered like streamers when the sun broke through and glanced off the water.

Most of the boats were painted either blue or red, with white cabins. The lettering of the names and registry numbers were mainly in white, black, or blue. Names like Santa Isabel, Prince of Peace, Luzitano, It Ain't Easy, and George's Banks. The boats were mostly draggers for cod and flounder, although there were a few scallop trawlers among them. The dragnets were rolled around steel spools some eight or more feet in diameter. She saw several paint-chipped wooden ships, but most were steel-hulled, seventy or more feet long.

And there, at the end of the dock, was the dragger named the "Azorean Queen." A swarthy, dark-haired man with a welder's mask was suspended by a rope seat over the side of the boat nearest the dock (she mentally recited "fore, aft, port, starboard" as though crossing herself). The sparks crackled and arced as he welded the hull.

'That must be John Estes,' she thought. And the woman with the bleached blonde ponytail who was mending the net would probably be his wife, Doreen. She was wearing jeans and a black sweatshirt, but even so, she was painfully thin. She would be a few years younger than Julia. Forty-two or so. But she seemed haggard and her skin looked tan and leathery. There was a focus, almost a desperation, in the way she mended the net. She looked like a woman who had been through rough times. Despite that, Julia thought she could see the pretty young girl she once had been.

"Excuse me," Julia called. "I'm looking for Doreen Estes."

"That's me," Doreen glanced down at Julia and continued mending. Her voice was a harsh combination of cigarettes and rough sea wind.

"Do you suppose I could talk to you for a few minutes...down here?"

"What about?"

"Nicole Fayette."

Doreen stopped mending and looked at Julia as though she were a loan officer from the bank, come to collect on their debt. Doreen took a deep breath, looked over at her husband—immersed in the noise of his welding—and nodded.

Minutes later, Julia and Doreen were walking on the dock away from the boat. Julia had rehearsed what she would say to the woman, telling her she was writing a retrospective case analysis for a new journal of the psychology of violent crime.

"Why?"

"I don't ask," Julia smiled conspiratorially. "My editor told me to. It's part of a series he's doing on unsolved murders over the past twenty-five years."

"I expect there'd be a lot of those."

"Yes, but he's doing it state by state. It's a Boston-based journal so we're starting with Massachusetts. Cold cases are all the rage on t.v. now, so that's where he got the idea. I'm just going to jot down a few notes while we talk, okay?"

Doreen nodded and Julia felt a pang of remorse about lying to her as she took out her pen and notebook. She couldn't tell Doreen the truth and still protect Sherry's identity. Doreen would guess it immediately.

"You were there at the junkyard the night Nicole Fayette died, weren't you?"

Doreen hesitated before answering. "Yes, for a while. I left the party early. I had a little too much to drink and got sick. My boyfriend took me home."

"Your husband, John?"

"No, someone else. I didn't know John then. Anyway, we didn't stay long, so I really don't know what happened. I already told that to the police."

"Were there other girls there?"

"Just Nikki, me, and Eileen Mann."

"Do you know where I can find Eileen Mann?"

"She's dead," Doreen answered, closing her eyes for a second as though in silent prayer.

"When did that happen?"

"A long time ago. A few weeks after Nikki disappeared. She died of an overdose. I wound up losing two friends in one summer."

"Did she ever tell you what went on at the party after you left?"

"I never actually saw her after the party. Except for the funeral."

"Were you two close?"

"Not as close as Nikki and me."

"Were there drugs at the party that night?"

Doreen shook her head emphatically. "No. We didn't do hard drugs."

"Except for Eileen."

"I didn't know that. I really didn't."

Julia nodded and wrote Eileen Mann's name in her notepad. "Who were the men who were there that night?"

Doreen frowned and looked impatient. "All this is in the police records. Do I really have to go over it again?"

"No, not if it's painful for you." Julia touched her arm. "But maybe something you forgot, or maybe something I'll put together from everybody's accounts, will shed new light on Nicole's death."

"You said this is a Boston journal. Do live in Boston?" Doreen asked skeptically.

"No. Pittsley."

"Then you know what it's like, living in a small town."

"Meaning?"

Doreen shrugged. "Everybody knows everybody."

"Yes, I suppose. If you grew up there."

"They were all my friends."

"The men at the party?"

"Yes. There were some from other towns who came and left, but mostly it was the regulars."

"Who were...?"

"My boyfriend, 'Blockhead'—that was one of his nicknames. Joe Block. Blockbuster, Around the Block—he had a lot of nicknames."

"Where is he now?"

"He owns an auto parts store."

"In Sipponet?"

"Yes. It's called 'Engine Block.'"

"Of course," Julia said with a smile.

Doreen smiled back and her face momentarily sweetened.

"Who else?" Julia asked, and Doreen's face slackened back into creases.

"George Cranshaw and his cousin, Conny."

Julia was startled. Conny Cranshaw had been the prime suspect—at least as far as Adam had been concerned—in Jeannine Bradburn's murder. He was never implicated, but Adam still mistrusted him. Julia didn't like him either, but he wasn't the killer and she shouldn't be surprised to hear his name pop up around town.

"But Conny Cranshaw lived in Pittsley, didn't he?"

"Yes, but George lived in Sipponet and he and George always hung together. George died of cancer a while back."

"Who else?"

"Joe Woods. We called him 'Little Joe' because my Joe was a foot taller. Little Joe was a farmhand for Ellis Chalmers. Still is, the last I heard. That's about the best he can do. Then there was 'Bucklure,' Dennis Buckley, he operated a front-end loader back then. He has his own construction company now. Lots of money."

"Would that be 'Buckley Builders'?" Julia had passed the huge construction site many times.

"Yes." Doreen absently looked down at her hands. "I used to get manicures." She rubbed her left hand over her right. "My skin was soft. I put lotion on them, but it doesn't help."

She looked at Julia's hands holding the pen and note-book and Julia felt embarrassed. She had just fixed her nailpolish and her hands looked so unworked compared with Doreen's.

"I use baby oil after I shower," Julia confided, "maybe that would help."

"Maybe."

"Why do you suppose," Julia resumed, "Dennis Buckley has his business in Pittsley rather than Sipponet?"

"I don't know."

"When did he start Buckley Builders? Before or after the party?"

"After. At least a year after, I'd say."

"Does he still live in Sipponet?"

"No, Pittsley."

"Have you seen him recently?"

"No. Not in a long time."

Julia wrote the names and nicknames down on her notepad.

"Who else was there?"

"The only other guy was Frank Leach. 'Leachy.'"

"Where is he now?"

"No idea. Nowhere around here."

"When did Frank Leach leave Sipponet?"

"Right after Eileen died."

"Were they together at the party, Frank and Eileen?"

"Could be. I don't know. Mostly Eileen free-lanced."

"What about Nicole? Did she have a boyfriend there?"

"No."

"She free-lanced too?" Julia watched for Doreen's reaction.

"Not the same way," Doreen said defensively. "Nikki just liked to dance."

"If she went alone that night, how did she get there? Walk?"

"She could have, it's not that far. I don't know. We got there after her."

"So you don't know if anybody brought her?"

"No, but it wouldn't matter. Somebody could have given her a ride, but she wasn't with anybody in particular. We just all hung out together."

Doreen put her hands in her pockets and turned her face into the wind and squinted her eyes. "I think you have to be born to the sea to love it the way my husband does."

"You don't like it?"

"You get lost out there. With no shoreline. Nothing but ocean as far as you can see. And just a few feet of decking from rail to rail. You start thinking about what's keeping you on top of the water. You look at the ocean then look at the size of your ship. Not a very good ratio."

"Speaking of ratios," Julia said. It was a terrible segue but she was desperate to get this back on track, "That was an unusual ratio at the party, isn't it? Three girls to six guys? Well, really, five to two, because you had a boyfriend."

"It wasn't unusual. That was the group."

Doreen sounded defensive again so Julia focused on the men.

"What about the guys who came and left. Who were they?"

"I don't remember. Guys just came and left. Once in a while they came with girls, but usually not. It was always that way. Some were townies but they weren't regulars in our crowd. Sometimes a few came from nearby towns, but they didn't stay."

"Why not?"

"They just came for a couple of drinks and a few laughs on their way to the next party."

A breeze came up and ruffled Doreen's ponytail. Julia wiped the stray hairs out of her eyes.

"Did any of the regulars in your crowd tell you what went on at the party after you and your boyfriend left?"

"No." Doreen looked away.

"Weren't you concerned when Nicole disappeared after the party?"

"No. Nikki took off more than a few times, you know? I just figured she found somebody to take off with again."

"And as time went on?"

Doreen brushed the thin wisps off her forehead and frowned. "I didn't connect the dots. I thought she'd just left town."

"Without her daughter?"

"It wasn't like she hadn't done it before."

It seemed to Julia that the only one who had really missed Nicole was Sherry. She wondered what Sherry's grandmother said to pacify the child when her mother didn't return?

A couple of fishermen passed them on the way to their boat. They nodded at Doreen, who nodded back.

"What was Nicole like, Doreen? You and she were best friends, right?"

"In high school."

"Did she have any other close girlfriends?"

"Nikki was always more into guys."

"Was she…flirty?" 'There must be a better word,' Julia thought, but she couldn't think of one that didn't sound derogatory.

Doreen snorted. "Yeah, I suppose. She liked to have a good time."

"Was she having a good time at the party?"

"Nikki always had a good time at a party."

Julia couldn't help feeling that Doreen was being evasive. "But she wasn't with anyone in particular?"

"Not that I know of."

She still wasn't satisfied, but obviously Doreen was not going to tell her what she wanted to know.

They had reached the end of the pier and stood there a moment looking back over the harbor.

"When they found Nicole's body, Doreen, and you learned that she'd been murdered, who did you think did it?"

Doreen was silent.

"Somebody came to mind, didn't he?"

Doreen began walking back. "No."

"It's been half a lifetime ago, don't you think it's time to tell?"

"There's nothing more to tell. That's all there is. Now I've got to get back to the boat. We've shipping out tomorrow."

Julia didn't want to leave her feeling pushed. "You always crew with your husband?" she said, keeping pace with Doreen.

"Have to. We can't get a full complement."

"Why not?"

Doreen gestured it off. "They think it's a queer boat. That's how we got it so cheap. But it isn't. And I've got work to do if you'll excuse me now."

Julia quickly wrote something on her business card and presented it Doreen. "My home phone is on the back. Please call me if you think of anything else that might be helpful."

Doreen put the card into her jeans' pocket without looking at it. "As far as Nikki goes, I don't know anything else."

"Well, just in case."

Doreen pursed her lips and nodded, then walked away.

"Thank you for your time," Julia called after her.

As Julia got back into her car, she watched Doreen climb back onto the boat. The panorama of boats and crew blended together in a portrait of life on the docks. She tried to imagine what New Bedford might have been like in Melville's day when it was 'the city that lit the world.' The dock would not have been concrete; all the ships would have been wooden with wooden masts and billowy sails; and the whaling ships would have had large crews. Today, the crews were small, their voyages short, and the ships would have electronic fish-finders. But the men would be the same—the men…and women…who go down to the sea in ships.

* * *

"You're not coming over tomorrow, then?" Adam asked. He and Cutter sat at the table in Cutter's kitchen. It would be the first Sunday in a long time that the three of them didn't get together.

"I can't drive on your roads no more."

"I could pick you up and bring you over to my house, then drive you back."

"Nope. Once I'm off the compound, they can get at me. They'll just stop your truck and pull me out."

"They wouldn't do that."

"The hell they wouldn't," Cutter said. "Don't you think the police have been driving up to my gate two, three times a day to try to catch it open? They taped a letter from the Selectmen's Office to the post. I had one of the kids pull it off, tear it up, and drop it outside. I'm telling you, Adam, they're not going easy with this. I didn't expect them to. But it's worse now that it was in yesterday's paper about me. Did you see that crap?"

"No. What'd it say?"

Cutter reached over to a pile of papers in the to-burn pile next to his woodstove and plucked one off the top.

"Driver brought it by. See here?" Cutter pointed to a headline and read aloud. "'Backwards Thoreau.'"

"Backwoods," Adam corrected.

"Anyway I had to look him up. I heard of him but I didn't remember too much. Honor—Angel's oldest—gave me her history book and I've been reading about him. Do you know that he only stayed in Walden for two years, two months, and two days?"

"I thought it was longer."

"Nope. And the ones who started those old back-to-nature communities? Hell, they were weenies, too. That Brook Farm only lasted six years. And that other one, Fruitlands, they only lasted six months. Never even got through the Winter. One growing season, that's all. Bunch of pantywaists. They weren't Swamp Yankees, that's for sure. That newspaper writer is full of bull." He tossed the new *Pittsley Chronicle* back on the pile.

The battle of the town newspapers—the *Sipponet Village Gazette* which covered only Sipponet news, and the *Tipisquin Gazette* which covered several towns in the adjacent county, including Pittsley—had heated up now that *The Pittsley Chronicle* began siphoning off subscribers from their limited readership. The *Chronicle* was hand-delivered (by Everett Holmes' boy, Asa) rather than mailed, so Cutter could keep up with local happenings, including his own.

"How did they find out about you?"

"Who knows? Maybe when we pulled the kids out of school, or I delivered the letter to the Town Clerk, or somebody-told-somebody-told-somebody, you know the way it is."

Cutter fell silent for a minute, then continued, "At first, they thought it was just about the money—because I'm not going to pay their illegal real estate taxes. But by now they're figuring it's more than that. Like Ruby Ridge, maybe."

'Ruby Ridge' was a clarion call for anti-federalism since the assault on the Weaver family in northern Idaho. Adam had met Randy Weaver at Ft. Bragg before Weaver got his discharge. At that time, he seemed like a normal Green Beret, tough and self-contained. There wasn't any evidence then of the religious extremist he'd become some ten years later. Like most Americans, Adam had followed the events during the stand-off between Randy and the U.S. Marshals in 1992.

Apparently, since Randy's Army days, he and his wife, Vicki, had become apocalyptic Christians. Not only were they convinced the end of the world was coming, they were paranoid about government conspiracies. Or, Adam wondered, is it really paranoid when the government actually does conspire against you? Anyway, if they hadn't gotten mixed up with the Aryan Nation's white supremacists, they might never have come to the attention of the government informer. The informer, Fadeley, was turned out by the Bureau of Alcohol, Tobacco and Firearms after dodging his own federal charges of gunrunning. Fadeley badgered Randy to sell him two sawed-off shotguns, which, ultimately, Weaver did. From there it went to an indictment against Randy for the illegal sale. He was offered the same deal as Fadeley—to become an informant on the Aryan Nation. Randy refused. He was apprehended, prosecuted, and released on bail, believing that he might lose his land if convicted.

Ruby Ridge, in the Selkirk Mountains above Ruby Creek, was a twenty-acre parcel that Randy and his wife bought in 1984 when they decided to wait out the apocalypse on a pristine mountaintop. They had no electricity or running water in their cabin for them and the five children—Sara, Samuel, Rachel, infant Elishaba (born later), and their 'adopted' son, Kevin. But it was their paradise.

Out on bail, Randy received a letter with his court date of March 20, 1991. It may have been one of the deadliest typographical errors in modern times. The actual date was supposed to have been February 20th. Randy did not show up in court on February 20th. (Adam wondered if he would actually have shown up on March 20th.) Randy was declared a federal fugitive. An arrest warrant was filled out, and the wheels of injustice began to grind slowly up the mountaintop.

The horrendous weeklong stand-off between Randy and the U.S. Marshal's Special Operations Group resulted in the deaths of a federal marshal, and Vicki Weaver, Sam Weaver, and Striker, the yellow Lab. It could easily have become the annihilation of the entire family except for an intermediary, Green Beret Colonel Bo Gritz, who finally was allowed to bring Randy out with his remaining children.

Randy was tried and exonerated on federal charges. He was found guilty only on failing to appear in court. Even that, Adam thought, was bullshit. Randy served four months in prison and was fined $10,000. But when he got out, he filed a wrongful-death suit against the government and was awarded $100,000 for himself and $1 million to each of his daughters.

Too little, too late, Adam thought.

After a two-year investigation into the incident, the Department of Justice concluded only that: "Although we do not find evidence of improper motivation, we remain concerned by the lack of timeliness of disclosures, and faulty judgment in assessing the importance of these issues."

"Don't get in that mindset, Cutter," Adam said gravely. "No armed resistance. That's taking it way beyond what it has to be."

"Nah, don't worry," Cutter waved it away. "I'm a family man now. I'm not itching for a fight. My old .38 is so pitted it wouldn't hit the side of a barn and my rifles haven't been fired in years. And I know better than to take aim at an army."

"You sure?"

"I'm sure."

Then, Cutter grinned. "There is one thing I like about that Thoreau, though. At least he was willing to go to jail for refusing to pay his poll tax. Even if it was only for one night because someone else paid it for him."

"Well, don't get any ideas. I'm not paying your real estate taxes."

"And I'm not going to jail," Cutter vowed.

* * *

After her interview with Doreen, Julia still had the whole afternoon free. Who should she see next? The easiest to find, she concluded, would be Doreen's old boyfriend in his auto parts' store in Sipponet. She got the address of 'Engine Block' from the phone book and headed for the Village.

As she neared the town green, she realized she hadn't even noticed how she got there. "Why am I doing this?" she said aloud to Cat. "It's not *my* job to solve the crime. It's my job to treat the patient." She shook her head at the dog. "And it really isn't critical to Sherry's therapy. Chances are, if Nicole had lived, she'd probably have run off with some ill-suited man anyway, and Sherry would have felt even more abandoned."

Yet, here she was, pulling up to the auto parts' store without a real reason for being there.

There were no other customers in the store so the owner focused his attention on her. Joe Block was tall, but thick about the middle, with a receding hairline, and glasses. Julia tried to picture what he might have looked like twenty years ago when he dated Doreen. But even being generous, it didn't seem as though he'd have been very handsome.

"Can I help you?" he asked, flashing Julia a smile that crinkled up his eyes. Suddenly, he seemed animated and Julia thought she saw what might have attracted Doreen to him—an unfailing eagerness to please. He would have taken Doreen anywhere she wanted to go and given her anything he had the power to give. But he was the sedan that got traded in for a muscle car. What a different ride it might have been for Doreen with him rather than John Estes.

'But what the hell,' Julia thought, referring to Phillip, '<u>I</u> chose a Land Rover who turned into a Mazzarati. So you really never know, do you?'

"Joseph Block?" she inquired.

"Joe." He stuck out his hand.

"Hi, Julia Arnault."

He shook her hand heartily. "What can I do for you, Ms. Arnault?"

"Doctor, actually. I'm a psychologist. I'd like to ask you some questions about Nicole Fayette, if you wouldn't mind." She used her most unthreatening tone.

Realizing she wasn't a customer, Joe Block's smile dwindled. "For what reason?"

Julia told him the same story as she'd told Doreen, after which Joe nodded his head twice then slowly shook it.

"I'm afraid I don't know anything. I wasn't there."

"You were there earlier, though. You and Doreen."

He nodded. "Yes, but we left."

"Why?"

He actually blushed. Julia found it quite disarming.

"We had an argument."

"Over what?"

"Oh, silly stuff. I don't even remember."

He was being gallant, Julia thought, not wanting to say that Doreen had been drunk.

"Have you seen her recently?"

"Doreen? No. Not in years."

"Are you married, Mr. Block?"

"Nineteen years. We have four children."

"I guess you didn't go out with Doreen for very long after the party, then."

"She broke up with me. She never said why. Turned out for the best though, because then I married Ann."

He began to get restless, rearranging the items on the countertop.

"Do you remember who was still at the party when you and Doreen left?"

"The same people that were always there. I told the police back then."

"Did you ever wonder which of them killed Nicole?"

Joe Block blinked. "It couldn't have been any of them."

"Why not? She never came home after the party."

"I don't know anything about that."

"And you've never heard anything since?"

"No."

"Not even a rumor?"

"Nope."

"You mean nobody cared?"

He scowled. "Of course people cared. But it wasn't any of *us*."

"Then who?"

"I don't know. Maybe she met somebody after the party."

"Like who?"

"I don't know."

His voice indicated nervousness even though his expression didn't change.

"She's the only person who was ever murdered in Sipponet, and nobody knows who did it? Even though Nicole partied with her friends that night? Don't you think that's strange?"

He glanced impatiently around the store. "I guess the police just couldn't find out anything. I don't know anything about police investigations."

"What did you think when Nicole never showed up again days and weeks after the party?"

"I thought she might have run off."

"With who?"

"I don't know."

"But she didn't run off, did she?"

"No."

"What was your opinion of Nicole Fayette?"

Joe Block shrugged and folded his arms across his chest.

"You didn't like her?"

"I didn't have anything to do with her. She was trouble."

"How?"

"She kind of spread it around, if you know what I mean."

"But not with you?"

He dropped his hands to his side. "No. Never."

Another customer entered and Joe's eyes immediately locked on him. "Excuse me, I better see what he wants. I really don't have anything more to say on the subject."

"Well, thank you for your time." Julia offered him her card. "Please let me know if you remember anything else."

"Sure," he said unconvincingly. "Glad to be of help." He placed her card on the counter as he walked swiftly towards the burly man in a green- and blue-plaid flannel shirt.

With half the afternoon left, Julia decided to keep going. The first two interviews certainly didn't yield anything. Except that both Doreen and Joe seemed almost indifferent to Nikki's murder. Or was it simply that they had moved on with their lives?

Buckley Builders was on the way home, so she decided she may as well visit 'Bucklure.' One thing that seemed consistent was that life had greatly changed for Doreen, Joe Block, and Dennis Buckley in the year following Nikki's death. What would Nicole be doing today, Julia wondered, if she had lived?

The bearded man in the front-end loader pointed her towards the office building that looked like a large corrugated metal shed. She was lucky to find the owner in, he said, because Dennis usually spent a lot of time out on his construction sites.

It was what Julia expected of a construction office, divided into a front room for the assistant and a back room for the owner. The front room was stark with a metal desk, old file cabinets, and an old wooden chair in front of the desk. The newest thing in the room was the computer. But all the piles of paper seemed organized into bins and there was a tidiness about the office.

As Dennis Buckley's attractive assistant escorted her into his office, Julia had an immediate and negative response to the man. She mentally coined the word 'egotesticle.' He appeared tall and trim, self-assured, with black hair and blue eyes. High, defined cheekbones. Strong chin. Handsome, actually, and well aware of it. As he motioned her to a chair, she felt him evaluating her looks. She would need, she thought, to take a different approach with this one.

"You must tell me how you got the nickname 'Buck-lure,'" she said ingenuously.

He laughed, revealing perfectly white teeth. Movie-star quality.

"I haven't heard that name in years. Who've you been talking to?"

"Doreen Crawford. Doreen Estes now."

"Good old Dory." He nodded with what seemed like a hint of a smirk. "How is she?"

"Very well."

"When did you see her?"

"This morning." She proceeded to give him the same story as the others and tried to make light of it, but she could see him pulling back.

"Estes," he repeated as though it were a slightly tainted taste in his mouth. "Her husband's Portuguese?"

"I believe so."

"What's he do?"

"He owns fishing boats." Inwardly she thought, 'Good grief, fishing boats, plural? Why am I doing this?'

"Out of where? New Beje?" He used the Portuguese term for New Bedford.

"Yes."

"Is she still a looker?"

"Oh, yes," Julia lied, not sure why.

"So you're making the rounds?"

"Trying to."

"Explain to me what the point is of writing about an old unsolved killing. You think you're going to turn up some new information?"

"No. It's just one case-report in a journal that focuses on violence."

He tilted back in his chair and crossed his leg. He wore jeans, as befitting a contractor, but they were expensive jeans, neither too old nor too new, with a wide brown-leather belt. The pants pulled up just far enough to reveal expensive brown leather boots. His shirt was button-down oxford cloth. All designed with the look of a Texas oilman.

"Why this case?"

"I didn't pick it, my editor did. Maybe because he knows I live here and he wants primary sources."

"How am I a primary source?"

"You were at the party the night Nicole disappeared."

"So?"

The intercom buzzed. He excused himself to answer it. "Tell him," he said to his assistant, "I'll call him back in a little while."

His fingers, Julia noticed, were long and tapered. Unlike Doreen, his nails were manicured just to the fingertips and buffed. There was no wedding band. Most women would find him attractive, but she didn't. All the elements were there, but something about him bothered her. Conceit, perhaps. Narcissism.

He turned back to her. "You were saying?"

"There are only a handful of people who saw Nicole alive that night, and you're among them."

He leaned challengingly towards her across the desk. "You're not suggesting that I had anything to do with her death?"

"Not at all. I just want to know what went on at the party."

He leaned back again and tilted his head. "Didn't Dory tell you?"

"No. She and Joe Block left early." Julia waited a beat, then added, "Didn't they?"

"I guess so."

"When did Nicole leave?"

"I don't recall." He looked levelly at her, as if to say that he did recall and had no intention of telling her.

"Did she leave before you?"

"Did she leave before me? Yes, I think she did."

"With whom?"

"Nobody. She just left on her own."

"Why?"

"Who knows?"

"What time?"

He arched one eyebrow accusingly. "I told you, I don't recall."

"How much longer did the party go on?"

"It wasn't like a real party. We just partied, you know, hung out and drank, listened to music, jawed, that's all. We were kids. We just had a few laughs."

"Any drugs?"

"Maybe a little weed. Nothing hardcore. Don't forget, we were just bumpkins."

He said that in a way, Julia thought, that was intended to make fun of her rather than himself.

"What else did you do?"

"We danced. That was the era of dir-ty dan-cing." The way he drew out the syllables made it seem salacious. "Or was that before your time?"

"Who supplied the liquor?" she asked, not responding to his question.

He smirked at her evasion, then said, "No liquor. Too expensive. Beer. Lots and lots of beer."

"Did Doreen and Joe drink?"

"Everybody drank."

"Including Nicole?"

"God, who remembers anymore?" He shrugged it away.

"I'm just curious why Nicole left. Everybody says she liked a good party."

"You could never predict what Nikki would do."

"So that wasn't the first time she left the party early?"

"No. Like I said, it wasn't really a party."

"Got it." Julia nodded. "Was she going with anyone then?"

He shook his head. "Dory would know better than me. I didn't keep tabs on Nikki."

"Did you have a girlfriend back then?"

He smiled suggestively. "I had a lot of girlfriends back then."

"Is that why they called you 'Bucklure.'?

"For that," he said patronizingly, "they'd have to call me 'Doe-lure.' No, they called me Bucklure because I lived for hunting in those days."

"And you used bucklure to attract the deer?"

"Bucklure. Saltlicks. I used whatever I could to bag as many as I could. Legal or not."

Julia said nothing in response.

"What, you don't like hearing about hunting Bambi?" He snorted. "Don't get your knickers in a twist, I don't hunt anymore."

"Why not?"

"I don't have time enough to do anything but work to pay alimony and child-support."

"Did you marry somebody local?"

"No chance."

"Why not?"

"Because you don't shit where you eat."

"Is that why you opened your business in Pittsley rather than Sipponet?"

He paused at that as though deciding whether or not to be offended. "I opened my business in Pittsley because it's a better location, and I got a good price on the land. That's it. And now I do have to get back to work."

"Yes, of course. You wouldn't happen to know where I can find Joe Woods or Frank Leach, would you?"

"Joe works for Chalmers' Farms. Leachy, I have no clue. You're talking to everybody who was there that night, are you?"

"I'm supposed to."

He snorted. "A futile enterprise. We all told everything we knew to the police." He eyed her appraisingly again. "You go with Adam Sabeski, don't you?"

Julia was caught by surprise. She should have realized that people might know her, have seen her with Adam, or seen her around town.

"Yes," she answered. "How do you know him?" Adam was older than Dennis, so they wouldn't have gone to school together.

"He grew up here." He smiled knowingly. "Everybody knew Adam Sabeski. He was what my mother used to call 'a hellion.'"

"In what way?" she asked tentatively.

He continued to smile, but now it seemed tantalizing.

"In every way."

Julia usually preferred spending Saturday nights at Adam's house because it was like a vacation. The evening temperature had dropped just enough for a feeble excuse to light the woodstove. The pot-bellied stove in the center of the rough livingroom warmed the house with a soothing heat. The stove door was open and they watched the flames hypnotically while they ate the dinner he'd cooked for her. He made a hearty lentil soup in his crockpot and they sat together in his large armchair, bare feet propped up and intertwined on the spool-table.

"I was over to see Cutter today," Adam said. "He's disconnected all his utilities and he and Angel are hunkering down for the duration."

"She's with him on this?" Julia couldn't disguise her shock.

"Completely."

"What about the children, how are they going to manage?"

"Angel has all the books and things she needs for home-schooling them. They've got the garden going and Cutter's got the place fenced off so no one can enter."

Just when she thought she was getting the hang of this country life and Adam's assorted friends, something new came along. "What do you think? Does he seem rational?"

Adam raised and lowered his eyebrows with a 'who can say?' expression. "Cutter's always been a bubble-off-plumb. But yes, I think he is rational. As rational as any outlaw, anyway. If it were somewhere other than here—like in some expanse in the prairie states—he probably would go unnoticed." Then he thought about Randy Weaver. "Or maybe not."

"Is the town doing anything about it?"

"Not yet, not that I know of. But a story about him appeared in *The Pittsley Chronicle*. Called him a backwoods Thoreau." Adam smiled. "Or 'backwards Thoreau,' according to Cutter."

"I hope they don't make a *cause célèbre* out of him." Julia was beginning to feel the heat combining with a hot flash and she sat up and fanned herself.

"It's getting too warm for a fire in here anymore," Adam remarked. "We'll have to do it outside next time. Like camping. Do you like camping? I don't think I ever asked you that."

"Do you know," she said, preoccupied, "we've never been away together? Not even for a weekend?"

He paused, then said, "Do you want to go away for a weekend?"

"I think I do."

"When?"

"Sometime this summer."

"Where do you want to go?"

"Northern Quebec. I'd like to see my grandparents' old farm. I haven't been there since I was a child."

"I'd have thought that would be a difficult memory for you."

She had told him how, when she was still just a child, her grandparents had been murdered by a serial killer. And how that became a reason for her to study psychology.

"Yes," she agreed. "But I never went to their funeral. Only my father did. My mother stayed home with me. I've never seen their graves."

"And that's meaningful to you?"

"I guess it is. It seems wrong somehow."

It suddenly occurred to her that she wanted to see where Nicole was buried.

* * *

Late in the night, the same two men from Dottie's Restaurant talked on the telephone. Their voices were low, but the one had become more excitable, more insistent.

"You said nothing would happen. But she hasn't stopped. She keeps asking questions. What if she learns something? Questions, questions, questions. She's going to find out."

"There's nothing to find out. No evidence, no witnesses, no suspicion, no motive. We worked all this out. Now get a grip on yourself."

"How do we know there's no evidence?"

"Because there isn't. If there was, you'd have been charged a long time ago."

"I don't like it. I don't like it."

"Stop repeating yourself. Everything's been taken care of. There are no loose ends. Do you understand?"

"All right," replied the other voice reluctantly.

"That's it, then."

The parties hung up. There was one loose end, however, just one. But never mind, that one loose end wasn't strong enough to make a hangman's knot.

SUNDAY, JUNE 13th

There wasn't much to Nicole Fayette's grave—just a small bronze plaque with her name and dates. But it had been tended recently. Julia noted that the border had been plucked clean to make the memorial plaque visible. Was that Sherry's doing? It was something she would ask her patient at the next session.

How very young had Nicole been at her death, only twenty-four. According to Sherry's birth certificate, her mother would have been nineteen when Sherry was born. Pregnant at eighteen. Maybe just out of high school. Back in 1975, Julia thought, unlike now, a child out of wedlock would have been a social disgrace. Particularly in a country town like Sipponet. People would have talked unkindly about her. Yet, she kept her daughter and lived with her parents. She didn't marry the father. So there she was for five homebound years. She didn't drive, or at least didn't have a car. Or a job. Or child support. All she did was take care of her baby and do chores at home, Julia imagined. Probably not the life she envisioned or wanted. Even though it was of her own making, it wasn't entirely her own making—there was still the absent father. At twenty-four, Nicole would have energy, lots of hormones. Obviously she liked to dance, liked to party, and was indiscriminate in her choice of men. And every now and then, she ran away from home, away from her child, her parents, and the drudgery of her life to go off with some man and have fun. But she always came back. She loved Sherry, Julia was certain. She loved her little daughter, but she needed to be free of her sometimes in the only way she knew how. Wrong, yes. Understandable, yes. Not something to die for.

Nicole was the only murder victim in the Sipponet Cemetery. She was the aberration. According to the newspaper article, hers was the only murder that had ever occurred in Sipponet until then. So how could the mystery of her death have gone on for so long? If she'd been the Mayor's daughter, or the town beauty queen, or a college student on the dean's list, would she be so neglected? Was there a 'she asked for it' mentality around her killing? Is that why everyone seemed to close ranks against Julia's investigating? Or were they protecting someone? Maybe someone whose life, they believed was worth more than Nicole's.

Church bells sounded off in the distance, dogs barked intermittently, a hawk called a piercing call overhead, and crows cawed as they did fly-bys. The morning sun warmed her enough to remove her jacket. It was a cloudless sky. The air was clean and a slight breeze stirred the leaves of the trees around the edge of the cemetery. Amongst all these graves, it felt good to be alive.

And yet, she acknowledged, everything is impermanent. "Someday, in some cemetery, someone may look at my gravestone and wonder what kind of life the woman lived who is buried there," she said aloud. Is that why was she feeling so urgent about finding some meaning in Nicole's death? And, thereby, her own life?

But no, Julia thought. It wasn't just Nicole she was concerned about, it was Sherry. It was Sherry who was at risk.

She stopped for gas at the nearby station and asked directions to the Sipponet junkyard.

"There ain't no junkyard," the skinny young blonde man told her as he filled her tank. "There used to be, but now it's a dump. Just down the road." He pointed off to the left. His forearm was barely thicker than his bony wrist.

She followed his directions and pulled up to the chain-link fence that surrounded the Sipponet Recycling Center. It was closed, but she could easily see through the chain-links. There were huge metal bins for bags of rubbish, cans, and bottles. To one side were mounds of metal discards—lawn mowers and other disposable equipment. To the other side was what looked like a landfill with shingles, wood, and everything plastic.

What might it have been like here twenty years ago, in this off-the-road site, when it was just a junkyard? Where would they have gathered to party Memorial Day night in 1980? There were no houses in sight even now, so it would have been even more secluded back then. They would have played their music loud and not have to worry about disturbing anyone.

Julia would have been Nicole's age, just about, in 1980. But Julia was in graduate school that year, finishing her doctorate. Still, she would have danced to the same music at the parties and clubs she went to with Phillip. They were already married, but Karen wasn't born yet. That would happen the year after. She closed her eyes and ran through her memory of songs. There was always Beatles' music, and the Rolling Stones. What else? Pink Floyd. Elton John. Billy Joel. Fleetwood Mac. Bruce Springsteen. The Spinners.

Sitting in her car, she began humming, and then started singing and moving to the music.

I keep working my way back to you, babe....

She kept humming, although she only remembered the lyrics to the first verse.

With a burning love inside....

It was a great beat. Everybody's favorite. She could almost imagine the group of friends in the junkyard dancing, singing, toking, drinking. Not so very different from what she and her friends were doing at the same time on Beacon Street.

'What if,' Julia asked herself, '*she* had gotten pregnant?' She and Phillip had been sleeping together throughout grad school. Would *she* have had an abortion? Or would she have had Nicole's courage to deliver the baby. Even then, it wouldn't have been the same courage as Nicole because Phillip would have married her sooner rather than later. He wouldn't have fled, leaving her alone with Karen. And she had the advantage of an education. She could get a decent-paying job if she had to. But the distance between her and Nicole seemed less than before.

As she drove away, she began singing another favorite from Bob Seger and the Silver Bullet Band:

Say I'm old fashioned
say I'm over the hill
Da-da da da da da da-da...
Still like that old time a-rock 'n' roll....

Cat looked up at her with wondering eyes as Julia beat time to the music on the steering wheel.

Finding the Ellis Chalmers' farm was easy enough, but finding Joe Woods wasn't.

"It's Sunday," Mrs. Chalmers declared. "Joe don't work Sundays."

"Do you know where I might find him?" Julia asked the grey-haired older woman. Actually, she was probably only ten years older than herself.

"Not in church, honey."

That was as helpful as Mrs. Chalmers could be. Julia would have to come back another time.

She still had two other people to talk with, Conny Cranshaw and Frank Leach. She hadn't a clue where 'Leachy' might be. She had hoped Joe Woods might know. And as for Conny Cranshaw, she was reluctant to meet with him. There was never any love lost between Adam and Conny, but when Adam accused him of murdering the little Bradburn girl, the line had been drawn. Conny hated Adam and probably, by proxy, her. She would have to talk with the man at some point, but not just yet.

* * *

Angel was looking somewhat less angelic than the last time he'd seen her, Adam thought. Her blonde hair was dark at the roots, and she'd lost weight. But she still seemed vivacious as she'd prepared delicious hamburgers and baked potatoes on the grill for all of them. He'd come to like

Angel. She was good for Cutter, although Adam still couldn't quite acclimate to the fact that his friend had inherited a passel of stepchildren with his marriage.

The children sat at their own picnic table next to the aboveground pool that wasn't filled with water yet. Adam, Billy, Cutter, and Angel sat in lawn chairs, watching them.

"Are they complaining yet about not having television?" Billy asked. "Billy Jr. would."

"Well," Angel answered coyly, "they go over to their cousins' house. They use the computers there, too. Mal made a path through the woods to both Driver's and Boomer's."

Adam wondered if Angel called her husband 'Malbone' when they were alone. Funny, how some wives didn't like their husbands' old nicknames. But Cutter would always be Cutter to everyone else.

"Of course," Angel continued, "we all go back and forth several times a week. They even come over here for Saturday night suppers."

"We're eating out of the freezer for now," Cutter explained. "I'm running it on a generator powered by a gas engine. I filled up the freezer and the drums of gasoline before I seceded. What we've got there'll take us through most of the summer."

"What about winter?" Billy asked.

"Don't need a freezer in winter."

"I mean food."

"Barter," Cutter answered, taking bites of his burger. "I'm planning to set up a barter table by the gate. We can barter our produce for the things we need. Like a free-trade zone."

"We'll have pies and cakes, too," Angel added. "And crafts. And of course the wooden items that Mal makes. Picnic tables and such. Even in winter, we can sell preserves and canned goods, and other things."

"Tessa's going to love that," Billy commented. "She'll be your best customer."

Adam glanced over at the old barn, which looked like it had a new coat of paint and repair to the broken boards.

"What's in the barn?"

"Two cows," Angel said proudly. "There out back right now. And we're getting a mule. I feel like a pioneer wife."

"The mules will help with the logging," Cutter added. "And we're getting a couple of goats from Driver." Then, he pointed to the plowed and planted area. "And we're going to have an ass-kicking garden."

Indeed, the tomato plants were nearly knee-high, lettuce plants were heading up, and the corn, squash, peppers, and everything else looked picture-perfect. From where he was sitting, Adam could see that each row was labeled with sticks as to what was planted and when.

"We put in some fruit trees—apple, peach, pear, and plum," Cutter continued, "but it'll be a couple of years before we get any fruit from them."

"That reminds me," Adam said, getting up, "we brought some treats for the kids."

From his truck, Adam produced a grocery bag full of boxes of cookies.

"These will keep them happy for a while." Privately, however, he doubted that by the time the treats were gone, Cutter and his family would still be waging this insurrection. But he had to admit, they were doing everything right.

"Have you heard anything from the town?" Billy asked.

Cutter finished his hamburger. "Driver says it's going to court and they'll probably issue a bench warrant for me. 'Course they can't serve it."

"You seem to be taking all this in stride. That's not like you," Adam commented.

Cutter laughed and Angel joined in.

"I'll tell you," Angel said gaily, "I have never seen this man so calm. It's like he's on Prozac or something." She turned to Cutter. "You haven't been secretly taking tranquilizers, have you?" she teased.

"Not when alcohol will do the job," Cutter replied. "You know," he said to his guests, "even the kids seem happier, and I wasn't so sure about that."

"We spend more time with them," Angel answered as she collected their plates, "that's one reason." She then excused herself and headed towards the house. "I have to check the chart to see whose turn it is to do the dishes. Maybe *yours*," she bumped Cutter with her hip, smiling as she left.

"It's more work to live like this," Cutter acknowledged. "But it's more peaceful." He paused thoughtfully. "I've been taking the kids into the swamp and teaching them things. Like I said, this used to be Wampanoag land. We've even found some arrowheads. I told them that I have Indian blood, so they think I know all about that stuff. But I'm just an old Yankee woodsman who's learned a thing or two about trees and plants and animals."

"You mean like the ones you used to poach?" Adam could not resist saying.

"Hell, if I didn't know how to hunt, we might not have food on our table next winter."

"I understand," Adam said. "But do it right, my friend, or the government will be far less of a problem to you than I will."

"Don't worry, Ski. I'll do it right. I'm an example now."

Adam nodded, privately marveling at the reformed man sitting next to him.

Driving Billy home, Adam was quiet.

"What are you worried about, Adam?" Billy asked.

"Worried?"

"Yeah. You're thinking so hard I can almost feel it."

Adam hesitated a moment. "I guess I just don't see a happy ending to this."

"It worries me, too," Billy sighed. "But I love what he's doing."

"So do I."

* * *

The two men sat on a bench in the town green. The younger man was hunched over, elbows on knees, shaking his head.

"I don't know where he is. Do you know where Leachy is?"

"No."

"He's hiding."

"Very likely."

"We have to find him. How do we find him?"

"His sister would know."

"What if this psychologist finds him first?"

"Well, we can't have that, can we?"

"I thought you said not to worry, she's nothing to worry about."

"She's Adam Sabeski's girlfriend. She's the one who found the Bradburn kid. She's responsible for Floyd and Babe being dead. She's tenacious."

"Then make her go away. Can't you make her go away?"

"Stop being a moron. How many people am I going to have to make go away for you? This is all your mess, you know. Now if something happens to her, it'll look like it's because of her snooping. Then it gets worse. It would be better to work from the other end."

"What do you mean?"

"We take away the sources."

"How?"

"Leave that to me."

* * *

By eleven o'clock that night, Julia's eyes were beginning to glaze over the journal article she was reading. She still had a massive amount of reading to catch up on, and would be up for several more hours. Next to her on the sofa, Cat stretched, pressing her large paws against Julia's thigh, then put her nose on Julia's lap gently petitioning to go out.

After letting Cat out through the kitchen into the back yard, she poured herself a glass of tomato juice. Just then, the telephone rang. That would be Karen. It was only eight o'clock in California.

"Hi, Mom, how are you?" said the girlish voice on the other end.

"I'm fine, possum, what about you?" Julia smiled, just hearing her daughter's bubbly voice.

"I'm great."

"Great? Well, that's good. And Paul?"

"Paul's great, too."

"Great, again? Well, that's good." Julia positioned herself cross-legged on the sofa.

You want to know why we're great?"

"You got a raise?"

"Nope."

"Paul got a raise?"

"Nope."

"Your father got fired? Your stepmother got a wrinkle? Never mind, didn't mean it."

Karen laughed softly.

"Okay, I give," Julia continued. "Why are you so irrepressibly great?"

Karen laughed again. "Guess."

Julia had a sudden premonition. "Karen, are you …pregnant?"

"Yes!"

"Omigod! That's wonderful! Congratulations, honey! When did you find out?"

"This afternoon. I didn't want to call you until after I told Paul. He flipped. He just ran out to get champagne, strawberries, and chocolate milk. Champagne for him, chocolate milk for me. We figure I'm due next January. You've got to come out then, can you?"

"Can I? You couldn't keep me away! Not to mention that your mother gets to go to sunny California in winter. Excellent timing, nibblet." Julia couldn't help smiling.

"We're so thrilled, Mom. We can't stop talking about it. Paul wants to buy a house so we can move out of this tiny apartment. And he's already treating me like I'm carrying an armful of Limoges. I never knew pregnancy affected *male* hormones."

Julia chuckled and refrained from informing her that the euphoria would pass.

"Anyway," Karen continued, "I just had to let you know right away."

"Well, you're going to have to budget your money from now on, so let me do the calling."

"E-mail me, it's cheaper. You're not exactly the Fortune 500 either."

"No, I'll call. I want to hear the sound of your voice."

"Okay, but call Sunday nights. The rates are lower. Oh, Mom, I'm so happy."

"Me, too, sweetheart. How are you feeling?"

"Terrific. No morning sickness."

Julia rolled her eyes. "I'll tell you a secret. The women in our family never get morning sickness. And we don't get stretch marks." On the other hand, she thought privately, we're in labor for days. But she wouldn't tell Karen that.

"Paul says I glow."

"That's the other thing about Arnault women. We always glow."

Julia felt a certain satisfaction in saying 'Arnault women.' Using her maiden name professionally had always irritated Phillip. Now she used it all the time.

"I'm so glad you're going to come out here to be with me. I miss you. I love you, Mom."

"I love you, too, possum. Give Paul a hug for me. I'll speak to you next Sunday."

After Julia hung up, she let Cat in. The Golden Retriever followed her to the livingroom and jumped back on the sofa, curled around once and snuggled against her. Julia stroked the dog's head and looked seriously into her eyes.

"Karen and Paul are having a baby. But don't you ever call me grandma."

The dog opened her mouth and panted. Was Cat laughing at her?

But as Julia went back to her reading, she couldn't help reflecting on her own pregnancy and how happy she and Phillip had been back then. Those years were good years together. She couldn't deny that. They were both so young and in love. Having Karen was a pure joy—well, after the painful, cramping, searing, wrenching, cursing labor. When their daughter was little, Phillip was a devoted father; he loved having her with them all the time. In retrospect, Julia couldn't help wondering if it was because he didn't want to be alone with *her*. For when Karen was school age, his interest seemed to wane. Towards both of them. Oddly, it wasn't until Karen was grown up that he took an interest in his daughter again. But not in his wife.

Julia's eyes began to close as she re-read sections of the journal. What page was she on? Soon, she was blissfully ignorant of snoring with her head tipped back against the sofa.

Until the phone rang, she hadn't realized she'd been sleeping. Startled, she glanced at her watch as she reached for the phone. It was two o'clock in the morning.

MONDAY, JUNE 14th

It was Sam calling to tell her that Sherry had made another suicide attempt. This time, he said, she was almost successful. She'd found a plastic fork under another patient's bed and managed to dig into a vein in both wrists again. If the other patient hadn't informed the ward attendant that Sherry was bleeding under her covers, she might have died before morning. She'd been taken to Bridgewater Memorial.

Although Sam didn't explicitly instruct Julia to go to the hospital, it was clearly his expectation. So she called Adam and asked if she could bring Cat over to his house. Adam was instantly agreeable and Julia reminded herself what a good guy he was. And she should thank him. Demonstrably.

Sherry was on an I-V and her wrists were bandaged and secured to the railings of the bed. She looked so pale and vulnerable. She was sedated and Julia didn't think Sherry would even know that she was there. But she pulled the mock-leather armchair over next to the hospital bed and tried to think what she should do.

'Here's the real dilemma of any psychologist who deals with psychoses,' Julia told herself. A neurotic is a neurotic, but a psychotic is dynamite. Potentially dangerous to themselves, maybe to others. And who was *she* to be able to stop it? She obviously had to be a whole lot better than she was right now.

She watched the slow liquid drip of Sherry's intravenous tube, aware of the slightly disinfectant aroma of the room, the muffled sounds of nurses' shoes on the tile floor in the hall, and the occasional groan from a patient in another room. Night sounds. It was only three a.m.

The last time she'd sat next to a hospital bed was when her mother was dying. Her mother had had a stroke and heart attack and was hooked up to an electrocardiograph in the cardiac unit. She waxed and waned in-and-out of consciousness. The stroke had paralyzed her left side and robbed her of speech. When she'd waken and see Julia, she'd try to speak but her nose and mouth were covered by an oxygen mask and she only managed to look imploringly at her daughter.

One afternoon, about a week after her mother was admitted, as Julia held onto her right hand, the EKG went abruptly flat and her mother's grip slackened. But Julia was unwilling to let go.

"Please don't leave, Mom," Julia whispered. "Please wait until I get my life straightened out. Let me make you proud of me."

But there was no response. Julia continued to hold her mother's hand, her head bent in a silent plea as Phillip came into the room a few moments later. Karen apparently had called him from the waiting room. He immediately assessed the situation and brought in the nurse.

The nurse turned off the heart monitor and gently removed the oxygen mask. She stood on the other side of the bed until Julia looked up.

"Do you need a little more time?" she asked kindly.

Julia couldn't remember anymore what the nurse looked like, but she remembered her voice being clear, calm, and patient.

"I think my daughter would like to say goodbye." Julia glanced over towards Karen.

"Of course. I'll get her."

Afterwards, after Julia and Karen said goodbye to her mother, Phillip took them home.

"I know you and I are having problems," he said before leaving. "But Evelyn is Karen's grandmother, and you and I have been married for a long time. So I just want you to know that I'm here to help you through this in any way I can."

It was, Julia thought, his finest hour. And it would have been a memory to offset that of their subsequent bitter divorce. Too bad he had to screw it up by bringing his girlfriend, now wife, the blonde beach-blanket-bimbo, to the funeral. But that was Phillip.

* * *

Although Adam went back to bed after Julia dropped off Cat, he couldn't sleep. His mind kept drifting back to Julia. He hadn't given much thought to where their relationship was going. Or even where he wanted it to go. For the past year, they'd simply had what used to be called 'an understanding.' She lived in her house; he lived in his. Even though they slept together at one place or the other, they didn't bring in closets full of clothing. They didn't have the same friends, or even the same hobbies. He liked being alone outdoors. He didn't want to be with her all of the time. She didn't want to be with him all of the time. When they were together, she rarely talked about psychology; he rarely talked about veterinary medicine. They didn't talk about the future. So what kept them together?

Yes, the sex was good, but it wasn't only that. They seemed so…Adam smiled inadvertently…synchronized. But there was more. And more than comfort. But what? And was it forever?

Cutter had shocked him by marrying Angel. Adam never expected his friend to settle down with one woman. Especially at his age.

Maybe age was it. Maybe Cutter was tired of living alone. Both he and Cutter were in their early fifties. So what did he, Adam, want for the rest of his life? Was he supposed to choose something?

Adam shook his head ruefully. There would be no sleep in him tonight. He decided to take Cat and Horace for a walk in the woods. Cat was eager with anticipation, but Horace was decidedly skeptical in a German Shepherd sort of way. Sally the pig continued to snore in her carpet-bed on the livingroom floor as they left.

* * *

"What are you doing here?"

Julia woke up to Sherry's slurred question. It was almost seven-thirty a.m. She must have dozed off. Why was she always so tired lately?

"Just keeping you company," Julia replied as she stretched her shoulders and neck. She thought she'd better get to a phone to reschedule the rest of her patients today.

Sherry tried to sit up and pull off her wrist binders. "Why am I tied?"

"So you don't cut your wrists again," Julia answered.

Sherry fell back on the pillow. "Is this a regular hospital or the psych ward?"

"This is Bridgewater Memorial. You were brought here late last night. You almost killed yourself this time."

"*Almost* doesn't count."

"I think it does."

"I don't care what you think." Sherry turned her head away.

"Are you hungry?"

Sherry turned back, surprised by Julia's change in conversation.

"Yeah," she said. "You going to make me breakfast?"

"No. But I'm going to press a button that you can't reach." Julia held up the call switch and pressed it. "Meanwhile, I need to make a phone call down the hall. Let's see who gets back here first. Me or the nurse."

"They don't call us patient for nothing," Sherry said without inflection.

The nurse allowed Sherry to have one wrist free to eat her breakfast as long as Julia was present. Scrambled-egg sandwich on toasted wheat, apple juice, decaffeinated coffee with a slim paper stirrer. No other utensils.

"Why now, Sherry?" Julia asked.

"Why not?" Sherry answered without looking at her.

"Do you want to hear my theory?"

"No."

"I think you got scared."

"Scared of what? You?" Sherry spit out.

"No. Scared of what you told me."

"It wasn't true."

"Oh, it *was* true. And now you have to deal with it."

"I don't have to deal with a fucking thing I don't want to."

"That's right, you don't. And you don't have to get better, either. That's your choice."

"Do you have to be here?" Sherry said, drinking her coffee. "Is it some sort of requirement?"

'Breakfast sure perked her up,' Julia thought. "No," she answered.

"Then why?"

"Why not?" Julia countered.

Sherry put down her cup. "I don't want to do this."

"Neither do I. Let's just have a little straight talk. Fact—you've been sporadically admitting yourself for treatment for the past ten years. You defy your therapist to find out what the problem is, and when it doesn't happen, or doesn't happen on your schedule, you sign yourself out until the following attempt. Right about the same time. This year, you took it a step further when you gouged your arms on the way to my office. Then you pushed it just about over the edge when you opened your veins last night. What it feels like, Sherry, is that you're giving me an ultimatum. Either I cure you right away, or you'll take your revenge on me by killing yourself."

"Not on you."

"On who, then? Your mother?"

"No," Sherry said softly. "Her killer."

"And how, exactly, does that make sense? You think your mother's killer is going to have remorse because her daughter commits suicide?"

"No," Sherry whispered. "But maybe somebody will take notice. Somebody will remember her. Somebody will care." Sherry began to cry quietly. "She's got to be worth something, doesn't she?"

Those were almost the words that Julia had said to herself.

"Because if *she's* not worth any effort," Julia said, "then *you're* not?" That was the same feeling she had had herself when her marriage was over.

Sherry turned away from Julia and sobbed into her own shoulder.

* * *

It was past Noon, Adam reckoned, and Julia still hadn't come back for Cat. Perhaps she went directly to work after seeing her patient in the hospital. He tried calling her pager, but the message said it was turned off. So he put both dogs, along with Sally, in the indoor-outdoor runs adjacent to his clinic, and left to pay his weekly visit to Goody.

As he entered Goody's cabin, Adam found the old hermit in bed, unmoving. His first impulse was to check Goody's pulse. As he did, the old man opened his eyes.

"I ain't dead, so git away from me."

"Are you all right?" Adam asked.

Goody tried to sit up then slumped back against his pillow.

"Are you in pain?"

Goody slowly shook his head 'no.'

"Can you get out of bed?"

Goody shook his head again.

"Okay, you need to be checked out. I'm calling an ambulance."

Goody tried to lift his hand in protest, but Adam took out his cell phone and made the call.

"He appears dehydrated and anemic. I'm ordering an I-V," the emergency room doctor declared after a quick physical examination of Goody, now lying in the ER hospital bed.

The ER doctor was young, most likely a resident, Adam decided. But it wasn't a very difficult diagnosis even for a first-year medical student no less a resident.

"We'll run some tests, but I'm pretty sure he'll have to be admitted. He'll probably have to be transfused. Meanwhile, we need to fill out some paperwork. Are you the next of kin?"

"No, he has no family. I suppose I'm the closest."

Adam looked at Goody for confirmation, but Goody's eyes were closed.

"Is there a healthcare proxy?"

"Not that I know of."

The young doctor flipped a page on the chart and made a scrawled notation, then swept his hand across his forehead, brushing away his hair in a nervous gesture.

"Well, that's something that needs to be done. Until then, we can only go by our hospital guidelines, but we'll call social services. Can you fill out some of this information on age, address, prior health conditions, insurance?"

"Some of it. He has a regular doctor here for his arthritis, so there's probably some information in the system. As for insurance, I think it's only Medicare."

"Does he live alone?" the doctor asked.

"Yes," Adam answered.

"Date of birth?"

Adam shook his head. "No idea."

The doctor then addressed Goody in a loud voice. "How old are you, Mr. Goodson."

The old man opened his eyes and scowled. "You think I keep count?"

The doctor looked helplessly to Adam, who shrugged.

"Over sixty-five anyway," the doctor said and wrote it on his sheet. "Did you have anything to eat or drink today, Mr. Goodson?"

Goody shook his head.

"What about yesterday?"

Goody shook his head.

"Well, we're going to take care of that just as soon as we can. After we get your tests and X-rays, how about a nice hot meal?"

He sounded as though he were addressing a child.

Goody stuck out his tongue. "Hospital food," he croaked.

The resident patted Goody's shoulder. "Maybe we'll let your friend smuggle in steak and mashed potatoes. How's that sound?"

"Pisser."

The young doctor smiled inadvertently. "Spunky, isn't he?" he said to Adam.

"You have no idea."

"Okay," the doctor said to Goody, "let's get those tests over with." He motioned to an orderly who began wheeling Goody's bed out of the cubicle.

"First week on the job?" Adam asked when the old man was out of range.

"What gave me away?"

"The steak and mashed potatoes."

The young doctor smiled again. "That just happens to be on today's menu. Hospital version, of course."

Adam nodded appreciatively.

Goody's red-blood-cell count was dangerously low, and he was, indeed, anemic. He was transferred upstairs to a hospital room with his I-V, and was immediately hooked up for the first of three transfusions. The kitchen sent up his meal and the Jamaican nurse's aide began cutting the chopped steak into bite-size pieces.

"You're going to enjoy this, Mr. Goodson," she said. "You got everyone waiting on you just like Donald Trump, for sure."

"I wouldn't mind a back massage while you're at it," Goody said in a scratchy voice.

"Oh, I'm going to give you a good massage, Mr. Goodson. But you got to give me something, too." She smiled brightly.

"Oh, yeah? What?"

"Here it is, honey." She produced a crook-necked plastic urinal.

"I'll leave you two alone for a while," Adam said. "I'll be back a little later."

From the public telephone the hallway alcove, he tried calling Julia's office but was told she wasn't in today. He tried her home, but there was no answer. That meant she could still be in the hospital. He went to the nurse's station around the corner from Goody's room where a middle-aged nurse was seated at a computer.

"Excuse me. I wonder if you could tell me, where would someone likely be if they had attempted suicide?"

"In a heap of trouble," answered the nurse, turning towards him.

"Right," he grimaced. "I mean what floor would they likely be on?"

"Why?"

"Long story. I need to find someone who's with that patient."

"We don't release information about attempted suicides."

"Then can you tell me who was admitted for an accident or trauma during that period?"

The nurse turned back to the computer as if to access a file. "Name of the patient?"

"I don't know. But the person would have been admitted last night or early this morning."

"Male or female?" She began searching a document.

"I don't know."

She stopped scrolling down the document page and turned back to him. "I'm sorry. I really can't help you."

"I understand," he replied, noticing a photo of the nurse along with a young boy with his arms around a Golden Retriever. "But I'm not interested in the patient," he continued. "Just the visitor. She's my neighbor. Anyway, she's a psychologist and because she had to come here without any notice, she left her dog with me last night." He tried to make it sound urgent, lying through his teeth. "She hasn't returned to get her and the dog needs seizure medication. I don't have a key to her house and I don't know her veterinarian. I'm not sure what to do. The dog doesn't look well. She's old and I'm worried about her…the dog, that is. Golden Retriever. Like that one."

"Oh," said the nurse as her gaze moved to the photo. "That's Buddy, my son's dog." She paused for a moment then wrote something on a small pad, tore off the page, and left it on the counter. Then she pretended to turn back to her computer.

Adam picked up the paper. It read, '404-D.'

"Thank you," Adam said. "Very much." He walked away expelling a deep breath.

Adam took the elevator up and walked down the two-tone beige and green hallway looking at the room numbers posted on the doors. At '404,' he stopped and glanced in. Julia was sitting in a chair next to the bed of a patient. The grey curtain was half-drawn, hiding the upper part of the patient's body, so he couldn't see the face. Julia, however, immediately saw him and got up. She excused herself to the patient and came out into the hallway. She looked tired.

"What are you doing here?" she said softly. "Is something wrong?"

He motioned her to walk with him down the hallway.

"Goody's been admitted. I found him in a pretty bad state this afternoon. Dehydrated, anemic. I'm sure he hasn't been taking care of himself. Anyway, he'll be here overnight, if not longer."

"Is there anything else wrong with him?"

"I don't think so. But I'm not sure what they'll do about letting him go home alone."

Julia nodded. "How did you find me?"

"A sympathetic nurse."

Julia frowned. "They're supposed to keep all information about psychiatric patients confidential."

"She didn't tell me who the patient was. Just the room number."

"Even that much is improper," Julia said brusquely.

"I'm sworn to secrecy, okay?"

"You have to be. I mean it, Adam."

"Yes," he nodded solemnly. "I promise. Are you planning to stay here much longer?"

"No," she glanced back toward Sherry's room. "I'm ready to leave. What about you?"

"I'll just go back for a minute to see how he's doing. Want to meet me in the cafeteria?"

"Sure. You take a girl to all the best places."

As Julia walked back into the room, he noticed the printed name on a card in the slot on the door. 'Doe, Jane.'

* * *

Later that evening, when Julia returned, she checked her telephone messages. There was only one.

"Dr. Arnault?" said the throaty female voice that Julia instantly recognized. "Doreen Estes. It's five a.m. We're going to be shipping out in an hour. I have something I want to tell you, but I want to do it in person. I'll call you when I get back at the end of the week."

That was all, but Julia could hardly contain herself. If she weren't so damn tired, she'd pour herself a celebratory *vino verde*.

TUESDAY, JUNE 15th

Sam removed his glasses and placed them on his blotter. How unshielded his eyes looked, Julia thought. Naked and lashless. It made him appear so young. He *is* young, she reminded herself. Younger than her, anyway.

"I…ah…have to talk with you, Julia."

It wasn't like Sam to stammer, Julia thought.

"I'm going to transfer Sherry Fayette to another therapist," he continued.

Julia was taken aback. "Why? Because she attempted suicide again?"

"No. Not because of that."

"You think I'm getting too involved? I'm not. But I think we're just beginning to connect."

"It's not my decision."

He looked, she thought, distinctly uncomfortable.

"Then whose decision is it?"

"The superintendent's. He told me to transfer the case."

"Then it is because she attempted suicide on my watch."

"Maybe." He picked up his glasses and put them on again. "The fact is, I don't know why Haskins made this decision. He didn't explain. He just said, 'That's how I want it.'"

"Has he ever done this before?"

"Not that I know of."

"I don't understand."

"I don't either, but that's the bottom line." He ran his fingers along the edge of the blotter as if to punctuate his statement.

"You didn't ask him why?"

"He's the superintendent, he can do pretty much whatever he wants to."

She looked at him for a moment, then shook her head. "I don't accept that. I'm going to talk with him."

"That's not a good idea, Julia," he said rapidly. "It won't change his mind and it may only become adversarial."

She took a deep breath and studied the framed diplomas on the wall behind him—Harvard University, Harvard Medical School.

"You know, Sam, that's the advantage of age. I've been through enough upheaval in my life not to let some minor political appointee bully me into silence." She rose from her chair and regarded him intently. "You should have stood up for me, you know."

"It wasn't about you. It was about Sherry."

"No. It was about me. And you should have challenged him."

Sam looked down at his desk. "I have to pick my battles, Julia."

"As do I," she said as she turned and left his office.

Haskins' secretary was reluctant to let her in until Julia said she'd sit in the reception area and wait until he came out. Within ten minutes, Haskins had cleared his schedule and allowed Julia into his office.

Although she had met Ed Haskins at the orientation session, she had never been in his office. She was surprised at how elegant it looked. It could have been the office of a Harvard dean—all crimson, black, and burnished gold—although there were no framed diplomas on the wall to indicate where he'd matriculated. She was certain that he, like herself, was no ivy-leaguer.

Ed Haskins did not look nearly as elegant as his surroundings. He was short and portly and balding. But Julia knew better than to underestimate him. Positions such as his did not come easily, but they came by connections rather than scholarship.

"Thank you for seeing me on short notice, Dr. Haskins."

He motioned her to sit opposite him. "And what can I do for you, Dr. Arnault?"

"As you might imagine, I'm concerned about the transfer of my patient, Sherry Fayette."

She watched him as she said this, but he remained impassive.

"Could you tell me," she continued, "why this decision was made?"

"Rest assured," Haskins said, "it does not reflect in any way, Dr. Arnault, on your competence as a therapist."

"Then why is she being removed from my care?"

"Certain…issues…have come to light about Ms. Fayette's situation." He gazed past her at the door. "We feel she would be better off in the hands of a psychiatrist. That's why I've asked Dr. Wu to take over."

"Sam? He didn't tell me that *he* was taking over."

He looked at her directly, narrowing his eyes. "He *is* the chief-of-staff."

Julia crossed her legs and folded her arms in front of her. If Haskins were more astute, he would been able to interpret her gesture and anticipate her question.

"You said 'we,' Dr. Haskins. Who is 'we?'" she asked.

"I beg your pardon?"

"You said, '*We* just feel she would be better off in the hands of a psychiatrist.' Who is we? Both you *and* Dr. Wu?"

"No. Dr. Wu had nothing to do with it. I was using the editorial 'we.'"

Julia nodded. "I see."

"The decision, you must understand, is irrevocable."

Julia got up to leave. "I do understand that," she said as she walked towards the door. "What I don't understand, is who made it."

"Why didn't you tell me you were taking Sherry's case?" Julia asked Sam, back in his office.

"Does it matter who?"

"Did you have any part in that decision? Be truthful with me, Sam."

"I had no part in it."

She believed him. He might cave in to Haskins, but he wouldn't lie to her.

"I have to be the one to tell Sherry," she said.

He shook his head slowly. "I'm afraid Haskins won't let you have any more contact with her. Besides, what would you tell her? Certainly not that you were ordered off the case."

"And what will you tell her?"

"I haven't decided yet. But nothing to cause her any distress."

The silence between them became palpable.

"Sam, don't you see something wrong in this?" she finally said.

He paused before responding. "Look, Julia, the girl tried to commit suicide while she was under your treatment. I'm not blaming you. No one is. But it looks bad. And in this facility, appearances are important. We're responsible to the state. Haskins is just doing what he thinks is in the best interest of the patient. And the hospital."

"Bullshit."

Sam frowned at her, and after another silence, he asked, "What did Haskins say to you?"

"He said 'we.' '*We* feel she would be better off in the hands of a psychiatrist.'"

Sam digested that. "Do you think he meant someone else, or was he just being expansive?"

"I somehow don't see Haskins using the royal 'we.' He's an 'I' kind of guy."

"Unless there's blame involved."

She nodded reluctantly.

Her gaze drifted to his window. Although all she could see was the tops of trees—maple, pine, oak—and a strip of blue sky, she reminded herself that there was a world of difference between out there and in here. This is only an institution, with an artificial hierarchy—she reported to Sam,

Sam reported to Haskins, who reported to the Commissioner of the Department of Mental Health. Although the Commissioner reported to the Governor, he was autonomous in running the Department. If pressure had been brought to bear on Haskins, it would likely have come from the Commissioner, but probably no higher. All she knew about the head of DMH was his name, Dr. Milton Barrington. But why Barrington would put pressure on Haskins was a mystery.

Normally, she would ask Sam about Barrington. And tell him what she'd found out about Sherry's mother. But Sam had not come to her defense, and she had lost confidence in him.

"Whatever his reasons, Julia," Sam was saying, "your relationship with Sherry is over. You do understand that."

"I hear you," Julia responded.

Dispirited, Julia returned to her office to resume her schedule. Mr. Warren would be her next patient, a 65-year-old farmer who shot his wife of 43 years. He was there for court evaluation. After him, Ms. Bianci. She was 45, mother of two, and manic-depressive manic phase. After her, Mr. Halberstrom. He was obsessive-compulsive. Julia steeled herself. Mr. Warren would be uncooperative. Ms. Bianci would be super talkative, super aware of every sound, color, smell, as though there were no filters on her senses. It would be difficult to make her focus, even with her meds. And Mr. Halberstrom, a young man of about twenty-two, would test her patience with his endless rituals and repetitions. It would be a long afternoon.

* * *

After work, Adam drove over to Cutter's place to tell him about Goody. He was only mildly surprised to see Driver inside the compound.

"Hi, Ski," Driver said as he swung open the gate.

"You doing guard duty now?" Adam asked jokingly as he drove through.

"Yep. Me and Boomer joined the secession," Driver replied.

"When did that happen?"

"Day before yesterday. We decided this separation idea was a good thing."

'Hmm,' Adam thought, 'there goes the t.v. and computers for the kids.'

"Between the three of us," Driver continued as he closed the gate, "we got over five hundred acres back-to-back, and it's all Liberty Nation."

"Well, how about that?" Adam said, not knowing what else to say.

He found Cutter in the garden, watering the plants with a hose attached to a submersible pump in his well, run by a make-and-break gasoline engine. The garden had been fenced in with six-foot high chicken wire to keep out the chickens that free-ranged around the yard, and any other raiders. There were two other men Adam didn't know clearing brush at the far side of the garden. They seemed to work in rhythm with the bang-bang of the gasoline engine.

"How's it going?" Adam asked.

"Gotta finish this while there's still sunlight. Lookit that lettuce," Cutter said, standing up and stroking his beard. "Organic." It was as though he was announcing he'd created Eve.

"Who are those guys?"

Cutter looked over towards the two men. "The Nash brothers. They've come to join us."

"Join you?"

"Yeah. They're going to make a cabin farther in so they have a little privacy, but meanwhile they're working on expanding the garden. They're going to put in winter vegetables and more potatoes. Driver and Boomer are enlarging the root cellar." Cutter nodded over towards the other side of the house, where Adam saw Boomer relaying pails of dirt to his eldest son. "The wives and kids are in the house making supper."

Cutter moved the hose over to a fifty-gallon blue plastic barrel and draped it over the top through a hole in the cover so the water went into the barrel. He closed the wire gate and Adam followed as his friend went over to the well and shut off the make-and-break.

"We've been getting peas and beans already. The gals are putting them up. And mulberry preserves, too. We all got together and made out a schedule of who does what and when."

"And the kids?" Adam asked as he trailed Cutter back to the house.

"We all take turns at that, too. Everybody has something to teach."

"How did all this happen?" Adam asked, marveling at the change in Cutter from a somewhat indolent woodsman to this…organizer.

"I was in the Army, too, you know," Cutter chuckled. He looked up at the sun. "What is it, about six o'clock?"

Adam nodded.

"Well, we've got a couple of more hours of sunlight before we go in to eat. I'm cutting some sticks out back, want to help? We need lumber for the cabins. I've got some boards curing, but I have a feeling we're going to need a lot more. Hey, what about your pig? You interested in finding a place for her?" Cutter headed towards the sawmill.

"Not for slaughter," Adam replied.

"Nah, breeding. Al Nash has got a hog." Cutter pointed far back to the side of the mill. A good-sized hog was staring back at them. "We'll get piglets, barter a few, eat a few, but not Mom and Pop."

Adam thought it over. Sally wasn't meant to be a house pig. She'd probably have a better life here. "I'll bring her by. If she likes him, she can stay."

"All right by me."

"Can you use a watchdog?"

"Probably. My hound died a while ago. I had him for sixteen and a-half years. Loved that old Wicked. He was good for chasing, but not much for watching. What'd you have in mind?"

"German shepherd."

"You mean Floyd's dog?" Cutter asked as he instructed Adam to help lift up a long log into place. "Why do you want to get rid of him?"

"Horace needs a job to do. I think this might be a better place for him. I don't think he's happy lying around the house. Want to try him?"

"Yeah, we can use him. Not near the kids, of course. And only if we can change his name." Cutter turned on the motor.

"You don't like 'Horace'?" Adam asked jokingly, lining up the log.

"Not here. Here, he's going to be Hercules."

Cutter guided the log towards the saw, with Adam on the back end.

"That suits him well enough. I'll bring them both by on Saturday."

The whining whrrr-rrr filled the air as the sawdust flew and as the blade cut through the scab end of the log.

WEDNESDAY, JUNE 16th

Julia woke up angry. Pissed off, in fact. How dare Haskins summarily take her patient away? And screw Sam Wu for letting him. And it wasn't just the indignity of it, or the feeling of powerlessness. It wasn't only the frustration of knowing that the head of DMH had pulled Haskins' strings, or the fact that someone had probably gotten to Barrington. Cave-ins all along the line. And there was nothing she could do about it. She didn't even have enough leverage to threaten to quit. She didn't matter enough. But the real issue was Sherry. What would she think? Would she feel abandoned again?

Julia decided she was going to have to re-think her promise to Sam about letting it go. As much as she really liked Sam, and as much as he'd been the one to encourage her to become a practicing psychologist instead of an academic, how much loyalty did she owe him for that?

It was personal now. Someone had pulled the plug on her and she didn't like it. More importantly, it wasn't going to help Sherry.

As she went about her work interviewing patients and writing reports, she mulled over her choices and the consequences. She was glad she would hear from Doreen Estes at the end of the week, but what would she do meanwhile?

By the end of the day, she had convinced herself to continue asking questions about Nicole Fayette. So on the way home, she stopped off to see Martin Ryman.

As they sat in his study, she deliberated how to approach him without seeming to send the wrong signals.

"I just wanted to ask you about someone else from Sipponet. I don't know if you know him. He might not even have been a parishioner here. His name is Frank Leach."

He shook his head. "No, but I know an Estelle Leach who lives in town. She doesn't belong to this church, but she comes to the Happy Hearts Club that I hold in the Council on Aging. It's a support group for people who are coping with chronic disease. Estelle has rheumatoid arthritis."

"Is she an older woman?"

"No, the group is for all ages. Estelle would be in her late thirties or so. Unmarried. A very caring person. Perhaps she's related to this man. Maybe a sister or cousin."

"Did she ever mention having a brother?"

"Not that I can recall. But that doesn't mean anything."

"Could you tell me where she lives?"

"Certainly."

He flipped open his notebook and copied out an address.

"Is this still in regard to Nicole Fayette's death?"

"Yes, it might be."

"How is that going?"

Without intending to, Julia began talking about Sherry. And, without mentioning any names, she told him about her interviews, ending with her call from Doreen Estes."

"Do you know the Crawfords?"

"They come to services every week. The family members have been parishioners ever since this church was built. But Doreen got married and moved away before I arrived."

"I think she's going to tell me something important. She may know who killed Nicole. But please, Martin, you must keep this confidential."

"I'm rather good at that, actually. It's part of the job, you know."

Julia sighed in relief. "It helps to be able to talk about it." Then she chuckled. "That's the mantra of my profession, you know."

"Not so different from mine."

She nodded. "I suppose. But you deal with *moral* dilemmas."

"Is there any other kind?"

"My realm. The products of a diseased mind."

"Ah, Disease *versus* Evil."

"If you believe in Evil. That's not one of our APA classifications. I don't treat illness of the soul."

"At least you admit there's a soul," he smiled.

"I was just using your construct."

"Were you?"

"Well, I'll admit there are times when I have doubts."

"Well, that's a start." He smiled again. "You know, it feels good for *me* to have someone to talk with, too." He paused. "I was wondering if you might have dinner with me some evening."

"Oh." Perhaps she had sent the wrong signal after all, without meaning to. "Actually, I'm still seeing Adam."

He looked chagrined. "I should have known that. I don't know why I'm surprised."

"I don't know, it surprises the hell out of me."

"Why?"

"He's just…not exactly the kind of man I'd have expected to…be involved with."

"In what way?"

"He's kind of maverick." She suddenly felt as though talking about Adam were somehow a betrayal. "Anyway, he's nothing like my ex-husband."

"Rebounds seldom are."

The idea crept in like a snake at the garden party. Was Adam a rebound relationship? She had never considered it. She pushed it out of her mind. It was not something she wanted to discuss with him.

"Well, thank you again for your help, Martin." She rose to leave. "By the way, why did Reverend Chauncy leave this parish?"

"He had some health problems."

"He was having some health problems when I saw him. Of the sobriety kind."

Martin sighed and rested his chin on his hands. "I'm sorry to hear that."

"Maybe he needs to talk with someone," she said pointedly.

Martin nodded as she left.

Seated in her car, Julia looked at the address on the notepaper that Martin had given her. She was already in Sipponet, she might as well talk with Estelle Leach.

When Julia mentioned Pastor Ryman's name, Estelle invited her in. The woman looked older than her thirties, but pain can do that, Julia thought. Estelle used a walker to lead Julia to the livingroom. Dark burgundy-colored rug and furniture slipcovers, white lace curtains, and a dark floral-patterned wallpaper made the parlor seem old-fashioned and dark. The accessories were old-fashioned, too. Paintings, ashtrays, picture frames, seemed as though they came out of the 1940s. This was probably the Leach family home, Julia thought. The furnishings must have belonged to Estelle's parents.

After inviting Julia to sit, Estelle used her walker for balance and lowered herself into a large simulated-leather chair that appeared to have an electric control on the side to help raise her up from a sitting position.

"I'm trying to locate a Frank Leach," Julia explained. "Would he be any relation to you?"

"Frank is my brother," Estelle said reservedly.

"Oh, good. Perhaps then, you could tell me where he is."

"No. I'm afraid I can't. He left here a long time ago."

"How long has he been gone?"

"Almost twenty years."

"My goodness, that *is* a long time. And you haven't heard from him in all those years?"

"No."

Julia noticed Estelle's hands resting on the stuffed arms of the chair. They were swollen at the knuckles and reddened, as though she'd held them in hot water, and bent so that her fingers balanced only on the tips.

"Why is that, Ms. Leach?" Julia asked tentatively. "Are you estranged?"

"Oh, no," she answered, showing animation for the first time. "We were always very close."

"It must concern you, then, that he's not in touch."

"Like I told—" She paused, then continued. "Frank has his reasons."

"Like you told *whom*?" That someone else was inquiring, was disconcerting to Julia.

"Nobody. Just that Frank has his reasons."

"How do you know? I mean, if you don't know where or how he is."

Estelle looked at her with understanding. "You mean, do I know he's not dead?"

Julia merely inclined her head.

"He sends me birthday flowers. Every year. June 6th."

"This year, too?"

"Yes. See?" Estelle pointed with her arthritic hand to a fading bouquet of flowers in a green glass vase. "Always pink and white carnations. That's what I like."

"Is there a card?"

"Just the florist's card."

"May I see it?"

"Certainly."

Estelle inclined her head towards the flowers. Julia retrieved the card and returned to her seat.

"'Happy Birthday, Sis,'" Julia read aloud, then smiled at Estelle. "It's very thoughtful of him to send you flowers every year."

"Frank is a sweet man. I miss him."

"Yes, I'm sure you do," Julia said warmly, noting the name of the florist in nearby Acushnet, 'Flower Power.' "You haven't shown this to anyone else, have you?"

Estelle looked uncomfortable. "No. Why?"

"Perhaps you shouldn't."

"Why not?"

"Did someone else come here recently asking for your brother?"

Estelle dropped her eyes and shook her head 'no.'

"Was it a friend of Frank's?"

Estelle continued to look down.

"Whoever came to see you, Ms. Leach, I'd be concerned. I'm not sure what their intentions are."

Estelle looked up at her. "Frank is gone. I don't know where he is."

"Can you tell me who was here, Estelle?"

Estelle simply shook her head 'no.'

Julia realized that the young woman was too frightened or too mistrustful to give her any more information.

"Would you have a picture of your brother that I might see?"

Estelle looked puzzled, but opened a drawer in the end table next to the chair and rustled through papers clumsily, unable to bend her fingers. She finally found what she was looking for and presented it to Julia.

The photograph was old but there he was, tall and thin and so youthful. Not bad looking. But what startled Julia was the person standing next to him. He had his arm around a pretty young woman wearing black shorts and a grey sweatshirt. She had a blonde ponytail.

"Is this Doreen Crawford with your brother?"

"Yes, that's Dory."

"Was she his girlfriend?"

"They went together for quite a long time. Before she left him for Joe Block."

On her way home, Julia decided to veer off into Acushnet to find 'Flower Power.' It was located in a little strip mall on the main street.

"You're lucky, Ms. Leach," said the woman behind the counter, probably the owner. She was in her forties, with very long black hair and no lipstick. The shop was painted in neon pink, orange, and turquoise, with multicolored curtain-beads in the doorway between the front and back of the store. The entire décor was 1960s hippie, although the owner, like Julia, had been too young for Woodstock.

"We only keep one month's receipts on hand, otherwise they go into storage." Reviewing the receipt, she said, "Yes, we delivered it to 954 Bayside, Sipponet Village on June 6th. Pink and white carnations."

"Are you sure?" Julia asked crossly. "They were supposed to be pink and white roses. That's what he always sends. Pink and white roses."

"No, see right here on the order slip, carnations."

"Well then, I'd like to call the florist that took the order on the other end. They must have gotten it wrong."

"I can give you the number, but I'm afraid you can't call from here. It's long distance."

"That's all right," Julia said. "I'll call from home." She wrote down the name of the originating florist, "Ka-Blooms," and the Iowa City phone number. Noticing the look of concern on the woman's face, Julia said, "It was a very pretty bouquet, even though they weren't roses."

"I'm sorry they weren't what you expected. But we only took the order, you know."

"Yes, of course. Thank you for your help."

Julia continued trying to look irritated despite being giddy with pleasure. She had located the elusive Frank Leach. How about that!

She drove home ridiculously happy at her success, but as she turned into her driveway, her smile vanished and Cat began furiously barking.

* * *

Adam surveyed the damage to Julia's house—broken windows and red and black paint splattered all over the shingles on the back of the house in some Jackson Pollock abstract. There was no sign that anyone had entered the house. Whoever did it was content to deface only the outside. The fact that it had been done in broad daylight wasn't so bold as one might think; there would have been very little traffic on this country backroad.

"This is supposed to look like random vandalism," he said to Julia. "But I don't think so. Any idea who might do this?"

Julia shook her head.

"A former patient, maybe? Or a student you once flunked?"

"I don't think so."

"Let me guess. You're still asking people questions about Nicole Fayette."

"Yes," she answered, as though she were caught ditching school.

"You think this might have something to do with that?"

"I don't know."

"I'd say it was a good guess," he said, irritated. "And I'd also say I told you keep out of it."

She looked up at him with a defiant expression.

"I told you," he said forcefully, "these are not people to mess with."

"Well, fuck them."

"Julia—"

"No, Adam, I mean it. They aren't going to scare me off with some broken glass and a bad paint job."

'Maybe not *this* time,' he wanted to say. But this wasn't the moment. Caught between anger and concern, he put his arm around her. It always surprised him how small and thin she was. She had a presence that made him think of her as tall and athletic. But the top of her head only came up as far as his nose, and beneath her cotton blouse, he could feel her shoulder bones.

Adam called the Pittsley police station and reported the vandalism. As expected, there was nothing they could do other than send an officer to look around and take the information. There was no likelihood of determining who'd done it. Then he let Julia use his cell phone to call her insurance broker, but the cost of repainting and replacing the window glass would probably be less than her high deductible, so she wound up not making a formal claim.

At least the glass company was more responsive. They said they'd send someone out tomorrow morning. So after he and Julia boarded up the broken windows, Adam invited her to stay at his house for the night. For a minute, he thought she might stubbornly refuse, but happily she didn't. He felt a lot better knowing she'd be safe for the night.

As they walked to his truck in the darkening evening, they saw the first fireflies of the season. They blinked on and off like random Christmas lights in mid-air.

Cat and Sally snuggled in the corner of his kitchen; Horace took his disdain into the livingroom. Adam and Julia sat at his kitchen table as he served the fish chowder they'd cooked together. He told her about Cutter's enclave and how he was giving him both Horace… Hercules, and Sally, and that it would be a good home for them.

"There are eight or ten more people that have joined Cutter and Angel beside Driver and Boomer and their families," he explained. "It's beginning to be a community."

"Isn't that kind of ironic?" Julia asked. "I mean, all this started because Cutter wanted to withdraw from government. But with that many people, there has to be some form of government, even if it's a true democracy."

"Cutter isn't against governance. Just government."

"A subtle distinction."

"But a real one."

He waited for a response, but she made none. Ordinarily, he thought, Julia would continue debating him and they would both enjoy the sparring.

"You seem distracted," he said. "Something happen?"

She nodded and he listened as she told him the story of how she was summarily taken off her patient's case by the hospital superintendent. How Sam had failed her, and how Haskins couldn't have made the decision by himself.

"Haskins is a toady," she concluded. "He just does what he's told. And the someone who told him to do it had to be the Commissioner of the Department of Mental Health, Milton Barrington."

"Uncle Miltie Barrington?" Adam said contemptuously.

"You know him?"

"If it's the same guy I went to high school with. We didn't hang together. He was a twit. But I heard he went to medical school."

"He was from Pittsley?"

"No, Sipponet Village. It was a regional high school." He watched her take that in.

"It does seem to put two and two together, doesn't it?" she said. "Someone from the Village could have gone to Barrington and had the Commissioner tell Haskins to dismiss me from the case. The question is whether Barrington was doing the someone a favor, or whether he had some part in Nicole Fayette's death."

"I doubt that he had any part in her death. He was a lot older. Twenty years ago, he'd be in his thirties. I don't think he was even living around here then. I think he'd already moved to Boston to do his residency."

"Then who would he owe a favor to?"

"Nobody I can think of. He wouldn't even know anyone in her crowd. Except maybe his younger brother. I think Joe hung out with them. Could be him."

"But nobody's mentioned a Joe Barrington who hung out with Nicole."

"It wouldn't be Barrington," Adam reflected. "Joe was Miltie's half-brother. By his mother's second husband. Joe was a good ten years younger than Miltie. Not too bright. Used to follow him around like a puppy. Then when he grew up, I heard he did some time for larceny." He thought for a minute longer. "Joe Woods."

"Joe Woods?" she repeated, looking stunned. "He was at the party the night Nicole disappeared. I've been trying to catch up with him."

Adam instantly regretted having told her that. But how could he know she was looking for Joe Woods? This was just what he wanted to avoid. There was little point, he thought, about remonstrating her about going to see Little Joe. It would make her all the more eager. And then what? Someone had already taken her meddling very seriously, and that someone was threatening her.

"Who else have you been talking to?" he asked.

"You know what I love?" Julia said.

"Changing the subject."

She smiled. "I love that when we're in your house—even when we make dinner together—you serve me."

"You do the same for me."

"Yes, but some men expect to be waited on all the time."

"Speaking of your ex-husband, I presume."

"Exactly."

"Don't you think we've exhausted that topic?"

He watched the expression on her face change.

She put down her spoon. "Do I do that a lot?"

Adam debated how to answer her. "Well... sometimes."

"I'm sorry. I'm really sorry," she said, looking genuinely unhappy.

"It's okay," he reassured her. "Comes with the territory."

"No, it doesn't." She shook her head. "It shouldn't. It's over. I just haven't let go of it. But I will," she said resolutely.

"Okay."

"I promise."

"Okay."

They both began eating their chowder in awkward silence.

"So," Adam resumed intrepidly, "who have you been talking to?"

She hesitated, then it all came out. "Doreen Estes, Nicole's best friend, and her then boyfriend, Joe Block. Then

Dennis Buckley. I haven't talked with Conny Cranshaw or Joe Woods, and nobody can find Frank Leach, but I think I've got a lead on him." She went on to tell him about Estelle Leach and the flowers.

"And I think," she said happily, "Doreen is going to tell me something important. She called me Monday morning when I was at the hospital with Sherry, but she won't be back until the weekend. She's out scalloping with her husband."

"I hope you're not planning to meet with Conny Cranshaw." Adam still believed the man was malevolent.

"Yes, I am. Saturday. I don't have to work this weekend."

"Don't, Julia," he said insistently.

"*Don't*?" Her eyes flared.

He silently admonished himself: 'It sounds as though I'm ordering her.' He amended, "I mean, don't go alone. Let me go with you."

"Why?"

"I don't trust Conny," he said slowly. "I just want to be there."

"You mean there when I talk with him? No. Not a chance."

"I don't have to be in the room with you. But let me drive you there and wait in the car."

"But you have clinic hours on Saturday."

"Only in the morning. We could go in the afternoon, couldn't we?"

In the end, he wheedled her into it. They would see Conny together, then go to the Chalmers' farm to see Joe Woods, then have dinner.

THURSDAY, JUNE 17th

Sam knocked politely at her open office door. "Are you between patients?"

"Yes," Julia said coolly. "For a few minutes. Come in."

He sat down and tapped his fingers on the arms of the chair. "Sherry's back from the hospital." He looked at her for a response.

Julia nodded perfunctorily.

"I had a session with her this morning."

It wasn't like Sam, Julia thought, to walk on egg-shells. She had the sense that an apology was coming and tried to decide whether or not she felt victorious. And whether or not she should show it.

"She threatened to leave or to hurt herself again, or both, if I don't transfer her back to you."

"And—?" Julia said, deciding not to gloat.

"You know we don't let patients manipulate their own treatment."

Julia nodded again.

"I asked her why she wanted you, since she already tried suicide again while she was in your care."

He paused and Julia waited for him to resume.

"She was testing you."

"I know that." Julia put her elbows on the desk in front of her and clasped her hands to her chin. She rested her chin on her crossed thumbs.

"I mean, she admitted it. She said she wants to work with you. She will only work with you. So I have a conflict."

"Yes?"

"Yes," he repeated. "Do I let the tail wag the dog, and give her back to you? Or do I try to overcome her resistance to me or to everybody else? What is in the best interest of the patient?" He took a deep breath. "I ultimately concluded that her best interest lies with you. So I went to see Haskins."

Julia sat motionless for a moment. There was no elation over her victory, just relief. And apprehension.

"Thank you, Sam."

"No, Haskins didn't agree with me," he continued. "He's having her transferred her to McLean."

Julia was stunned. This was not the outcome she expected. Nor could she have foreseen a transfer to McLean Hospital. That was a private facility.

"But she can't afford McLean," she sputtered, not knowing what else to say.

Sam looked up towards the ceiling. "They're recruiting subjects for an experimental program treating younger suicide patients. Sherry is eligible. They'll take her as a state patient."

Julia shook her head in disbelief. "This didn't happen all of a sudden. Haskins must have been engineering this ever since we talked."

"Perhaps so. But she's going this afternoon."

"Can I talk with her?"

"Haskins said 'no contact.' Not here, or there."

Julia put her arms back down on the desk and leaned forward. "You can't possibly say this is normal procedure."

Sam inclined his head.

"Nor," Julia continued, "does this have anything to do with the fact that Sherry cut her wrists while she was my patient. This has to do with me. And with my looking into her mother's murder."

"Murder?" Sam was clearly broadsided.

"Oh, yes," Julia said between her teeth, "Sherry's mother was murdered twenty years ago and the killer has never been found."

"You didn't tell me," Sam scolded.

"You…didn't…ask," Julia replied, her words dripping accusation. "You were too busy telling me I was off the case. You disappointed me, Dr. Wu."

Sam silently accepted her rebuke.

Before work that morning, Julia had tried to call the Iowa City florist, forgetting the one-hour difference in time zones. When the phone rang several times, she realized it was only seven a.m. there and she resolved to try again at Noon. But she became so busy after Sam left that she never stopped for lunch and never got to think about it again until the end of the day.

Finally, at six forty-five, she picked up the phone and charged the call to her home number. She hardly expected anyone to be at the shop after hours and the phone on the other end rang five times. She was just about to hang up when someone answered.

"Ka-Blooms-s," said a harried young male voice with a sibilant 's'. "May I help you?"

Julia went through her fabrication about the flower mix-up.

"I'll have to look that up and I'm afraid I can't do it immediately. This-s is prom week for the high school and graduation for the university. Plus weddings-s, and showers-s, and there's a funeral, and a...well, we're just over-whelmed right now. I'll be glad to do it. But just not right away. Could you please call back in a week? I'll make a note to myself to look the first chance I get. Please be patient."

What else could she do? Nothing, absolutely nothing. So she graciously agreed to call back.

* * *

Pittsley Selectmen Albert Carriou, Todd Kingman, and Madison Wentworth sat in Albert's livingroom after hours.

"This is getting out of hand," Albert said. "He hasn't paid the demand, so Barstow issued the collector's warrant for delinquency. Briggs didn't answer the court summons, and now there's a bench warrant. What next?"

"Ordinarily," Madison answered, "the police would have to take him into custody. Then it becomes a real mess. Is this what we want to do?"

"The police haven't been able to get onto the property," Albert said.

"If the police can't get in to take him, what happens?" asked Todd.

"It depends on how far we want to push it," Madison replied. "I certainly don't think we want to send in some sort of SWAT team. I talked with the District Attorney and he doesn't want to touch it. It's a civil matter. Would the public good be served having a SWAT team to storm the place? No. I don't think we want that here."

"You're not suggesting, I hope," Albert said, "that we let this ride. Don't forget, it's not just Malbone Briggs' property that's part of this tax revolt. His brothers are in it, too. That sets a dangerous precedent."

"I believe that if we do anything confrontational," Madison countered, "it will only exacerbate a bad situation. Let's take it slow and easy."

"Maybe we should have a talk with Barstow. He's not up for re-election as collector of taxes for another two years," Albert said. "Maybe he can rescind the demand."

"I don't know," Todd said, "I think it's gone too far."

"Maybe he could just put a lien against Briggs' property and leave it at that," Madison said.

Albert looked at the other two members of the Board. "Is that our consensus?"

"I say 'yes'," Madison answered. "What about you, Todd?"

Todd Kingman grimaced and nodded.

"Do you want to call him, Albert, or do you want me to?" Madison asked.

"You're the lawyer," Albert replied. "Why don't you do it on behalf of the Board?"

"Damn Cutter Briggs," said Todd, shaking his head. "He was always a problem."

"It's in the genes," Albert said. "His whole family back to his highwayman ancestors has been a problem. Swamp Yankees, all of them."

* * *

The State's Attorney General, Marsha Mayhew needed advice. The matter at hand required, she concluded, a constitutional historian. So she called in Lawrence Karajian for an impromptu consultation about a unique situation.

"I received an informal inquiry from Davis Johnson, of Breedon and Corcoran, town council for the town of Pittsley. He faxed me this," Marsha handed a copy of Cutter's declaration, "and mailed this." She passed him a copy of *The Pittsley Chronicle*.

As Lawrence read the articles," she continued. "Apparently he sent a copy of the letter of secession to the governor, as well. But the governor's office filed it in their crank file."

When Lawrence finished, he looked up and smiled an acknowledgment that this was, indeed, a unique situation.

"Johnson called me this morning to get a read on how to advise the Pittsley Selectmen to handle this. Frankly, this is out of my domain. It's beyond a simple tax matter. The man has barricaded himself and some others—family and followers—in an enclave that the town cannot breech without using force." She looked at him earnestly. "I'm assuming this secession thing is a lot of hooey, but I need to check with someone who knows the issues better than I do."

"He raises an interesting point," Lawrence said.

Marsha shook her head. "Those are not the words I want to hear. There aren't any legal precedents here."

"Well, there are historical ones, of a sort. The American Revolution, for example."

"Meaning?"

"The American Revolution was arguably a secession rather than a revolution. The colonists didn't want to unseat the monarchy or Parliament. They wanted the right of withdrawal and self-government."

Marsha shook her head again. "Even so, that was a body of people. Not one person."

Lawrence smiled again. "That's where it becomes dicey. What role does individual rights play in self-determination?"

"Let's cut to the chase," Marsha said impatiently. "Is what he's doing constitutional?"

"It's neither constitutional nor unconstitutional. Most rights of secession—if one wants to argue that secession is legitimate, and we'd have to look back at the Civil War to argue that one—apply to groups of people."

"Okay, so—"

"But," he interrupted, "there is nothing that would specifically exclude an individual secession, such as he's doing. That's the legal conundrum."

"Whose issue is this? The Fed? The State? Or the town?"

"Has he broken any income-tax law at the state or federal level?"

"Apparently not. He doesn't file."

Lawrence nodded knowingly. "That's actually good. Better not to get the Fed involved. They haven't always dealt well with these situations."

She nodded knowingly. "So what do I do?"

He shrugged. "Do you want to come down on him? Realizing all the ramifications?"

Marsha expelled her breath so hard it looked like she was blowing up a balloon. 'Next year would be an election year,' she thought. 'Is this the rocky hill I want to fight and die on?'

SATURDAY, JUNE 19th

As it turned out, Adam couldn't go with Julia to see Conny Cranshaw after all. He phoned her to say that Goody was going to be discharged later that afternoon. After he closed his clinic at Noon, he was going to deliver Horace and Sally to Cutter and would have to go directly to the hospital from there.

Arriving at Cutter's, Adam was met by two new men whom he didn't recognize. A burly fellow with long black hair who wore a cap low on his forehead peered through the gate, observing Sally in the bed of the truck. Horace began barking vigorously. The man asked Adam his name then relayed it by walkie-talkie to someone on the other end. Cutter instructed them to open the gate.

Adam drove up the path wondering who the men were. As he reached the cabin, Adam was surprised to see even more unfamiliar faces—men, women, and children—working in the expanded garden and in several clearings like spokes out from the hub of the cabin.

When Cutter came around from the rear to greet him, Adam asked, "What's going on?"

Cutter shrugged. "Boomer's friends. They all want to join Liberty Nation."

"You're kidding," Adam said as he led Horace out of the cab on a leash. Horace lunged for Cutter.

Cutter stood his ground. Then, in a firm voice, he commanded, "Hercules, sit."

The dog stopped barking and stared at him. Cutter stared back. In the silence that followed, the dog finally sat, still with unwavering eyes.

Adam passed the leash to Cutter, who snapped it smartly, saying, "Hercules, heel." The dog did not move.

Cutter snapped the leash again, harder, and the dog walked to his side and sat down again.

"Good dog," Cutter said, then turned to Adam. "Well, it's not exactly heel, but it's a start."

Cutter then walked the dog over to a long chain attached to a tree and hooked Hercules' collar to the end of it. "I'll leave him here for now until I can work with him later. I want him to be off-lead as soon as he gets to know the property and the others here."

Adam was duly impressed. And relieved. Certainly, Cutter was the right person for Horace-Hercules. The dog would do well here.

As Cutter moved around the back of the truck to set up a ramp for Sally, Adam said, "She likes a scratch behind the ears."

Unloosening the harness that held the pig steady in the truckbed, Adam led her by a makeshift collar down the ramp. Cutter kneeled down and scratched Sally behind the ears.

"Hello, little lady. We have a gentleman named 'Hamlet' who's anxious to meet you."

Sally garrumphed in response.

Cutter and Adam led her over to the pen where a very hammy Hamlet eyed them from a far corner while he was feeding from the trough. Cutter let Sally in and she stood still for a moment, assessing the situation. Then, slowly, she sauntered over to the trough and began eating alongside Hamlet.

"I'll keep an eye on them to make sure they're okay," Cutter said, leaning on the fence. "I figure it'll take a day or two 'til they work it all out."

Adam nodded with a small pang of regret at giving her up. He would miss her. Then he turned to Cutter. "So what's been happening here?"

"Damndest thing," Cutter said as they walked back to Adam's truck. "There's a whole bunch of people who want to do this with us."

"How many?"

"We got seven more families, so far. One of the guys knows how to do solar and windmills, so we can probably generate some amount of electricity. I figure we can handle maybe ten or fifteen more people, but that's about the limit."

"What's the town think about this?"

"Far as I'm concerned, they got no say in it. 'Course we'll see what happens down the line. Maybe they'll try to take me to jail. Or maybe they won't. Maybe they'd try to seize the property or maybe put a lien on it. It's up to them. Come on, have lunch with us and meet everybody. We're building a mess hall, but right now we're just eating out on picnic benches."

Adam would like to have stayed longer but told Cutter he couldn't because he had to pick up Goody. He related what had happened.

"Bring him by when he's feeling better," Cutter invited as he walked Adam back to his truck. "What's Tully been up to these days?"

"I saw him a few days ago. He's all upset because Doris doesn't want to have sex with him anymore after the last miscarriage."

"About time. How many misses has she had now? Two hundred? Three hundred?"

"I don't know."

"Tully needs to put a lid on it, so to speak.

Adam shrugged. "You know Tully."

"Well, say 'hey' for me the next time you see him."

Although Adam nodded agreement as he got into his truck, he thought Tully wouldn't much care whether Cutter said 'hey' or not. Whenever they got together—usually at Adam's house on a Sunday afternoon—Tully and Cutter always would up arguing vehemently about something, no matter how insignificant. Oil and water.

"These are the prescriptions for the medication he'll need," the nurse explained as she went over the chart. Adam helped Goody put on his clothes while she went through the instructions. "He needs to be at bed rest for at least a week, and closely monitored for the next several weeks. As for diet, I have a list of the things he can and cannot eat. We'll show you how to give him his shots and test his blood sugar. Then, you'll teach him when he's up and around. In the beginning, he needs to be tested three times a day. I'll get you some test packs to take home with you."

As soon as the nurse left the room, Adam looked questioningly at Goody. "Did you tell them you were coming home with me?"

"Had to. Otherwise they wouldn't let me go. Don't worry, I ain't lived this long depending on somebody nursing me. You just drop me off my house, I'll be fine."

"There's no way you can go home alone, Goody. No way."

"Well, I ain't staying here, and I ain't going to no old-age prison."

When Goody pulled his mouth up into a bunch, Adam knew there was only one choice.

"I'll sleep down here on the sofa," Goody announced as Adam closed the door behind them.

"That's good," Adam said, "because there's only one bed and that's mine and it's upstairs."

"You got television?" the old man asked, looking around.

"No."

"Hmph."

"Since when do you watch television? You don't have a t.v. in your cabin."

"Had one in the hospital." Goody looked around as he sat on the sofa. "I thought you lived better than this."

Adam couldn't help laughing.

"Don't that Julia-woman care that you got bare-board floors and ratty old furniture?"

"No, she doesn't."

Goody nodded approvingly, then looked meaningfully towards the kitchen. "What's to eat?"

"Didn't they give you lunch?'

Goody pointed to the clock on Adam's desk. "It's four-thirty. That's when they give me supper."

"Okay. I'll go see what's in the fridge."

"It's gotta be on my diet," Goody announced. He lifted his legs one by one to swivel himself into a lying position on the sofa.

'Oh, this is going to be fun,' Adam muttered under his breath.

* * *

She had ignored Adam's admonition and gone alone. Not exactly ignored it, she told herself, because, after all, he was tied up with Goody, and what else was she supposed to do?

Conway "Conny" Cranshaw kept Julia waiting in the outer office for twenty minutes after his secretary announced her. She hadn't made an appointment, so she couldn't really object. She stared out the window of CranLand Trucking watching the big rigs come and go. All the trucks looked bright and clean with cranberry red paint and the name of the company emblazoned in gold with black outlines on the doors of the cabs.

When she was finally admitted, Conny motioned her to sit. He was a short stocky man with a plentiful crop of wavy silver hair and an outdoors' complexion. His expensive blue polo shirt did not disguise his bulk. He looked the part of a retired boxer. As he opened a gold case on his desk, she noticed his fingers were thick at the fingertips, and his hands were coarse. His fist, she judged, would deal a formidable blow.

On the wall behind him hung a commendation from the Chamber of Commerce, a framed Realtor's license (Conny's secondary occupation), and a painting of a large boat with the name "Sea-Cran" painted on the hull in cranberry-red script with the same black outlining. The awning over the flying bridge was the same cranberry red. Beneath the painting, a two-foot long replica of the boat sat on the credenza. Even the model looked extravagant.

"Lovely boat," she said to ease into the interview. "Is it new?"

"I've had her about a year."

"It looks large."

"About fifty feet. Custom built."

It might not have qualified as a yacht, Julia thought, but it certainly was impressive. Conny Cranshaw obviously had expensive taste. Adam had driven with her past Conny's house a while ago; it was a monument to his success—a large colonnade decorated the front of what could easily be called an estate. After seeing his thriving company and observing his 'accessories,' she knew that to think Conny Cranshaw was anything less than an astute businessman would be foolhardy.

"Do you get out often?" she asked, prolonging the conversation before getting to the topic of Nicole.

"As much as I can."

"Where do you keep her?'

"Right now, she's moored in Padanaram."

Julia had driven around Padanaram with Adam. It was a picturesque area of South Dartmouth. The beautiful little harbor had easy access to the sea.

"Cigarette?" he asked.

"No thank you."

He reached in his pocket and removed a gold lighter with the initial "C" embossed on it. "Sometimes I want a cigarette and sometimes I want a cigar. And sometimes both." He lit his cigarette.

"At the same time?" she asked facetiously.

"If I want."

There might have been a state ban against smoking but as far as Conny was concerned, Julia surmised, it did not apply to him. She got the distinct feeling that he regarded all laws that way.

"You're Adam Sabeski's girlfriend," he said between puffs.

"Well, 'girlfriend'—" she stopped mid-sentence. She did not want to give him an invitation to call her anything else. "—will do."

"This have anything to do with him?"

"No." If it had, she wondered, would he have ejected her immediately?

"Well, I presume you're not here on trucking business. Are you looking for real estate?"

"No, not at the moment."

"Then what can I do you for?"

He leaned back in his swivel chair and looked at her impassively as she gave him the same story about the journal that she'd told the others. He did not register any surprise.

"I'm afraid you're wasting your time. I don't know anything about it."

"But you were at the junkyard that night."

"Was I? I really don't remember. We partied there lots of nights back then. They all blur together."

"But that was the last time Nicole partied there."

"So I'm told."

"You don't remember the night she disappeared?"

"I'm afraid not," he said unblinking.

"Didn't the police interview you?"

"Yes. But I didn't have any information for them back then. And now," he waved his cigarette, "I can't recall a thing."

"You did know Nicole, didn't you?" ('Or is that a blur, too?' she wanted to say but didn't.)

"Everybody knew Nicole."

"Did you have a relationship with her?"

"Hell, no."

"Not that you remember," she said with a false smile.

He took a deep drag on his cigarette and blew the smoke towards her.

"What's the point of all this questioning?"

"As I said, it's for the journal."

"Yeah, some kind of case report. But for what? It's all over. What makes it of interest to some…journal?" He said the word distastefully.

"It's a chronicle of unsolved murders."

"Why?"

"Because it hasn't been done before."

"You mean to say you're going to 'chronicle' every single unsolved murder in Massachusetts since it was a colony?"

"No, that wouldn't be possible."

"Then why *this* one?" He used his cigarette like a pointer.

"Because my editor assigned it to me." His stare made her uncomfortable. No one else had interrogated her like this.

"And your editor didn't tell you why?"

"I suppose it was because I live in the area."

"You 'suppose'?"

"Yes."

"You didn't ask?"

"No."

He took another drag and inhaled deeply. She was suddenly aware of a clock ticking on the wall. She felt a strong sense of scorn from him.

"Sorry I can't help you with your 'chronicle.' Whatever happened to Nicole Fayette, she probably brought it on herself. But that was a long time ago and I have nothing to add. So I think we're done." He smiled just as falsely back at her. "Don't you?"

Julia plunged out of his office, out of his truck yard, and into her car as though being chased by a rabid dog. She locked the doors and gripped the steering wheel, breathing deeply to stop from shaking.

She drove to the nearest Dunkin' Donuts drive-through. She badly needed a large caramel latté with sugar and whipped cream.

As she sat in the parking lot waiting for the hot coffee to cool, she admitted that the man had completely unnerved her. She understood now why Adam felt there was something malevolent about him, and why Adam had wanted to be there with her. She wished he had been. She felt as though she had glimpsed into a dark cave and discovered a monster lurking there. It wasn't anything he said explicitly. It was his mannerism, the tone of his voice, and look in his eyes. If someone were to tell her that Conny Cranshaw was the devil himself, she would not have denied it.

She wished she had brought Cat with her, but the day was warm and breezeless and she didn't want her dog confined to a hot car while she did her interviews. But she missed her companion, especially now.

After finishing her coffee, Julia headed toward Ellis Chalmers' farm. "In for a penny, in for a pound," she declared.

As she wended her way through the back roads, she realized she was traveling the area where Nicole Fayette had been found. There was the street sign for Pondview Avenue. As she turned right onto the street, she sighed in disappointment. What must have once been acres and acres of woods was now a large housing development. She turned in and slowly drove the wide circular road around the development. There were no trees left. House after house was surrounded by grass, with some bushes planted here and there. As developments went, this one was high-end. The houses were designer large, with lots of windows, three-car garages, architectural interest. But no trees. No privacy. How could anyone live that way?

She tried to envision the area as it had once been. It would have been thickly forested. Perhaps with a cart path into the woods and a little clearing where couples might park. Did the killer pull in there and drag her already dead body out of the car? Or did the murder occur while they were parked there in his car or truck?

He would have pulled or carried her through the trees, and laid her down on the ground. Face up? Or face down? She didn't know.

There was no possibility of telling where Nicole's body had been found now. It was disheartening to think that in just twenty years, so much of the landscape had changed everywhere in town. Sipponet Village was on its way to becoming just another suburb. She couldn't even get a feeling for what it had been like to leave Nicole there in the woods.

Ms. Chalmers recognized Julia with a smile and a shrug. She was wearing an apron dusted with flour.

"If you're looking for Joe, he and Ellis have gone for the day. Joe doesn't usually go with my husband to market, but you missed him by just half an hour. I can't say when they'll be back. Do you want to leave your name and phone number?"

Without optimism, Julia scribbled her name and number on a pad from her purse. She thanked Ms. Chalmers and left.

Was it only a coincidence that Joe Woods wasn't there? Or might Conny Cranshaw have warned him? There was nothing she could do about it. Lacking any other ideas, she decided to swing down to New Bedford to see if the Azorean Queen was in. Doreen said they'd be back by the end of the week.

As she walked along the busy dock, the sun beat down on the water and bounced back up at her. She looked in the slip where the boat had been when she met with Doreen, but another scalloper was anchored in that spot. She hailed a crew member and asked him about the Queen, but he did not speak English.

Twice she walked up and down the dock, inspecting the names of each of the boats. The one she was looking for wasn't there.

'Perhaps,' she thought, 'they were having trouble getting their catch and had to stay out longer.' Which was exactly what the harbormaster told her when she sought him out in his office. He said they'd likely be in later in the day.

Discouraged, she walked back to her car. But reaching the parking space, she stopped dead in her tracks. All four tires were flat.

"Oh, no," she murmured.

As she got closer, she saw that the car had been keyed—there was a deep gouge all along the doors on the passenger side. On closer inspection, she discovered the driver's side window had been smashed. She looked around helplessly to see if there were any witnesses. But she had parked at the end of the lot and no one was around.

Inside, she found that her radio had been ripped out. The seat on the driver's side was slashed open. A dead codfish with blank eyes had been placed in the fold of the torn leather.

When the New Bedford police arrived, they took her report but could not be helpful. Theft of car radios, they told her, was rampant in that area. As was vandalism. The fact that the dead fish had been put in the car was probably just a prank. Luca Brazzi sleeps with the fishes. Kind of funny.

Julia thought differently.

They advised her to have the car towed to a local shop to have the tires replaced so she could drive it home.

* * *

"Why the Christ did you do that?" The other man on the telephone was angry.

"Because she didn't stop after we trashed her house."

"I didn't tell you to have her house trashed. What did you think you were going to accomplish by that?"

"I wanted her to stop, but she didn't get the message."

"So you thought she'd get the message if you had her car vandalized?"

"I told him to leave a dead fish on the seat. You know, like in 'The Godfather.'"

"You asshole. That's just going to make her think she's on to something. Sometimes I think you're just as dumb as he is. Now is not the time to go off the reservation. Now the police are involved."

"Nah, the cops just think it was routine stuff. He stole her radio and slashed her tires. Happens all the time there."

"Well, at least he did it out of town. But I doubt that's going to stop her."

"Then what is?"

"I've already taken care of it."

"How?"

"Never mind 'how.' And for God's sake, don't have him do anything else without clearing it with me."

* * *

When Julia returned home, she sat on the floor and hugged Cat tighter than usual until the dog began to squirm. "If you'd been with me," she said into the dog's ear, "they might have hurt you."

The phone rang and she left the dog looking at her with somewhat bewildered eyes.

It was Adam calling to say he wouldn't be able to see her that evening either because he had to look after Goody. He asked if she would come over tomorrow morning while he had clinic hours and babysit his new housemate.

She readily agreed. She then proceeded to tell him what had happened at Conny's and at the docks. He was silent for a moment and when he spoke, his voice was uncharacteristically harsh.

"All right now, that's the end of it. No more amateur detective, Julia, you've got to stop. The next time, it might be serious."

"I know," she said quietly.

"Good. I'll see you tomorrow then at eight. "

As she hung up, she felt a little guilty that she'd let him take her response as agreement. But she did not want to make any promises about quitting until she heard from Doreen Estes.

With a free Saturday night, she debated what to do. She was too tense to stay at home and read, but she didn't feel like going out alone. Ordinarily that wouldn't bother her, but she acknowledged she was spooked by what had happened that afternoon.

She picked up the telephone again and dialed Tessa Jensen, Billy's wife. She hadn't talked with Tessa in several weeks. It was unusual for them not to keep in touch, but Julia'd been so busy. No excuse, she told herself, then repeated that to Tessa.

"Billy and Billy Jr. have a gig at the American Legion tonight," Tessa said. "I'm not up to it so they've got someone filling in for me. Why don't you come over and keep me company?"

"Sure," Julia replied. "But why aren't you up to it?"

There was a pause at the other end. Then, "I had a lumpectomy a little over a week ago."

"Tessa!" Julia reacted with alarm. "Why didn't you call me?"

"It all happened so fast. It was just a routine mammogram, then it was a biopsy, then it was surgery. It all seemed to happen before I could even think about it. I didn't want anybody to know."

"Billy didn't tell Adam?"

"I asked him not to. I was going to call you, but I just wasn't ready to talk about it. But I'm a feeling better about it now. Come on over. And bring my favorite furry baby."

"On our way."

Julia hung up smiling, knowing that Tessa loved Cat almost as much as she did. But her smile faded as she thought about Tessa's breast cancer. How fast. How unexpected. How frightening.

Tessa wore jeans and a large pink sweatshirt that read, "My husband's a leg man."

"Billy got it for me," she explained while Cat jumped up on the sofa and nuzzled her ear. "It's just his way of saying it doesn't matter that I've got a chunk out of my breast." She looked at Julia teasingly, "I've got enough to spare anyway."

"Yeah, yeah," Julia replied. "Rub it in. If I lose a pennyweight of breast tissue, I'm officially a boy."

Julia poured them both some iced tea from the pitcher Tessa had on the table, and took a large oatmeal raisin cookie from the tray.

"They're supermarket cookies," Tessa apologized. "I didn't bake them."

"So what? They gonna take away your Betty Crocker crown?"

Tessa chuckled.

"Are you hurting, Tessa?"

"Not really. I'm just tender."

"Did they get it all?" Julia asked matter-of-factly, trying not to sound worried.

"They think so."

"Do you have to have chemo?"

"Yes, I've started. Then radiation after. Just a precaution."

"How are you doing?"

"Okay," I guess. "I still have my hair so far." Tessa took a deep breath. "It puts things into perspective, you know? For weeks, Billy and I were more afraid about my dying than anything else. It makes you re-think your priorities."

Julia nodded. How minor her concerns seemed by comparison.

"So what's been going on with you?" Tessa asked.

Julia gave her an abbreviated version of the past several weeks' events, concluding with her going down to the docks to look for Doreen.

Tessa squinted. "Her boat's out of New Bedford?"

"Yes," Julia answered. "The Azorean Queen. Why?"

"Did you listen to the news on the way over?"

"No." Not wanting to alarm her friend, Julia had omitted the story about her vandalized house and car, so she said nothing now about the missing radio. "Why?"

"There's supposedly a late boat out of New Bedford. I don't remember the name, but I think it might have had 'Queen' in it."

"Are you sure?"

"Not one hundred percent on the name, but yes on a boat being overdue. It's the local New Bedford station. They carry all that information."

"But all the boats have ship-to-shore or something, don't they? Wouldn't they be in contact with someone?"

"I don't know anything about fishing boats," Tessa said.

Julia felt an overwhelming urge to drive immediately down to the dock. But she doubted that would yield any information. "I don't suppose they'll know anything more until tomorrow."

"Or later," Tessa added. "They might just have had to go out farther for their catch."

"I'll go down there in the morning and find out," Julia said, then corrected herself. "Not in the morning, in the afternoon. I have to babysit Goody in the morning." Then she explained all about that to an amused Tessa.

"Adam and his strays," Tessa commented. "But are you sure you can get away in the afternoon? That's when Billy is planning to go over to Cutter's with Adam. You know, the Sunday social club," she added.

"Adam didn't mention it," Julia said.

"Maybe he forgot. They moved it to Sunday evening, but that didn't work out as well. That became the time the families got together to meet. So they went back to Sunday afternoons."

"Damn. I really need to get down to the dock tomorrow."

"I could stay with Goody while you go, if you want me too."

"He's not the easiest person to tend to, Tessa."

"It's just for a few hours. No problem. I'd just be hanging around here not knowing what to do with myself."

"Oh, that's great. I owe you dinner for this."

"If he's as cranky as you say, you'll owe me a banquet."

"Done."

"I really don't mind at all. It'll take my mind off things. I'm still scared, you know," Tessa confessed.

In her own way, so was Julia.

SUNDAY, JUNE 20th

"He's already had his insulin and his breakfast and he's gone back to sleep," Adam explained. "I don't think he'll be too much trouble. I'll close up at Noon and take care of lunch."

"I'll make lunch, don't worry. But what about this afternoon?"

"What about this afternoon?"

"You, Billy, Cutter?"

Adam rubbed his forehead. "I forgot. Billy's coming over. I'll call him and cancel."

"No. You go. Tessa said she'd stay with Goody while I run some errands. I'll be back before you."

"Sure?"

"Sure."

"Thanks. I could use a few hours away from here."

"I know," she said smiling.

"That's why I love you," he said flippantly. He tipped up her chin and kissed her. And then he was gone.

"Love?" she repeated silently.

She sat in the armchair with Cat lying next to her, one paw on her foot, while Goody slept on the couch. She'd always thought of him as a craggy mountain of contained energy. A force of nature. But here he looked as still and pale as paper. The sadness of growing old and infirm overwhelmed her, so she buried herself in reading about neurotransmitters in her journal.

By mid-morning, Goody awoke and looked around, as though orienting himself to unfamiliar surroundings.

"What time is it?" he asked gruffly.

Julia checked her watch. "Almost ten."

He swung himself into a sitting position. He was fully dressed.

"Going to the can," he announced as he hoisted himself up.

"Would you like a cup of coffee or tea?" Julia asked.

"Beer," he said as he left the room.

As they drank their tea in the livingroom, Julia broke the silence by asking, "How are you feeling, Goody?"

"Like a damn invalid," Goody replied. "I don't see why I can't go home."

"I'm sure you can, as soon as you're up to it."

"I'm up to it now. But I got no way to get there."

"I'm sure Adam will take you back when he thinks you're ready."

"I'm ready now. Why don't *you* take me?"

"Strict instructions," she lied.

"Phfff," Goody snorted derisively and puckered his lips as if to spit on the floor. But when he looked down, he apparently decided against it.

"What would you like for lunch when Adam comes back?"

"If it don't include a hunk of meat between two pieces of bread, I don't much care. This diabetes is a pain in the ass."

"I could make some soup later. Would you like that?"

"Whatever."

This wasn't going very well, she thought. If she was going to have to make conversation with him until Adam returned, she'd better think of something more interesting than his health or his diet. Then she had an idea.

"You know, Goody, Adam says you know just about everything that goes on around here."

He shrugged indifferently.

"Does that include what goes on in Sipponet?"

He looked at her curiously. "Some."

"What do you know about the murder of Nicole Fayette about twenty years ago?"

"Never caught him."

"Who?"

"The one who done it."

She was going to say she knew that, but quickly decided that wouldn't get her anywhere.

"Who would that be?"

Goody paused for a minute. "Nobody says."

"What do *you* think?"

"Don't know for sure."

Goody was being cagey, she thought, and that wasn't like him. It was rare for Goody to not know something as juicy as this. Maybe she could come at it from another direction.

"Do you know if Nicole had a particular boyfriend back then?"

"From what I heard, she always had one."

"Do you know who it was?"

"Some say it was the mayor's son. But he was married."

"What was his name?"

"Marvel Kane."

That wasn't a name that had come up in any of her interviews. No one mentioned a Marvel Kane at the party that night.

"Where is he now, Goody, do you know?"

"He's the mayor."

"The mayor of Sipponet?" she said.

Goody nodded.

"He was the mayor's son then, and now he's the mayor?" She couldn't help repeating herself in astonishment.

"Ain't that what I said?"

If the mayor's son, now mayor, had killed Nicole, it would certainly explain a lot of the secrecy around her murder, Julia thought.

"Was he at the party the night she was killed?"

"Nobody says."

"Would he have been friends with the men who were there?"

"They was all around the same age. Of course, he didn't run with them anymore, after being married and all. Not openly anyway."

She leaned back in her chair, silent as her thoughts raced around the possibilities. Goody finished his tea and put down the mug, and regarded her knowingly.

"That's no proof of nothing, you know," he said.

When Adam returned, Julia was ready with lunch. She had raided his refrigerator and kitchen cabinets to put together a hearty vegetable-bean soup, and cooked a pot of brown rice to go with it—reminding him that Goody could only have, at most, a small portion of the rice.

After they finished eating, Billy and Tessa arrived and Billy and Adam left to go to Cutter's. Adam said he'd bring take-out food for all of them for supper. Tessa stayed in the kitchen to help Julia with the dishes while Goody went back to the sofa.

"How is he?" Tessa asked softly, taking the dishtowel from its rack.

Julia stood at the sink, filling it with soapy water. "He seems to be doing all right."

"I mean," Tessa whispered, "is he grumpy?"

"Actually," Julia said pondering it, "he seems a little mellow. I don't think he'll be any trouble."

"Hmm, famous last words." Tessa smiled. "You think he's a banjo kind of guy?"

"As opposed to what?" Julia asked slyly.

* * *

Adam and Billy were admitted to Liberty Nation by the same man who recognized Adam from the day before, but not before calling Cutter to give him Billy's name.

As they drove in, Billy said, "This feels like another country. Like I should have a passport."

"I think that's the idea," Adam replied.

"I wish I could see what's going on. Can you describe it to me?"

Adam told him about the two men at the gate, and the long driveway up to the cabin. He parked in front and helped Billy out of the truck.

Leading Billy around the cabin, Adam said softly, "Cutter and about twenty people are under a new shed he built. They're sitting at picnic tables. Cutter's standing in the center addressing the group."

"Who are they?"

"I don't know most of them. Driver and Boomer are there, and some others I recognize from yesterday, but they're mostly strangers to me."

They fell quiet, listening to Cutter speak.

"We'll try to keep to the same schedule every day. We'll work together on the garden and community chores in the morning like we did today, and in the afternoon you all work on your own homes. We've got a list of who has what skills to teach you. We'll rotate cutting the trees and milling the lumber. For right now, we'll take all our meals together. We can continue or not, once you build your own homes. Until then, cooking and cleaning up afterwards is voluntary, but everybody will take turns, men and women. We'll make up the schedule once a week. Everybody works in the garden and putting up the produce. For the summer, we'll have volunteers doing daycare for the children while you work. Come Fall, we're going to have a one-room schoolhouse, like the old days. We'll make out a plan for each age group. Any questions?"

One man sitting with a woman and three children raised his hand. Cutter acknowledged him.

"We're going to need supplies eventually—things we can't make ourselves." He looked at his children. "Toilet paper, for instance."

They all laughed in agreement.

"Right," Cutter said. "That's why I gave each of you a list of the things you needed to bring with you when you came to live here. But yes, we're going to run out of things that we'll need to replace. We're going to set up a barter system with some reliable outsiders. People we can trust."

Billy leaned over and whispered, "I think that includes us."

"I have that same feeling," Adam replied.

"Some of this," Cutter continued, "we're going to have to figure out as we go along. One evening a week, we'll all come together and discuss what's next and what we need and how we're going to get it. Anything else?"

Nobody else spoke.

"We don't have anything in writing about this secession," Cutter continued. "But I want to give you my thinking on it. That way you can choose to stay or not." He looked around to make sure he had their attention.

"Governments derive their power from the consent of the governed. I read that. And that's what this is about. I do not give my consent to this, or any government that deprives me of my independence. No one on earth has dominion over me, unless I permit it. And I have dominion over no one, and do not seek it. Self-government, is what *this* is about."

Heads were nodding throughout the group.

"What is the point of having a government? Most people think it gives them a certain security. Doing some things cooperatively makes sense. We see that right here. None of us, alone, can make all the goods and provide all the services that we're used to. We can get by. But together, we can do more. Government offers us many comforts and many advantages. It's like a hive with everybody working together. That doesn't sound so bad, does it? But the fact is, the more government does to make you secure, the more liberty it has to take away from you as an individual.

"And what happens as governments grow larger, is that they desire and acquire more and more power. It's just inevitable. But government is not a real thing. It's not a mountain. It's not an ocean. It's closer to religion than to reality. What makes it possible? We're back to consent of the governed."

There were murmurs of assent from various parts of the group.

"What governments run on is money. Business money and individual income. And land ownership. Governments do not exist in limbo. They're tied to the land. Look how many wars have been fought over land.

"When the first settlers came to America, what did they do? They squatted on land. Then they bought land from the Indians. From the Wampanoags right here. Indians didn't have any concept of land ownership. They didn't believe they *owned* the land. They used it, lived on it, hunted it, protected it, but they didn't *own* it. They sold it to the settlers, thinking they were putting one over on them. As though they were selling air. Or water. Things that could not be sold, because no one owned the air or the water. Oh, but they learned. How they learned. And now they know what it's all about, don't they?

"So we have to learn, as well. Land can be owned. And I own this land. My brothers own that land." Cutter swept his hand in a semi-circle. "Together, we are a country."

Billy let out a "phew" under his breath. Adam whispered back, "Here we go."

"We're a country. But we're not a government," Cutter went on. "You are welcome to live in our country. We will make some rules together. Not too many. Just so we can live peaceably and cooperatively. But know this—I own this piece of earth. If you do not want to stay, find your own piece of earth to live on and take your house with you. Like I said, this is about self-determination." He looked around. "Any questions now?"

No one spoke.

"If you want to go, then go. Go now, or go later if you want. No one will think less of you."

No one got up.

"Well," he concluded, "that's all then."

Cutter walked over to Adam and Billy to greet them. Hercules walked beside him, off his lead.

"What do you think?' Cutter said.

"You sound official," Billy commented.

"Well, it's my land and my idea, so I guess I'm leading the secession. But everybody here's going to have a say. That's the only way it'll work."

Adam didn't want to say that what Cutter had set up seemed as much like a benevolent dictatorship as a cooperative. But he didn't think his friend would take kindly to that idea.

"Let's go back to the house and have a pop."

What Cutter offered was neither a soda pop nor a popsicle. Having a pop meant liquor, pure and simple.

Hercules followed as they walked to the cabin door where he laid down on the step.

Inside, the three men sat at Cutter's kitchen table with tumblers of shine.

"I have to admit," Billy said admiringly, "I never thought you'd go through with this, but it sounds as though you really know what you're doing."

"Shit," Cutter said, "I'm just flying by the seat of my pants. The problem is, more and more people want to get in, even though they know how hard it's going to be. I guess it just took someone like me to finally say 'no more government' to the government and mean it.

* * *

Julia left Goody at Adam's house, resolved to ask Doreen about Marvel Kane. Perhaps that's what she'd called Julia to talk about. Cat accompanied her, seemingly happy to be invited along. She jumped joyously into the car, but stood stiff on the seat. She nosed the cushion covering the rip where the fish had been, and sniffed the empty space where the radio had been.

"Cat? Can you smell who did this?"

The dog looked at her with loving eyes and no comprehension whatsoever. Julia just sighed and put the car into drive.

There was a crowd of people mulling along the dock, many were women, speaking in Portuguese. Julia thought their voices seemed agitated. It would be difficult to press through all those people to look for Doreen so she decided to go directly to the harbormaster's office.

"Is the 'Azorean Queen' in?" she asked.

He shook his head. "You were here yesterday, weren't you?" he asked.

"Yes."

"Are you a relative of a crew member?"

Julia felt the hair on the back of her neck prickle. "No. But I'm a friend of the owner's wife. What's going on?"

He took a breath then answered. "According to the crew's families," he inclined his head toward the crowd on the dock, "she's overdue."

"Have you called the Coast Guard?"

"About an hour ago. I expect they're out there looking."

"Is that all you know?"

"For now."

Julia left with her stomach in knots.

When she arrived back at Adam's, Tessa and Goody were singing a duet. They were on the second chorus of "*Why-o, why-o, why-o, why did I ever leave Ohio?*" Tessa sat on the floor playing banjo accompaniment.

* * *

Adam laid out the cartons of Portuguese food for Goody, Julia, Tessa, and Billy, on the spool table in the livingroom. He'd been careful to order dishes that were within Goody's program, but the old man bunched up his face.

"I don't eat Portagee," he announced.

"Suit yourself," Adam said. "But this is supper, take it or leave it."

Goody turned his head away in defiance.

As each carton was passed around, Adam surreptitiously added food to Goody's plate. And when the old man finally deigned to look back, he stared at his plate like a man who'd found an electric eel curled up there.

"What's that?" he said accusingly.

"This is shrimp Mozambique. That's *bacalhau a braz*. It's eggs and potatoes and salt cod. And this is…never mind, just try it."

"I don't want any."

"If you don't like it, you don't have to eat it."

"So tell us," Tessa said to shift the conversation, "what's happening at Cutter's place?"

"You mean Liberty Nation," Billy said earnestly.

"Is that what he calls it?" Tessa asked.

"He's got it posted on his gate," Adam answered. "Along with 'Sovereign territory. Do not enter' and 'No trespassing,' with a couple of guards to make sure no one uninvited gets in."

"I didn't realize it had gotten that far," Julia commented.

Goody, meanwhile, had begun moving the paprika-colored shrimp around with his fork. Finally, he took one in fingers, examined it, and bit.

"I'll take you over there during the week sometime," Adam said. "You'll be surprised. There are probably ten or more other families living there now. Building cabins, working the garden."

"He's got them all organized," Billy added. "Who'd have believed it? I mean, *Cutter*."

"But what about the town?" Tessa asked. "Are they going to let him do this?"

"That remains to be seen. Or, in my case, heard," Billy answered. "But I was bowled over. Cutter really seems to be a leader. I mean, he's not the same old Cutter, is he, Adam?"

"No. He's evolving into a spokesman for the group. He makes a good case for what they're doing."

"And," Billy added, "he's got everybody working together. Building things, gardening, everything. It's amazing."

Adam snorted. "He even has old Horace behaving."

"You're kidding," Julia said.

"Nope. Calls him Hercules now. He's not only got a new name but a new disposition. He's actually becoming obedient."

"Now *I'm* bowled over," Julia said. "What about Sally?"

"I forgot to ask," Adam said. "But I guess it's working out. Cutter didn't mention her."

"I just wonder where this is all going to lead," Tessa said.

"I suggested he declare himself a religious community and get himself a preacher's license," Billy said. "You can do that, you know. But Cutter didn't want to."

"That didn't help David Koresh in Waco," Adam said. "The Feds did a number on them anyway."

"But that was because of the weapons thing, wasn't it?" Tessa asked.

"Maybe," Adam answered.

"Cutter isn't stockpiling arms, is he?" Julia asked.

"He says he's doing everything right, now, because of the kids," Billy answered.

"I hope so," Adam said. "But Cutter was never one to worry about what's legal and what's not."

"Didn't you tell me he was a poacher?" Julia asked.

"Used to be," Adam answered. "Percy and I were always after him, but we could never catch him. One time, we went into the woods in Percy's police car the night we knew Cutter would be out jacking deer. We laid a big camouflage tarp on the ground and drove the front wheels over it." Adam illustrated with his hands. "Then we pulled the tarp up over the car so you couldn't see it, and we waited there until we heard his truck. As soon as we thought we had him, we took off, driving over the tarp which just went right under our tires. We chased him through trees and gullies and we almost had him when suddenly, he and Boomer jumped out of the car while Driver kept going. They ran behind two trees on either side of the clearing and pulled up a chain that was lying across the opening. They hooked it on the trees and Whomp!, we drove right into it. Smashed the grill, the radiator, and practically broke our teeth with the impact. The two of them went off laughing and there were Percy and me, sitting in a broken down car with steam coming out under the hood. We had to walk out through the swamp about three miles back to the police station. Boy, did we catch hell from old Chief Kerwin."

"What's Cutter's doing now is a lot riskier than jacking deer," Tessa said. "He's taking on the government."

Between mouthfuls, Goody croaked, "Damn fool to call attention to himself. Shoulda done it quiet and gotten away with it. But that's a Briggs for you."

* * *

Later that evening at home, Julia telephoned Karen. Her daughter sounded bright and eager when she answered.

"It's going to be a boy!" Karen announced.

"You could tell from the sonogram?" Julia asked in surprise.

"I had an amnio. Paul was willing to wait, but I just couldn't stand not knowing."

"That doesn't surprise me, your father and I couldn't put your presents under the tree until Christmas morning. You could never keep your hands off them. Have you told your father yet?"

"I told him we're having a baby, but I haven't told him it's a boy yet."

"I'm sure Grandpa and step-Grandma will be as happy as I am," Julia said cattily.

Karen chuckled. "You don't let up, do you?"

"Never," Julia replied pleasantly. "So everything looks good with you and the baby?"

"Absolutely perfect. Oh, Mom, I'm so excited."

"And you're feeling well?"

"Fabulous."

"I'm so happy for you both, 'possum."

"Paul and I have been looking at houses and we found something we liked right away. It was just put on the market and it's exactly what we want. We made an offer and we should know in a couple of days if we get it. It has four bedrooms and a finished basement where Paul can put in a complete photography studio. I'd love you to see it."

"I'd love to, too. Maybe I could fly out for a couple of days in a week or two, once you find out. I'll plan my trip around your schedule. "

"That would be great, Mom. Everything's going so fast now, I could use your sensible input. And some decorating ideas. "

"Four bedrooms is a lot, isn't it?"

"We're figuring there'll be our bedroom, the baby's room, a guest room, and the fourth room as an office so I can work from home. There's no reason I can't do most of my editing at home and just go in one day a week. That way I'll be able to spend most of my time with Pookie."

"Pookie? Please tell my you're not thinking of naming him Pookie."

"No," Karen laughed. "We're just calling him that until we agree on a name."

"Good, you just saved me from cardiac arrest."

After they had talked for a little while longer, Julia hung up with Karen's words repeating in her thoughts, "sensible input."

'Is that what I am', she pondered, "sensible"? It's probably not very sensible to go and see Mayor Marvel Kane.'

But she was going anyway.

* * *

The Pittsley Selectmen were meeting in private again with Tax Collector, Josiah Barstow to discuss the mounting problem of Malbone Briggs. It was their biggest irritant right now and it needed to be solved quickly and quietly. He'd had a court date for which he did not appear and a bench warrant had been issued. Cutter's two brothers, Driver and Boomer had neglected to pay real estate taxes, as well. Barstow had issued a delinquency notice to both of them.

"If they follow the same course as their brother," Josiah informed them, "they will get bench warrants, too. What you boys have to determine, is whether or not to send in the police."

"I talked with Davis Johnson this afternoon. He talked with the State's Attorney General this morning."

"Are we going to get charged for that?" Albert interrupted.

"No, it was all very informal," Madison answered. "But the A.G. would like this handled on the local level. No, let me revise that. The A.G. has required us to handle it."

During the silence that followed, the four men did not make eye contact.

"What about bringing in the Feds?" Todd asked. "Don't they have a stake in this. I don't suppose Cutter or any of the others are paying income tax, either."

"Hold on, Todd. The last thing we want is the Fed to come in," Albert said. "We don't need some kind of Waco situation here."

"That's unlikely," responded Madison. "The Briggs boys probably never paid income tax to begin with. The Fed would only be interested if they posed some sort of threat, stockpiling arms or something. This has got to stay as low key as possible."

"If it was just the Briggses, we could look the other way. Play a waiting game," Todd said. "But what about all these other people who are living there now? They're probably not going to pay taxes either."

Madison mulled this over. "As for income taxes, they probably won't have any taxable income."

"I'm compiling a list," Josiah said, "of each property. I know some of them have deeded their land over to relatives. I suspect there was some money exchanged, but we can't prove that. Some of the smaller lots will probably be declared abandoned and come to the town by default for back taxes. But the Briggs brothers collectively own several hundred acres. That's a lot of revenue to ignore both now and in future. I think you don't have any choice here."

"I strongly recommend that we do nothing to provoke a show-down," Madison responded. "That could get real ugly."

"But we need to do something," Albert said. "And we need to keep it out of the papers. If the local news gets hold of it, they'll pump it up into some kind of headline and before we know it, it'll be on CNN. We don't want that. Let's think of another solution."

MONDAY, JUNE 21st

Before going to work that morning, Julia called the harbormaster's office to ask him about the Azorean Queen.

"We now believe the boat may have gone down," he answered.

Julia's hand rose involuntarily to her mouth as he continued.

"The Coast Guard found wreckage of the boat in the shipping lanes. By the tide charts, they figure it went down a few days after leaving port."

"Did they find any survivors?" Julia asked, her voice sounding hollow in her ears.

"Not yet. They're still looking."

"How many were on the boat?"

"John Estes and his wife and three crew members."

"Does anyone know what happened?"

"No," he answered. "But it must have been sudden because there was no 'Mayday' on the radio."

"What could cause a boat that size to go down like that?"

"Sometimes the weather is bad, but that wasn't the case here. Most times they go down because they're overloaded. They have such a good catch they can't resist overfilling the hold and adding more on the deck and even loading the tenders. They get too heavy, roll over, break up, and eventually wash ashore. Happens two, three times a year."

"But the Azorean Queen wasn't out that long, was she? I mean, to overload?"

"You just never know. The Queen, she was a queer boat to start with."

"What do you mean?"

"Just built wrong. She's had her problems over the years. It was just a matter of time."

Doreen's words echoed in her mind. "Thank you for the information," Julia said weakly as she hung up. She sat frozen and stunned.

She had planned to call the Mayor's office and make an appointment to speak with him at four o'clock, but after the phone conversation, she debated whether to continue. Finally, she decided she shouldn't give up, despite the tragic news about Doreen. She left work early, reshuffling her last two patients to the following day.

As Julia waited for his secretary to show her in, she tried to decide exactly what she'd say. She had made the appointment using the same story she'd given the others, but it was lame since she couldn't pretend to interview him as a witness.

"You probably meant to speak with my father; he was the mayor back then," the current mayor said uncomfortably when Julia explained what she wanted.

Marvel Kane had wispy blonde receding hair. He was tall and thin, with fine features and large blue eyes that did not make contact with her.

"But your best source would have been the old Chief of Police. Unfortunately, he retired to Florida ten years ago and I heard he died recently. The current Chief comes from Winthrop. He's only been in Sipponet for five years. In fact, the whole force has turned over in the past twenty years."

"Is your father still in Sipponet?"

"Yes." He answered as though he hadn't expected her to ask that.

"Do you think it would all right if I contacted him?"

"I can give you his phone number. Although his memory isn't quite what it used to be. He's getting a little forgetful."

"Thank you, I might try anyway. While you and I are speaking though, perhaps you could tell me what you remember. I imagine Nicole's murder would have been very big news in town twenty years ago. What did people think about it back then?"

He gestured with open hands, looking past her. "There was a lot of speculation, of course. But most people thought she was killed by someone out of town."

"Why is that?"

"Well, Ms. Fayette liked her fun wherever she could get it, they say. It was rumored that she was going out with some Black guy from Fall River or New Bedford. Some druggie."

Julia bit her lip in anger. But she decided not to confront him on it. Not right then. "Funny, her best friend didn't mention it," she said instead.

"Who is that?"

"Doreen Crawford. Doreen Estes now."

He shrugged. "Maybe she didn't know. That's the kind of thing a girl around here might keep secret."

"So that's what you think happened?"

"Me? I haven't a clue. But I can't imagine anyone from Sipponet doing it."

"Really? Why not?"

"Well you know how small towns are. If someone local did it, people would find out eventually. After all this time, it would have to leak out. No, I'm pretty confident it was a stranger. Who, I don't know. And I guess the State Police don't know either because it's still unsolved, right? They were in charge of the investigation. Maybe you should talk to them. If any of them are still around."

"Anyone in particular?"

"I wouldn't know."

"Perhaps your father would."

Marvel drummed his fingers on his desk. "Maybe, maybe not. He has his good days and his bad days." He looked at her for the first time. "Tell me again why you're dredging all this up."

"As you say, it's still unsolved."

"And you're trying to solve it?"

"Oh, no, not me. I'm basically just reporting the circumstances for an article and then I'll go on to the next assignment."

"Another unsolved murder?"

"Yes. Although I don't know where, yet. My editor decides that."

"And this is for a journal of psychology? Sounds more like the *Police Gazette*."

"I don't think it's the individual cases he's considering so much as the patterns."

"Umm hmm. Well, I'd be interested in seeing the article when it's published. Will you send me a copy?"

"I'd be glad to. If it makes the cut, of course."

"Then, is there anything else I can do for you today?"

"Just your father's telephone number, if you don't mind."

As he was writing down the number, she asked. "Did you know Nicole well?"

"No. She was a lot younger than me. I knew who she was, of course. Who didn't?"

"You probably knew some of the young men that were at the junkyard that night, right? They would be around your age."

He kept his focus on writing. "I knew all of them. But I didn't hang out with them. Only through high school. After that, I got married and had a family. My social life was pretty limited. I was working two jobs, no time for friends. Not single ones, anyway."

He handed her a piece of paper with his father's telephone number on it and she left Mayor Kane's office feeling that he didn't for a minute believe her ruse. Nor did she believe his.

That evening, she made the mistake of telling Adam about her encounter with the Mayor. He blew up at her.

"I thought we agreed you weren't going to pursue this. Don't you listen? This is dangerous business. You almost got yourself killed over the Jeannine Bradburn murder, do you want to finish the job now? Didn't we talk about this?"

"You talked, I listened, but I didn't agree to stop. What am I supposed to do? I might have information about Nicole's killer."

"Damn it, let it go. It's not worth risking your life. Turn it over to McDermott. Let him investigate."

"I don't have anything to turn over to him. It's all…" she fumbled for the word, "speculative."

He shook his head. "Then let him speculate and you get the hell out of it."

"I don't think," she said slowly, "I want to be told what to do. Or what not to do."

He remained silent for a moment, staring at her.

"You mean you don't want *me* telling you what to do. Even though I care about what happens to you."

"This is something I have to do, Adam."

"Why? Why do you have to do it."

"Because it's important. For my patient. And because there was a woman clubbed to death and left to rot and nobody cares who killed her because she wasn't the Right Kind of woman. Don't you see? It's like saying her life didn't matter."

"Your patient isn't *your* patient anymore. And who appointed you the crusader for unsolved crimes? That isn't your job."

"And it's not my business, is that it? Just forget about it?"

"Yes."

"No."

He paused again, then said, "If you keep this up, I don't want to hear about it."

"You're right. I shouldn't have told you about it. Obviously, you're not going to back me up."

"I think this goes a lot deeper than finding out who killed Nicole. Maybe you need to figure out why you're so obsessed with this."

"Maybe *you* need to figure out why you're giving me an ultimatum."

"It's not an ultimatum. Unless you take it that way."

"If it looks like a duck and quacks like a duck—"

He stood up. "That's your ex-husband. Not me."

"Ya could've fooled me."

He took a deep breath. Then he turned and left.

After he was gone, she closed her eyes and put her hand to her forehead. 'Oh, God,' she thought, 'what did I do?'

* * *

Goody was improved enough, Adam decided, to leave him alone for a while. He just didn't feel like dealing with Goody right this minute. So he headed for Cutter's.

A police car was parked in front of the gate. A yellow light flashed in the entrance. Percy Davis was on detail.

"Picking up some extra money," he explained to Adam. "Though I hate to have to do this to Cutter. Were you going in to see him?"

"Yes."

"Can't let you. Town ordered us to close access to the property."

"For how long?"

Percy shrugged. "You got me. The longer the better as far as my pay goes. They got Boomer's and Driver's property blocked, too. Of course," he winked at Adam, "you and I might remember another way in from the old days."

Adam nodded. "Anybody else know?"

"Know what?" Percy smiled.

Adam drove down the street and around to a dirt road where he parked. He took a small flashlight out of his glove compartment and got out. There was no path into the swamp, but Adam knew his way.

It was slow going through the underbrush and the tangle of ferns and tree roots. The damp smell of mold and rotting vegetation filled his nostrils. He held onto low branches as he made his way along the flat part of the swamp. The wet packed leaves were deceptive—he knew you could step on them and sink up to your knees. As soon as he came to the stream that ran through the swamp, he kept to the graveled moraines abutting it.

When he finally emerged, he came face-to-face with Hercules. The dog lunged at Adam, growling and barking, holding him at bay. But within seconds, Cutter was at the back door of his cabin in his white longjohns and a rifle.

"It's me, Cutter, Adam. I had to come the back way."

The other men began assembling on the perimeter of the clearing. "It's all right," Cutter told them. "It's a friend." Cutter lowered his rifle. "Come on in, Ski."

Inside, Angel joined them in the kitchen as Cutter explained that the police detail had begun that afternoon. He wasn't sure what was coming next.

"Shit," Adam said, "whatever you do, don't come out with a rifle in your hands again. If it was the police, they'd shoot you."

"That's just what I told him," Angel said.

"It's beginning to look like that's what they want," Cutter replied.

"No, I don't think so," Adam said. "At least not yet. But I don't know how long the town is willing to pay for a twenty-four hour police detail at your gates."

Angel shook her head in consternation. "I was hoping they'd just leave us alone."

"Not likely," Cutter said, exchanging looks with Adam.

"You anticipated this?" Adam asked.

Cutter simply raised a brush-thick eyebrow and cocked his head.

"Have you got a stockpile of arms here?" Adam pressed.

"No. I thought about it. But no good would come of it. Then again," he added, "it might not make any difference. Especially if people get riled up."

Adam leaned back in his chair. "You got any shine?"

"Hell, we got enough shine to supply New England. Angel, here, wants to barter quilts and crochets." Cutter broke into a toothy grin. "But likker is quicker."

Angel giggled as she pulled over the curtain under the sink and reached on a shelf and brought out a giant plastic bottle of dishwashing detergent. She poured the clear white liquid into two glasses.

"We figure we can ferment just about anything," Cutter said pleasantly as she passed the glasses to him and Adam.

Adam tasted it and rolled his eyes. "Whew. Good stuff."

"We're calling it Liberty Juice," Angel said, giggling again. "Well you two enjoy yourselves, I'm going back to bed." She patted Cutter on the shoulder and left the room.

"So what's up?" Cutter asked as he took a swallow.

"Nothing. I just felt like some homemade spirits."

"Oh, yeah?" Cutter said skeptically.

"So, how's it going? Other than the barbarians at the gates."

"It's going okay. But I been thinking maybe this is the wrong place to try this. Maybe I ought to sell the land and move west. Or south."

"You'd actually sell?" Adam couldn't imagine Cutter giving up his heritage. This secession must be more important to him that Adam realized.

"I don't want to. It's my last option, not my first choice. But I believe in what we're doing here. The more I think about it, the more I'm sure that I want my independence."

"There's got to be some compromise, Cutter. You can't live the way you want to live in the real world. Not in this country, not in this time."

"Any compromise is too great. That's how the Briggs came to be here in the first place, ain't it?" Cutter smiled crookedly.

"Tell me about your ancestors," Adam said.

Cutter looked at him quizzically.

* * *

"Why in hell did you give her my phone number? What were you thinking? Or do you think at all?"

"But she asked and I couldn't say no. She'd have found it anyway. You're in the phone book, you know. I thought it would look suspicious if I didn't."

"She is suspicious. Why the hell do you think she went to see you in the first place? You are such a fuck-up, Marvel. Now you're going to have to clean up your own mess. And this time, make sure Asshole doesn't leave any traces."

TUESDAY, JUNE 22nd

The telephone rang in Julia's office, startling her as she was writing up her notes from the previous session. She rarely got outside calls.

"Dr. Arnault?" queried the baritone at the other end.

"This is she," Julia answered not recognizing the voice.

"This is Dr. Raymond Alonzo at McLean Hospital. I'm Sherry Fayette's therapist. Do you have time to talk right now?"

"Yes, I'm between patients," Julia answered, wondering what he wanted and fearing the worst. "Is Sherry all right?"

"Yes and no. She's physically fine. But she refuses treatment. I was hoping you might be helpful."

"I don't know how much you know of this transfer, Dr. Alonzo, but I'm not her psychologist-of-record."

"I realize that. When I spoke with Dr. Haskins, all he would say was that he had thought Sherry would be a good candidate for our experimental program. Quite frankly, I felt his explanation was somewhat…shall we say…incomplete. Perhaps you could give me some background."

Julia took a deep breath and considered how much to tell him.

"Would it be easier if we met in person?" he asked.

"Yes. It probably would."

"Can you come up here this afternoon?"

She explained that she wouldn't be through until five-thirty, and it would take at least an hour to drive to Belmont. Alonzo said he had to be there until eight that evening and would wait for her. He seemed, she thought, rather anxious.

The Pavilion at McLean looked like a hybrid of New England colonial and Southern plantation. The spreading lawn in front of the pillared building, with a scattering of large full trees, made the hospital look unlike a hospital. But, to Julia, it had the same misleading façade as any upscale nursing or funeral home. On the other hand, it beat walking into an underfunded state institution. It was advertised, after all, as the largest psychiatric teaching facility of Harvard Medical School.

In his office, Dr. Alonzo was more forthcoming than he had been on the phone. She liked his demeanor right away. Straightforward and confident. He was quite tall, African-American, heavy set, with penetrating eyes.

"Dr. Shin Wu, as you may know, has an appointment here at McLean as well as Bridgewater. He's told me the circumstances of Sherry's transfer. In confidence. He seems to be taking an uncharacteristic risk by urging me to facilitate contact between you and the patient." He looked at her expectantly.

"Yes," Julia conceded. "If Dr. Haskins found out, I think Dr. Wu's position at Bridgewater might be in jeopardy."

"I hold Sam in very high regard. I don't believe he would do this without strong justification. So I'm treating this as a strictly private matter. I expect you will do the same."

"Of course." Julia replied. "You say that Sherry has refused treatment?"

"I understated the situation on the telephone," he said. "Sherry was in restraints during her transfer, but when she got here, we attempted to remove them and put her on twenty-four hour watch. Before anyone could stop her, she managed to run headfirst into the glass partition of the nursing station and she broke her nose. I think she thought the glass would shatter and she'd cut herself. She's in isolation right now. She won't talk with anyone."

"How can I help?"

"I've read your notes. I have the feeling she might talk with you."

"Do you want me to try?"

"If you will."

"Yes, of course."

"Good." Dr. Alonzo's expression showed relief.

As Julia looked through the small window of the isolation room, she could see Sherry sitting on the padded floor. The walls were covered with tan padded blankets and there was only a blow-up mattress to sleep on. Sherry sat in the corner with her arms wrapped around her legs and her forehead resting on her knees.

As Dr. Alonzo unlocked the door and as Julia entered, Sherry looked up. Julia could see her bandaged nose and black eyes.

"What do *you* want?" the young woman said in a hostile tone.

"I heard that you hurt yourself."

"What do you care?"

"I care because you were my patient."

"You dumped me."

"No, Sherry, no," Julia shook her head. "That was not my decision."

Julia nodded to Alonzo and he closed the door behind her. It automatically locked.

"I didn't ask for you to be transferred," Julia continued, approaching Sherry. "I was informed that I was being relieved."

"You didn't ask to get rid of me?"

"No."

"Then why didn't you tell me that? "

"I wanted to. But that wasn't my decision either. None of it was."

"You didn't send me here?"

"I had nothing to do with it."

Sherry was silent as Julia moved closer to her and sat down on the mattress. "I didn't want to stop working with you."

Sherry looked away and began to say something but her voice cracked and her eyes teared up. Julia remained quiet until the young woman wiped her eyes and looked at her again.

"Then why?" Sherry asked, trembling.

"I'm still trying to find out," Julia answered. She paused, then added, "And I'm still trying to find out who murdered your mother."

"I *know* who murdered my mother. I know and *he* knows and everybody in town knows and nobody will do anything about it."

"Who, Sherry?"

"Marvel Kane. Mayor Marvel Kane."

Julia tried to conceal her surprise. She didn't like the man, but she didn't peg him for a killer. "How do you know that?"

"Because Aunt Doreen told me. Ask her."

Julia swallowed hard. Should she tell Sherry about her aunt?

"Doreen is missing, Sherry. She went out scalloping with her husband on their boat and something happened. The boat broke up with everyone aboard." She decided not to tell Sherry yet that Doreen was probably lost. "The Coast Guard is searching for them."

Sherry took a few minutes to process that, then said, in a low voice, "He killed her."

"No. They think the boat was overloaded. That kind of thing happens sometimes when the catch is good and they take on more than the boat can handle."

Sherry looked her in the eyes. "It was sabotaged."

"That's not likely, Sherry. Doreen and her husband were always with the boat, right until it sailed. The boat was well maintained. I saw it at the docks."

"Then it happened at sea."

"How could anyone scuttle the boat out at sea?"

Sherry looked at her as though it were self-evident. "From another boat, of course."

Instantly Julia's thoughts went to Conny Cranshaw's painting. 'No,' she told herself, 'that's crazy to think that. No one would sabotage the boat just to get at Doreen. Not risk the lives of five people. Not even Conny Cranshaw would do that.' But her mind kept racing. 'He might have let someone else do it though.' But she was getting ahead of herself. Maybe they would find the survivors and it would all be explained. It was just a horrible accident.

"I doubt that," Julia reassured Sherry. "We'll probably find out there's a rational cause for what happened."

"Don't you believe it," Sherry answered, looking away and fingering her bandages.

"Does it hurt?" Julia asked.

"Of course it hurts," Sherry said acidly.

"Good. Maybe it will remind you not to do that again."

Sherry snapped around angrily to look at her. Then, seeing Julia's maternal expression, she smiled a little.

"You know," Sherry said, "nobody else talks to me like that."

In fact, Julia never spoke to any of her other patients that freely. But somehow she knew it was the right way for Sherry.

"I think Dr. Alonzo might, given half a chance," Julia said. "I think you lucked out with him. He seems to be one of the good guys."

"You think?"

Julia nodded.

"Yeah," Sherry said thoughtfully. "I could bang him."

As Julia drew a deep breath to think of a response, Sherry said, "Just kidding."

After spending another half-hour with Sherry, Julia promised that she would come back. She would let Sherry know the outcome of the Coast Guard search for her aunt.

As Julia went to bed that evening, she could hear the rain begin soft as a lullaby. It soothed her to sleep. But around Midnight, she began to hear the sounds of thunder like canons booming on a distant battlefield. Then the lightning came, illuminating the room like fireworks. The lightening was followed by loud crashes overhead that seemed to rock the room. Cat pawed her way closer and lay up against Julia's back, shivering at each thunderclap. It continued throughout the night.

WEDNESDAY, JUNE 23rd

By morning, the thunder and lightning had stopped but the rain and wind continued to lash against the roof. Julia let Cat out into the yard and she quickly returned soaking wet. Julia toweled her off and turned on the television for a local forecast. Over breakfast, Julia heard the very brief announcement that the search for the crew of the Azorean Queen had been called off. The newscaster mentioned only that the ship had been lost at sea the previous week with five hands on board, no sign of survivors. There would be a memorial service at the Seaman's Bethel in New Bedford on Saturday afternoon.

"Come in, Julia," Sam said, looking up from the pile of folders on his desk.

Julia took the seat opposite him and smiled. "Thank you, Sam."

"For what?"

"For talking with Dr. Alonzo."

He put down his pen and sat back in his chair. "I thought it was the right thing to do. You saw Sherry then?"

"Yes. She was in rough shape. But she was responsive to me."

"Good. Are you going to see her again?"

"I have to call Dr. Alonzo to ask him if I can go there this afternoon. I have bad news for her."

Sam looked concerned as Julia explained about Doreen.

"I promised to let her know."

"Yes," he agreed. "I think you should. But there's a risk here. It may just feed into her paranoia about her mother's death."

"I don't believe it's paranoia, Sam. There *is* something going on."

She told him the full story about the vandalism and the Sipponet connection between Commissioner Barrington and Joe Woods.

"Haskins was just following Barrington's direction to take me off Sherry's case. I can't prove that, but I'm certain of it."

"You're saying Barrington is connected with Nicole Fayette's death?" Sam said skeptically.

"No. But I think his half-brother is connected somehow. Maybe not directly, but who knows? They all seem to be in a conspiracy about it."

"And you think that this Doreen's death wasn't an accident? That's way off the chart, Julia." He unconsciously removed his glasses and began wiping them.

"I know. Who would kill five people just to eliminate one? It doesn't seem possible. And yet, what if it's true?"

He shook his head. "I frankly don't know what to believe."

"Neither do I," she confessed. "But the immutable facts are," Julia raised one finger at a time, "*one*, that Nicole Fayette was murdered. *Two*, that the killer is still at large. *Three*, that my house and car were vandalized after I began interviewing suspects. *Four*, that Doreen Estes had something she wanted to tell me. And *five*," she raised her pinkie, "that now Doreen is dead." She lowered her hand. "Plus the fact that I was summarily taken off Sherry's case after I began investigating her mother's death."

Sam sighed and put his glasses back on. "You make a convincing case, Julia. But it doesn't get you any closer to knowing who killed Nicole Fayette. And if all this is true…and I do mean *if*…then you're dealing with someone, or ones, who are capable of anything to prevent Nicole Fayette's killer from being exposed. You may be putting yourself in grave danger. Why don't you talk with that Lieutenant McDermott you spoke of? He's the one who should be investigating this, not you. You should turn the whole thing over to him."

Back in her office, she pondered Sam's advice. She *had* told Lt. McDermott, after all, that she would keep him informed. Perhaps she ought to turn it over to him. Did she really want to continue on this risky path? Checking her schedule, she decided she had just enough time to make two phone calls before her first patient. The first was to Lt. McDermott, the second would be to Dr. Alonzo.

"Yes, I remember you," Lt. McDermott said when she identified herself over the phone.

"I've been looking into the matter," Julia said, "and I have some information to give you. I don't know how substantive it is from your point-of-view, but I'm convinced I'm on to something. But I don't have time to go into it over the phone. Can we meet?"

"Let me check my calendar," he said. After a moment, he asked, "How about tomorrow morning at my office?"

"Late afternoons are better for me," she said. "Could we possibly do it around four o'clock?"

There was another short pause, then he said, "Yes. I can do four o'clock tomorrow."

Dr. Alonzo wasn't in his office when she arrived late that afternoon, but he'd given Julia permission to speak with Sherry when she'd called that morning. He told her Sherry was out of isolation and back on a locked ward.

She met with Sherry in the supervised visiting room outside the ward. A female attendant in her early forties, with short dark hair and a white hospital jacket led the patient in and sat in a corner. Julia and Sherry sat across from each other at a large oak table. The young woman's bandage was off, but her nose still looked red and swollen.

"I have some sad news for you about your aunt. The search was called off yesterday. They presume Doreen and her husband and the others drowned when the boat broke up."

Sherry nodded silently.

"I'm so sorry," Julia added.

"Is there going to be a funeral?"

"There's a memorial service on Sunday. At the Seaman's Bethel."

Sherry unconsciously folded her hands in front of her on the table. "I'd like to go. Do you think I can?"

Julia rubbed her palms together. "I don't know. I can talk with Dr. Alonzo about it."

"Maybe he'd let me go if you went with me."

Julia had every intention of going to the service herself. But she wasn't sure it would be wise to take Sherry.

"Aunt Doreen is the only one left that was close to my mother. It would mean a lot to me. I'm doing better now; you can see that, can't you?"

It was far too soon to know if Sherry was really doing better, Julia thought. But this might make a difference in her recovery. Yet, it wasn't a judgment she felt qualified to make. And, in any event, it was out of her hands.

"I'll talk with Dr. Alonzo, Sherry, but I can't promise anything."

Julia found Alonzo in his office after she left Sherry and explained the entire situation to him.

He thought about it for a while, concluding with, "You're asking a difficult series of questions. 'Is Sherry well enough to go?' 'Would it be helpful for her to go?' 'Is she safe in your care?'" He paused, then continued, "Whether she would be safe in your care is probably the easiest to answer. I can confer with Sam about that. But assuming the answer is 'yes,' there are still the other two important issues. Is she well enough? I don't know yet. Let's see how she behaves over the next two days. That still leaves the question of whether this exercise would be helpful or not. Frankly, at this moment, I have no way of knowing. Today was the first session I've had with her where she actually talked with me. I need to explore this more with her."

"I didn't promise her anything," Julia said, "only that I would bring it up with you."

"Good, because I'm inclined against it. But I won't exclude the possibility until I've had more time with her. If I'm not satisfied in all particulars by Saturday, I will have to say no."

"Of course," Julia said.

"You'll notice I haven't asked your opinion," Alonzo said.

"She's not my patient," Julia replied.

"Exactly."

Julia rose to leave. "Thank you for arranging for me to speak with her, Dr. Alonzo."

He smiled. "That part, I'm convinced, *was* helpful."

"I'm glad it worked out that way," Julia replied.

As she turned to leave he said, "By the way, what *is* your opinion?"

Julia paused, then answered, "Sherry gets very few of her emotional needs met. I guess I'd risk it."

Dr. Raymond Alonzo did not respond to that and Julia could not determine anything from his expression. Instead, he said simply, "I'll call you Saturday afternoon."

THURSDAY, JUNE 24th

In State Police Headquarters, Lt. McDermott listened carefully to what Julia told him, but his face betrayed no reaction until she was finished. Then he leaned back in his chair, crossed his arms, and lowered his head. He sat this way for such a long time, Julia almost thought he was asleep.

Finally, he looked up at her. "Let me follow-up on Frank Leach. I'll contact the florist and get his address."

She nodded assent. "What about Joe Woods? I never got to speak with him."

"Let that go. You wouldn't get anything from him, anyway. I interviewed him at the time. He's a sullen, brutish fellow."

"Did you talk with Marvel Kane back then?"

"Yes."

"And his father?"

"Yes, both. And they both stonewalled us."

"Do you think Marvel Kane killed Nicole?"

"There's no evidence of it."

"That's not what I asked."

"That's all I'm prepared to say." He leaned forward. "From here on, I want you to stay out of it."

Julia was split by a shiver of apprehension in the way McDermott said this, and a feeling of relief. She really didn't want to continue this all by herself. It frightened her. And now she could withdraw on his order.

"All right," she agreed readily. "I'm done."

SATURDAY, JUNE 26th

Mashpee was only an hour's drive from Pittsley and Adam thought it would make a good afternoon outing for Goody. But the cab was too high, so Adam had him stand on a cinderblock to get in. The sun was too strong, so Adam put down the passenger-side visor. The motor was too loud, but there wasn't anything he could do about that. The open window blew too much air on him, but it was too hot if it was closed. Adam opened the side vents. Even then, Goody grumbled.

"What if I have to take a leak before we get there?"

"If you do, I'll stop. Just let me know."

"How'm I going to get out of the truck?"

"Use the parachute under your seat," Adam replied. "Or piss out the door."

Goody pulled his mouth into a frown and went silent for the twenty-five miles down Route 495 to the end, onto Route 6 and around the rotary. As they crossed the Bourne Bridge over the Cape Cod Canal onto Route 28, Goody fidgeted.

"I ain't been down here in sixty years. We used to hook school and come down to Buzzards Bay. Sleep out, go swimming. It was real pretty then. It don't look like anything I remember. It's all built up."

"It's built up everywhere, Goody. Cape's no exception." Adam had never thought of Goody as ever being young.

"I don't like it none."

"I don't like it none, either, but it is what it is."

"Houses and stores. Stores and houses. People want this, do they?"

"They don't know any better."

Goody shook his head. "Pity on them."

"What else did you do as a kid, Goody?"

"Worked, mostly. Worked the farm. Worked my grandfather's bog. They were good days."

The soil became sandy with white pine and scrub oak as Adam turned onto Route 151. They drove past Mashpee Commons to another rotary and then right onto Great Neck Road.

"Where the hell are we going, anyway?" Goody asked.

"Not far."

At number 483, Adam turned into a bare parking lot in front of a fair-sized grey and white building.

"Do you want to wait here or come inside?" Adam asked.

Goody looked at the house askance.

"Imagine that," he said. "Indians living in big houses and driving big cars."

"SUVs," Adam said. "Sports utility vehicles."

"Ain't that a bitch."

As Adam got out of the truck, Goody said, "Can you still get chow mein sandwiches these days?"

Southeastern Massachusetts—particularly around Pittsley, Taunton, New Bedford, Fall River—was probably the only place in Massachusetts—maybe the only place in the world—to find a chow mein sandwich. It consisted of vegetable chow mein on a hamburger roll, full of onions and crispy noodles in a brown sauce, sometimes a white sauce, sometimes with ground meat, sometimes not. You had to eat it with a fork.

"Sure can," Adam replied.

"You think we could get a chow mein sandwich on the way back?"

"I don't see why not." If Goody didn't eat the top bun, Adam thought, it would probably be okay for his diabetes.

Goody nodded and Adam thought he saw a faraway look in the old man's eyes.

SUNDAY, JUNE 27th

"Cripes," Sherry said as she got into Julia's car and sat on the duct-taped seat. "You don't much worry about status, do you? What happened in here?"

Julia had been genuinely surprised that Dr. Alonzo gave her permission to take Sherry to the funeral service.

"Oh," she replied nonchalantly, "somebody broke in to steal my radio and vandalized the inside. My fault for parking in a bad area."

Sherry looked at the hole where the radio had been. "They must have been pretty desperate."

During the long ride back from Belmont and to New Bedford, Sherry told her everything she remembered about her mother. Her happiest memories were in the summer when she and her mother played for hours in the little wading pool in back of the house. Nicole read her bedtime stories and they spent winter afternoons making hot chocolate, or making snowmen when it snowed. Grandma Fayette did all the cooking and she made French meat pies and brownies with cherries. Sherry didn't talk about Grandpa Fayette.

When her mother disappeared, her grandmother told her Nicole died in a car accident. She didn't know until she was fifteen that she'd been murdered. Her Aunt Doreen finally told her. And now her Aunt Doreen was dead. Sherry just knew she'd been murdered, too.

Julia took this last information with more than a grain of salt.

They were fortunate to find a parking space alongside the New Bedford Whaling Museum. The Seamen's Bethel was just across the cobblestone street.

Entering the foyer, they stood at the end of the line behind a hundred other people. Julia picked up a brochure from the rack and began reading it as they slowly moved forward into the chapel.

When Melville came to New Bedford in 1840, the Bethel—Hebrew for house (Beth) and God (El)—was relatively new. It was built in 1832 to "promote the interests of seamen" whose numbers had become nearly equal to that of permanent residents, but with distinctly different inclinations. The saloons, brothels, and gambling clubs proliferated, much to the dismay of the solid citizenry, many of whom were Quakers.

Most people today, Julia imagined, probably know the Bethel less from *Moby Dick* the book, published in 1851, than from *Moby Dick* the movie, made in 1956. More from Gregory Peck than Herman Melville. (The famous cinema star actually visited the Bethel, most likely to promote the film, and older New Bedford residents still talked nostalgically about it.) How many people, besides college students, actually read Melville anymore? True, the Whaling Museum had an annual 'round-the-clock reading of *Moby Dick* during the first week in January, but she had never been to it and suspected it attracted only tourists. Julia made a mental note to go to the next reading.

The Bethel housed a Whalemen's Chapel and "few are the moody fishermen," Melville wrote, "shortly bound for the Indian Ocean or Pacific, who fail to make a Sunday visit to the spot." Himself included. Although the Bethel was nondenominational, it was really a product of the apprehensive Quaker whaling merchants who formed the New Bedford Port Society for the Moral Improvement of Seamen. It embodied many of their values, including a school—not for children, but for illiterate whalemen. Cleverly, the merchants never called it a school, but named it rather the 'Salt Box.' A salt box would have been familiar to whalemen as it was the term for the area located beneath the deck of a ship where the salted meat was kept and also the term for the boxes that salt was actually shipped in, and kept in. Julia had found, at a yard sale, an antique blue-and-white porcelain saltbox with a wooden lid that she kept salt in on her kitchen counter. 'Salt Box,' too, had since become a familiar architectural style from New England to Newfoundland for compact houses with a pitched roof, short slope in front and longer slope in back. It made the house, from the front at least, look taller.

The wooden floor of the Bethel, with cutout-iron heating vents, creaked as people took their seats. There were two shorter center rows, flanked across the aisles on either side, but two longer rows of pews. Organ music began playing dirge-like hymns, solemn and sad.

Because they were towards the end of the line, she and Sherry wound up sitting in the second-to-last pew on the left-hand side. Julia smiled when she read the pamphlet indicating that this was Melville's pew. Most people would think his pew should be at the front of the chapel. But, because of the fire of 1866 and subsequent reconstruction, the front and back of the chapel were reversed.

'How could they say this was his pew,' Julia wondered, 'when he was only here for a few weeks before he shipped out?'

Around them on the walls were tablets that looked a little like hanging wooden gravestones. "Cenotaphs," she read, which is Greek for "empty grave." As she viewed the cenotaphs immediately around her, she saw a memorial from the Officers and Crew of the Emily Morgan to Lewis Cheshire, who fell overboard on April 17, 1840, at age 23. Certainly, Melville would have heard of that. More than one young whaleman was memorialized for falling overboard, possibly from a chase-boat.

There were many cenotaphs and many more names listed, right up to present. But the pamphlet particularly mentioned one in memory of Captain William Swain, "Master of the Christopher Mitchell of Nantucket. This worthy man, after fastning to a whale, in the 49th year of his age, was carried overboard by the line and drowned."

In back of her to the right, was the original spot for the chaplain's lectern. There never was a high prow-shaped pulpit with a rope ladder, as in the novel. The real Bethel preacher never climbed up into it and pulled the rope up after him. But at the front of the chapel now stood a half-prow facsimile of a ship. Why? Because when tourists came to see the Bethel, they were disappointed not find what they had seen in John Houston's popular movie. So, in 1961, the New Bedford Port Society installed a mock-pulpit to fit their expectations.

Sitting in the front pews were, Julia presumed, family members of the crew. As her eyes swept over the back of their heads, a man turned slightly towards the older woman beside him and she recognized Martin Ryman. There was an older man seated next to the woman on the other side, holding her hand.

She leaned over to whisper to Sherry. "Are those Doreen's parents in the front row?"

Sherry followed her gaze and nodded.

The organ music stopped and a ship's bell clanged five times. The reverend in black robes was seated to the side of the pulpit and when the bell stopped, he mounted the pulpit in the prow of the boat. He was a middle-aged, tall, dark-skinned man with a shock of white in the front of otherwise black hair. He addressed the congregation first in Portuguese, then in English.

"We are gathered today to pay homage to our brethren lost at sea. John Estes. Doreen Crawford Estes. Manuel Arruda. Joseph Cabral. David Souza."

At each name, there was single ring of the ship's bell, with sobbing emanating from various parts of the chapel.

"Fellow mariners. We are all sailors on this vast sea. Our lives are small fragile vessels pitched and tossed beyond our control."

The reverend gripped the sides of the upturned prow as though steadying himself in rough waters.

"There is naught but the heavens to guide us ashore. And naught but perils to navigate on our way home. But we sail forward, plowing through the turbulent water, mindful that there are creatures below that will rise up to harm us and thunder and lightning above that will come down to strike us. From the Book of Jonah, this is the lamentation of the drowning soul:

> "*You hurled me into the deep,*
> *into the very heart of the seas,*
> *and the currents swirled about me;*
> *all your waves and breakers*
> *swept over me.*
> *I said, 'I have been banished*
> *from your sight;*
> *yet I will look again*
> *toward your holy temple.*"

"Jonah," the reverend paused to look around the congregation, "was saved from death in the belly of the whale by his repentance of his sins and his love of God. His rescue was physical as well as spiritual. The whale, being moved by the Almighty, heaved Jonah back into the sea and thus he lived. So, too, have our brother seafarers been rescued, but not in the physical sense. As the waves closed over them, every one, I am certain, called upon God and rebuked all wickedness in his life. And God, in His mercy, stretched forth His hand and raised their souls out of the depths. Mourn not for them, for they are saved in the Lord."

As he continued, Julia looked around. All the pews were filled, but in the crowd, she spotted more familiar faces on the other side of the aisle. Estelle Leach was seated on the opposite side of the chapel. Was she, Julia wondered, that close to Doreen? She was much younger than Doreen, and besides, Doreen had broken up with Estelle's brother. It seemed strange somehow that she would be there. Then, stranger still, several rows behind her, Julia recognized Joe Block. He was alone.

After saying "Amen," the reverend sat down, but the services went on for another half-hour with recitations and hymns.

At the end, the reverend rose again and stood next to the prow. The bell clanged, then clanged again at the end of each verse of the poem. Five times in total: one for each of the five dead.

"Sunset and evening star,
And one clear call for me!
And may there be no moaning of the bar,
When I put out to sea.
"But such a tide as moving seems asleep,
Too full for sound and foam,

When that which drew from out the boundless deep
Turns again home.
"Twilight and evening bell,
And after that the dark!
And may there be no sadness of farewell,
When I embark.
"For tho' from out our borne of Time and Place
The flood may bear me far
I hope to see my Pilot face to face.
When I have crost the bar."

The organ began playing again, but this time the music was uplifting, inspiring, suited to the message of hope and resurrection. Julia turned to Sherry, to see how her charge was reacting to the service.

There were tears in Sherry's eyes that she hastily wiped away. She shrugged. "I don't know. I kept expecting to hear the theme of Gilligan's Island."

Julia laughed involuntarily and several people looked to see who was being so inappropriate.

They filed out of the chapel by rows, from front to back, with Julia and Sherry being among the last to exit.

Standing on the top steps, Julia looked over the crowd and noticed Estelle Leach off to the side. A man approached her and Estelle nervously looked around while they talked. Estelle saw Julia on the steps, said something to the man, and he turned around. Julia recognized him from his photograph, despite the man's age. It was unmistakably Frank Leach. She wondered what Estelle had told him.

As she continued to watch, another man approached Frank whom Julia didn't know. He was about the same age, but shorter and thicker. He looked like someone who'd spent all of his time doing hard outdoor work and Julia wondered if he were a fisherman. After a brief exchange, the man dissolved back into the crowd and Julia lost track of him. When she looked back, Frank Leach, too, had disappeared.

"Julia?" Martin Ryman called, as he mounted the steps.

"Oh? Hello, Martin. What are you doing here?"

"I came with the Crawfords and Estelle Leach."

He looked pointedly at Sherry, so Julia introduced them by simply saying, "This is my friend, Cheryl."

Martin extended his hand to Sherry politely, but she caught his quick, knowing glance. Julia was sure he guessed her identity.

"Is Adam with you?" he asked.

"No."

"Well, I have to take the Crawfords home and drop Estelle off. Perhaps I could call you later?"

Was there something telling in the way she had said 'no' to his question about Adam? Too abrupt, perhaps. Too final? Because Martin seemed to take it as an invitation. Or maybe he just wanted to talk about Sherry.

"All right," she answered.

He nodded to her as he said, "Nice to meet you, Cheryl," and left.

"How are you feeling, Sherry?" Julia asked as they walked back to her car.

"I'm all right."

"Are you?"

Sherry nodded. "I think if I had actually seen her body, it would have been worse."

As they were driving away from the Bethel, Sherry looked back. "It still doesn't feel finished."

"I know," Julia replied.

Julia drove Sherry back to McLean by five o'clock. It was after six by the time she returned home. As she pulled her car into her gravel driveway next to the house, Cat began barking from inside.

"I'm coming, girl," Julia called out.

As she went around to the back door, the man she'd seen with Estelle was sitting on the steps.

"Please let me in for a minute. I need to talk with you. My name is Frank Leach."

Startled, Julia nodded. She unlocked the door and Cat came to her side, growling. Julia reassured the dog and let her out into the yard as Frank Leach followed her in.

"You talked with my sister."

"Yes," Julia answered noncommittally. She sat down on a kitchen chair and motioned him across from her. Up close, he looked haggard. Like a man who didn't sleep well, or slept in hard places.

"Estelle said you were looking for me."

"I don't think I'm the only one."

"I know that." He sat hunched over.

"Who else is looking for you?"

"Joe Woods. And he found me."

So that must have been the man talking with Frank earlier, she thought. "What does he want?"

"He wanted to make sure I don't talk to you. Or anyone else. But I think he really wants to make sure I don't talk to *you*. I made a mistake in coming back here."

"Why did you?"

"I had to see Estelle before I go away for good. This time, I won't come back. And I wanted to say goodbye to Doreen"

"Would you like a cup of coffee? I'm going to make some coffee."

"No, thanks."

She got up and began running water for the coffee-pot. "Why doesn't Joe Woods want you to talk to me?"

"Because I saw him take Nicole Fayette out of his truck and put her dead body in the woods."

She shut off the tap and turned quickly around to him. "Joe Woods killed Nicole?"

"No," Frank answered. "No. He just disposed…I don't know how else to say this. He disposed of Nikki's body. I'm sure he didn't kill her."

"Who did?"

"Are you sure you want to know?"

"Marvel Kane?" she said.

He looked stunned. "How do you know that?"

"From Doreen." Well, she thought, that was half-true. "And now *she's* dead."

As he began breathing rapidly she was concerned he was going to hyperventilate.

"So tell me," she said to calm him down, "how you came to see Joe Woods doing what he did?"

"We both saw him. Eileen Mann and I. We were parked there, off a bit into the trees so no one would see us. We had a little weed and we were making out when Joe drove in. We watched him. He never saw us. We didn't know it was Nikki until I got out to look after he left. Eileen went a little nuts. Nikki was seeing Marvel. But that night at the party, Nikki told him she wasn't going to see him anymore."

"Marvel was at the party?"

"Yeah. He came late. Probably to take Nikki home. Well, not right home, you know."

Julia nodded.

"Anyway, Nikki told Marvel she'd found somebody else. Some guy from New Bedford, and she was going to live with him. Marvel was furious. She said if he didn't leave her alone, she'd tell his wife. They argued, then Nikki left with him, and that was the last I saw of her. Eileen and I left together after the party. I think Marvel must have gone berserk and hit Nikki. Then he must have paid Joe to dump her body. Joe was just a lackey. He did whatever Marvel told him to.

"Eileen wanted to go to the police, but I told her to stay out of it. I knew Marvel's father controlled the police chief and it would only get her in trouble. But I think she must have said something to somebody, because a few weeks later she was dead. They said it was an overdose, but I knew Eileen didn't do drugs. That night we were together was the first time she'd even tried weed.

"Woodsy came to see me at the funeral. He said I better not say anything about that night, or something bad might happen to me and Estelle. I figured I'd better get out of Dodge, fast, and stay out."

"Who else saw Nikki leave with Marvel Kane?"

"All of us."

"Who, all?"

"Conny Cranshaw, Joe Woods, Dennis Buckley, Joe Block—"

"I thought he left with Doreen," Julia interrupted.

"Only because she had a curfew. So they went off for a while, then he took her home, then he came back. I knew he was the one Nikki was really seeing on the side. She lied about a guy from New Bedford. But Marvel didn't know it. Blockhead…Joe Block…and I were tight back then. I never thought it was serious between her and Joe. I thought Nikki just wanted to make Marvel jealous, so he'd leave his wife for her."

"Why are you telling about this now? Why didn't you say something back then?"

"Don't you understand? Somebody killed Eileen because of it. Woodsy told me if I said anything, I'd be killed, too. I'm only telling you so you don't keep messing around with this or they'll hurt Estelle. That's what Joe said to me. They'll kill her." He shook his head. "I should never have come back. But I was afraid for my sister. She told me Woodsy came to her house and threatened to hurt her if she told you where I was. I had to talk to him, to tell him Estelle doesn't know anything."

He got up and the chair scraped the floor. "Now I'm going away. Far away, and nobody will ever hear from me again. And I'm warning you that if you keep nosing into this, you're putting my sister in danger. And yourself. Leave it alone. Nicole wasn't worth Eileen getting killed. And she's not worth anybody else getting killed."

He opened the door to leave and Cat stood guard on top of the steps.

"It's all right, Cat," Julia said. "Let him go."

As soon as he'd gone, she telephoned Lt. McDermott. But it was Sunday, and he wasn't there. She left a message for him to call her as soon as possible.

After that, she phoned Martin.

* * *

"Joe said he followed Leachy to that psychologist's house," Marvel reported. "Maybe he told her what happened. Now he's disappeared. This is getting all fucked up. What're we going to do?"

"Don't worry about Leach. He's a weak link, but as long as he knows we have Estelle in our sights, he won't do anything. He'll be far away forever."

"But what about the shrink?"

"That's a problem we're going to have to deal with more decisively. Tell Joe Woods to take care of it. You talk to Conny and arrange to borrow his boat again. This time, you do not want Asshole leaving any bodies around to be found."

"Conny knows what we used his boat for the last time. I don't think he's going to let us use it again."

"Yes, he will. You just remind him that he's an accessory from the beginning, and if he cares about his hide, he'll

let Little Joe take out the boat again. Or he'll have to deal with me."

* * *

Billy and Goody sat in lawn chairs as Cutter finished up his day's work. Cutter sat next to them and poured himself a modest drink.

"Where'd Adam go?"

"For a walk in the woods," Billy said.

"So what's with him?" Cutter asked.

"Him and his girlfriend split up," Goody answered.

"What happened?" Cutter asked.

"He didn't say," Goody replied. "One minute they're all lovey-dovey, and the next minute he's moping around like a lonely box turtle."

"It's not the first time. They split up last year for while, too, remember?" Billy said. "I think maybe Julia's just a little prickly sometimes."

"It's probably the Change," Goody declared. "They get like that."

"How's it been going, Cutter?" Billy asked.

"It's been working so far. I'm just waiting to see what happens on the outside. What do you think, Goody, you want to join us here?"

"Thought about it," Goody said. "But it's too much community for me."

* * *

"I've never seen you in your civvies," Julia commented as she preceded Martin into the livingroom. He was wearing jeans and a black tee-shirt with an open denim shirt over it.

"Shucks," he said looking down, "I forgot to put on my minister clothes. I almost never take them off. Even to shower."

"Right," she smiled self-deprecatingly. "I made iced coffee, want some?"

"Sure."

"Or would you prefer a brandy?"

"I'd much prefer a brandy."

As she poured them both a Courvoisier, Martin said, "You mentioned on the phone that Frank Leach came to see you?"

"He was at the funeral service this afternoon. He must have been waiting for me after I took Sherry back, because he practically followed me into the driveway."

"Sherry is Nicole's daughter?"

"Yes," Julia sighed. "But code-of-silence, Martin."

"I promise. So what did Frank Leach want?"

When she'd finished telling him, he sat swirling the brandy around in his glass for a moment.

"I think you did the right thing by calling Lt. McDermott. You can tell him about Frank Leach and let him handle it. And I'll do what I can to watch out for Estelle."

"The problem is, without Frank, there's no evidence."

"There's still Joe Woods. Maybe the Lieutenant can get something out of him."

She nodded without saying anything.

"Now may I ask you a personal question?" he said, finishing his brandy.

"You can always ask," she answered trying to sound light-hearted about it.

"Are you not seeing Adam anymore? I mean," he said awkwardly, "you called *me*."

Suddenly she felt very tired. So much had happened over the past month. Not the least of which was her break-up with Adam. Is that what it was? Yes, probably. He hadn't phoned her afterwards. Neither had she called him. In nearly a week.

"I'm not really sure," she answered truthfully.

"Not really sure whether you're still seeing him?"

"Yes."

"How does that work?"

She had done enough confiding for one day, she thought. So she merely replied, "I'm not sure of that, either."

"Well," he mulled, "it's nearly seven o'clock. Can I interest you in dinner?"

Ordinarily, she would have declined. She had no intention of starting up another relationship, especially when she wasn't sure about the existing one. In fact, she wasn't sure she wanted *any* relationships. They were just too much damn trouble. But dammit, she was not going to let this thing with Adam get her down. She'd already done that once, last year, when they'd had a falling out. She wasn't going to mope over it like some silly teenager.

"All right," she answered.

"Would you like to go to Dottie's? I'm not dressed for anything fancy," he said modestly.

Anywhere but Dottie's, she thought, where she might run into Adam. "How about the Pocasset Inn?"

The Inn was a huge three-storied house more than one hundred years old. It overlooked the Nemasket River at a bend where, a century ago, barges and sloops traveled up the river from New York and ports south. The barges brought coal and left with wood. The sloops brought visitors to the inn. The current owners kept the inn pretty and painted on the outside but the inside was maintenance free. The old bar, tables, booths were as unpretentious as a picnic, but the food was good old-fashioned homestyle dinners. The Inn had its own clientele, separate from Dottie's.

"Sounds perfect."

* * *

The telephone rang only twice on the other end before Karen picked it up.

"Hi, Mom," she said cheerily without Julia's having to announce herself.

"How are you, sweetheart?"

"We got the house!"

"You did?"

"Yes, isn't that great! The owners really wanted us to have it. They're moving back east to be near their children and grandchildren. Their daughter has a cottage on their property that she and her husband fixed up for them. But it's small and they can't take everything with them. They're leaving some of their furniture, including things for the baby's room they had stored in the garage. We're going to pass papers in two weeks and move in on July 31st. I can't believe this is all going so fast. It's like a dream. You've got to start planning to come out."

"I will, honey. And congratulations! I love you both and I'm so happy for you."

It was, in fact, the happiest news in a very long time. First, about the baby coming, and now about Karen and Paul's new home. She hoped with all her heart that Karen would never have to go through what she went through. But Paul was very different from Phillip. He wasn't pretentious or self-important, and he was clearly devoted to her daughter. Julia hadn't thought that much of him at first. A wedding photographer, she'd called him, even though he did more than take photos of weddings. But when she got to know Paul, she could see how unassuming and caring he was. That was what she wanted for Karen. Everything else was a bonus. And now that they were on the west coast, Paul had been doing portrait and landscape photography. Lately, his pictures had been hung in several galleries. He might just be, Julia thought pleasantly, an artist.

"I know you are. I can't wait for you to visit us. Even Dad likes the house, and you know how McMansion he is."

"Your father's already seen the house?'' Julia tried to keep the irritation out of her voice.

Karen paused. "I suppose I should have told you. Please don't be offended. But Dad helped us with the down payment."

Julia said nothing for a moment, cautioning herself to be civil.

"Don't be mad, Mom."

"I'm not, darling. Not at all."

"Paul's parents don't have any money. And I know you don't, right now. So—"

"It's okay, honey. The most important thing was to get the house. That's what rich fathers are for."

"Mom—"

"I know."

Karen quickly changed the topic. "So tell me what's been happening with you. How's Adam?"

Julia rolled her eyes. "We're taking a little break from each other for a while."

"Oh? Again?"

"So I had dinner with someone else tonight."

"Re-ally?" Karen said in a sing-song way. "Who?"

"The Reverend Martin Ryman."

"I don't believe it, Mom. You went out with a *minister*?"

"A minister and a very good kisser."

"E-yeu-u-u," Karen said in mock disgust. "I don't even want to think about it."

"Hey, I didn't want to think about you and Paul, either. But I'm not on the shelf yet, you know."

"What about Adam?"

"I don't know right now."

"You like this reverend guy?"

"He's very nice."

"Hmph. Since when have you been attracted to nice?"

Julia chuckled.

"And don't tell Dad I said that."

They both laughed.

MONDAY, JUNE 28th

"Dr. Alonzo? This is Dr. Arnault. I was calling just to see how Sherry is faring after our excursion yesterday."

"No repercussions that I'm aware of. I received your e-mailed report first thing this morning, thank you. I take it the journey was uneventful."

Julia breathed out audibly. "Yes, as far as she's concerned."

"Do I want to hear more?"

"No. She did fine. I don't know about closure, but I do think it was important for her to attend."

"Good. Well, we'll take it up in therapy today. Thank you, again."

"You're welcome. Thank you for letting me take her."

After hanging up, Julia sat quietly staring at the door. Sherry was in good hands and now that she'd turned the case over to Lt. McDermott, could she let it go?

* * *

A week had gone by since he and Julia had argued. She hadn't called him and he debated whether or not to call. In the end, Adam decided he needed to get it sorted out. He waited until six-thirty when he knew she'd be home from work, then drove over to her house.

Her car was in the driveway. But he sat in his truck for several minutes before going to the front door and ringing the doorbell.

Cat barked from inside and came to the window.

"Hi, girl," Adam said, expecting her to wag her tail at him, as usual. But she didn't. Cat kept barking. Then she disappeared from the window, reappeared and barked again. Adam rang the doorbell again as Cat kept barking.

Was Julia inside, but refusing to answer the door? The least she could do was talk to him. He was beginning to get angry. After ringing several more times, he spun around and headed back to his truck.

As he went by Julia's car, he automatically glanced in.

That was odd. There was a bag of groceries on the back seat.

He turned around again and went back to the house. This time, he pounded on the door, yelling, "Julia!"

His anger gave way to alarm when she didn't answer, but Cat seemed to go into a frenzy. He knew Julia kept a spare key under a loose brick on the porch wall, so he immediately went to it. Yes, there it was.

With Cat still barking, he opened the front door to the livingroom. Cat circled him now, agitated.

"Julia?" he called loudly.

No answer.

"Julia!?"

He searched downstairs first—kitchen, diningroom, bathroom, foyer, backyard, all the while calling Julia's name. Nothing. Then he ran upstairs and checked each bedroom, bathroom, closets. Nothing. He flew back downstairs to the basement. Nothing. Where was she?

Maybe she went off with a friend. Maybe Tessa.

He called Tessa on Julia's kitchen phone, but Billy answered. Tessa was in the shower and no, they hadn't heard from Julia. Why?

"Well, I'm at her house and her car is here, but she isn't."

There was a pause at the other end. Then, Billy said, "I thought you two had split."

"Yes and no," Adam answered.

"But I heard she's been seeing Martin Ryman. Maybe she's with him."

"The pastor?" Adam asked, stunned.

"I don't know much about it. Tessa said Julia's gone out with him a couple of times."

"I see," Adam said, subdued. "Well, thanks, Billy."

"Hey, why don't you come over here for dinner, Tessa's cooked up great eggplant parm and banana cream pie."

"Thanks, Billy, not tonight. Maybe some other time."

"Okay, Ski, see you Sunday."

"Right."

He stood still for a moment, letting the news sink in. He felt sucker-punched. He looked aimlessly around the room then down at the dog sitting at his feet.

"What do you say, Cat, do you have to go out?"

The dog jumped up and did a full-body wag. Adam let her out into the front yard and put the house key back under the brick. Instead of going to the grass, Cat went to Julia's car and barked. Then she sniffed around the side of the car, and barked at Adam.

"What?"

Cat barked again, so he walked over to the car and looked in. There was that grocery bag on the back seat. Puzzled, he opened the car door and looked in the bag. There were cans of dogfood, milk, a loaf of bread, and a container of what would now be melted chocolate-cherry ice cream.

"That's not right," he said aloud.

He noticed the grocery slip on top of the cans of dog-food and picked it out. It was stamped with today's date, the 28th, at "5:13 p.m."

She had obviously shopped on her way home. But why wouldn't she take the milk and ice cream into the house? Should he do it? Bring in the bag and put the milk in the fridge? But then she would know he was here, and in her house while she was out. Not a good idea.

As he debated it, a two-tone taupe Volvo turned into the driveway. His first thought was that it Julia might be in it with someone else and he would have a lot of explaining to do.

But the driver was Martin Ryman, and he was alone.

Martin got out of the car and extended his hand.

"Hello, Adam."

"Martin." Adam shook his hand. Awkwardly he said, "I just came over to see Julia for a minute, but she's not here. I…um…got worried because Cat was barking, so I looked in the house just to make sure everything was okay."

Martin was looking at him very skeptically.

"Then I thought she might be out with someone, so I thought I'd let Cat out before I left and I was going to put her back in the house and lock up when she started barking at Julia's car."

Martin nodded at him without saying anything, which made Adam feel as though he were some kind of Peeping Tom.

"Anyway, there was a bag of groceries on the seat of the car, so I looked inside." 'Boy,' Adam thought, 'this does sound like I'm a stalker.' He hastily added, "They're today's groceries, according to the slip. But there's milk and ice cream in the bag. And it's too hot to leave that in a closed car, so I was going to put in the refrigerator. Except that it's not like Julia to do that."

Adam finished and waited for a response. The reverend was dressed in khaki pants with a navy blue blazer and a blue shirt open at the collar. He didn't look very reverential.

"I was coming to pick Julia up at seven." Martin looked at his watch. "It's just seven, now." He frowned at Adam. "She should be here."

"Something's wrong," Adam said.

Martin nodded. "Has she told you what's been happening with the Fayette case?"

Adam pursed his lips. "Not in the last week."

Martin quickly filled him on the episode at the Bethel yesterday and later at her house with Frank Leach. And the possibility that Mayor Kane was Nicole's murderer.

"I'm going to the police," Martin said. "You wait here and see if she turns up."

"No. There's no time. You go. Meanwhile, I'm going to have a little talk with Marvel Kane."

Adam took Cat with him to Marvel Kane's house, but the dog did not seem interested in the man who opened the door. Whoever took Julia, it wasn't him.

"Hi, Marvel, Adam Sabeski."

Marvel looked at Adam without recognition.

"You don't remember me, but I've heard a lot about you. Can we talk privately for a minute? Out here?"

"What about?" Marvel said suspiciously.

"About Nicole Fayette. Eileen Mann. Frank Leach. Julia Arnault. Especially Julia Arnault."

"I know of the others, but I never heard of a Julia Arnault."

"Sure you have, Marvel. She had an appointment with you. I drove her to your office," he lied.

"Oh. Was she the writer?"

"Psychologist."

"Oh. Yes. She was doing some research on Nicole Fayette's murder. But I didn't have anything to tell her, so she didn't stay very long."

Adam reached over and pulled Marvel out of the doorway by his shirt, and closed the door behind him.

"What do you think you're doing?"

"I'm beating the crap out of you."

Adam slammed him against the porch railing and Marvel fell over it into the bushes, landing on his back. Adam jumped over the railing next to him and punched Marvel in the face.

"Where is she?"

Blood spurted from the mayor's nose. "I don't know what you're talking about, I'm going to call the police."

Adam kicked him between his legs and Marvel curled up on his side, groaning in pain. Adam knelt down held him by the throat.

"I said *Where is she*? I swear to God I will kill you right here if you don't tell me. And I think you know I mean it, don't you?"

Marvel looked into his eyes and weakly nodded.

"Where is she?"

"She's dead," Marvel croaked in a whisper that was close to a wail.

Adam sat back on his heels. He could feel the blood rushing away his face and hands. He steadied himself on the step. As Marvel tried to crawl away, Adam leaned over and grabbed Marvel by his hair.

"Where is she? Believe me, you are better off going to jail then dealing with me. Because I will tear you to pieces." Adam jerked his head back with a snap.

Marvel lifted his hands and Adam eased off. The mayor struggled to sit up.

"Joe Woods killed her," he said between breaths.

"Where is she?"

"I don't know."

Adam raised his fist and Marvel cowered.

"Don't. Don't hit me again. He's going to dump her body at sea." Marvel found a handkerchief in his pocket and blotted his nose.

"Where's his boat?"

"He took Conny Cranshaw's boat. Out of Padanaram."

Adam looked at his watch as he got up. Seven-thirty.

"What's the name of the boat?"

"The Sea-Cran."

Adam ran to his car and called Police Chief Burke in Pittsley. Martin was still there. Adam didn't say Julia was dead, only that she was abducted. He told Burke to get the Coast Guard to intercept the Sea-Cran. The fastest response site to where the boat would probably be was the First District out of Boston. Then he told Burke to have the state troopers arrest Marvel Kane. He didn't trust the Sipponet Police to do it.

* * *

It was black. She was under something stiff and it smelled musty. Like plastic linoleum. It crackled as she moved. Oh, God, her head hurt. And her throat hurt. She put her hand to her throat and felt an indentation. She tried to make a sound but couldn't. She didn't think she could speak at all.

What was that motor? It vibrated through the floor she lay on. Where was she? She tried to remember what had happened.

She recalled leaving work and stopping at the convenience store. Then what? Then she drove home. Got out of her car to get her grocery bag. Then Cat was barking from inside the house and she felt something around her neck and she struggled. Then she blacked out. That was it. Someone had strangled her. Or tried to. They must have thought she was dead when she fainted. But where was she now? And what was that droning motor?

* * *

Adam arrived only minutes before Martin at the Coast Guard field station near the Cape Cod Canal railroad bridge. It was the closest place to get first-hand information about the search and rescue operation.

Martin looked as grim as Adam felt.

They sat on uncomfortable orange-vinyl chairs as the sole operator took information over his radio. He looked like a cadet, but his voice was deep and confident.

"We will probably call back the plane and helicopter within the next ten or fifteen minutes. The fog is thick and it will be too dark. But we'll keep the cutter out. Since we don't know the sea route, however, it won't be easy to find them tonight."

Adam put his head in his hands.

"If you gentlemen would like some pretty bad coffee, there's some over on that table."

Martin got up and poured himself coffee while Adam sat back again in the chair. "Want some?" Martin asked. Adam shook his head 'no.'

Martin sat back down with his coffee but didn't drink it.

"So what's the story with you and Julia?" Adam asked.

"No story. We've gone out a couple of times, that's all."

"Then what are you doing here?"

Martin looked down at Adam's knuckles. "There's blood on your hands."

"Yeah, well there's blood on Marvel's face." Adam looked sidewise at Martin. "I suppose you would have just preached the information out of him."

"Don't be an ass," Martin said, "I'd have knocked him from here to Sunday." Then he raised his eyebrows. "That doesn't sound very Christian, does it?" he said rhetorically.

"Don't kid yourself."

"What else did he tell you?" Martin asked perceptively.

"Marvel said she's dead."

"Dead?" Martin shook his head in disbelief.

"That's what he said."

"He killed her?"

"No. Joe Woods did, he said."

"Marvel saw it?"

"No."

Martin lowered his head and Adam got the distinct feeling that he was praying.

* * *

It didn't take long before she realized that she was on a boat. Under a tarp.

She slowly and quietly lifted a small corner of the tarp to see what part of the boat she was on. She seemed to be in the cabin area. She didn't hear anyone and couldn't see anyone. Her first thought was to grab a life preserver and jump off before anyone saw her.

But it was too dark and she had no idea how far out into the ocean she might be. Or how many of them were on board. She wasn't even sure whether there was anyone watching her right this minute.

She pulled back the tarp a little further. The cabin door was open and she could see her surroundings dimly in the night. There was a kitchenette and what was obviously the head, and some sort of sleeper. There were several steps up to the doorway. Then glass sliders onto the deck. There didn't seem to be anyone around.

She listened intently but heard no voices. Maybe there was only the one. He must be on an upper deck, piloting the boat. But why was she there?

'Of course,' she realized, 'he thinks I'm dead. He's going to dump me overboard. Who is it?' she wondered, 'Marvel Kane?'

Should she try to come up behind him—whoever 'him' was—at the wheel and knock him out? She looked around to see if there was anything heavy within reach. Nothing. No, wait! There was a fire extinguisher.

The question was, could she get up and get it without betraying herself? Maybe. If she moved quietly.

Little by little, she inched out from under the tarp, keeping an eye on the glass sliders at the top of the steps. She stood up to reach the small red wall-extinguisher and gently lifted it off its mount.

'There's no way that I can get out of the cabin and up the steps to the deck without him hearing or seeing me,' she concluded. 'I'll have to take him by surprise.'

She had the advantage, she thought, because he believed she was dead. If she slipped back under the tarp, she could wait for him to come to her.

'I'll do it the way Adam said he and Percy did to catch the poachers.'

She painstakingly repositioned the tarp so that half of it was under her. She pulled the safety pin out of the fire extinguisher, nozzle pointed away from her. Then she lifted the other half of the tarp lightly over her as she lay down. When he came in, she would spring up and the tarp would drop away. If nothing else, it would frighten him out of his wits and buy her time. She lay with her finger on the cold metal trigger of the extinguisher, and waited.

* * *

"The air rescue teams have returned to base," the Coast Guard cadet told Adam and Martin. "The cutter is still out there but, without eyes or ears, they won't be able to do anything until daylight. You guys might want to go home."

"Are you here all night?" Martin asked.

"Yes, sir," said the young man.

"I'll give you my phone number. If anything happens, please call me right away. Otherwise, I'll be back in the morning."

"Yes, sir."

Martin looked at Adam. "You're staying?"

"I'm going to walk Cat for a bit. Then I'll probably head home."

The two men left together. As they walked outside, the mist was cold and wet on their faces.

Adam walked towards his truck.

Martin said, "If she's alive—"

"If she's alive," Adam said, turning around, "she'll make up her own damn mind."

"Well, I wasn't suggesting we have a knock-down drag-out fight over her," Martin responded brusquely.

"Look, reverend, I'm sure you're a real peach of a fellow. You just happened to slide in line when I blinked, that's all, right?"

"What do you mean, 'slide in line'? Julia came to me about this Fayette case before I ever asked her out. In fact, she came to me to talk about the Bradburn girl over a year ago. As far as I know, she's not married to you. In fact, she stopped seeing you, didn't she? And I'm not sliding in line. She and I have not—we haven't done anything except have dinner. But if we did, it wouldn't be any of your business now, would it?"

The two men glared at each other in silence.

Then Martin said, "This is…wrong."

"I know," Adam answered, looking away.

"We both want her to be alive, and that's all that matters," Martin said.

"Yeah." Adam did not trust his voice.

Martin turned to get in his car. "I'll see you in the morning."

"Yeah."

As Martin drove off, Adam drove with Cat out of the station gate and around to the parking lot alongside the Canal. They walked to the edge overlooking the water, Cat following him as though it were perfectly natural to be at the Cape Cod Canal at night. It was only about five hundred feet to the other side, but the water was over thirty feet deep and choppy with a fast current that reversed every six hours. He felt the sharp breeze off the water even in this warm evening. The wind ruffled Cat's blonde fur as she stood next to him.

A canal across the seven-mile isthmus of Cape Cod connecting Buzzards Bay and Cape Cod Bay had been the dream of no less than Miles Standish. Back then, a canal would have made trade between Plimouth Colony and the Dutch merchants from New York a great deal easier. But it took until 1914, almost three hundred years, to accomplish it.

When Adam was a young boy and his father took him here, there were always large barges and boats going through the Canal. These days, the traffic seemed to be mostly pleasure boats. The thought of pleasure boats suddenly reminded him of Conny Cranshaw. Did anybody arrest Conny Cranshaw?"

He had to see Chief Burke.

"Conny's in custody," Burke said when Adam arrived at the police station.

Adam had come to respect Police Chief Carson Burke. Burke was just a well-intentioned rookie when he took over the former Chief's position. At first, Adam thought he was a twit. Well, he actually *was* a twit, but he had grown with his responsibility and Adam quite liked him now. He just wished Carson would dress a little more casually. The man must wear a tie when he's rogering his wife, Adam suspected.

"Can I have a few minutes with him?"

Burke grinned. "No. He's being interrogated the *normal* way."

"Does he know where—?"

"No. He just handed over the keys to Joe Woods. As far as he knows, Joe was going to do some fishing tomorrow. Conny probably told Joe not to tell him anything, just in case. That would be the smart thing to do. And Conny is smart enough for that. We're probably going to have to cut him loose. Eventually."

Adam shook his head in disgust. "What about Marvel?"

"He's lawyered up, of course. But I think we can charge him with something."

"Is he going to press charges against me?"

"What for? Marvel fell off his porch. Did a helluva job on his nose. Caught himself on the railing. He's getting patched up in Morton Hospital. Don't worry about him." He hesitated. "I'm very sorry about Julia, Adam. "

"She's not dead."

"I saw Marvel's statement."

"She's not dead."

"I know. But she might be, Adam."

"She's…not… dead."

"Okay." Burke patted him on the shoulder. "Either way, there's nothing more you can do right now. Go home."

It was only ten-thirty. Long night ahead. Adam couldn't face going home. Cat was comfortably asleep on the seat of his truck, so he decided to go to Dud's Suds.

Adam was the only customer. Dudley was tending bar, as he usually did. He'd be in his seventies now, Adam estimated, but Dud was timeless. Adam ordered a whiskey and ginger.

"Monday's are lousy bar nights," Dudley said from the other side of the bar. "I'm thinking I might close Mondays. I been open seven nights a week for forty years, and Mondays have never been good bar nights."

"Has it been forty years? Yeah, I remember coming in here before I was legal. That was at least thirty years ago," Adam said. "I think you even had hair back then."

"Yeah, and you didn't have grey in yours."

"Those were good days."

"Yup. We had a band every Saturday night. Meat raffle on Sundays. Clam boils Friday nights. Pizza on Thursdays. Standing room only."

"Why don't you try pizza again, on Monday nights this time? Might bring in a crowd."

"Oven's been broke for years."

"What about the other stuff?"

"Bands are too expensive now. Can't make any money on them. Especially since people aren't drinking like they used to. Used to be Peter Sampson would come in here and have twenty beers at a clip. Now, he does ten, twelve at the most. Same with the others. They've all got D.U.I.s from leaving here gonzo. Pittsley cops would park down the road and nail them when they drove out. When people don't drink, I don't make money. What the hell is the matter with the cops? It's a bar, for godssake."

"I heard Driver was in here a while back, kickin' it up with a trio of townies."

Dudley chuckled. "Oh, Adam, you shoulda seen it. It was just like old times."

Adam smiled appreciatively. He finished his drink and tapped the glass for another.

"So what's going on with him and Cutter and them over there to Libertyville?" Dudley asked as he poured whiskey then gingerale into Adam's glass.

"Well, they're holding out."

Dud shook his head. "I don't like the odds."

After Adam's sixth whiskey, Dud said, "You haven't been drinking like this since you came back from 'Nam. What's up?"

Adam shook his head and motioned for a refill.

"Alright," Dud said, "but take it over to the booth. That way, if you pass out, you won't fall off the stool."

He steered Adam over to the booth and handed him the drink.

"You can stay here, but I've got to close up for the night."

Adam nodded. His eyes were heavy. What was Dud saying? Something about hearing something?

* * *

Suddenly, she heard the motor cut down to an idle and she realized there was a flaw in her plan.

She couldn't throw off the tarp and at the same time spray him from a prone position. But neither could she spring upright from a lying position. She needed both hands on the fire extinguisher. If he had a gun, he'd have time to shoot her before she ever got to her feet. And if he didn't, he'd still have time to tackle her, or knife her.

If she was going to get repositioned, she'd have to do it quickly. She swiveled one leg under her until she was kneeling on one knee. She hoped it would look as though the tarp had just bunched up. It was dark. Maybe he wouldn't notice right away. She tried to regulate her breathing so he wouldn't be alerted. She told herself that when he got in range, she mustn't stop to think. She must just act.

She heard the footsteps coming down from the bridge to the deck. She imagined him at the doorway, looking in. What if he put the lights on?

But no, he didn't.

He opened the glass slider and took the three steps down to where she lay.

Julia jumped up, screaming, "Now," at the top of her lungs. At the same time, she pulled the lever and sprayed the extinguishing foam into the man's face.

She was like a madwoman.

As soon as she sprayed him, he yelped in a combination of surprise, fear, and distress. As he put his hands up to his eyes, she was on him. One solid crack on the head with the extinguisher and he went down like a sack of sand.

She stood over him, breathless and shivering, watching to see if he moved and shocked by her own rage. She wanted to hit him again. She wanted to open his skull and let the inside fall out like fish guts. But she didn't.

In the moonlight, she recognized him as the man who met Frank Leach outside the Bethel. Joe Woods.

She stood swaying over him, looking for signs of life. Yes, he was alive. But she had better tie him up before he regained consciousness.

TUESDAY, JUNE 29th

Adam opened his eyes and saw the top of the dark wooden table an inch away from his nose. His head was resting on his arm. A shaft of light came through the side window and lit his face. There was forty years of shiny grime on the tabletop. Initials were carved randomly over the surface. The table had the smell of a thousand beers in it.

"Ouuu," he murmured as he lifted his head out of the sunlight. He looked around at his surroundings, then closed his eyes for a moment and stretched his head back. His shoulders hurt. He was stiff all over.

"Stiff, being the operative word," he said aloud.

He looked at the clock over the bar. Six-fifteen a.m. His thoughts went first to Julia, then to Cat in the truck.

He slid out of the booth and went to the men's room. Then he laid a twenty-dollar bill on the bar and let himself out.

Cat was still sleeping soundly in a Golden Retriever sort of way, so that he had to shake her to wake her up. After letting her out back of Dud's, they got back into the truck and headed for the Coast Guard station. Cat laid her head on his thigh and looked up at him inquiringly.

"Don't worry, girl," he said, patting her head.

Martin was standing next to another on-duty cadet when Adam entered the station office.

"She's alive," Martin said fervently. "They found the boat and she's alive. I tried to call you after they phoned me about an hour ago, but there was no answer."

"She's alright?" Adam repeated. "Really alright?"

"Yes. They're bringing her in by helicopter to Boston right now. "

"What happened?"

"I don't know," Martin replied.

"We don't have any details yet, sir," the young cadet said. Other than they're bringing your friend in and, I guess, the man who kidnapped her. They'll be medivac-ed to Massachusetts General Hospital, and I called the State Police."

Adam felt the color drain from his face. He felt woozy. "Why does she need to go to the hospital?"

"It's routine, sir. She's apparently unharmed."

"You look like you should sit down," Martin said.

Adam nodded and made his way to the uncomfortable orange chair.

"I thought she was gone," he said.

Martin took a deep breath. "So did I."

Martin offered Adam a ride up to Boston with him, but Adam declined. That was just a little too brotherly-love for him. He'd go on his own. Besides, he had to put a notice on his clinic door that he'd be out, and give Cat breakfast before putting her in the dog run. And he badly needed a cup of coffee.

He arrived at MGH about an hour after Martin.

Checking the records, the nurse told him that Ms. Arnault was seen in the emergency room.

But by the time he got to the ER, the clerk said the Ms. Arnault had been examined and discharged. A Mr. Ryman was driving her home.

He cursed under his breath and went back to his truck, paid the parking fee, and drove home.

There was no point in going to her house. Ryman was there. What were they going to do, sit around in the parlor like two Victorian suitors scrambling over a dropped lace handkerchief?

But he *did* have a legitimate reason to go to her house, he realized. He had to bring back Cat.

* * *

Her throat still hurt so she didn't want to talk. She slept all the way home in Martin's car.

"Where's Cat?" she said raspily as soon as they entered her house.

"Adam has her for safekeeping. Why don't you lie down on the sofa and sleep a while more? I'll just sit here in that chair until you wake up."

She sat on the sofa but did not lie down. "I don't want to sleep any more." She rubbed her throat.

"Would you like me to make you some tea with honey? Do you have honey?"

She nodded. Then, abruptly, she began to cry.

He sat down next to her and handed her his handkerchief. "You've been through so much."

"I was so frightened," she croaked. "And then," she said, wiping away her tears, "I was so damn mad. I scared myself. I didn't know I could be so violent. I hit him so hard. And I just wanted to keep on hitting him."

"But you didn't."

She shook her head. "But I could have."

"You used the amount of force you needed to save yourself. No more."

"Do you know why I didn't hit him more?" She unconsciously balled up the handkerchief in her fist.

"Because it's not in your nature."

"No. Because I wanted him alive. To testify. That's the only reason."

"Whatever the reason. You didn't kill him. And you didn't hit him more than once."

"Does that count?"

He laughed. "Oh, yes. That counts."

She looked down at her hand. "Look what I've done to your handkerchief."

"That's what they're for," he answered.

Who has handkerchiefs anymore, she wondered, in this age of Kleenex? Adam would probably just pass her a napkin, hopefully unused. She dabbed at her eyes for the final time. "How did the Coast Guard know where I was?"

"Chief Burke called them."

"How did he know?"

"Adam coaxed it out of Marvel Kane."

Julia raised an eyebrow at 'coaxed.' "How did Adam know I was missing?"

"He was here when I arrived to take you to dinner. We were both concerned for your whereabouts, so I told him what had happened yesterday. He decided to…talk…to Marvel and I went to the police station. Marvel told Adam that Joe Woods had killed you and took your…you…out to sea. Adam told Burke, then both he and I went to the Buzzards Bay station house to wait. We were both pretty frustrated when they called off the air search last night."

"So you thought I was dead?"

"It looked that way."

"Adam, too?"

"We didn't want to admit it."

They sat in silence until Martin finally said, "He had to put a notice on his clinic that he wouldn't be there today. That's why I arrived at the hospital first."

"You mean he was driving up to Mass. General, too?"

"Yes."

"But you didn't tell me. We should have waited. He would have come all that way and found me gone."

"I should have said something," Martin said remorsefully. "I just wanted to see you first. I didn't realize they would discharge you right away. I wanted to be the one to bring you home. I wasn't thinking about him. I'm sorry, Julia."

"I think your apology should go to Adam, not me."

"Yes, you're right." He hesitated before speaking again. "It isn't like me to be competitive this way." He looked at her contritely. "I guess it's because I think I'm losing a chance to get closer to you. Losing the chance that something might develop between us. There is no chance, though, is there?"

Julia reached over and took his hand.

"I wanted there to be, Martin. But the fact is, when I thought I might die there in the boat, the person I thought about was Adam."

He gave her hand a squeeze and let go. “I think I need to get back on track myself.” He got up, saying, “Well, everything’s turned out for the best. And you’re alive and well and that’s what matters.”

As he walked to the door, Julia said, “Thank you, Martin. For all your help. I mean that.”

He turned towards her. “You can still stop by once in a while for conversation, can’t you?”

“Depend on it,” she said.

“I will,” he answered as he left.

She felt like an absolute heel.

* * *

Adam stopped at the police station to speak with Carson Burke before going to Julia’s. When he arrived at her house, Cat was scratching at the front door even before he got up the steps. When Julia opened it, the dog jumped on her so enthusiastically she was almost knocked over.

“Thank you for taking care of her,” she said.

“You’re welcome. I’m glad you’re all right.”

“Come in.”

In the livingroom, he looked around expecting to see Martin Ryman even though his car wasn’t in the driveway.

“I thought the good reverend brought you home.”

“I didn’t know you were coming to the hospital.”

“*He* did.”

“Yes. He owes you an apology for that.”

Adam shrugged as he sat in the armchair.

She sat on the sofa. Cat immediately jumped up and lay on her lap. She stroked the dog lovingly.

“How are you?” he asked.

“My throat’s still a little sore. But I’m all right.”

“What happened?” he asked.

She told him the story of being nearly strangled and her lying in wait under the tarp, the way he and Percy had done.

"It didn't work exactly the way I thought it would. But it worked."

"And you got him good. He's still in the hospital but he's under arrest," Adam said. "As is Marvel Kane. Woods is a coward. He made a full confession. Said Marvel Kane told him to do it. Marvel denies it, but between what Woods says and what Marvel told me, I think it's over. Woods also said that Marvel killed Nicole and he only took care of getting rid of the body."

"Then they were right all along, Sherry and Doreen. I've got to tell Lt. McDermott."

"Chief Burke said he already notified him. I expect you'll be hearing from him soon."

"What about Conny Cranshaw? It was his boat."

"He claims he doesn't know anything about it. He gave the keys to Woods just to go fishing."

"I don't believe it."

"Neither do I. But unless Woods gives him up—which I doubt—there's nothing we can do about it."

"What about Doreen? Did Woods say anything about the Azorean Queen?"

"No. Nothing."

She paused and there was an awkward silence between them. Finally, he spoke.

"I always seem to be a little bit late to the rescue with you. Not much of a knight in shining armor."

"I don't need shining armor," she said.

"What *do* you need?"

He waited for her answer, prepared for the worst.

"I need someone who's by my side. Or no one."

"I suppose I failed in that department, too," Adam said self-deprecatingly.

"I wouldn't say 'fail.' I'd say 'incomplete.'

He accepted than, then said drolly, "What do you think? Can we arrange a make-up test?"

She smiled slightly. "I'll take it under consideration."

WEDNESDAY, JUNE 30th

"It's solved, Sherry. Marvel Kane will be tried for murdering your mother and for conspiracy to murder me. Joe Woods will be tried for attempted murder and as an accessory to your mother's murder."

Julia and Sherry sat in the visiting room at McLean. Sherry had been taking her medication and going to therapy, and she seemed improved, Julia thought. But the young woman said nothing in response to Julia's news.

"Do you understand what I'm saying, Sherry? They've got him."

"I understand." Sherry paused. "It doesn't stop me from hating her," she said fiercely.

Julia was stunned by Sherry's tone.

"Why do I hate her?" Sherry asked rhetorically, then pinned Julia with a look. "Why do you think?"

Julia took a moment before answering. "Because," Julia said tentatively, "by dying, she left you unprotected with your grandfather?"

"It was always all about *her*. She'd get tired of being at home, so she'd go off for a weekend. Or a week. Or she'd go to a party. If she hadn't been such a pig, she wouldn't have been killed. And I wouldn't have had to grow up in that house alone. So you got her murderer. And what about the others?" she asked grimly. "The ones who knew all about it and kept silent."

"There really isn't anything the police can do about them."

"And what about Aunt Doreen?"

Julia shook her head. "There's no proof of anything about your Aunt Doreen's death. But the charges they're facing are enough to put them both away for life."

Sherry looked down.

"You're going to have to let that part go, Sherry."

Sherry looked away from Julia. "You almost got killed for me."

"Well," Julia answered breezily, "that wasn't part of the plan. But I survived."

"Thank you," Sherry said solemnly.

"You're welcome," Julia answered sincerely.

They were silent for a moment, then Julia said, "You need to work with Dr. Alonzo. I know you have a lot to get through, and it's going to take time. But I need you to promise something."

Sherry looked back at her.

"One day soon, you'll be discharged. But I know how things can build up when you're on your own, so if you ever need to talk with me, you can. And if you ever get to that point where you feel like hurting yourself again, I want you to immediately get in touch with Dr. Alonzo or me. Will you remember that?"

Sherry nodded.

Julia knew that that was as much as she was going to get. It would have to suffice.

"I have something else to tell you," Sherry continued. "A juicy little tidbit."

"Oh?" Julia expected something humorous. Maybe something about Dr. Alonzo.

"Just a piece of information I think you've earned."

Julia's curiosity was frankly piqued. "What is it?"

"Marvel Kane is my father."

Julia felt blindsided. Blonde hair, blue eyes, fine features. She had never put it together.

Leaving McLean an hour later, Julia didn't know whether or not to feel optimistic for Sherry. Even though her mother's murder had been solved, she had suffered so much at the hands of her father and her grandfather. Would she be able to overcome that? The odds were against it. But she had to have confidence in Dr. Alonzo. If anyone could help her, Julia thought, he could. She could only hope.

FRIDAY, JULY 1st

The Pittsley Board of Selectmen met in emergency executive session at the town offices at four o'clock in the afternoon with secretary, Mary Washburn, attending.

"Please indicate," said the chairman to Ms. Washburn, "that all members, Albert Carriou, Todd Kingman, and Madison Wentworth are present, Albert Carriou presiding."

Ms. Washburn diligently took notes as Albert continued.

"I will now read into the record the contents of a letter which was received this date at the Town Offices."

He held up a piece of paper and adjusted his glasses.

> "'*This is to inform the Board of Selectmen, Town of Pittsley, Massachusetts, that a claim for aboriginal land in your township has been lodged with the Commissioner of Indian Affairs, U.S. Department of Labor, pursuant to a lawsuit filed in Federal Court to enjoin the United State Government to acknowledge the indigenous property rights of the Wampanoags. We have determined that Malbone Briggs of Pittsley (Pittsley County, Massachusetts), his brothers and sisters, are of quantum blood, and are full members of the Wampanoag Nation, and that their properties belong, by right and by deed, to this Tribal Council. As such, this land is immune to taxation. Any communications may be directed to our legal representative, Attorney Birdsong Goffe, Mashpee, Massachusetts.*'"

Albert put down the paper and looked at the others. "The Wampanoags have been Federally recognized and this is on official stationery signed by the Tribal Council Chief."

Madison chuckled.

"A copy of this letter," Albert said to the others, "should be forwarded to Josiah." He turned to Mary Washburn. "Please see that a copy is sent to the Collector's office." He thought for a moment. "And send a copy to the town Treasurer, the State Department of Revenue, and the Governor." Then he added, "Mark all copies 'confidential.' We do not want this to become a newspaper circus."

She nodded and made a note.

"Off the record," Todd said, looking at Mary before addressing Albert. "What the hell does this mean? It's not their land, is it?"

"By right *and* by deed," Milton answered. "It's covered either way."

"You mean we're going to have an Indian reservation in town?"

"I don't think it's going to be anything other than what it is. A Briggs enclave. Untaxable."

"That's a lot of money in lost revenue, when you consider year after year. We can't afford to let this happen. Barstow is going to have a shit-fit."

"We'll have to talk with town counsel," Madison said. "But I don't think we're in a position to do anything about it until it's been settled in court."

"You haven't said anything, Albert," Todd said. "Do you have a plan?"

Albert nodded to Mary, indicating that she could resume taking notes.

"Our plan will be to contact town council for advice. It is likely that we will have to let the issue be settled in court. Until that time, we will not take any action against Mr. Briggs, *et al.*" He made a hand-gesture to Mary. "Please note that the executive session adjourned at," he looked at the Waltham clock on the wall, "Four-fifteen p.m." Then he added, "That will be all, Mary. Thank you for coming in and have a Happy Fourth of July."

"Thank you, Mr. Carriou," Mary replied, taking her notepad and closing the door behind her.

Albert turned to the two other men and breathed a deep sigh. "Gentlemen, we're off the hook."

Madison laughed. "You got to give him credit for being a clever sonovabitch."

* * *

Nine white-robed men gathered in Usha Kane's finished basement.

"Sorry about your boy, Usha," each of them said deferentially to the former Mayor of Sipponet.

Usha nodded and sat at the head of the circular table. "We have lost two more members. My son, Marvel, and Joe Woods."

"Joe was no loss," said another. "He didn't have the brains of a haddock."

"More importantly," Usha said, looking around the table. "we are down to only nine. It is time to recruit new members."

"And time to get rid of that woman for good," said the man to Usha's right.

"Not yet. For now, we must concentrate on recouping our numbers so that we can continue our rituals. We'll deal with her later. When this storm has passed."

SUNDAY, JULY 4th (Independence Day)

Adam, Julia, Tessa, Billy, Billy Jr., and Goody sat with Angel under the canopy at one of the picnic tables in back of Cutter's cabin. The rest of the residents sat at five other tables forming two parallel rows. The men, in relays, brought the platters of hot food to the tables—piled with barbecued ribs, hamburgers and hot dogs for the kids, grilled corn, baked potatoes. Already on the table were salads, cornbread, watermelon, lemonade, and layer cakes—much of which had been brought in by the guests.

As the last platter was set down, Cutter stood between the rows of tables and addressed the group.

"Let's all raise our glasses to toast Adam Sabeski in gratitude for helping us to stand here on Wampanoag land. Up Liberty Rez! Happy Independence Day everybody!"

"Happy Independence Day!" echoed from table to table.

"And screw the bureaucrats," growled Goody.

—The End—

LaVergne, TN USA
08 December 2009
166315LV00001B/15/P